ADVANCE PRAISE FOR *NERMINA'S CHANCE*

"*Nermina's Chance* in less expert hands would have ended up as a drifting trilogy. Dina Greenberg has kept her story together in one tight and suspenseful narrative, intricately woven. She has given us a cast of main characters each worthy of their own novel. Rarely does a story blend so meaningfully the horrors of war, the possibilities and limits of love, and the human need for family. If you give *Nermina's Chance* a chance, you will soon be turning the last page."

**-Clyde Edgerton, author of *Walking Across Egypt*
and *The Night Train***

"The day I became a refugee was the day I bore witness to the trauma of the war in Bosnia, especially as my relatives were tortured and raped in concentration camps. Not many people are quite so capable of writing about other people's tragedies as Dina Greenberg did in *Nermina's Chance*. The book is a witness statement of the trauma that exists still years after the brutality has ended. You can tell Greenberg has put her heart and soul into the writing of this book. I've read *Nermina's Chance* in three days, and I highly recommend it."

-Nadina Ronc, Foreign Affairs Analyst

"In *Nermina's Chance*, Dina Greenberg weaves the horrors of a nearly-forgotten war with the ongoing plight of the immigrant experience to create a riveting story about survival and perseverance. It's a story that reminds us of the humanity that underlies every experience, no matter how alien it may seem, and one that is perfect for our divisive times."

-Joe Ponepinto, Senior Editor, *Orca, A Literary Journal*

"I stayed up so late reading *Nermina's Chance* because I had to know what would happen next. Each time I put it down, I found myself ruminating about these characters I had come to love—what would happen to them? Would they find their way toward peace? This is a novel of remarkable self-assurance and wisdom. Dina Greenberg has written a gripping story of love, loss, war, and the things that people do to create family."

-Dana Sachs, author of *The Secret of the Nightingale Palace*

"*Nermina's Chance* is an intense, riveting read that is hard to put down. In Dina Greenberg's stories, one always has the feeling of being dropped right into the center of her protagonist's world. The author takes this connection to a new level in *Nermina's Chance*. Well placed details like "delicate gold-plated dishes" in the family home in Bosnia, reveal Nermina's privileged upbringing. All too soon, though, readers are perched on the edge of their seat beside Nermina—the "truck jerking and lunging" along a dark, mountain road, explosions in the distance—wondering if she will escape. Nermina's will to survive is extraordinary. *Nermina's Chance* is a wonderful achievement. Highly recommended."

-David Bright, Editor, *Gemini Magazine*

"With passion, compassion, and wise storytelling, Ms. Greenberg renders the brutality of the Bosnian War, and gives us Nermina, a traumatized refugee of that war, who comes to America and faces the challenges of a bewildering new culture. Alone, unmoored, she strives to reclaim her identity and to replace the family she lost. *Nermina's Chance* is a novel that's psychologically keen, told with exquisite detail about a protagonist who soars off the page and into your heart."

-James Rahn, founder of Rittenhouse Writers Group
and author of *Bloodnight*

NERMINA'S CHANCE

DINA GREENBERG

atmosphere press

TABLE OF CONTENTS

PART THREE

FOREWORD

Give us your tired, your poor, your huddled masses...
— Emma Lazarus, 1883 ("The New Colossus")

Give us your refugees?

Our humanity disappears with the label assigned us: the label of refugee. Our lives are transformed, our dreams wrenched away from us. For a brief moment, our catastrophes are your headline news. We're asked myriad questions about the war, and then another catastrophe takes place, and the world moves on.

As refugees, we consider ourselves lucky when we find sanctuary. We continue our lives, each in our own way, trying to make sense of what has happened to us, trying to come to terms with the loss of family, country, identity. Of who we might have been if only our journeys were not so brutally interrupted.

As refugees, our memories play cruelly upon us; nightmares that we try to forget still haunt us. Happy memories that we try to hold onto fade with time. The world has moved on, but as Tolstoy wrote in Anna Karenina: "All happy families are alike; each unhappy family is unhappy in its own way." As refugees, we carry our sorrows—our personal catastrophes—each alone. Each uniquely.

Nermina's Chance is the story of one such catastrophe—the brutal war in Bosnia in the 1990s that destroyed countless lives and communities. But *Nermina's Chance* is more than a story of war. It is a story of survival.

Through Nermina, Dina Greenberg intelligently gives voice to hundreds of thousands of women, women like me, rebuilding our lives in our new countries. Like us, Nermina takes a chance on a new existence and, despite everything she knows about the evil side of humanity, brings new life into a world still shifting beneath her feet.

As a refugee and survivor, I worried that *Nermina's Chance* might not do justice to the historical facts of my war, to my city, and it's people who had suffered so deeply. Though forensic in detail, the novel eludes the trap of a single narrative—as important as this one is. Instead, Dina Greenberg performs the job of a skilled fiction writer, wielding her imagination to bring to life one woman's healing journey with empathy and humanity.

— Zrinka Bralo, CEO, Migrants Organise

PART ONE

CHAPTER 1
THE TUNNEL
Sarajevo — May 1992

The six other passengers in the truck are silent, though Nermina feels the shudders of the old woman pressed to her right side and knows she is crying. The little boy Esmer sleeps, his head nested against Nermina's shoulder, his breath and body warming her. At first, the circuitous route made no sense to her. Three additional trucks in their convoy, their headlights off, crawl behind one another in a hideous steel caterpillar. She hears a shout from the driver in the truck ahead of them, and their own vehicle rolls to a creaky halt. This is the third such stop in as many hours. Their driver—a grim man who could be twenty-five or fifty—had told them that traveling through the mountains on unmarked roads is the only way they'd escape Serbian gunfire. By now Nermina understands the presence of the white UN vehicles throughout Sarajevo will do little to stave off the siege; only these men who drive the trucks—Bosnian Muslims and Croats—have a chance of delivering Nermina and the others to the relative safety of the airport tunnel.

But the mountain roads have proven treacherous. Rocks cut into the trucks' thick tires and have now punctured the oil pan of the truck ahead. She hears the men whispering terse instructions to one another. They'll have to improvise a repair now since they've depleted the only spare parts the caravan carried the last time they'd broken down. Along with the others, Nermina dutifully climbs out at the driver's order. Her body feels bruised and sore from the truck's constant jerking and lunging. The women take advantage of the stop, though, each squatting in the dark to relieve themselves while one of the men keeps watch. The old woman holds tight to Nermina, clutching at her sweater, while Esmer's small hand grips her own. Exhaust fumes from the truck announce the temporary fix and they all clamber back inside.

Once they are in motion again, Nermina's mind begins to race; too exhausted to stop their chaotic dance, she sees the images of the past weeks and months flash one after the other. But now as the convoy comes to yet another stop, her heart pounds harder inside her chest. She looks down at the black mirror of water below them, the narrow bridge that seems unlikely to support the weight of their truck, let alone the others behind them. She thinks of her father, the last time she'd seen him alive. She remembers how he'd forced the cash into her hands, the emptiness in his eyes. They reflected her own weariness, a sorrow that still hasn't reached its full power. He'd pushed her away—had she been a parent she would have done the same—but she'd felt only the ruthless cruelty of this action like a slap.

The truck crawls across the rickety wooden bridge and the fear that had overtaken Nermina just moments before now folds into her general state of tense exhaustion. And then as the truck's engine whines into its lowest gear as they climb yet another ridge, a flash of light streaks across the night sky. In the distance, Nermina sees fire leaping against the darkness. "Dobrinja," the driver whispers. "They've taken Dobrinja." She remembers the house and her room. Her face crumbles. *Mirsad*, she mouths, seeing again the blazing office tower. *They took my brother, too.*

The trucks near a low stone house and the driver, cigarette dangling from clenched lips, jumps from the cab. He hisses at his passengers to wait and then a second later to gather up their belongings. No other instructions come for what seems a very long time. And then suddenly they're all scuttling through a low entryway, the driver aiming a weak stream of light ahead of them from his flashlight. They walk along a set of railway tracks, each—even little Esmer—carrying his own load, no one speaking a word except for the driver's hushed instructions.

And then Nermina realizes they're climbing a set of cement stairs. And the stairs deliver them into the bombed-out airport that still holds a small terminal. Two uniformed UN officers hurry them through a short corridor that reeks of urine and smoke. She hears a brusque conversation between their driver and the uniformed Americans. A misunderstanding? A mistake? Nermina hears the Americans' terse words, words her brain is too rattled to decipher, and then she's carried along with the others in another rush of movement. The old woman clutches again at Nermina's arm and torso and she fights the urge to push her away. Another UN peacekeeper—British this time—motions the group across the tarmac and onto the steps of the plane. With Esmer pressing against her leg and the woman grasping the flesh of Nermina's arm through her sweater, she cares only about getting aboard. She feels the collective tension of all of them now, a great wave of fear and exhaustion, but also a flicker of hope. If she can make this first, most critical leg of the journey, the war will be behind her. Her lips form a grim smile. She sees her father's face, determined, prideful. "I'm getting you out," he'd said. "There's nothing here for you now." She pats her side, feels the thick envelope, which had been even thicker before she'd boarded the truck.

Now they're buckled into their seats, and the jet's engines drown out her thoughts. But once they're in the air, the old woman asks timidly: "Do you have people in London?" In the dim light of the cabin, Nermina sees how dark circles spread above the woman's hollow cheeks—she appears to be starving—and she swallows the bitter taste of guilt for the harsh feelings she'd had earlier. She runs her hand softly over Esmer's jet-black hair. The child had fallen asleep again as soon as the plane lifted off. She hears her father's instructions once more: "First Ancona, then London, then Portland, Oregon. America."

"No, no one there," Nermina murmurs.

"Where then?" The woman's expression eases ever so

slightly.

"I'm continuing on to the United States where I have some friends." She hears the artificial cheerfulness she'd used so often with Esmer in recent weeks. She feels she might laugh or perhaps she will cry. "And you?" Nermina asks then, as though she were making polite conversation at a party.

"London," the old woman says. "My niece will meet me in London."

"Good," says Nermina. She pats the old woman's hand, the skin worn like the hospital linens they'd used those long weeks without laundering, and looks into her wrinkled face. She sees her mother's face then, bruised and beaten. Her parents would never grow old together. This, too, the soldiers have stolen.

CHAPTER 2
DOBRINJA
November 1991

⸻

Her father slammed his hand down on the table. Four salad plates rattled atop the dinner plates below. Nermina flinched. Everything was changing. Her family was being impossible, her father—Suljo—behaving the worst. She sought her mother's eyes, but then no sooner had Nermina registered her still-placid look, her older brother Mirsad nearly overturned his chair getting up.

"Sit down," said Suljo, the hard edge of his voice as forceful as his palm on the table the moment before. "We're not done here."

Mirsad gripped the top of the chair in front of him. Nermina feared he might leap across the table and shake their father senseless. She knew—they all knew—the war was coming, but her father continued to deny it. Even now. Nermina stared down at her salad greens and counted three breaths as her finger traced the delicate gold-painted edge of the plate. Again, she sought her mother's eyes. Again, her mother cast them down. The light from the chandelier purpled dark circles beneath them, paled the smooth planes of her face.

Still standing—though a bit unsteadily Nermina thought, Mirsad faced their father. "I'm an adult," he said. "I want to fight and I don't need your permission—"

"We were having a discussion," Suljo said. "That's all. And you—sit, please—were making no sense." Suljo leaned back against the heavy upholstered chair, chose the smaller silver fork from his place setting.

"I *am* making sense," Mirsad said. "You're just not listening." He slid his lean body back into the chair beside Nermina's. She followed her brother's glare. It seemed to Nermina they'd argued about the possibility of a coming war a million times, but in this regard, Nermina *didn't* disagree with her parents. Like her, Mirsad was a child of privilege. He wasn't expected to fight. And even if he were, their father's connections and status would assure his exemption. Their mother's hand—glossy-red manicured nails, perfect ovals—now rested on their father's.

Mirsad shook his head. "It's the educated, the wealthy," he stuttered. "Us. It's people just like *us* Milošević wants dead."

Her father's face remained impassive. He'd regained his regal composure, and now tilted his head to the side, as always, the full shock of gray hair meticulously groomed. "It's not our war, though," Suljo said.

"Why? Because we're not Croats?" Mirsad shot back. "The

Serbs hate us just as much as they hate them. We're next. You only have to look as far as Croatia to see that. Of course, it's our war."

Nermina's pulse quickened as Mirsad glared into their mother's face, and then the heat of his gaze shifted to her own. They'd both failed him, Nermina thought.

"The strength of the Republics of Yugoslavia is in *bratstvo i jedinstvo*," Suljo said. "This is where our hope has always been and this is where it must remain. This is our safeguard."

"No," said Mirsad.

Mirsad flattened his hands on the starched white damask and Nermina saw how they trembled.

"Brotherhood and Unity," Mirsad chided their father. "That's the *old* Bosnia. Can't you see? It's over. Slovenia's independent. Macedonia—"

"With Tito, we were one people—" Suljo began.

"Tito's dead, Papa! That was a long time ago."

Mirsad slammed his hand down on the table and then withdrew it, as though from a searing stovetop. Again, Nermina flinched. She remembered when she and Mirsad were little—even teenagers—how they'd both worshipped their father. She saw the circle of men that seemed always to surround him. "Listen to Suljo Beganović," they would say. "Suljo will know the answer." Nermina had always believed her father's authoritative baritone—forceful yet still melodic— to be the source of his influence. But now this same voice grated on her. She patted her fingers, damp with perspiration, on the linen napkin in her lap.

"You were only a child then. You don't remember," said Suljo.

Now Nermina watched as her brother's fingertips found the pulse at his temple, touched the tender spot as their mother always had.

"But I'm not a child now," Mirsad said. "That's my point. And I see what you can't. What you *won't*. Bosnia's next."

Suljo shook his head dismissively. He shifted his gaze from his son, leveling it next on Nermina. With his thumb and pointer finger he smoothed the wide and neatly trimmed mustache, the same silver color as his hair.

"So, your brother is suddenly an expert," Suljo said, his voice rising and falling rhythmically. "He knows more than his father now. He wants to join the fundamentalists. He wants to be a soldier. What do you think about that, Nermina?" He could have been asking whether she favored coffee or tea.

Nermina reached for Mirsad's hand, entwined her slender fingers with his own as they'd done when they were children racing into the surf.

"She doesn't need to answer you," Mirsad said. "This isn't about her."

Then Nermina met her father's gray eyes.

"I don't want him to fight," she said, "but I can understand why he'd want to." Her voice held steady. "In Vukovar... hundreds were murdered..." She paused, lowered her eyes. "I'm sorry, Tata, but it's true."

"That would never happen in Bosnia," Suljo answered, his voice low and somber. "Zulfeta," Suljo said then, "speak to your daughter. She's gotten herself hysterical for no reason." He sent a withering look toward Mirsad. "Your son has spoiled our dinner."

Zulfeta withdrew her hand from Suljo's—Nermina saw

how the gold bangles at her mother's wrist caught the light from above—and turned to face her husband. "Neither of them is a child anymore," she said.

Nermina drew in a breath. She understood that this was true, but at that moment, wished that it were not.

Two months later, Nermina understood a great deal more. She rinsed off her breakfast plate in the sink and stacked it among the others in the dishwasher. From the kitchen window, she made out the ridgeline where terracotta rooftops emerged from the early morning mist. She'd grown sentimental about her life in Dobrinja, knowing now how soon she'd have to leave it. She remembered her father's pride when he'd first moved them here—a brand new house, a pristine suburb, a world away from the bustle and grit of the city.

In the dining room she kissed her father's cheek. He smiled up at her but Nermina saw this came with great effort.

"Take care, and remember to call us when you arrive," he said.

"Yes, Tata."

She waited for her father to crease his newspaper and tuck it beneath his breakfast plate, just as he'd done for as long as she could remember. Since Mirsad's exodus to his own flat in the city, Nermina had felt a renewed ease with her father, the absence of daily bickering between him and Mirsad, a reprieve, if only temporary. Like Mirsad, Nermina still hit the brick wall of their father's obstinacy.

But unlike her brother she'd given up trying to change their father's views. Despite his public declarations of Bosnia's invincibility, Nermina knew her father was gravely worried. She knew that—behind his bluster—at the heart of this worry were those he loved. She imagined him in his rounds at Koševo Hospital, calculating the distance between each of them. Her mother, a gynecologist, shuttled among three medical clinics in Sarajevo. Mirsad worked in a financial firm at the city's center. And Nermina spent five days a week in classes at the university. To her surprise, it was her father who first gave voice to the potential danger of her commute into the city and she, Nermina, who defiantly refused to consider taking a leave from her program.

Now Nermina watched as Suljo stroked his wide mustache. She registered his stern look, taking in almost for the first time the gravity of his instructions as she bundled her waist-length hair beneath a woolen hat and wound her scarf twice around her slender neck.

"Your mother and I must always know where you are," he said with even more severity.

"I understand, Tata." Nermina placed a kiss on each side of her father's stoic face.

She then walked the few short blocks to the trolleybus and, after several stops, exited at the bus station where she waited with several other passengers for the bus that would deliver her to the university.

CHAPTER 3
NERMINA'S TEST
Sarajevo — April 5, 1992

∼◦◦∼

Nermina looked down onto the Miljacka River, gray and muddy like the rest of the city today. She peered beyond the wrought iron fence of the narrow terrace and saw how the stone walls along the river glistened beneath globed streetlights. An old man, bearded and wearing a *shalwar kameez*, turned a crank that slowly raised a red awning covered with the familiar Coca Cola logo. He propped open the café door with a stick and proceeded to carry out, in stacks of three, twenty-four chairs. The slate roofs of houses that clung to the hills beyond the river—a collage of salmon, ochre, and brown—were slick with rain. Nermina wondered at the old man's assurance that the weather would clear, that the thick cumulus clouds would give way to bright azure, a color she had been dreaming about since she noticed the first crocus flowers pushing their way through a thick carpet of molting leaves along the riverbank.

Nermina felt the tightness in her jaw and realized she'd been standing silently at the window for several minutes. It hadn't been her choice to leave her parents' home, but now that she had, she felt an almost manic determination to go about her life as though nothing had changed. Some days, like this one, were more difficult than others. Tracing a series of loops with her finger in the misty film on the window, her heart quickened as she recalled the uncharacteristic quiver in her father's deep baritone. Was it patriotism or pure stubbornness that had allowed him to remain optimistic for so long? She would not permit herself to use the word "stupidity," though it had certainly crossed her mind more than once.

Nermina turned abruptly from the window when she heard Mirsad's quick steps in the hallway a moment later. She smiled at the slim young man, freshly showered and dressed in a suit and tie. "I was just watching the river," she said.

He brushed each of her cheeks with a brotherly kiss.

"It's pretty from here, isn't it?"

"Yes, but in the rain today, it makes me sad."

Mirsad ran his hand through his thick brown hair, which he now wore in a short, stylish cut, a change Nermina attributed to his move into the city. He looked steadily at his sister, his eyes shaded with long, dark lashes he had been teased for as a boy.

"Don't be sad," he said. "I've asked Tatjana and Kemal and some others to come celebrate with us. What do you think?

Will you join us?"

Gathering herself, Nermina said, "How sweet of all of you to celebrate the outcome of my exams. I intend to do quite well today, you know."

Impulsively she hugged her brother, inhaling the citrus-sweet aroma of his cologne. Mirsad's handsome face registered embarrassment and he stood motionless when his sister held him at arm's length.

"I'm only teasing," Nermina said, the false brightness drained from her voice. She dropped her hands from his shoulders, but held his gaze, reading her brother's face more closely. She saw how the purpled vein pulsed beneath opaque skin at his temple and resisted the urge to touch her finger to this tell-tale of her brother's moods.

"I know what you think," said Mirsad, "but I need to do this. I can't just sit here and wait like a coward."

At first Nermina had been angry, then frightened, when Mirsad revealed his determination to join Izetbegović's Muslim Patriotic League. Now she was far from resigned, though she knew her brother's mind was set.

"Does Papa know?" she asked.

"Of course, he doesn't know. You think I'm crazy?"

"I don't know what to think."

Mirsad broke free from his sister's gaze and paced for several steps before turning to face her again.

"Look, I agree with Papa," Mirsad said. "Bosnia's independence is a wonderful thing, but what exactly does it mean? Does he really think we all just wave the flag around and the Serbs will let us go about our business?"

"Of course not. I'm here, aren't I? Papa was worried

enough to have me stay here with you." Nermina splayed her fingers against the cold glass of the window, leaving an imprint of her small hand when she removed it a moment later. "I'm really not sure what he thinks, though...maybe what's happening in Mostar now won't happen here in Sarajevo..."

"I love you, *mala sestra*, and I don't want to frighten you unnecessarily, but none of us knows what will happen next." He plunged his hands into his pants pockets and looked down at the colorful, woven rug Nermina remembered from the sunny back room of their childhood home. She and Mirsad had spent countless hours sitting cross-legged on that rug, playing card games in which Nermina was rarely the winner.

"I'm not frightened," said Nermina. "I just don't want you to do anything careless."

Mirsad drew back from his sister and straightened his tie, a gesture she immediately found endearing and, yes, now that she thought about it, somewhat comforting. Her brother had grown into a competent young man. No matter what, she told herself, he would know what to do to take care of himself. And to take care of her.

"Have you ever known me to be careless?" he said, with a new edge of bravado that was not lost on his younger sister.

Standing outside the gates of the university, Nermina smiled and waved as her brother pulled away from the curb and onto a road still choked with rush-hour traffic.

Fifteen minutes later, Nermina stretched her legs beneath the desk, took two sharpened pencils from her bag, and began the exam when the proctor gave the sign. She moved quickly through the first section but scolded herself when her mind began to wander. As a second-year medical student, she'd been inundated with horror stories about the demands of the program, particularly the difficulty of the exams. Last year, it seemed the thousands of words describing the human body and its myriad systems and parts were imprinted onto her brain. She was able to summon these words and images from a seemingly endless and expedient storehouse of memory. This language of the human body was one Nermina believed she'd been born with. But now when she thought of the pages of highlighted notes she'd made sitting at Mirsad's kitchen table, she regretted how she'd taken for granted the relative ease of that first year.

When she was done, Nermina handed her exam to the proctor. She exited the room quietly, catching her classmate, Hasan's, furtive glance as she swept past him. They'd arranged earlier to meet up in the courtyard when they were through with the exam. Obsequious with the professors, the rail-thin boy was shy and awkward with Nermina and the other female students. For this reason, her father had deemed him the appropriate male classmate to accompany his daughter to her brother's flat each evening where the boy waited dutifully on the street until she'd safely entered the building.

Out in the hallway, Nermina worried her scores would never match her first- and second-quarter exams. She worried because she'd finished early. This could be either a very good thing or a very bad thing. Even so—with the test behind her now—she felt infinitely lighter as she pushed through the double doors that led to the courtyard.

Outside, the rain had stopped and the still-brisk air carried the newborn scent of damp soil and spring grass. Nermina peeled off her heavy woolen sweater and tied it around her waist. She tilted her head upward and drank in the dappled sunlight warming her face. She felt, for the moment, carefree and invincible. Stretching herself out on a wooden bench, beneath which the ground was strewn with cigarette butts, she untied her sweater, rolled it into a pillow, and laid her head against it. Then she willed herself to ignore the damp planks against her back.

When Hasan touched Nermina's shoulder twenty minutes later she jolted awake. She laughed when she saw his face.

"What's so funny?" Hasan said.

"You looked so frightened," said Nermina. "What did you think I'd do to you?"

"I thought you were feeling unwell," the boy mumbled. "I didn't want to disturb you."

"I'm feeling fine," said Nermina, swinging her legs to the ground and grabbing her sweater from the bench. "How did you do?" she asked.

Hasan shook his head slowly from side to side. "I'm not sure. The section on the autonomic nervous system was difficult, didn't you think?"

"Well, sort of," Nermina lied.

The boy kicked the toe of his shoe a couple of times into the dirt beneath the bench before meeting Nermina's eyes. "Ready?" he asked.

"Sure. Walk or tram?"

"It's up to you," said Hasan.

"It's early. Let's walk. The fresh air will do you good," she said and took a few long strides that left the boy scuttling behind her to catch up.

They followed the river wall toward Šeher-Ćehajina's Bridge. The stately, old, government buildings they passed, with their filigree of iron window grates and rooftop spires, reminded Nermina of the prissy 19th-century English dowagers pictured in one of the oversized books her mother liked to leave piled on the coffee table. When they reached the ornate *Sebilj* in the center of Baščaršija Square, Nermina suggested wandering through a few of the stalls before crossing the bridge to Novo Sarajevo.

"We should really get home," said Hasan warily.

"Oh, just for a little while." Nermina's tone was purposely indulgent. "Who's going to care?"

"Well, your brother…" Hasan began as Nermina walked off briskly, weaving her way along the cobbled lanes, clotted with shoppers.

She stopped in front of a crowded stall brimming with copper goods. She smiled at the grizzled old man who sat on a small stool behind his wares, a cigarette dangling from his lips. She took in the tightly packed rows of plates and bowls, the samovars, and delicately tooled plaques.

Hasan appeared at Nermina's side, a bit out of breath. "What are you looking for?" he asked.

"A present for Mirsad. I thought I might find something for his flat."

The old man paid no mind to either of them, conversing loudly in Turkish with another vendor at the next stall. Nermina picked up a small copper figurine of a cat. The eyes were inlaid with what looked to her like garnet. It reminded her of a porcelain figure of a Persian cat their mother had kept on a table at her bedside. She and Mirsad had been arguing and Mirsad—perhaps he'd been ten—whirled around to face her. His intention was never to strike her, she knew. But his wrist caught the figurine and it flew into the hallway where it shattered against the tile floor. This figurine would make a perfect gift for her brother now.

"*Koliko?*" she asked the man.

The old man eyed Nermina with sudden interest. "For you, ten *dinara*."

"Five," said Nermina, her green eyes sparkling with amusement.

The old man gave his customer an injured look and spread his hands in a gesture of submission. "Such a beautiful girl and you try to cheat an old man like me. Seven, then."

"Six," she said decisively, counting out the bills into the man's wrinkled hand. The man wrapped the figurine in a scrap of newspaper, but before he could place it into a bag, Nermina plucked it from his hands and wedged it into a front pocket of her jeans. "*Hvala!*" she called, already turning away.

Leaving the busy marketplace, Hasan and Nermina fell into an easy rhythm. They walked in silence for some fifteen minutes. The sky had clouded over again and Nermina was thankful she'd worn such a heavy sweater. She liked that she didn't have to jabber away with Hasan every minute they were together. He was a nice boy, she thought, then corrected herself: young man. Hasan was a young man. He was from a good family, a secular Muslim family, like her own. Had things been different, perhaps she would have been interested. She let the thought go then, realizing how quickly she would tire of Hasan's docile nature, the quiet adoration he'd shown her since their courses began the previous year. Then she silently scolded herself for being so unkind.

Just before the bridge, Hasan pointed to a thick cloud of black smoke. The plume spreading across the sky in an ugly swath.

"It could be one of the factories," Nermina said. She thought of the ever-present vapor clouds hovering in the sky whenever the family had driven north to visit with their grandmother—Zulfeta's mother—in Maglaj, the last time for her burial.

"You think we'd see smoke from the factories from here?" Hasan asked.

"Maybe," she said. Then Nermina realized that what she'd taken for clouds a while earlier was actually a sooty layer of ash. Bits of white and ochre—perhaps plaster or brick—flecked the gray-black haze. Although it was only a little past noon, it felt to Nermina like midnight. A pungent odor pricked her nostrils and Nermina felt a chill race up her spine. Her mouth went dry. She purposely avoided Hasan's eyes and kept walking at what she told herself was a casual gait. Mirsad's office stood only a couple of blocks from the far side of the bridge, the flat several blocks west from there, along the river.

As they got closer, she saw that flames engulfed the top floors of one of the modern office buildings on the wide avenue of Zmaja od Bosne. A sickening stench filled the ash-laden air. A large crowd of people—their faces and clothing covered in the stuff—raced toward them, frantic and sobbing. They looked to Nermina like ghosts. Hasan grabbed Nermina's hand and tried to pull her back the way they'd just come, but she remained frozen where she stood.

"No! What are you doing?" she yelled.

"We're going back," yelled Hasan. "We need to go back."

"I can't," said Nermina. "I have to go to Mirsad."

"How do you even know he's there?"

Nermina pointed to the burning office tower, the top floors pocked with gaping black holes where window glass shattered in the blaze.

"That's his office in the Financial Tower," she said. "That's where Mirsad works." Her voice caught. "That's where my brother works." Nermina looked up again and realized the building to the left—its twin—had also been hit.

Nermina saw that Hasan was trembling. His eyes were glazed with fear and disbelief. He was waiting for her to tell him what to do next, she thought sadly.

"We need to help them," Nermina said finally. "People are hurt."

"We're only students. What can we do?" Hasan's voice sounded weak and frightened.

"You don't have to come with me," she said.

"No, no...I can't leave you," he said in a sad, desperate way that struck Nermina momentarily as touching. But the moment vanished instantly when her long strides soon surpassed his on the footpath. The two were jostled several times by men and women pushing past them in the opposite direction, and after a time, their faces became a confusing blur. Nermina pulled the collar of her sweater over her mouth and nose, but her eyes stung relentlessly from the caustic fumes. The closer they got to the burning office towers, the more certain Nermina was of the origin of the awful smell.

For the remaining one-kilometer span of the bridge, neither had spoken a word, yet as they neared the Novo Sarajevo side, once on the downside of the rise, a barricade of steel drums and crates suddenly blocked their way. A gasp escaped Hasan's throat. Nermina's heart beat a wild staccato. Hasan kept a tight grip on her hand and, this time, she didn't pull away. In the street below them, heaps of debris were strewn everywhere. Small fires blazed in storefronts. An overturned car belched greasy, black smoke and flames. Amidst the smoke and ash and chaos, Nermina was nearly blinded. Here, in a place her brother had been so proud to show her, so proud to be a part of, she now felt immersed in a hellish nightmare she'd pay anything to escape.

Two men emerged from behind the barricade. One was bearded and wore a black jumpsuit, but the other wore tan slacks and a clean white button-down shirt like the ones she sometimes ironed for Mirsad. Both men had AK47 rifles slung over their shoulders. Nermina began to cry silently and Hasan clung to her hand more fiercely. As they got closer, Nermina recognized the Četnik badge, a double-headed eagle, pinned to the dirty black cloth on the bearded man's chest. Hasan and Nermina stood motionless as the men walked up to them, close enough that Nermina could smell the rank odor of the bearded man's body. The other man had light brown hair, cut short, and Nermina saw that he was handsome, much younger than the other.

"You are Muslims?" the bearded man asked bluntly.

Neither spoke, but Hasan looked into Nermina's eyes, now fixed in an impermeable stare. She shook her head from side to side, almost imperceptibly. The younger man casually circled the would-be captives, sidling up to Nermina and roughly grasping her long blond hair, then wrapped it around his fist. He yanked, pulling her face to his. Nermina's eyes hardened as she felt his warm breath against her cheek, his other hand clenching her breast.

"Leave her alone!" Hasan yelled. He loosened his grip from Nermina's hand and swung wildly at the man with both fists.

"Pitiful," said the bearded man. He lifted the spindly Hasan, placing a beefy paw under each armpit, and threw him to the ground as though the boy were a scarecrow. Hasan scrambled upright and swung again, this time clipping the bearded man ineffectually on his right cheek. Towering above him, the man glared at Hasan. "This is your Muslim girlfriend?" he snarled. "Or is she just your whore?" He jabbed his right fist into Hasan's gut, sending the boy to the ground where he curled up tightly and still.

"She's *our* whore now," said the younger man, reaching for Nermina again.

"Not yet," said the bearded one. "She needs to see this first." He grabbed the back of Hasan's thin jacket at the neck and pulled him to his feet. "So, you're a *šahid*? A brave man? You look more to me like a coward." He spat thickly into the boy's terrified face. "Kneel down!" he shouted.

"No!" Nermina shouted. "He's done nothing to you." The younger man laughed, grabbed Nermina by the throat.

"Watch!" he demanded.

Hasan dropped to his knees and stared up at his captor, wild-eyed. Straddling him, the man took hold of Hasan's dark hair with one hand and pulled his head backward. He reached inside a pocket with his free hand and, in one clean arc, struck the boy across the face with the cold, gray bulk of his pistol.

"Open your mouth, coward," he demanded.

Hasan wept loudly, his body convulsing as though possessed.

"I said open your mouth! Or, you want to suck my cock first, *šahid*?"

Hasan gagged as the man thrust the pistol between his open lips. Nermina fell to her knees and vomited onto the pavement. The younger man kicked her hard in the ribs several times and she fell forward into the mess of her own sickness.

"Look at this, the little boy is frightened," the bearded man called out. Still straddling Hasan, he began to laugh and the spittle from his mouth shone on his filthy beard. The man's laughter cut through Nermina's pain—a steady throbbing in her side—and reverberated inside her. She was uncertain how long the vulgar, barking noise had continued or when it had stopped, but when the younger man dragged her to her feet, she saw that her friend was still alive. The bearded man shoved him forward a few steps at a time.

In the street, Nermina saw that amongst the smoking debris, bodies lay smoldering, as well. The bearded man shouted to another black-clad soldier for his attention.

"What have you got there?" he replied jovially, making his way to his comrade.

"What do you think? Another *šahid!*"

The bearded soldier shoved Hasan forward and the other grabbed him, slapping an iron handcuff to his captive's wrist and the other to his own. He dragged Hasan along, forcing him to match his long strides.

"She's my responsibility," Hasan pleaded, his voice sounding distant to Nermina in the vast chaos.

She watched, too numb to call out, as the soldier led Hasan away to a cluster of men—young and old—who were gathering the dead from burning storefronts and cars and piling them at the curb. She watched as the soldier cuffed Hasan to an old man, the old man's clothing covered in blood. The old man pointed at something on the ground and, when Hasan did not respond, he bent and retrieved what Nermina could then see was a foot, placing it tenderly on top of the pile of spent life he and the other prisoners had already gathered.

The young soldier and the bearded one dragged Nermina a few hundred yards down the street to a burned-out, two-story building that had recently housed a restaurant. The bearded one kicked out the remaining glass in the doorway and the two lifted-dragged her—each grasping an elbow—through the metal frame. The pain engulfed her and its ebb and flow felt nearly comforting, so complete and overcoming was the sensation. The young soldier kicked several chairs and small tables out of their path as they made their way in the dank, darkened space.

"Over there," said the bearded one, pointing to a pile of flattened cardboard boxes. Together they threw Nermina to the ground. She felt the roughness of their hands as they pulled the clothing from her body, and the solid blows to her face and again to her ribs. Something pressed heavy and hard against her chest and at first, she fought to move, to breathe, to live, but when her lungs began to burn—a searing so harsh it blinded her and all thought gone then—she knew she must surrender.

CHAPTER 4
MIRSAD'S TEST
Sarajevo — April 5, 1992

Mirsad closed his office door. He'd spent the morning trying to make his way through the thick report his supervisor had assigned him, staring at the same columns of figures for hours, their meaning swimming beyond his grasp. Throughout the long night before, he'd wrestled with his options and, even as he watched the first swaths of sunlit pink brighten the sky, he still hadn't reached a conclusion to join the frontline fighters. He thought of his sister as she'd turned back to wave at him in front of the university, the brave smile plastered on her face. Could he do this? Did he really have the guts to follow through? He looked south now to the high peaks of the Jahorina, the blue-gray mountains shrouded in mist. Mirsad could barely make out the terracotta rooftops. He returned to his desk and placed a call on his office phone. He waited through several rings until someone answered.

"Yes, this is Mirsad Beganović," he said in response to the terse question emitted from the receiver before he'd had the chance to say a word. His expression hardened as he listened to the voice at the other end of the line.

"I agree..." he said. He stood up and, cradling the large phone beneath one arm, paced as far as the cord would allow him. "Of course," he replied after a few moments. He felt a trickle of sweat at his temples as he strained to keep track of the instructions the voice on the phone parceled out. Was the man being condescending or merely cautious? Mirsad paced back and forth on his short, tethered path between the desk and window. His thoughts turned to his father, how angry he would be that his son would defy him. But the voice on the phone drew him back to the moment at hand, the moment he'd longed for. Why, then, was he now so frightened?

"If this is Izetbegović's purpose, then I'm prepared to contribute. I've raised the money, as well," he said with quiet authority, though his palms were moist with sweat and the starched blue shirt his sister had pressed the night before now clung to his back. "I'll be there," he said with what he hoped sounded like certainty.

Then he placed the phone on the desk, set the receiver back into the cradle, and strode to the window. He closed his eyes and pressed his thumbs to his temples. The TV images of last week—the grieving bride and groom, the Orthodox priest in blood-soaked vestments, the groom's father, face down and adrift, it seemed, in a burgundy pool of his own blood—were vivid behind his eyelids. His own image, that of a tall, slender man with brooding brown eyes and the same angular cheekbones as his mother, looked back at him through the window glass.

Maybe his father was right, Mirsad admonished himself. Maybe it wasn't his responsibility to fight. But he knew, as well, the carnage the Serbs had already unleashed on the Croats in recent months. His decision to join had come painfully but also inevitably. But now he wished for the conviction of the young men he'd met at the meetings, Muslims who called themselves *Patriotska Liga*. It would be much easier to see the issues in black and white, as these men did.

Today Mirsad saw the purity of his father's beliefs and, for the moment at least, he envied his single-minded faith, just as he envied the men he'd join in battle. He squinted into the distance where a plume of thick, white smoke billowed against the mackerel sky. In his exhaustion, he became transfixed upon this image, watching as the wind buffeted the smoke, first elongating the rising pillar, and then compressing it into a squat, amorphous cloud.

Still dazed, he felt the first blast before he understood what was happening. When the second rocket shattered a window a few floors above his own, though, his heart began to pound with terror as fragments of glass rained down from the sky. They glinted in the still-weak April sunlight, the image almost beautiful.

It's begun, Mirsad thought. The war has begun without me. The notion seemed at once childish and rational. He'd wanted to be among the warriors who would preempt the first strikes on the city. Clearly, that wouldn't happen now.

He heard the fire alarm and the ear-splitting blare pulsed through his body, the racket throbbing inside his skull. The next moment, one of Mirsad's co-workers flung open the door.

"Get out of here!" he yelled. "We've been hit."

Without waiting for a response, the young man turned and ran down a corridor already choked with workers from other offices on their floor. Mirsad grabbed his messenger bag and, slinging it across his shoulder, he waded into the crush of people in the corridor, the crowd thickening tenfold at the doorway to the stairwell. Unable to discern individual voices, he heard instead what seemed a collective howling. He noticed two older women, their faces streaked with tears, saw how they clung to one another desperately, shoving their way through the throng as one person. Mirsad felt himself being pulled into the depths of this fear-driven body. All one, its frenzied movement compacted by terror.

He thought of his sister, Nermina, and cursed again under his breath. He should have fought his father on this point. He should have fought his headstrong sister, for that matter. They should have sent her to Rome where she'd have been safe. He tried but couldn't bring to mind now the name of the boy who'd been delivering her to the flat every day after her classes. Why had they all been so stupid?

In the stairwell with the others, the acrid stench of smoke overtook him. The smoke hung heavy, viscous and dark. When two men at the head of the crowd pushed open the door at the building's mezzanine level, Mirsad saw flames lapping at the walls, devouring the thick wooden frames, the paintings installed when the steel and glass office tower had first been dedicated. The raging fires now cut off two steep sets of escalators. Mirsad gagged as he saw several bodies, inert on the glassy marble floor, suddenly engulfed in flames, the fire devouring anything that would burn.

"The ground floor!" someone yelled, and Mirsad felt himself forced back into the stairwell by the crowd. He wanted only to be freed of these people packed so tightly all around him. *I have to get out!* This thought overtook all others. He was frantic, wild now with fear. And as the reality of his situation took hold of him, the building shook with another blast. This time, he couldn't tell if the rocket had hit above or below them. He recalled some bits of what the men at the meetings had talked about—Howitzers, AA rocket launchers, most if not all left over from the Soviets, they'd said. He felt another, stronger surge of panic and, with this, an aching swell of cowardice rising in his throat.

The more insistent press of bodies against his own brought him back again. He noticed for the first time the stench of perspiration. His own? The people around him? He heard shouts from the front of the crowd. The howling persisted beneath the shouts—and now he remembered a silly fight with his sister. He'd swung at her, shattered the figurine. A Persian cat. He'd lied to his mother. An accident. His mother held him as he sobbed. Shame washed over him now, just as before.

He sensed the crowd pressing back against him, harder now. The soldiers appeared in the narrow corridor. Young men. Teenagers. Three of them? A dozen? Staccato pulse of automatic weapons fire, relentless, unyielding. The screams of the wounded raised gooseflesh on his neck and arms. Those who could run did so, while the others cowered against the walls. He saw a young woman—no older than his sister—slumped against the wall. A hole in her forehead, the wound blackened and oozing bright red blood. He went to her, put his ear to her heart.

When he rose, he felt the bullet enter his chest, the white-hot pain that wasn't pain but rather a slow drowning—*The pieces of porcelain scattered on the tile floor, and his sister put her hands to her face, her eyes wide with fear*—precise, undisguised, and in those final moments, a surrender that felt to Mirsad like forgiveness.

CHAPTER 5
AWAKENING

Nermina uncurls her limbs, releasing bit by bit the tight small creature she's become. Gingerly, her fingers touch the cardboard beneath her, the rough wooden floorboards beyond, all of this, sticky, cold, wet. The ruined restaurant, half-lit and still now. The men gone. She cannot remember which man had been first or how many times they'd each been inside her. Her mouth tastes of blood and she remembers how she'd bitten down hard into a hand stifling her cries. Which one? Which man? She sees the three earrings that studded the bearded man's right ear, gold crescents in graduated sizes. She feels the weight of him slamming against her broken body. And the other one, his cologne still sharp in her nostrils, how she'd gagged when he thrust himself inside her mouth. How she'd vomited each time after that.

She raises herself to hands and knees. A wave of pain and nausea crests and recedes, crests and recedes. She forces herself to stand—legs sore and throbbing and far too weak to hold her. Her body is pale in the half-light, raw like meat. She shrouds her blood-streaked body as best she can with the remains of her clothing, torn, soaked in the rust-colored swill that surrounds her. She is the creature again—unable to hold herself upright—reduced to hands and knees. An animal.

She crawls, palms cut, bleeding from broken glass, chunks of concrete, shards of aluminum, all of this strewn across an expanse of destruction, a vast and impossible distance she must traverse. She crawls and rests, crawls and rests. Finally— miraculously—outside: cold. She feels but doesn't quite feel this sensation on her face, her hands. She is surprised to see the streetlights still burning, surprised as well to discover how close she is to her brother's flat, how close she has been all along. Has it been days, she wonders, or perhaps only hours? She cannot be certain.

She drags herself along the streets—hobbling now, half-crouched. The smell of fresh-baked bread from a small *pekara* seems to belong to another lifetime. Has she dreamed this place? This familiar, warm smell? Lights come on in the houses across the river. Mirsad's flat appears and she drags herself up a long flight of stairs. Her fingers find the extra key from under the mat—damp with rain—and she winces with the effort of this.

Inside, she calls out for her brother and her voice sounds strange to her, as empty as the darkened rooms. Finally, she removes the figurine from her pocket—another small miracle—and places it carefully on top of her brother's bureau.

She sees his frightened little boy's eyes, eyes fearful only of their mother's displeasure. She knows the danger Mirsad surely faces. She won't allow herself to believe that he is dead. Above all, she aches for the childhood they'd once shared; she knows now with certainty that those children are gone. If she were ever to see her brother again, they would meet as near strangers.

Nermina struggles from sleep to near-waking. She drifts. Wooly darkness surrounds her. A damp chill saturates her bruised body, the soreness permeating deep into her bones. The leather of Mirsad's sofa is moist against her cheek. Her mind skitters—frantic—trying to determine where she is. Her sleep had been fitful. She'd dreamed of running and running through endless dark streets and alleys, splashing with each footstep into foul-smelling sludge that nearly reached her thighs.

She jolts to complete awareness, heart pounding, mouth rank and thirsty. Her fingers travel the length of her arms, her legs. She is, indeed, alive. She wraps herself in a deep hug—*alone, alone*—and rocks. She drifts into half-dream. The streets. The alleyways. She rocks and rocks in the silent flat, only the creaking springs of the mattress remind her—again—she is alive. She's certain now, but also certain that her brother has not come home; if he had, he surely would have awakened her. She sees Hasan, the metal cuff around his wrist, the bloody foot he places on the pile. She shivers but no tears come, no cry escapes her caged heart.

She understands now that Mirsad is either a captive—like Hasan—or already dead. She *feels* this, rather, and the feeling sickens and frightens her, but no less than what comes next: a flash of sweat-slicked faces hovering above her own. The bearded one. The other. The men who raped her. One and then the other. *This happened.* The stench of sweat and blood clings to her skin and hair and clothing. *This happened.* With remarkable effort, she raises herself on one arm. The jabbing pain in her ribs reminds her, it has been with her all along, the companion of her nightmares, relentless and deliberate, but familiar and therefore not wholly unwanted. The pain feels hot to Nermina, like a live electric wire, and the burning draws a tight belt around her ribcage that throbs with each breath.

When she sets her bare feet onto the cold floor, she can hardly believe that she is whole; these are her ankles, her calves, her thighs. She holds her arms out in front of her, tries to make out the mud-caked silhouette of her hands. She realizes—remembers again—that the mud is not mud. Thin lines of dried blood stain the paleness of her wrists and forearms. She stands and the pain wraps her even more tightly. She takes a step. She feels the rawness inside her, remembering how each man had thrust himself deep into her until the pain was nothing but a sound, a tuneless, low hum that, thankfully, mercifully, had drowned out everything else. Her stomach tightens when she's forced again to see their faces, to feel the blows to her ribs, to her face. The pictures flash and flicker, flash and flicker.

The bile rises in her throat and she stumbles to the washroom, retching into the sink until she feels her body is drained of all life. She is a corpse, like the burned and blackened bodies she and Hasan had seen in the street. But when? How long has she slept?

Panic washes over Nermina now. She cannot remember, can't place the events in proper order; she can make no distinction between *then* and *now*. Her mind grasps only snippets, the terrible miasma of images. Hasan. The pistol inside his mouth. The bearded man's face. The pile of smoldering logs that turns into human flesh. One picture bleeds into the next. Several pictures overlay one another in strange, opaque veracity. The images speed up and slow down, speed up and slow down, before disappearing all together. They wait.

In the washroom Nermina tries the switch but no light comes on. No water flows when she turns the faucet at the sink. Finally, she peels her filthy jeans from her body, sits on the cold toilet seat, and pees into the bowl. She reaches instinctively for the toilet paper still in its holder; the thought seems almost ludicrous to her, that something, this small thing, has remained just as she'd left it. She wipes the slime from between her legs as best she can, then rises and lifts the top from the toilet tank. The lid rings against the silence as she sets it on the cold, tile floor. She dips the corner of a blue hand towel into the tank and feels the sting of cold water, first blotting gently the painful abrasions, then rubbing harder at the insides of her thighs as the men's faces flash again before her. She winces as she touches the soft, dry part of the towel to her labia, registers the rusty stain on the cloth when she takes it away.

The throbbing pain in her ribcage returns, stronger having waited its turn. Her attention grows clearer, and clearer still. She suspects a break but knows there's nothing to be done. And then—improbably, irrationally—a tender smile plays briefly on her lips; had Mirsad been more of an athlete, perhaps she'd find an elastic bandage among his things to wrap herself. She watches for a few moments as fourteen-year-old Mirsad storms across the court, red-faced and indignant, conceding another match to his twelve-year-old sister. The summerhouse. The air perfumed with lavender and sage. Mirsad's sweaty palm grasping her own in a handshake. Nermina swallows the lump of pain that grows larger with each breath, these images bleeding into all of the others.

She opens the mirrored door to the medicine cabinet and grabs the plastic pill bottles from the shelves. In the poor light she is unable to make out the labels but remembers Mirsad's most recent bout of bronchitis, an illness he'd suffered perennially since childhood. She hopes at least one of the bottles contains an antibiotic. She takes nail scissors, the box of Band-aids, a bottle of antiseptic, a tube of hydrocortisone cream, and the bag of cotton balls. These she lays on the floor.

Peering into the near-darkness of the mirror, her face is a misshapen shadow, swollen and purpled. Her lips, her tongue, her throat raw and aching. She remembers the bag of Epsom salts under the sink and she scoops a fistful with her fingers, forces herself to dip the washroom cup into the tank, to sift the grains into the cup. Stinging and burning, she rinses the filth from her mouth. Next, she dabs antiseptic on the deep cut below her left eye. It's stopped bleeding but is tender and throbs when she touches it. Finally, she pulls the remaining dry hand towel from the bar and wraps the supplies inside.

Timid now, Nermina enters the small room that Mirsad had readied for her in another lifetime. She feels inside the drawers for clean underwear, a sweater, and jeans, her fingers confirming each garment without difficulty. She dresses slowly, resting from time to time, and when she's done, she gathers the small sum of money that's folded neatly inside her jewelry box. Here, too, is the gold necklace her parents had given her when she'd graduated gymnasium—such big plans then, medical faculty, all of it gone now. She slides the gold chain, the engraved locket into her bra, feeling the silky coldness against her skin. Then sitting on the edge of the bed, she wills herself to stuff the backpack she'd used as a schoolgirl with her meager cache of medical supplies and a change of clothing. I cannot stay here, she tells herself, though she longs to curl up beneath the covers of her bed. To sleep and sleep, shutting out forever the terrible images that cleave to her even in their intermittent absence. But she longs even more for her family. She needs to know they're safe. She needs to feel her mother's cool hands pressed to her cheeks. And her father. Her father will know how to find Mirsad. Her father will know how to fix this.

In the kitchen she forces down a slice of bread she's spread with peanut butter, shoving the rest of the loaf into a cloth bag she'd used at the market. She throws in, as well, the jar of peanut butter, two oranges, and one of the plastic bottles she'd long ago filled with tap water and stored in the small refrigerator. Her eyes then alight on the telephone; it sits mute like a stoic witness on the small table in the corner, beneath the room's only window. The pinkening sky casts the phone's beige plastic in an eerie glow. Her hand trembles when she lifts the receiver, places it to her ear; the dense silence confirms what she already knows. She picks up a pen and jots a note on the top sheet of paper from a thick pad Mirsad keeps next to the phone. She uses one of the magnets—a likeness of the cartoon cat Garfield that Mirsad had found at the *Baščaršija* when they were children—to clip the note to the refrigerator. She marvels then at how her brother had kept such a silly thing all of these years. She thinks of the tiny porcelain figurine she'd left on his bureau the night before. How long ago even this now seems.

Finally, she grabs her slicker from a peg on the wall and ties it around her waist. The momentum of her actions carries her to the front door of the flat. These actions supplant deeper thought, and for this, she is if not consciously then instinctively grateful. She's set herself on a course of action, as yet undetermined, although this is of little consequence just now; she understands only that she needs to keep moving forward. One step at a time. She needs to keep moving and she needs to reach her parents. Perhaps Mirsad has contacted them by now. Perhaps they've had some word from the people at his office. She refuses to believe that her parents are anything but safe in their own home in Dobrinja. It's unlikely the trolleybuses are running. She tells herself she'll walk. She'll rest when she has to, but she'll make Dobrinja by nightfall.

CHAPTER 6
RESCUE

Out in the street the air carries the acrid smell of smoke, though there's no other sign of the hellish scenes she remembers from the bridge, the barricade. Not a single vehicle moves in the still-weak light of morning. Not a single person walks past her. Nermina shoves her hands into the front pockets of her jeans and strides in the opposite direction of the barricade where she'd last seen Hasan. She thinks of his hand—soft, even girlish—clutching hers so forcefully. She thinks about the terror she had seen there in his eyes and begins to cry silently, though without slowing her pace. She wonders if she'll ever again see this gentle boy, her friend.

And then before she's had the chance to comprehend the sound of an engine, the car is upon her. Her heartbeat pounds in her ears. Cold sweat instantly chills her. She sees the soldiers' faces from her nightmare hovering above her broken body. Though her intention is to run, her legs refuse. She stands dumbfounded and trembling as brakes screech and a young man jumps from the car. "Get in!" he yells. "Are you crazy?" Nermina's arms swing wildly as though fighting through a thickly treed forest. Her fists strike at the man's chest, his gut. Two hands—stronger than her own—grasp her shoulders, then pin her arms to her sides. "Get in! Move quickly," he demands.

In one swift motion he shoves her into the back seat where two other young men, bloodied and inexpertly bandaged with torn clothing, lie back against the seat, inert and groaning. The man slams the door a split second after Nermina is inside, sprints to the front of the car, and slides into the passenger seat. Nermina hears herself screaming and kicking at the door. The sound of her voice frightens her more than the men—soldiers—she thinks. She remembers the one from the bridge. The ruined restaurant. His pressed white shirt, how her vomit had splattered it.

"Let's go, Tata!" the young man shouts to the driver, a man at least as old as Nermina's father.

"Where are you going?" Nermina demands of the older man. Her voice sounds shrill in her ears. "Where are you taking me?" The old man remains silent. His hands grip the steering wheel.

"We're taking my brothers to the hospital," the young man up front says. "You can't stay here." He's no longer shouting. "Do you know what's happening?" He throws his left arm across the top of the front seat and turns to face Nermina.

"They're taking the city. The Serbs, the filthy pigs—They've got snipers in the hills." His voice is almost calm now, pleading, but Nermina feels the impact of his words like a blow to the gut.

Of course she knows the siege has begun, just as Mirsad had warned. The war has arrived, had been upon them all along. Mirsad knew this. He'd warned them. He'd warned their father. But now, hearing the truth confirmed, the words of a stranger, Nermina is forced to comprehend even more than she's gleaned from her time with the soldiers. *This happened.*

"I'm sorry if we frightened you, but you can't stay here," the man continues when he gets no reply. "Do you know this? Do you know what they're doing?"

"Yes," says Nermina, her voice barely audible. "They took my friend. And my brother. He's...he's missing."

"I'm sure you will find him," says the father, his voice so filled with kindness that Nermina begins to sob. "We'll take you to the hospital and this will be the best place to be. The safest place. You are injured."

Following his father's example, the son in the front seat says, "The doctors there will see to your wounds."

Nermina's mind floats. She thinks of nothing. Tears continue to slide down her cheeks. She warms her hands—dirt packed under jagged nails—inside her slicker. She doesn't want to remember. She doesn't want to think or feel. But she feels the warmth of the injured man next to her and realizes that the bandage wrapped around his thigh is soaked with blood and that this is the source of the warmth. The man—a boy, really, she thinks—has begun to whimper.

"Thank you," she says quietly, bowing her head as though in prayer.

CHAPTER 7
ESMER

A large writhing crowd has amassed in the parking lot, surging in waves it seems, toward the main entrance to the hospital. As Nermina gets closer, she sees that many people are gravely wounded, some with limbs and torsos wrapped in makeshift bandages. Their clothing is torn and stained, faces streaked with blood and dirt and ash. Still, others seem unharmed but frantic in their efforts to push forward in the mob. Nermina hears a great deal of shouting, the moaning of those in agony, and then the wail of an infant slicing through the chaotic drone in its urgency. She realizes that people are calling out the names of missing loved ones, searching in the desperate hope of finding them bloodied and injured rather than reaching the more likely conclusion. She thinks she should be doing the same—perhaps Mirsad is here—but when she shouts her brother's name, her voice is wholly consumed by the others'. She feels small and powerless. She tries to recall the last words she'd spoken to Mirsad, but her thoughts refuse to come clear.

An ambulance pulls into the emergency bay, and within seconds two men in blue EMT uniforms jump out, race to the back, and fling open the doors. Even from a distance, Nermina can see that the woman they wheel out on the stretcher is charred from head to foot, only recognizable as female from what remains of her blackened skirt and leggings. The rescue workers shout above the din, the crowd parts for an instant, and then the three are swallowed up in the swirling sea of people.

Nermina had told the men who'd brought her here—the old man and his sons—to rush on ahead of her, that she would be all right on her own. The injured son had gone into shock during the car ride and she prayed now that he would live. She'd done what she could, checking that his airway was clear, bundling him with the others' spare clothing, but she understood his life depended on the immediate attention of a surgeon. And now, even knowing her own wounds are minor, she is frightened for her life, as well. The closer she gets to the doors, the more insistent the pushing from the crowd. It isn't until she's gotten within thirty feet of the building that she realizes where she is: Koševo Hospital. Her heart skips and a rush of frantic hope supplants her fear; her father will be here. This hospital is his workplace and, with any luck, she'll find him.

Now she begins to push in earnest along with the others and she notices that the same soot and ash that had hung in the air that day on the bridge surrounds them here, as well. She realizes that aside from the yelling, people are coughing, and her own throat and eyes begin to burn. The acrid smell of smoke is now chillingly familiar. She pictures Hasan on the bridge, what the soldiers had done there. What they'd done to her later. Then her thoughts jump to Mirsad's empty flat, and then to their family's house in Dobrinja before she'd moved into the flat with Mirsad. She sees her parents' faces and begins to sob. And then, just as suddenly, she feels an urgent tugging on her hand that frightens her, jolting her from these thoughts. She looks down to see a little boy, perhaps five or six years old at most.

"*Upomoć! Treba mi vaša pomoć!*" he yells.

She sees the boy's dark brown eyes, wide with terror. Pleading. He wears a spotlessly clean and pressed school uniform—blue pants and white shirt—and aside from his frantic grip on Nermina's hand, appears to be unharmed. "*Majka, Majka,*" he cries now, craning his head back and forth, searching for his mother.

Her first instinct is to pick up the child and carry him with her, but then her next thought is that he'd slow her down; she is ashamed to be struggling with what now seems an impossible decision. She understands the boy could be trampled in the crowd—or worse—if she leaves him here, and yet she is frantic to get inside the doors. She knows her father would never abandon the flood of wounded and dying and that, if he is here, she will find him. And if Mirsad had made his way to this hospital, they will all be together. She will be safe.

But as the crowd presses in all around them and the boy

continues to clutch her hand, another wave of panic washes over her: Where is *her* mother? In her confusion she cannot remember what day it is and, therefore, at which clinic her mother would be working. Was her mother still in Dobrinja or in the city center? She can't work it though. The events of the past days seem surreal, the boy's crying and the desperation in his small hand suddenly the only sensations she can grasp with any certainty. This she understands. This is happening now. All of the rest she pushes away.

"Listen to me," Nermina cries in a much sterner voice than she'd intended. "You stay with me! Do you hear? You stay close!"

The child looks up at her with enormous, frightened eyes. *Of course, he would stay close to her.* She scolds herself for likely scaring the boy even more. *Where else has he got to go?* She squats down so that she's eye-to-eye with him. "What is your name?" she asks.

"Esmer," comes the boy's response. The child's voice lingers only a moment before evaporating in the chaos.

"Can you run?" she shouts.

The child shakes his head mutely in the affirmative. And then Nermina musters all her remaining strength, pulling the boy close beside her as she charges into a clump of people ahead of them, not caring who she pushes. She feels a moment of shame, then quickly dismisses it. The same rules of social convention that had guided her such a short time ago seem wildly out of place here. Everything has changed in an instant. She feels herself being pummeled by elbows and shoulders, not realizing that she's squeezing the boy's fingers harder and harder as they near the doors. She thinks again of her father.

The way he'd held his hand to her cheek like a blessing. How long ago? Again, the fear of this void.

Then suddenly she can make out a green-scrubbed hospital worker at the glass doors—a nurse perhaps, or a doctor? She sees that they've set up a makeshift triage; some people are being waved in while others were being turned away. Rows of gurneys stand outside as well as beyond the glass entryway in the hospital lobby. Nurses move swiftly between the moaning patients. Nermina pushes even harder, never letting go of the boy's hand.

"*Molim! Molim!*" she cries when it is finally her turn in the queue. The man at the door—the gatekeeper she understands now—is her father's age, the purpled circles beneath his eyes depicting the horror of the last several days. "Doctor Suljo Beganović! I'm his daughter," she shouts. The man ignores Nermina but squats down to examine the boy. He presses his fingers gently to either side of the boy's throat, shines a penlight into his frightened eyes.

"No, no, the boy is unharmed," she says, trying to summon a rational, civilized tone. "I just need to find my father. Dr. Beganović." She looks down at the man's ID badge, reading the name and title when, still, her words fail to elicit any response. "Dr. Sidran, I can help," she pleads. "I'm a second-year medical student!" She's begun to shout again, incensed at the doctor's seeming disregard of her plea as he continues to examine the child. And then finally, slowly, with the barely contained mob of people beyond him, Dr. Sidran pats the boy on the head and rises to face Nermina.

"I heard you, Miss Beganović," he says with a voice hoarse from exhaustion. "You may go in. Your father is here; he's been here since it began." He shakes his head sadly. "You'll keep the boy with you?" he says, already dismissing her as he turns toward an old woman with a large gash in her forehead.

"Of course," Nermina shouts as she pulls the child along with her, the two now running as the automatic glass doors to the hospital shush open to admit them.

Inside, the relief that fills her is overwhelming. She feels as though she might laugh and cry and the same time. No matter what happens now, her father will keep her safe. He will keep all of them safe. She looks down into the child's frightened eyes and then stretches out her arms to him. She lifts him easily—he seems nearly weightless to her—and his legs clasp snugly around her waist, his thin arms around her neck. She forces herself to slow her gait, peering into first one hospital room and then another. The rooms are filled. People are lying in hospital beds and in chairs. Curled up on the floors. Each room holds a different but similar scene of despair. And yet, surprisingly, the panic has left her. The boy is no longer a burden, but instead feels to Nermina a part of her. She doesn't question this. Her progress through the corridors is efficient now but unhurried.

And then she sees her father coming through a stairwell door at the far end of the hallway. His habitually pristine white physician's coat is stained with blood, his thick gray hair more disheveled than she's ever seen it. And yet Nermina sees the quicksilver wash of relief that spreads across his face as she runs straight toward him, the boy clinging tightly to her neck. Without understanding how she's traversed the distance that separates them, she feels her father's arms around her, and the tears slipping down her cheeks as he tassels Esmer's dark hair. Was this a moment later? An hour?

Then still feeling the gentle pressure of her father's hands on her shoulders, Nermina hears the question that jolts her back to her new reality. "Where is your brother?" She sees that her father's expression has changed completely. His eyes hold hers until she's forced to look away.

"I don't know. He wasn't at the flat when I...when I returned. Or rather...when I left."

"I don't understand," says Suljo. A look of annoyance flashes across his brow, one that Nermina recognizes and, until quite recently, would have evoked a somewhat defiant response. But in this moment Nermina realizes just how much she has changed. The days of arguing with her father about which university she would attend or which course of study she would follow are long gone. What a spoiled child she had been then. A defiant brat.

She sees again how she'd dragged herself up the stairs to Mirsad's flat, remembers how she'd not wanted to awaken. And yet she *had* awakened and the nightmare had clung to her even in the daylight. She sobs now, understanding that the nightmare will never leave her.

"What is it?" Suljo demands, but when Nermina's cries grow even more urgent, he crushes her to his chest, the little boy, Esmer, standing mute beside them. Nermina allows the pain to pour out from inside her. Her mind forms no thoughts; she feels, instead, minuscule, nearly nonexistent.

CHAPTER 8
HOSPITAL
April 23, 1992

Nermina picks her way among the rows of makeshift bedding. She wants to be certain the child is asleep. They've used whatever supplies they can—thin hospital blankets, sheets, and towels—packing as many bodies into each room and hallway as possible. It seems improbable to her that people could find any sort of respite here. For her part, Nermina sleeps only briefly between the shifts she's worked out with the others. She's lost all track of night and day, moving robotically from task to task, perpetually exhausted. But she refuses to abandon the boy, to leave him with no one.

She looks down now at his sleeping face, at the long, thick lashes that remind her of Mirsad's and, therefore, stop her breath each time she makes this connection. She leans over, pulls up the wrinkled sheet that coils around his spindly legs so that it now covers him to his chin. Then kneeling down close to him, she sweeps back the nearly black tendrils that lay matted against his forehead. "Sleep well, little one," she whispers. She stands—her back aching—and leaves him then, making her way through the stifling hallways for the rest of her rounds.

The little boy Esmer told her that he is five years old. From what Nermina has pieced together from the child's story, his mother had been shot in the street in front of their house. An aunt brought him here in her car, but then they'd lost one another in the crowd. The boy knew his aunt only as *Strina Lela*, no last name to go on. So, on the first day, Nermina and some of the others made signs and added the boy's name to the list for those who would come looking for missing loved ones. She'd expected that Esmer's aunt would turn up eventually. But then after the shelling had begun in earnest it became more difficult to circulate even the simplest message throughout the city. Now, like the others, Nermina fears for her life each time she steps outside the hospital doors. She knows that Esmer's aunt will not come back for him now. If she's not already dead, she'll make an easy target for the snipers should she be desperate or foolish enough to try to cross the main road to the hospital.

With the phone lines down, the doctors and nurses who've stayed on take turns with the satellite phone whenever one of the rescue workers manages to breach the front line to bring in the wounded. While most of her time here has been a continuous haze of activity—days and nights indistinguishable from one another—certain moments are etched permanently into Nermina's memory.

For instance, it had been the third day from her arrival when they'd brought in her mother's body, her face so badly beaten her father had only identified her by the birthmark on her thigh. He'd tried to push Nermina away—she was part of the triage team—but she refused and stood over the bloody remains of her mother. Her father's sobs confirmed her worst fears, but she continued to stand there. Mute, and as she now remembers, perhaps even blinded. One of the other doctors led her father away, pulling him gently at first, and then using a much greater force when necessary. When her father's wailing had become unbearable to the others. But Nermina had remained as one of the nurses wrapped her mother's battered body in an already soiled sheet. She placed her hands on the blood-soaked cloth, feeling the outline of her mother's face, trying to remember how beautiful that face had once been, willing her fingers to divine what the soldiers had destroyed. She'd felt herself choking, then turned her head and vomited at her feet. She heard the ugly guttural cries that surged from inside her and she longed for the cool silence of death.

Suljo had spent the following week using his connections—doctors and administrators at the other city hospitals, some of his old political cronies—to try to locate Mirsad. Finally, when news reached them that rescue workers had turned up scores of charred bodies in the lobby of the East Financial Tower, Suljo risked everything to make his way there. A day of futile searching through the rubble, another at the morgue and makeshift holding areas in adjacent buildings. Finally, they surrendered to the inevitable. After that, neither Nermina nor her father had anywhere else to go. So, they stayed.

Staying, Nermina understands, is a relative term. She sees in her father's eyes, and in those of the others, confirmation of the ghostly limbo they inhabit. The grieving that would have consumed them in most any other circumstance absurdly eludes them here. A wholesale numbness displaces the expected emotions of grief. And strangely, Nermina thinks now as she approaches her father in one of the dimly lit operating rooms, this is likely a blessing of sorts. She doesn't trust herself to release the sadness and anger that lie welled inside her for fear she would never staunch its flow once it started. She watches silently as her father changes the dressing of an old man's leg wound, one of the hundreds they've seen that is likely already infected.

"How is the boy?" her father asks, his famous baritone weakened with sleeplessness. He cleans his hands with the antiseptic that is now a sparse commodity, and turns to his daughter, kissing her on the cheek.

"Asleep," says Nermina, putting her hand to her father's face. His cheeks are covered with days-old stubble, something the meticulous Suljo Beganović would never have tolerated in the past. "He's stopped crying for his mother. I don't know if that is good or bad."

"Likely neither," he says, helping the old man down from the low table he was sitting on. He hands the man a wooden crutch that leans against the table. "Keep it clean as best you can," he says sternly as the man hobbled away. Then turning back to Nermina, "The boy's stopped crying because his little heart is empty now."

"I think you're right," says Nermina. "Maybe this is best." She scans the cluttered room, sees that her father and the other two doctors have used the last hour and a half of generator time to complete four surgical cases. She knows, however, that no amount of rationing will allow them to keep up.

"I've signed up for the water team," she says flatly, deliberately avoiding her father's eyes.

"That's foolish," says Suljo. "We need you here."

Looking up now, Nermina sees how gaunt her father has become. The clothing that he wears—a dingy white button-down shirt and black pants that were once part of a well-made suit—now hang loosely from his body.

"There weren't enough people on the list. I haven't taken a turn—"

"You're not listening to me," he says, his words clipped with the curtness she'd heard him use with staff, more and more each day.

"I *am* listening," says Nermina defiantly. "I'm needed. We don't survive here without clean water. You know that. I'm one of the youngest. I'm one of the strongest—"

"And you could be shot!" Suljo shouts. One of the doctors, a nearly skeletal and balding man, turns quickly to look at his colleague, but Suljo ignores him and glares at Nermina.

"I'm getting you out of here. I'm getting you out of Bosnia," he hisses, his voice frightening Nermina in its steely intensity. "If you think I'm going to allow you to stay here to die then you're sorely mistaken."

She thinks of the ridiculous arguments she'd incited with her father the year of her acceptance to the medical faculty.

She was going to care for underprivileged people in the countryside. She was going to become a general practitioner rather than follow her parents' path in medicine. Now this notion is irrelevant, her idealism a perverse joke.

"Tata," says Nermina, her voice threatening to break. "I'm not leaving you," she says softly. "I *can't* leave you." She holds out her hand to him, but he slaps it away. The movement is harsh. Precise. She feels the brutal sting of it, remembering the blows to her ribs and to her face. Remembering the soldiers. She especially remembers their animal smell. Her breath catches sharply in her lungs.

"You're not the one who chooses," says Suljo, seeming calmer now to Nermina, but still fixing her with a cold stare. "I've already put plans in motion. I need only another few days. Then it will be done. It's out of your hands now, Nermina."

She catches a momentary glint in her father's eyes, but then he turns from her and strides toward one of the gurneys. Nermina stands still for several moments, her entire body tense with anger and exhaustion. The image of her father—she'd not once seen him break since her mother's death—dogs her, though. It saddens her and for a heartbeat, she feels that the floodgates will open. Her thoughts loop back to the soldiers. Then she walks to the set of swinging double doors and kicks the right one so fiercely that it swings wide open for her.

CHAPTER 9
WHITE LIES
Ancona, Italy — June 1992

Nermina watches the swath of shoreline and turquoise waters as they materialize below. The plane takes one last dip, banking sharply toward the little airport. The effect of this movement and her perspective from the oval window makes Nermina feel as though she is floating alone in space. The earth below seems as far away as a distant star. As the plane dips lower a thick patchwork of farmland and villages, terra cotta rooftops, and winding streets, seems unfathomably remote. There lies below her a civilization beyond the war, a civilization Nermina can barely imagine.

Next to her Esmer stirs. She shifts his weight gently from her side, feeling the warm spot where his head lulls against her ribs. She'd refused to leave him behind. Instead, she will see him off in Ancona where an aunt will meet them and take the boy back to Rome.

Nermina's own plans are much more complicated, but she is still too dazed by fear and exhaustion to consider the difficulties that might lie ahead. Her father had been insistent, meticulous in his instructions. She has the thick yellow envelope pressed against her skin, snugged inside the waistband of her jeans. She has her mother's ring. This she will sell. She'll need the cash, first for the hostel in Ancona and then in London. For food, of course. And then finally for the flight to the United States. She has no expectation of what will come beyond that. She doesn't count the bills now, doesn't consider how long the money will last her, what will happen when it runs out. She doesn't worry about dying because she suspects she's crossed that thin perimeter between the living and the dead already.

But she worries about Esmer because he is just a child and there is no one left in Bosnia to care for him. She thinks of the other children. Day after day, they'd foraged for food in bombed-out basements and kitchens along with the rest. Children younger than Esmer in the UN queue with plastic jugs for water, scrabbling for kindling in public parks already barren. Always, the snipers on the rooftops, in the mountains. Always the dry-mouthed fear. She wouldn't leave him to that. Her father had reached the aunt and the aunt said she would keep the boy for as long as necessary, this, her father's last rational act.

Now as the plane screeches onto the runway, Nermina rouses the child. "We're here," she says, not completely certain what this means for either of them. The first leg, she tells herself. The first step. One step and then another. She needs to repeat this mantra again and again because even the simplest things—washing her face, drinking from a bottle of water, peeing it out later—seem at once alien and unnecessary. She must breathe. She must sleep. She must eat.

Nermina smoothes down the messy shock of dark hair that sticks straight up on the boy's head like a rooster's crown. "See, I told you we'd be here in no time." She winces at the forced cheerful tone of her voice.

"Will we sleep in a big hotel tonight?" the boy asks.

"Something like that," she answers. One more white lie to ease the child's burdens. In another day, she will leave him, too.

Nermina pays in British pounds. A cot for herself—she'd begged the clerk to allow the child to stay with her—in a dormitory room with seven other women. She is the child's guardian, she said. The child is alone. She held him throughout the night, her knees bent and the boy's small body filling the space she made for him beside her.

In the morning, Nermina holds Esmer's hand as they wait in the queue with the other hostelers. A young man about Nermina's age heaps pastries on a plate, fills a Styrofoam cup with coffee. He wears a pair of dirty blue jeans, ripped at the knees, his hair a bundle of dreadlocks tied with a bandana. He smiles at Nermina and when she doesn't reciprocate he says "Whatever" in English, a bemused look on his face. "That your brother or something?" he asks then.

"He's my cousin," Nermina says in perfect English, her voice a flat line. Esmer turns his face to her, a look of confusion clouding his features. He says nothing. The child's clothing hangs wrinkled on his body, his large eyes growing limpid with distrust as he assesses the American.

"You...like...traveling?" the man persists.

"Yes. We're on holiday," Nermina says. She places two pastries on a Styrofoam plate and hands them to Esmer, then pours herself a cup of coffee. Next, she ushers the boy to the furthest table from the queue. The American stares after them a second or two before biting into his pastry.

The high season has not yet begun and only a few small clusters of tourists walk the cobblestoned streets. At precisely 1400, a short, blocky woman approaches the Fontana del Càlamo where Nermina waits with Esmer. The woman walks quickly, a large brown handbag hanging from her shoulder. Nermina sees that the woman is likely no older than her mother, though she dresses like a woman closer to her grandmother's age, a thick pair of black shoes, black skirt covering her short legs to the ankle, the collar of a crisp white blouse peeking out from under a beige overcoat. Nermina imagines her mother, her dark hair twisted gracefully into a knot, the hem of a navy silk dress brushing her knees. And then the next moment she sees her mother's face, purpled and raw, her dark hair thick with blood. She feels the bile rising in her throat.

The woman, Maria, greets Nermina by name, and Nermina jerks herself back from the edge. "This is Esmer," she says, placing her hand on the boy's shoulder.

Maria speaks in rapid Italian until Nermina responds in French. The conversation that the women conduct is one little

Esmer cannot comprehend. Nermina wonders if his not knowing is similar to her own ignorance of her future; she no longer fears the unknown. Nothing that lies ahead of her could ever eclipse the horror of her past. And if it did, she now has the benefit of no longer caring.

Nermina shifts the small duffel she'd packed for Esmer. Inside are the few items she'd scavenged from the hospital. These bits and pieces of the life they'd led before the war seem in some ways trivial and also unspeakably precious—a worn piece of blanket, a child's book of fairy tales, the ball and jax the boy had mastered in the past several weeks. These artifacts of a life no longer possible for Esmer. For any of them. There would be no papers, no official search, no legal documentation of the child's whereabouts. A lawless state of chaos had brought Nermina and Esmer to their present circumstance and Nermina believes that once she's seen the child into what she judges to be capable hands there is no more that she or anyone else can do.

She feels the boy's sticky-warm hand inside her own and senses his fear now, but this comes to her as one might observe a play or a movie. This sense takes place outside of her, hovering only at the edges of her perception. She sees but doesn't see, feels but doesn't feel. Not completely.

Fog still blankets the city, the coastline floating in a ghostly-pale sea, and through this Maria leads Nermina and the boy to a small café on the palazzo. Beautifully dressed men and women swirl in and out of Nermina's view. She pulls the bulk of a thick gray sweater around her shoulders against the damp morning. Everyone here seems to have a place to go, men and women carrying briefcases, delivery men pushing carts and shouldering cartons, a few tourists crawling along with cameras and guide books. Nermina remembers the city square in Dubrovnik where her parents had taken her and Mirsad when they were children. The bright sunlight that turned the cobblestones golden, the startling turquoise-blue of the sea. This memory—like the others—feels to Nermina now like a lie, chunks of her life locked away beyond her reach.

Maria speaks in rapid Italian to the waiter and, when the young man disappears inside, she turns to Nermina and takes her two hands inside her own. "I know your father thought it safer for you in the United States...until things get better..." Nermina hears Maria's words as her thoughts unravel and she knows—would have known even before her father's death—that nothing will *get better* for a very long time. If ever. There was no going back now.

"I want you to know," Maria continues, "You are welcome to stay here, welcome to stay with us." For a moment, the woman's earnestness, her kindness, seeps into Nermina's open wounds like a salve. She imagines the purpling around her father's neck once Dr. Sidran had cut him down. He'd taken his own life rather than giving the Serbs the pleasure of killing him. And he'd given her—his daughter—no other choice but to leave her homeland. "Thank you," she says, "but my father has—" The hard knot of tears stops her from saying more.

The waiter returns with a small silver tray. He removes two delicate porcelain espresso cups, a steaming cup of hot chocolate for Esmer, and a plate of cheeses, biscuits, nuts, and jams. All around them patrons are delivered food of similar beauty. Nermina thinks of the sacks of rice and potatoes she'd carried through the hospital doors, her heart still racing, sweat-slicked with fear and adrenaline. The bundles had been heavy and awkward to carry. She feels the ache again in her arms, tendons taut, fear a sickly taste in the back of her throat.

But now Esmer smiles, a thin moustache of foam from the chocolate on his upper lip. Nermina feels the rush of caffeine inside her chest, tastes the rich coffee on her tongue. She uses a little silver knife to spread some blueberry jam onto a wafer, its edges browned. Maria hands Esmer a small white plate loaded with bits of all of this feast and the boy, his eyes wide and still somewhat frightened, eats heartily, spilling some of the jam onto his shirt. He seeks Nermina's eyes, momentarily pausing, and when she doesn't scold him, wipes away the jam with a quick swipe of the white linen napkin she'd placed on his lap.

Maria pays the check when they are finished and Nermina gets up from the table. She squats down to meet the child eye-to-eye. "You're going to be very happy with your Strina Maria." She uses a special tone, perfected since becoming Esmer's surrogate mother, and swallowing back tears, Nermina knows she'd modeled this tone—her manner with the boy all along—on her own mother's, the way she'd spoken to her and Mirsad. "You're such a brave little boy," Nermina says, but when the child begins to cry she pushes him away, then leads him by the hand toward the older woman where she waits with his duffel. Nermina cannot take the chance that Esmer's sorrow will break hers wide open. "I'm sorry," she says to Maria. "I've got to go now."

Her terse words sound cruel but already distant as she hears them in her mind hours later. "One step and then the next," she says aloud now. "One step and then the next."

PART TWO

CHAPTER 10
DIRT MOUNTAINS
Clementon, New Jersey, 1975

At the far northern perimeter of his neighborhood, the Dirt Mountains loomed majestic over the silent *cul de sac*. For months, those red-clay peaks had drawn Carl like a magnet. All throughout the summer, a small forest of milkweed and Joe Pye weed, oak and elm seedlings, flourished on the windward side. The stalled construction project—more than a bit of an eyesore—aggravated neighbors but held endless possibilities for Carl. Now that school was back in session he'd taken to waiting until his dad had left for his shift. His mom would be at the sink finishing up the last of the dishes, and Jeff up in the bedroom he and Carl shared, doing every last bit of his homework. Most of the neighborhood boys would be at home doing the same.

Had he pondered the question in his twelve-year-old mind, Carl may not have made a clear distinction between the lure of the Dirt Mountains—that maze of trails, endlessly traversed—and the thick spool of copper tubing. The value of *this* gleaming treasure grew exponentially as September's sunlight waned and the metal took on an almost magical patina.

It would be dark soon. Carl shifted his wiry frame on Jeff's hand-me-down bike. His hands, damp and coated with moon-dust-colored sand, squeezed the rubber handlebar grips. The empty backpack felt hot against his shoulder blades. He inched the bike closer and closer to the chain-link fence, to the gate, to the padlock whose U-shaped jaws hung—unexplainably— open. Carl tasted the orangey dirt in the back of his throat. He heard his mother's voice, the harsher, scarier tone that cut through his sleep many nights. In answer, his father's voice deeper, no less threatening for its measured cadence, its edge of bitterness. Of danger.

He eyed the long stacks of lumber, pallets of red brick, cinderblock left over from the sixteen foundations that squatted along a dredged creek bed, long gone dry. According to Carl's mother, this new neighborhood was to be much nicer than theirs, with houses they'd never be able to afford. What their family could and *couldn't* afford was a frequent topic of conversation. His father balked at the fee for the community pool; instead, Carl and Jeff swam in the nearby lake when it wasn't choked with algae. Their family *could* afford Jeff's uniforms for football and baseball, but the science camp Carl's teacher recommended was out of the question.

According to Carl's father, the money for the new

subdivision had run out. The construction workers disappeared then too, giving free rein to the cavalry of boys astride their banana-seated Huffys. But for now, the other boys were gone, as well. Carl felt his aloneness in the pit of his stomach. A sour, jumpy feeling somewhere between taste and smell that churned amidst the mac 'n' cheese and Sloppy-Joe dinner he'd gulped down earlier. This feeling was not unlike the one he got when he stuffed a failed test into the bottom of his book bag. Had he already decided?

He'd learned during that first post-Labor Day week at school about the periodic table. About precious metals, like gold and silver and copper. While the Indian summer breeze still carried the fragrance of roses and honeysuckle through the room's open windows, Mr. Seton's science class dozed. But the colorful chart and its symbols mesmerized Carl. Mr. Seton explained positive and negative charges. He said that copper was a valuable commodity because it conducted both heat and electricity so efficiently.

Outside the chain-link fence, Carl dropped his bike in the dirt. The back wheel clicked lightly as it spun. Adrenaline carried him inside the gate. He swallowed the block of fear lodged at the back of his throat. Swallowed it down with the red-clay dust, thick on his tongue and inside his nostrils. Carl already saw the fat yellow envelope stuffed with money. He'd slip it inside his mother's beat-up brown pocketbook. He'd never tell her it was him. He'd be just like Robin Hood, a secret hero, and his parents' nighttime arguments would stop.

Carl's sneakered feet crunched in the gravel. He slipped the bulky padlock from its hasp and, when he peeled the straps from his shoulders, he felt the release of a burden much heavier than the sodden pack. It's unlikely he could have shed completely the dead-weight memories that haunted him: his mother's voice, so often now choked with tears, his father's stony silence, or his quick temper with Carl. The bubble of assurance that surrounded Jeff, and kept Carl—the little brother—always, always a step behind. Carl thought of all of this or none of this. His eyes locked onto the copper coil that would fit with more than a little ingenuity into the backpack he'd emptied of books and papers and wadded-up gum wrappers. His fingers explored the thin tubing, quietly calculating the small fortune he'd collect.

But then the single bleat of a siren sliced through the twilight. Carl's heart flip-flopped inside his chest like the catfish he caught but always tossed back into the lake. A carnival swirl of red light swept across the Dirt Mountains, Carl still hunched inside the chain-link cage. Gravel skittered as the police car rolled to a stop. Frozen, a wave of shame—more potent than fear—washed over Carl as the beam from the policeman's flashlight found him. Even at this, *especially* at this, he'd failed her. Just as bad, he'd proved his father right again. Hot tears cut runnels through the coppered dust on his cheeks. Words tumbled out of Carl's mouth before the officer spoke, a long-winded apology that would never erase his stupidity.

"Stand up, son," the officer said. And after he'd spent several long moments eyeballing Carl: "You're Jeff Ingram's brother, right? Richard and Patty's kid?"

Carl nodded. The man towered above him, no taller than his father, but significantly more muscular. Carl swatted away his tears with the back of his hand.

"Yessir."

"See that sign over there? No Trespassing. You know what that means, right?"

Again, Carl nodded. He remembered an identical sign at the edge of the woods, a little beyond the lake. The taste of rotting leaves. The older boys' jeering laughter. "Pussy," they'd called out as Jeff dragged him to his feet.

"You have no business here," the officer said.

"But the lock was open—"

"This place is private property. Off-limits. Got it?"

Carl stared down at the unyielding light the flashlight cast, the circle of coppery earth it captured. Almost gently, the officer placed his free hand on Carl's shoulder and guided him outside the gate. Carl stood motionless while the policeman replaced the padlock in its hasp and turned the dial. And just as carefully, he wedged Carl's bike into the trunk of the squad car. The ride home from the Dirt Mountains lasted only moments but sparked a white-hot pain the boy would carry always.

CHAPTER 11
SHELTER
Portland, Oregon — November 1992

She lies awake on her narrow cot. Trying not to awaken the three other women in the room, Nermina stifles her sobs. She presses her face into the pillow and feels the cold and damp against her cheeks, the familiar weight of fear inside her chest. Even with the rhythm of the other women's slumbering breath, these hours are Nermina's most desolate. Under her thin blanket, she's bundled in nearly every item of clothing she owns: a pair of faded denim jeans, a thick pair of gray woolen socks, a Seattle Mariners sweatshirt whose waistband reaches to her knees, and a brown, hooded ski parka. All of these items, she'd plucked from a carton of donated clothing at the refugee center. Still, she shivers.

Although it had been early summer, Nermina arrived in

Portland to cold, gray drizzle. Now, after six months of wakeful nights, she listens to the blare of truck traffic on the interstate that severs a neighborhood nicknamed *Felony Flats*. Police sirens cut through the bleak nighttime hours like a knife through flesh. She lives here, along with thirty-five other Muslim refugees from Bosnia, in a homeless shelter in one of Portland's poorest neighborhoods, a place her parents would surely compare to Sarajevo's meanest slum.

This neighborhood—whose proper name is Lents— is different in every possible way from the Sarajevo Nermina remembers from before the war. In Lents there is no library with stacks of musty-scented books. No grocery with fresh vegetables, fruits, and cheeses. And no sidewalk café to sit and drink a cup of strong Turkish coffee.

Beverly, the sturdy-looking American caseworker who'd helped Nermina settle in this place, had warned her she shouldn't walk alone after dark. But when the daylight hours began to wane Nermina hadn't the energy to dispute the necessity of her nighttime journey. Setting out after work from her new job—riding two city buses, and finally walking six long blocks from the downtown bus stop—darkness descends now before the shelter doors lock behind her.

Nermina feels these lessening hours of daylight like an internal tide, each moment of darkness diminishing with equal measure the liquids and mass she'd once embodied. Days and nights flow in numbing sameness, just as they'd done those last weeks in Sarajevo, *that* place and time at once crystalline and shrouded like the fog-covered banks of the Willamette in *this* place.

But now Nermina's mind circles back to one particular

morning—though she cannot name the day or month—and her heart pounds again with fear. At 6:00 a.m., she'd passed the ramshackle strip club with its exterior of black-painted cinder block. She held the collar of her coat close to her throat with one gloved hand, pressed a cloth tote bag to her side with the other. Wary, she scanned the parking lot, empty but for a stand of tall weeds near the driveway where slivers of broken beer bottles and food wrappers collected. She walked quickly, anxious to cover the distance between her new home and the bus stop. But *that* morning, she'd felt the rough push of a male shoulder against her own as she rounded the corner at Ninety-second and Foster. The man's eyes held Nermina's for the split second it took to determine he meant her no harm.

Shutting her eyes tight now against this image, Nermina runs her fingers along the compact handle of the knife beneath her pillow. With her index finger she traces the three-inch blade, exerting just enough pressure so that the sharp edge draws pain without cutting. She tests the sharpness at the tip of the blade—just as she's done dozens of times— then slips it into her coat pocket. Soundlessly, she lifts the paltry bedding and feels with one foot for the track shoes she keeps by the bed. She bends to retrieve them and carries the shoes with her toward the slit of light that cuts across the floor from beneath the door. She turns the doorknob gently, waiting for the click. Then just as gently, she pushes the door back into place. In the dimly lit hallway, she lets out a long breath.

At first she hears only the pounding of her heart. Yet once she's collected herself she recognizes the wailing of a child. Esmer! How long ago had she left him? But an infant produces this crying now, not a little boy. The cries persist and escalate in volume. The cries penetrate the solid wooden door, the depth of despair so complete—the infant's, her own—that Nermina covers her heart with her open palm. With the other hand, she holds tight to the smooth handle of the knife and paces the lonely corridor end to end, then starts back again in the opposite direction to continue her nightly circuit.

She remembers the sticky feel of the child's small hand inside her own, the weight and warmth of his body as he'd clung to her. She sees his sleeping face, long, thick lashes—so much like Mirsad's—the wide brown eyes veiled, at rest. At peace. She hears his even breath beside her, feels with each exhalation the suspension of pain, his as well as her own. Tears sting her lids but she refuses to release them. She feels her heart, huge and pulsing. She presses her fingertips to her eyelids. A pinprick of light draws her inward and she follows, slowly at first but gaining momentum and assurance as the light guides her.

Like a sleepwalker, she is startled to find herself at the north stairwell. Here, she slides down along the wall until she is sitting, knees to her chest, on the cold tile floor. A constellation of images—initials, names, crude drawings—is scratched into the metal exit door like pictographs emerging from stone. Her eyes scan the cacophony until again—half-wakeful, startled—she finds herself on her knees before the door as though in prayer. Nermina slips the knife from her pocket and carves E S M E R. With each stroke the door's blue paint reveals the black beneath. Her blade traces each letter again, the cuts sure, deep. She etches a circle around the child's name and when she's finished she runs her fingers over the lines like braille.

CHAPTER 12
DISCARDED
Prescott, Arizona — November 1989

Carl stood on the front porch. He could already smell cat shit and rotting wood. And all the other God-awful stuff that was probably inside. The dispatch girl at Kwik Klean said to expect a mess. Some old woman had died in her sleep and the daughter was there now cleaning out what she could but needed some help.

He rang the bell and, holding his breath, half-hoped the daughter wouldn't answer. Almost instantly, though, a slim woman who looked to be in her forties opened the door. A pale- yellow bandana covered her hair, the cloth holding back a tight mass of reddish-blond curls that reached her shoulders. She wore faded jeans and a darker denim work shirt, the sleeves rolled up. The cats—a black one with white paws, a gray runt, a fat one with orange stripes, and a few more that he couldn't keep track of—intermittently rubbed up against the woman's legs and darted beneath a coffee table piled with magazines and newspapers, teacups and plates.

"Come on in," she said. "It's not as bad as it seems." She pushed the screen door wider so he could get past her and kept her eyes on the cats. She moved quickly and with a jauntiness that reminded Carl of the sorority girls who wouldn't have given him the time of day during his first and only year of college.

"When I called, they said you could stay as long as I needed you. I'm thinking together we can knock this out by Thursday."

"Um, well—" Carl began.

"Listen, what's your name?"

"Carl—"

"*Carl* then. I'm Lovisa."

He fought back the nausea that reminded him of his last hangover, penance for staying out all night drinking with his buddies.

"I guess I could work through Thursday."

When the Lovisa woman said nothing more, he followed her into the kitchen where she grabbed a stack of newspapers from a glass-topped dining table and started to bundle them with twine. Every time she touched something, a flutter of cat hair was set in motion.

"Come with me. You'll start in the attic," she proclaimed.

He followed her up a flight of carpeted stairs. The woman pulled down an attic ladder from the ceiling and he followed her up to a wood-planked room. With the room's sharply angled ceiling Carl could stand only in the center. The odor wasn't so bad up here, but the heat was stifling. He shrugged out of his coat and tossed it onto one of the cartons that clogged most of the floor space. He heard the cats meowing below them. They sounded frenzied, desperate.

The woman moved directly to the window and struggled with the rotting wooden sash.

"Damn," she muttered.

"Here, let me," he said. He waited for her to move aside. Unable to budge the window on his first try, a wave of annoyance washed over him. The woodwork was thick with layers of paint, caulk, and the remains of some old weather stripping.

"Jeeeez," he grunted, trying again. "When was the last time someone opened this?"

"Knowing my mother, probably never."

The window came unstuck with a screech. A cool breeze blew in, rustling the pile of plastic bags, wrapping paper, and ribbons that littered one corner of the floor

"Great, okay...so everything here..." she said, scanning the room. "Everything up here can go."

"Like, all of it?" he asked uncertainly. "Don't you want to...you know...to go through it or something?"

"This stuff? There's nothing here worth saving."

"You sure? I mean, didn't you grow up in this house?" The woman gazed at him, smugness creeping into her blue eyes, Carl thought.

"Hold on a second," she said. She took a step toward him. "You some kind of expert?"

He thought of his mother, how fast she could turn from

hot to cold. How her voice would drop a full octave when she was angry, the edge sharp and vengeful. Her entire face would change, her mouth going slack like a flat tire. It was his father she couldn't stand then—her life with the bastard—not him or Jeff. Carl had decided this a long time ago. But once the switch was flipped, she'd go after any of them. Her digs weren't as bad as the old man's, but scary in their own way. His brother had been smart to get out when he did.

Carl squared his shoulders now. "What? Me, an expert? Nah. Just thought you might want to, you know, save a few things, is all."

The woman cocked her head and eyed him silently. "How about you just let me decide what to save," she said.

"Sure." He looked down at his boots. His jaw clenched. "I get it. It all goes."

When he looked up again, the woman was tucking away a curl that had come loose from the bandana. The gesture reminded him that her mother had just died. His mood flicked to sadness like a wiper blade across the windshield.

"I'll get the trash bags from the truck," he said, his anger drained.

Two and a half hours later Carl sat cross-legged on the attic floor, eighteen 55-gallon trash bags stuffed full and twist-tied at the top. A photo album lay open on his knees. He saw Lovisa here, beautiful and fresh-faced, her hair a near golden halo, and her shoulders bronzed beneath the pale-blue halter-top. In another photo he saw her sitting next to a gawky, red-headed boy, and her parents, he supposed, the father tall and lean like the boy, the mother a pixie-faced, petite woman, standing behind them with their hands resting on their children's shoulders. Carl wondered what sort of family they'd been. They looked happy, he decided. Normal. This thought tugged at him until he found himself tearing up. He felt ridiculous and ashamed now. But then he slipped back into the familiar anger and this seemed a little better. He knew he was right. This woman couldn't just throw away her past. Nobody could.

He thought about the last time he'd been home. More than three years now. The old man barely acknowledged him. His mom waited till his father had left for his shift before she'd asked Carl if he needed anything. Then she'd pressed the bills into his hand. He remembered the way she'd looked at him. There was love in her eyes, but also pity. Had it always been like that? Carl wondered now if she'd known he'd only come back for the money. He'd felt bad leaving her—all alone with the old man. Knowing, like always, she'd bear the brunt of his mistakes.

"Lousy bastard," Carl said aloud. He closed the photo album and placed it behind one of the rafters in the slanted ceiling. It was time for a break, he decided. He slung down to the second floor landing the bags he'd already filled—lots of crap (boxes of old Christmas cards, a set of electric curlers, a bunch of old-time games like *Candy Land* and *Chutes and Ladders*)—most barely holding his interest for the few seconds it took him to decide if it was recyclable or not. This was the only instruction she'd given him. From the second floor, he dragged the bags down to the first-floor landing. He found the woman still working in the kitchen. Cold air blew through the windows and diluted the smell some.

"Hey," he said. "I thought I'd take what I can from here,

plus what I got up there, and head over to the dump." He'd pick up some lunch on the way.

Lovisa surveyed the room, still a disgusting mess, but Carl could see she'd made some headway. Several neat rows of bundled papers and magazines were stacked against the wall and she'd emptied the sink of crusted-over plates, pots, and pans. The refrigerator stood wide open, emptied of its rotted contents and gleaming white and clean. Only the gray cat and the fat one with orange stripes hung around now.

"Yeah, I suppose that makes some sense," she said. "We can free up some space for later when we start to move out the heavier stuff."

"Sure," said Carl.

When he got back, the woman was on the phone, her voice professional, no-nonsense. She was giving someone directions to the house from the interstate. Carl stood there, not sure what to do next.

"No more than six or seven," she said into the mouthpiece; then after a pause, "I have no idea if they've been spayed or neutered. What difference does that make, anyhow?" She listened to whatever the person on the line was saying. "Okay, okay," she said finally. "So your guy should be here by what?...Four? ...Great...thank you...thank you."

Lovisa hung up the phone and walked to the sink. She let the water run awhile then soaped up her hands and rinsed them, drying them hurriedly on her jeans.

"So, what's next?" Carl asked. The sandwich he'd eaten in the truck had taken the edge off his hunger and dispelled the bad feelings from earlier.

"Well, let's see," she said, looking around. "How about the basement? *God* knows what she's got down there. Let's check it out."

The door to the basement had been fitted with a cat flap and Carl braced for the worst of it. The woman flipped the switch at the top of the stairs. The unmistakable stench of cat piss was ten times stronger. He wondered again why he was here. Sure, his prospects weren't all that great right now, but this was *bad*. He thought about the hundred bucks he still owed Joey, his buddy back in New Jersey. "Screw Joey," he muttered under his breath. "He can wait for his money." He told himself he'd finish out the day. No more, no less.

The woman led the way and Carl saw that, aside from four litter boxes overflowing with mounds of cat shit, the basement held nothing out of the ordinary. The space was remarkably organized. A washer and dryer filled one corner alongside a deep, utility sink. There was a workbench and a decent array of tools, clipped or hanging to a pegboard on the wall, a bunch of baby food jars holding nuts and screws of all different sizes, and a nice circular saw that Carl thought he wouldn't mind asking Lovisa about.

"My dad..." she began. Carl turned toward her, but she made a fluttering motion with her hand and stalked toward the back wall where a bunch of plastic storage bins were stacked high. She reached up on her toes and opened a small window. "Here," she said. "Start here."

"Um," he said, unsure of himself all over again. "Should I...look through this stuff? Sort it?" The woman set him on edge. He couldn't tell what she was thinking, couldn't figure what she might do. This was the same way he'd felt as a kid.

He'd come home from school and never know what to expect. His mom could be sweet as pie or ready to let loose on him and Jeff. At those times, her words just got meaner the more the two of them would cry.

"It's all junk," she said. "Don't bother sorting it. You can haul them out just the way they are." She walked past him to the stairs without so much as a glance, but when she was halfway up the steps she turned suddenly. "Oh. I'm going to need your help when the Animal Welfare guy gets here."

"Um..."

"What's the matter?" she asked.

"Nothing," said Carl.

Lovisa's fingers trailed the wooden banister. "All right then," she said, smiling.

"I'm not a big fan of cats," he added.

"*Really?*" This information seemed to amuse her. "Are you scared of them?" She widened her eyes comically.

"No, I'm not *scared* of them. I just don't *like* them, is all."

"Well, neither do I, but as you can see, my mother did."

Carl thought he heard something soften in her voice. Maybe her bravado was just a cover. Maybe she'd really loved her mom but just didn't know how to show it. And now it was too late. First she'd lost her dad. He thought he could tell—just from the way the man kept his tools—that the dad had been an okay guy (nothing like his old man). Maybe the mom wasn't even a crazy cat lady till after the dad died. Maybe that's what sent her over the edge.

Carl had finished hauling the bigger stuff out of the basement and was breaking up some dilapidated pieces of wooden furniture that had been left to rot on the tiny cement patio out back. He heard someone pull into the driveway and glanced down at his watch. The Animal Welfare guy was on time. He wondered about the cats and if the old lady had loved them more than people. He'd heard about people like that. Loonies, mostly. He wondered if the old lady had loved Lovisa and her brother. He walked around the house to the front and saw a man pulling a bunch of cages out of the double doors at the back of the van. The guy looked to be sixty-five or so. Carl wondered why they'd send someone so old. Carl figured *he'd* be the one doing most of the work now.

"Hey," said Carl. He stood with his arms folded, a few feet from the man.

The man eyed him nonchalantly. "Afternoon," he said, continuing to unload the cages.

Carl stood watching him.

"The lady of the house in?" the man finally asked.

"Yeah," said Carl, relieved. "I'll get her. Uh...follow me." He waited for what seemed a long time for the old guy to clip a jangling set of keys to his belt loop before he led him in through the front door. A few of the cats milled around a scruffy, pee-stained sofa, the fabric on the armrests ripped and clawed beyond repair. They scattered toward the kitchen as the men approached. Carl called to Lovisa and, when she didn't answer right away, told the man to wait.

She appeared on the staircase, her arms loaded with neatly folded linens. She gazed evenly at both men, holding the stack of linens in place with her chin, then set the pile down on the dilapidated sofa.

"Okay," she said to the man. "I guess we should get

started."

"Can you get 'em all out here, ma'am? Shut all the doors to the other rooms?"

"Yes. Of course."

"We'll set some food out here," he said, directing the request to Carl.

"Check the rooms on the second floor," Lovisa said to Carl. "I'll take care of the food." Then turning to the man, she said politely, "May I speak with you a moment?"

Upstairs, Carl saw that the old lady had kept her kids' rooms fixed just like when they were teenagers. For Carl, that was a time he hated to think about. His parents had been at their very worst then; his mom had even gone off to stay with his aunt in Connecticut. She'd cried and told him she wouldn't be his father's doormat anymore. She'd spit out the word *doormat*, making it sound filthy and filled with implications that, as a boy, he'd been reluctant to explore. He remembered being scared but also a little excited. He'd wanted to deck the old man, but when his mother returned two weeks later, she'd left red scratches on Carl's forearms as she pleaded with him, *forbade* him to cause any trouble. And somehow Jeff—as always—stayed above the fray.

In Lovisa's old room, Carl checked under the bed, mauve carpeting dusty but otherwise clean and free of cat shit. He scanned the closet, the top shelf crammed with books and a milk crate filled with old albums. Two wooden tennis rackets rested in the corner against the back wall. He shut the closet door, flicked off the overhead light, and closed the door behind him. The boy's room didn't look all that different from what Carl remembered of his own room when *he* was a kid—a shelf packed with baseball trophies and team photos, the perfectly worn-in glove smelling of linseed oil, leather, and sweat. Here, he shooed a couple of white cats from under a wooden desk and out into the hallway. As he shut the door, he wondered where the hell Lovisa's brother was now. Why wasn't *he* helping with all this? Carl thought of Jeff again. He couldn't remember what they'd fought about, why he'd blown off Jeff and Lisa's wedding. He pushed this thought away, just like the others.

The old lady's room was every bit as disgusting as Carl had imagined, but he could see Lovisa had already done some work here. One small closet was empty. She'd stripped the bed. A pile of dirty blankets and sheets was heaped in the corner, the gray cat nestled on top. He approached slowly and put out his hand, though he had no idea how to deal with cats. His family had never had one and for some reason, cats made him nervous. All that sneaking around; maybe that was it. *Lurking* best described it, he decided.

The cat regarded Carl calmly then darted under the bed. Reluctantly, he got down on the carpeting—the odor sickening—and tried out the pssss pssss pssss sounds everyone made with cats.

"Come on out now. It's okay," he heard himself saying. The cat sat and stared, its green eyes glinting back at him. He felt ridiculous but crawled on his stomach until he was eye to eye with the feline. He waited a little to see what it would do. Then he inched his hand out slowly and stroked the fur, which felt dry and cool. "Pssss pssss pssss," he tried again. The cat began to purr loudly. He spent a few minutes stroking the fur. He felt peaceful. He felt the warmth of the cat's body beneath the fur, felt the vibration of the purring in his fingertips. The cat closed its eyes and drifted to sleep.

Then, feeling guilty, Carl grabbed the cat with both hands and pulled it toward him. He felt the friction of the thing's claws digging into the carpet as he struggled to crawl backwards from beneath the bed. He stood up awkwardly—nearly tripping over his own feet—and unhooked the cat's rear claws from his shirt. It fought hard, nearly thrashing its way out of his hands. He held the cat out stiffly at arms' length. Then he stalked around the room—somewhat frightened even—trying to hold the writhing thing away from his body.

"You gonna behave now?" he asked, sweating. "You gonna calm down?" He paced a while longer, muttering under his breath. And then miraculously, Carl thought, the cat began to purr again. He held it to his chest, walking slowly down the stairs. He felt the purring warmth of the cat against his heart.

Lovisa and the Animal Welfare guy had corralled the others in the living room; they'd stacked a bunch of cages and some of the filled cardboard boxes, blocking the entrance to the kitchen. The cats ate from several bowls set out on the floor, meowing but not in that desperate way like before. The man wore a heavy quilted jacket. He motioned to Carl to put the gray cat down near the food. Again, he felt guilty, but gently set the animal down with the others. Lovisa stood watching, her hands on her hips.

"Gimme a hand here," the man said to Carl. "We're gonna shove this bookcase over there and block the stairway." Even emptied of books, Carl doubted the old man would be able to shoulder his end. This pissed him off. But then he remembered the dad's tools hanging neatly in the basement; he admired the obvious care the man had shown them. There was something almost loving about it, Carl thought. Something honorable. And this old-timer here, he was just doing his job. So really, he reasoned, it was the same sort of thing. The man was doing what needed to be done. He was doing the *right thing.*

"Okay," Carl said, determined to kick in the extra muscle if necessary. But when they tilted the thing on its side, it slid easily on the carpeting. Carl gave it an extra heave anyway when they righted it in front of the staircase. Brushing his hands on his pants, the older man reached into his pocket and pulled out a plastic bag of cat treats. He squatted down and picked up the first cat within his reach. He held it gently and offered one of the treats in his open palm. Then standing, he brought the cat close to his chest, stroking it, just as Carl had done, and walked slowly over to the cages. He opened the door and flung the animal inside, just as the hinge sprung back in place.

"Your turn, now," he said to Carl. "We'll have this wrapped up quick if we work together." The old man scooped a handful of cat treats from the bag and gave them to Carl; he stuffed all but two into the front pocket of his jeans. Squatting down the way the other man had, Carl put his hand out to the gray cat. The cat instantly lapped up the treat and he felt its sandpaper tongue on his palm. The cat rubbed against his leg, generating a low, lulling purr. He reached into his pocket and gave it another treat, then lifted the animal and carried it to the cages. Sensing something, though, the gray cat began to thrash around in his arms. It hissed and emitted a long yowl that frightened him so that by the time he'd gotten the thing inside the cage Carl's heart was racing. He looked down and saw three identical red gashes on the inside of his forearm.

"Shit," he muttered. "Goddamned thing clawed me."

"They'll do that," said the man, chuckling. Then he took a bottle of antiseptic and some cotton balls from his duffle and swabbed the cuts.

"Occupational hazard," he said, chuckling again. "You'll live." He peeled the backing from a large bandage and gently covered the wounds. Then he dug around in the bag and pulled out a pair of thickly padded work gloves. "Try these," he said.

The woman showed no sign of concern. Now with his own coat on, and with the gloves the man had given him, Carl worked as efficiently as possible at this ridiculous and sadistic task. The collective yowling and whining of the caged cats made Carl feel like he was in a horror movie. Finally, though, with the last of the animals behind bars, the two men began to transfer the cages to the van, all the while enduring the relentless crying Carl thought he'd never get out of his head.

Lovisa hung back a little and when Carl glanced at her he thought he saw sadness in her face. The streetlights had come on and the glow picked out the glints of blond in her hair. Maybe now that the worst of the mess was behind her, she'd start to grieve her mother. He'd only been to one funeral in his entire life—he'd been fourteen—and he still remembered the way his Uncle Pete had broken down as everyone took their turn praying over his aunt's casket, whispering a few embarrassed words into his uncle's ear.

The man walked over to Lovisa with a clipboard and now Carl hung back. He thought about the homely girl at Kwik Klean, the one he'd settle up his hours with, once he was done with this God-awful job. He calculated his pay and felt a little better. Lovisa signed the paperwork, then crossed her arms in front of her.

"Well, that's it," the man said as Carl joined the two.

"So, at least they'll all go to good homes," Carl said. He'd suddenly decided he needed to say something uplifting, something kind.

"Oh, these kitties'll be goin' to their final resting place straight away," the older man said. His tone wasn't somber, but it also wasn't insincere. He exchanged a knowing look with the woman.

"What? I thought the Animal Welfare place was a shelter, and people could go pick out their pets—"

"Or, they exterminate the animals," Lovisa said evenly.

"What do you mean?"

"Exactly what I said." She stood with her arms crossed in front of her, a jaunty lift to her chin that made him want to shake her.

"That's not right. You can't do that," he said.

"Sure, I can."

Her face remained a mask of disinterest and this further infuriated him. "You throw away all the stuff in the house and *now* you're putting down all these animals. Just like that?"

"Yes." She enunciated the word carefully.

"Just like that?"

"*Yes*, just like that."

Carl felt close to losing control and it scared him. He'd heard that sometimes people act crazy when a loved one dies. Maybe that's what was going on here. Maybe this woman was crazy with grief. He remembered the way the gray cat had felt against his chest, how his heartbeat had been swallowed up in its purring.

Lovisa narrowed her eyes at Carl. "What would *you* have me do with all these cats?" Her cheeks were rosy now from the cold, her skin glowing under the streetlights. "What would you know, anyway?"

The Animal Welfare man left them where they stood and headed toward the van. Without another word, Carl followed. He easily overtook the older man.

"Hey!" said the man.

The double doors stood open. Carl unlatched the first cage and then the next and the next. The cats flew from the cages and disappeared into the darkness.

"*Something's* getting saved today!" shouted Carl.

CHAPTER 13
DR. CHONG

Nermina scans the posters on the walls in the doctor's office. She examines an illustration of the female reproductive system, remembering with bitter fondness the medical textbooks she'd pored over just before her last exams in Sarajevo. Her eyes move to a poster exhorting the benefits of a new low-estrogen birth control pill; another seeks women who suffer from painful menstrual periods to participate in a research study at the university; participants will receive compensation and two free medical exams.

She shifts around on the table, feeling the paper crinkling beneath her, sticking a little to her legs. Earlier, the nurse had handed her a cotton hospital gown and a folded paper drape, instructed her to remove all of her clothing. She'd held the thin garment closed at her chest with one hand and smoothed down the drape across her lap with the other. Now, after waiting more than forty minutes she feels herself growing ever more anxious. She breathes in the sharp smell of alcohol and antiseptic; a smell identical to that of three interchangeable medical offices in Sarajevo where her mother had examined both pregnant women and old women, women long past their child-bearing years.

Setting aside the paper drape, she steps down from the table and inventories the instruments the nurse has set out for her exam: the speculum, a clear gob of lubricant jelly on a small tray, a vial for the cervical cell samples, and the bristle-ended swab. Nermina flushes as she remembers how her mother had explained (as she'd put it then) 'the menstrual cycle and sexual intercourse between a man and a woman.' Her mother had methodically provided this information—so long ago, in another lifetime it seems—with none of the implied shamefulness that always infused the whispered discussions among her girlfriends. In Nermina's memory, her mother had been pragmatic throughout those years of her adolescence and early adulthood, but also kind. She feels the tug of longing, feels it slide like a stone along its grooved trail. She wants her mother here with her now. And then clutching the thin gown to her chest she remembers the soldier's knife against her cheek, the weight of the first man, the bits of crumbled plaster scraping the skin from her shoulders. It doesn't matter now, she mouths silently. It doesn't matter.

A moment later, she's startled at a brisk knock on the hollow door, and before she's had the chance to climb back up onto the exam table, a young, Asian doctor—a woman who looks to Nermina not much older than she is—sweeps into the room. She holds Nermina's medical file to her chest, against her starched white coat. The woman is trim and petite with glossy, dark hair that ends abruptly at her shoulders.

"I'm Dr. Chong," she says, thrusting her hand at Nermina. "Sorry to have kept you waiting so long." Nermina doubts the doctor is truly sorry but appreciates the firm pressure of her hand as it grasps her own. I could be her, she thinks only fleetingly, but she forces this notion from her mind like the others. She needs to be clear. She needs this doctor's help. This is the very first step.

"No problem," says Nermina, reciting the phrase, one of many she's learned from her coworkers, a whole lexicon of American sayings she's determined to memorize like the anatomy terms from her old textbooks.

Seating herself on a low swiveled stool, Dr. Chong opens the folder and makes herself busy studying Nermina's chart. Nermina is grateful that her medical records carry no trace of her life in Bosnia, yet she fears that her body may still reveal her past. She climbs up on the exam table and slides back awkwardly. She places her heels in the stirrups without being instructed to do so and a feeling of helplessness sours in the pit of her stomach. She is open, exposed, even before this woman, the female doctor she'd insisted upon. Her mother had ensured that she received annual gynecological exams ever since Nermina had turned sixteen. There is nothing in *this* room—so like those others—that should frighten or confuse her. But she freezes, her legs trembling beneath the paper drape.

"Just slide down toward me." Dr. Chong glances up from the chart. "A little more, please." Nermina inches forward.

"That's it," says the doctor, her face impassive. Nermina thinks back to the first of those exams and how her mother had explained the necessity for using birth control 'once a young woman becomes sexually active.' At the time, Nermina's face had burned with embarrassment; one of her mother's female colleagues had conducted the exam while her mother spoke professionally about the responsibilities that every woman has in this 'next step toward maturity.' These memories—so silly, really—thread through the others, the soldiers, the bloody slice along her cheek, the slime she'd wiped from between her legs. Her jaw clenches.

"Okay, the first thing you'll feel is a little goo and then the speculum," says Dr. Chong, her voice chipper but not condescending. At the first touch of cold metal, Nermina cringes.

"Are you all right?" the doctor asks.

"Yes," says Nermina. She fights the urge to push the doctor's hand away, imagines the steel instruments, the tray, crashing hard against the tile floor. A deep, sharp pain engulfs her as the instrument spreads her labia, probes deeper into her vagina. Her legs shake uncontrollably now. Shame washes over her body in a rush of heat. Her skin is slick and sticky now against the paper that crumples beneath her.

Dr. Chong's dark eyes peer over the drape, "Are you sure?" she asks. Her tone is softer now, tentative.

Nermina nods her head 'yes,' afraid her voice will betray her. She cannot for a moment submit to this doctor's compassion or, worse yet, her suspicion. When the nurse pads into the room, Nermina's eyes are clenched shut. She hears the crinkle of plastic as the nurse unwraps another instrument from the tray.

"Okay then, I'm going to use the swab now," says Dr. Chong. "This will only last a second or two." Nermina feels the scraping inside her and holds her breath until the doctor withdraws the swab. The steel instrument contracts with several precise movements of Dr. Chong's hands. Relief floods Nermina.

"Now just go ahead and put your hands up next to your head like you're relaxing," Dr. Chong instructs. Despite herself, Nermina almost laughs at this. The doctor's tiny fingers probe methodically in a circular motion around first one breast and then the other. "Do you conduct a breast exam each month?" she asks.

"Yes," says Nermina dutifully, though she hasn't done so since arriving in the United States. The thought of touching herself this way is repugnant now, impossible.

"You can put down your arms. I'm going to do an internal exam and then we'll be done."

The relief that Nermina had felt moments earlier evaporates completely. Her eyes clench shut again. Nermina feels the doctor's gloved fingers probing inside, the pain—not sharp like before but persistent—pulsing in synch with her heartbeat. She forces back tears.

"Okay," Dr. Chong says. "We're all done now." She strips off her latex gloves and deposits them in a bin marked Medical Waste. "Just get dressed. I'll be back in a few minutes and we'll..." The doctor hesitates. She directs a fleeting smile at her nurse as she slips from the room with the sealed and labeled vial. "We'll have a little talk," the doctor says.

Nermina dresses quickly, pulling on her jeans and

sweater, then slips on a pair of brown leather loafers. She studies herself in the mirror, traces the scar on her scalp with her fingertip, then trails it gently along her right cheek. It strikes her as strange, how quickly the cut on her cheek had healed over, barely a trace of it now. She smoothes down the strands of blond hair that have escaped her headband—the chin-length style accentuating her angular cheekbones, the overall effect bringing to mind a nearly starved street urchin—then turns away from the mirror.

When Dr. Chong returns Nermina is sitting in a straight-backed plastic chair, leafing through an old issue of *Ladies Home Journal*. She notices for the first time the rose-scented perfume the doctor wears and, when she tucks a few strands of ink-black hair behind her ear, the delicate links of a gold bracelet that encircle her tiny wrist.

The doctor seats herself directly opposite Nermina in the other identical chair. She places the medical chart gently on the counter as though the papers within require care equal to that of her patient. She leans forward. "Ms. Beganović," she begins. Again, she tucks the errant strands behind her ear. "May I call you Nermina?"

Nermina nods.

"Nermina, your exam—" She stops, begins again. "I need to ask you, Nermina—as a physician—Have you experienced trauma? Sexual abuse? I know these are difficult questions." Gone is the doctor's chipper efficiency from the beginning of Nermina's appointment. She hears the concern these words and tone convey. Professional yet genuine, personal, the same tone the psychologist produced when Nermina had first arrived in Portland. The same tone *that* doctor had used to convince Nermina to begin a regimen of anti-depressants.

"No," says Nermina. "Nothing like you ask me."

Dr. Chong crosses her legs. "I know you'd hoped to talk with me about artificial insemination." Her voice is softer still. "We can certainly discuss IVF...when, if, the time comes..." She leans in further, places her tiny hand on Nermina's forearm. "Nermina, there's some scar tissue that I suspect—"

"No," Nermina interrupts, her voice much louder than she'd intended. "This is not..." She searches for the correct English word. Her mind races through the medical texts she'd consumed in Sarajevo, the dozens of journal articles she'd read on the computer at the medical library in the hospital where she works now. She'd digested the medical concepts easily and thrilled to the idea her baby could be derived—if not miraculously then scientifically—through a sterile and anonymous process completely of her doing. IVF was the perfect choice, the *only* choice she had. "This scar tissue is no een-de-ka-shon," she dredges out finally.

Dr. Chong tilts her head to the side. Her eyes, expertly edged with soft liner, are painfully kind. "Nermina, if someone has hurt you—"

"As I say before, *no*." Unable to control the impulse, she nods several times in quick succession.

Dr. Chong's gaze holds steady on Nermina. "All right," she says. "Assuming you are a healthy young woman..." She picks up Nermina's records, opens the folder, and glances at the top page. Her gaze returns to Nermina's face once more. "You're twenty-four. A perfectly fine age to get pregnant. A perfect age to have a baby. If you're *ready* to have a baby," the doctor adds gently.

Nermina squelches the urge to reach out and clasp the doctor's delicate hands. Her voice is unsteady as she begins, "I am ready—"

"But I must tell you it's highly unusual," Dr. Chong cuts in. "Most of our patient referrals to fertility specialists are women who've been trying to conceive—unsuccessfully—for a very long time. IVF is usually the *last* option, not the first."

"Yes," Nermina says. "I read this." She concentrates, choosing each English word carefully, deliberately. "I read about this, too." Nermina takes a deep breath. Her eyes alight on the red script embroidered on the doctor's white coat. Elena Chong, M.D. Silently, she repeats the words to herself several times until they all run together like an incantation. Dr. Chong clears her throat and folds her small hands in her lap.

"I do know this," says Nermina. "What I ask you...what I ask is not so common thing." She hears her own voice now—the halting English, her accent exaggerated and clumsy—and worries that perhaps she's misspoken. Still, she continues. "But I must giving very good reasons, Dr. Chong." Nermina feels her words gathering speed and emphasis. She hopes she hasn't ruined her chances of sounding like a rational, responsible adult. "I have for you many good reasons for wanting my baby now."

"I've no doubt," says the doctor. Nermina detects a sad smile tugging at the corners of Dr. Chong's plump lips, a look of pity.

"Dr. Chong, I do understand your...um...your *reluctance*—this is correct word?—your reluctance to refer to me specialist reproductive doctor. I'm not married woman." For a split second she thinks of telling Dr. Chong the truth—that she has no family, no boyfriend, no desire to have one—but her intuition warns against this.

"I am new to United States," she says finally. "But I have very good job. And soon medical insurance. So now, I must…I want very much a child."

Nermina forces a wide smile, but the doctor shakes her head. Again, she places the chart on the counter. Nermina's heart thumps hard inside her chest. Her parents' faces appear then. Her father with his head of thick silver hair and her mother's dark hair swept back from her face, her green eyes, the tiny flecks of amber at the edges of her pupils. These details of her parents' features swim in and out of focus. She feels her mother's moistened fingers on her forehead when she tamps down the cowlick there. Tears sting Nermina's eyes but if Dr. Chong notices she politely pretends she hasn't.

"The procedure," Dr. Chong says finally, "is very expensive. Medical insurance doesn't normally cover this sort of thing except, of course, in extremely dire circumstances. And even then…" she trails off, looking down at her tiny fingers, then directly into Nermina's eyes. "It's likely you'd need more than one treatment. Most women do. There's no guarantee that a pregnancy would occur on the first try."

"Oh," says Nermina abruptly. "I know this too," she continues, though she clearly hadn't considered this, certainly not the part about insurance. Since arriving in America, all of her medical costs have been covered through the refugee center. Beverly prepared the paperwork and Nermina complied by visiting whichever doctor she was required to see. But her primary aim since starting her job at the hospital is reaching the time when her medical benefits begin.

She'd never inquired about whether the benefits would cover this procedure. *Who would I have asked? Who could I have trusted?* She'd relied on scholarly articles only, statistics on successful pregnancies among women in the age group of twenty-four to twenty-eight years, and the generally poor results of women above the age of thirty-eight. There'd been nothing there about the cost of artificial insemination or medical insurance not covering it.

"Nermina," says Dr. Chong, "I'm sorry. I can see I've upset you." She leans forward in her chair. Once again, Nermina fixes what she imagines to be a composed smile on her face.

"No, not upset," she says. "Well...with honesty, I am not so familiar with American insurance." In Bosnia, socialized medicine had covered everyone. If you were rich then you offered a bribe and your medical care was better. A great deal better. "I am not understanding..."

She searches for words, English words, that refuse to surface. She sits primly, mildly aware that she is holding her breath, hoping that Dr. Chong is about to offer another option. Maybe there's something Nermina has missed.

"I don't want to discourage you," the doctor says after what seems a very long silence. "But...how can I say this? The patients we usually refer for fertility treatments are generally quite comfortable financially. These procedures can run into thousands of dollars, tens of thousands sometimes."

Nermina's throat goes dry. *Thousands of dollars.* These words drown out anything else Dr. Chong may have said. The doctor glances down at her watch. Nermina notes the beveled glass, the square face offset with two small diamonds. She sees now that the young doctor also wears a plain gold wedding band and a diamond solitaire, both rings perfectly proportioned for her tiny fingers. *How had she missed this?* She knows the doctor is letting her know her visit is over. That another patient is waiting. But she remembers a photo of her parents that hung in the dining room of their home in Dobrinja, a close-up of the two facing one another. Their hands are entwined, and her father's lips brush her mother's cheek. Nermina pictures the diamond ring her mother wore in the photo, though she'd rarely seen it on her finger during the workweek; her mother had been a practical woman. And now Nermina wants Dr. Chong to know what sort of family she'd had. Wants her to know that her parents were loving— with one another and with their children, with her brother Mirsad and with her. That they were strict parents, but also fair. That she, Nermina, had learned so much from each of them about how to love a child.

"I do understand," Nermina says. She looks into the doctor's deep brown eyes. "Thank you for this time," she adds when Dr. Chong's expression tells her there's nothing more to discuss. She presses her cloth tote bag to her chest, a gesture that sometimes comforts her, but now only makes her feel needy and lost and poor.

"I'm sorry, Nermina," Dr. Chong says again. Nermina rises along with the doctor. She registers the doctor's slight touch to her shoulder yet not much else. "Please call if ever you'd like to talk."

CHAPTER 14
RITUAL

She hates sitting in the noisy hospital cafeteria, thick with the greasy smell of French fries and the incessant chatter of her co-workers. She's done this a couple of times—though only at her supervisor's insistence—but found it too difficult to smile at the right times, to respond in kind to the rapid-fire wisecracks. Nermina understands perfectly well what these boisterous young women are saying. She just has no interest in joining this daily ritual.

But since her visit with Dr. Chong, she's begun another ritual of her own design and more to her liking. Nermina carries her lunch outside where she eats alone at a picnic table, just beyond the parking garage, and adjacent to the new construction site. She does this whenever she can, whenever the summer showers hold off their abrupt, sun-streaked deluge until mid-afternoon. Today the bench feels warm beneath her, the air perfumed with lantana from a large concrete planter, a welcome relief from the frigid and sterile environment inside the hospital.

For thirty minutes each day, she manages to fend off a tangle of feelings so entwined she's not even certain she can name them. At the very center, though, is fury, and this she directs at herself. Only *she* is to blame for being so stupid, for believing that Dr. Chong would conjure a baby for her like a wizard with the wave of her tiny hand. How had she convinced herself that a gynecologist—a specialist like her mother— wouldn't find traces of her past? She'd thought only of the biological outcome of IVF, not the cost of treatments. She'd fooled herself on both counts and walked out the door with nothing more than Dr. Chong's pity.

For weeks after the exam, twice daily she'd hunched against the window of the cross-city bus, her sullen face staring back at her like a stranger's. But over time, she's learning to stifle the pernicious noise her mind produces, just as she's learning to tune out the drone of construction. No longer an annoyance, the drilling and pumping and screeching have become an odd source of comfort. From her vantage point, Nermina can peer across the sea of mud and gravel to follow the project's progress. From here she's witnessed the setting of steel rods and cinder blocks, the pouring of concrete that's formed the building's foundation. She admires this process, the precise, right angles that have emerged in recent days. With just a bit of imagination, she's able to foresee the final project—an L-shaped, two-story building that will house the Veteran Administration's new in-patient post-traumatic stress clinic she'd read about in the employee newsletter.

Today, she unpacks her lunch from its brown paper bag: an egg salad sandwich on whole-wheat bread, a nectarine and, in a square plastic container a small portion of bean soup called *grah*—a leftover from her dinner—that sends up a sweet scent of paprika and smoky meat when she pries open the lid. She takes a bite of her sandwich and watches as the men fire nails into the wooden frame the crew has erected. She's squelched her alarm—at first, thinking the snipers had tracked her to America—and grown to anticipate the echoing rounds. The rhythm is rapid and steady as each nail enters the yielding wood. Each shot a staccato note of finality.

Together, the crew works efficiently, and Nermina admires this. When she looks up again, one of the workers is heading toward her. His wavy, blond hair hangs in ringlets, the sweat-damp ends reaching his shoulders. His body is compact and muscled. He tosses a couple of soda cans into the trash bin at the perimeter of the concrete pad where Nermina sits. He could be thirty, she thinks, or maybe younger. She watches the man as he walks, head down, back toward the worksite. He stoops to pick up a stone from the ground then sends it high up over a set of power lines. He does this twice more, then stands—hands on his hips—peering up at the wires, a silly, child-like stance, Nermina decides. Then she remembers Hasan, timid, apologetic. Peering down at her on the bench in the medical faculty courtyard that last day before her life unwound. Such sweetness there in his face—just a boy's—as she'd awakened. And then the more familiar nightmare images: Hasan, clinging to her hand. His face a mask of fear and terror.

The image dissipates as she watches the man again. Now he climbs the rungs of steel scaffolding on the building's east side, his movements economical and sure. The warm breeze stirs and carries for several seconds the new-birthed scent of fresh-cut wood. She breathes as deeply as her lungs allow. She remembers how the daffodils emerged each spring through frozen soil, their yellow blooms nodding on the banks of the Miljacka. Reluctantly, she turns away from the construction site, away from the boyish-seeming man. She gathers the debris from her lunch and stuffs it into the paper bag. Then she shoulders her tote and prepares to enter the frigid building to finish out her workday.

CHAPTER 15
NERMINA'S REHEARSAL

Nermina lets herself in with her key—taking care not to let the screen door slam behind her—then tiptoes through Raifa and Samir's living room. She remembers Raifa's instructions: Don't ring the bell! And she reminds herself to watch out for the books and toys and shoes that will surely be strewn across the carpeted floor. She doesn't want to frighten Raifa, but she doesn't want to awaken the little ones, either. With her hand on the rounded finial of the staircase, she stands a moment, undecided whether she should go up or wait downstairs. But before she takes a step, Raifa appears at the top of the landing, baby Sabrina a tightly wrapped bundle of pink, snugged at her shoulder. Raifa shifts her wide hips, swaying softly from side to side. "I'll be right down," she mouths. She flutters her free hand toward the sofa and Nermina obeys, sinking into the worn-out cushions, as comforting and familiar to her now as her own bed in Dobrinja had once been.

She smiles broadly when a few moments later Raifa joins her. The women hug and after they've pulled away from one another, Nermina feels the slick spot of baby spit-up—or is it breast milk?—on her cotton blouse. She touches it gingerly with her finger. Raifa laughs. "I'm sorry," she says. "Like they say here, comes with the territory."

"It's fine," says Nermina. "I will learn this, too?"

"Absolutely."

It's Saturday and Nermina knows that Samir is working. She'll have an hour, at most, with Raifa before the baby or three-year-old Taki get up from their naps.

Nermina seeks out her friend's gray eyes. Purplish-blue shadows beneath them confirm how little sleep Raifa is getting these days. This reminds her how frightened and exhausted Raifa looked the first time they'd met. Both women waiting their turn in the queue at the refugee center. Little Taki clasping Raifa's leg. Samir slumped in one of the molded plastic chairs. She and Raifa had built a kinship based on loss, instant and likely permanent. But Nermina wonders now—not for the first time—if she's made a mistake asking her friend's help on this matter. Raifa is married, already a mother. She'll never have to pilfer a child the way Nermina intends.

Raifa trains a guileless look on Nermina that dispels her earlier hesitation. "We get down to business," Raifa says. "Tell me about this guy at your work."

Nermina feels her face flush, hearing aloud what she's been thinking about for days on end. It isn't that she doubts Raifa's abilities so much as she doubts her own.

"He is not my workmate," Nermina says. "He's on the construction crew for the new building."

Raifa sucks in her lower lip. "So, he's not educated man."

"I don't know," says Nermina. "Does this matter?" She recalls the man's body, solid and compact. How he'd stood like a petulant child gazing up toward the heavens.

"You want a man with intelligence." Raifa says this with convincing authority.

Nermina kicks off her loafers and tucks her feet up beneath her on the sofa. She hadn't thought much about intellect. Maybe she should have.

"Wait a minute," Nermina says. "Samir's educated, but he paints houses—"

Raifa waves her hand in the air. "That's different. He's a foreigner. Samir takes what he gets here. But this guy, he is American, yes?"

"Yes," says Nermina. She loves her friend but resents having to defend her choice now. Nermina has watched him and he seems adequate. She wants Raifa's help, not—as her co-workers might say—the second degree.

"So, the American men, maybe you want professional instead—"

"But this is the one I chose," Nermina says. Raifa puts a finger to her lips. "I'm not looking for a husband," Nermina continues in an exaggerated whisper. "You understand this part, right?" Again, the words sound absurd. She's *chosen* a man with little more thought than she'd given to plucking second-hand clothing from bins at the refugee center. She'll *take* the baby she wants, the baby she needs, from a man she neither knows nor cares about. She sees the look of pity on Dr.

Chong's face and feels a rush of impatience, nearly panic. She has no other choice now.

Raifa gathers the thick bundle of her shoulder-length brown hair and slips a rubber band from her wrist. She catches up the wiry mass in a ponytail. With her hair drawn back from her forehead, Nermina thinks her friend looks much younger than her actual age—thirty-five—but no less wise or experienced.

"I do," says Raifa, though a mischievous expression lights up her gray eyes. "Still, you never know…"

"But, I *do* know," says Nermina, the soldiers, of course, ever-present. She remembers those first days of shock and shame and grief. And still, here—thousands of miles away—these feelings follow. The idea of a man's body—a man inside her—repulses her. But this will be different, Nermina believes. This time she'll get what she wants. She'll get her baby. "You said—"

Raifa grabs Nermina's hand, the playful expression instantly extinguished. "I understand," Raifa says. "I hear you the first time. I do." She curves her palm to the contour of Nermina's cheek, then draws it back a moment later. "So, this construction man …"

"He's strong," says Nermina, relieved. She wants only to be moving forward now, not backward, and only her baby will help her to do this. She thinks of the man she's been watching, how purposefully he moves when he's working, how easily he seems to accomplish each task.

"Handsome?" Raifa asks.

Nermina pictures her brother, Mirsad. His dark, sullen eyes. Twinned arcs of lashes. Not a handsome man, her brother; his features too soft, feminine, she thinks now. Mirsad had been *beautiful*, but this man is quite different.

"Yes, I would say this," Nermina says.

Raifa claps her hands together lightly. "Okay. Handsome and strong. This is good," Raifa says. She sinks her hands into the soft cushions and levers herself up from the sofa. Once she's on her feet, she stretches out both hands to Nermina and pulls her up, too. They'd had a good laugh with Samir about this couch, a "rescue" that Raifa and Nermina had lugged from the curb in front of a neighbor's house. Despite her apprehension, Nermina feels excited now; she's about to take the next step in her plan.

"Okay," Raifa says. She squares her shoulders and sets her legs wider apart. Then she hitches her thumbs into the front pockets of her jeans.

Nermina laughs. "You play the man, then?" she says.

"Of course. How else do you learn this?"

"So now what?"

"You tell me where you meet this man again," Raifa says. "Where you find him next?"

"Hmmm...on the construction site. I see him when I walk from my bus—"

"No good," says Raifa. "Outside? With the other men? No good."

Another point Nermina hadn't considered. "Where then?" she asks. She's watched him only from her outdoor spot at the picnic table. Once, though, she'd seen him carrying out a tray of six coffees to his workmates. "I know," she says, forgetting the sleeping babies upstairs and almost shouting. "The coffee kiosk in the lobby."

Raifa smiles. "Good. This is perfect place." She waves her hand toward the tiny kitchen. "Come now," she says. Nermina follows Raifa through the archway. She watches as her friend crosses her arms across her ample breasts then saunters to the kitchen counter. "Two double latte," she says, making her voice low, and then with her voice returned to its normal register, "Now your turn."

Nermina clears her throat. "One black coffee, please."

Raifa mimes paying the cashier and picking up two cups of coffee. She turns toward Nermina and says, "Oh, hi there."

Nermina stands mute.

"Say something," Raifa says.

"Hi there?" says Nermina.

Raifa laughs. "Wow, I cannot believe I see such a beautiful girl like you here," she says in her lowered voice.

Nermina's face flushes. She stands with her hands balled at her thighs.

"No, no," Raifa says. She juts out her right hip and clasps her waist with her right hand. "Like this," she says. Then she pulls her hair out of its ponytail and plays with a strand that falls across her cheek, winding it around her finger, letting it go. "See, now?"

Nermina draws herself up to her full height and mimics Raifa's stance; she feels at once silly and powerful. She frees a strand of hair from her braid—it's grown quite a bit since she'd visited Dr. Chong—and she likes the way it feels now, silky on her fingers, still crimped from the braid.

"Good," says Raifa. "Now, talk to your construction man."

Nermina smiles. "Thank you," she says. "Thank you. I see you, too, sometimes outside."

Raifa claps her hands together again. "So much better!" She hitches her thumbs in her front pockets again. "So...maybe sometime," she says in her lowered pitch, "I take you out for a date?"

Nermina lowers her eyes seductively like she's seen one of her co-workers do with the man from accounting when he delivers the paychecks to her department every Friday. "This would be my pleasure," she says.

"Oh, good," says Raifa. "You learn fast."

"But now I have to wait to see him, right?" She doesn't want to wait, not even until Monday. She wants her life to begin now, now at this very moment.

"Of course," says Raifa. "We all wait for what we want."

CHAPTER 16
WHITE TRUCK/BLACK COFFEE

Nermina has added a new element to her ritual, one she completes now each morning. She exits her bus and, rather than crossing immediately to the stretch of sidewalk that leads to the hospital's east entrance, she follows the temporary wooden walkway that takes her past the construction site and, as Nermina believes, closer to her baby.

Even before she reaches the larger machinery—two cranes, a cement-mixing truck, and a noisy generator—an uneven row of vehicles presages the building's progress. This changing array of cars and trucks signals the arrival of new workers—bricklayers, electricians, HVAC contractors, or plumbers—as the construction enters each new phase. The scene changes incrementally now and provides Nermina a satisfying point of reference. Without completely understanding this, she now measures her own progress toward her goal—her baby—against that of the new building.

On this particular morning, Nermina notices a white pickup truck parked beneath the shade of a large birch tree. The plot of land had been cleared recently of dozens of other trees, though this one, Nermina realizes, has been arbitrarily spared. As she gets closer, she sees a man—her man—get out of the white truck and walk around to the flatbed. His back to Nermina, he unlatches one of the metal cabinets and lifts out a canvas tool belt. This he fastens around his hips. She watches as he walks to the front again and scrapes something from the bottom of his work boot along the running board then ducks back inside the truck.

She imagines walking right up to him—how simple this would be—but a knot of panic grips her. Her heart races and she feels the nuisance of several tiny pebbles as they lodge between her toes and the thin soles of her summer sandals. The thought of finally meeting him frightens her, but the thought of *not* meeting him frightens her even more. What if his part in the work here is coming to an end? What if he moves on to another job somewhere else? She'd have to begin her process all over again. She thinks of Raifa, of the lessons they'd practiced together. Raifa had said to wait, to be patient.

She walks faster, her face burning. She remembers how she'd run from her bus stop after work, the first day that she'd seen him. The idea had emerged slowly but once it took hold she'd clung to it the way passengers on her bus held tight to the overhead straps to keep from falling. If Dr. Chong couldn't give her a baby with IVF she'd have to conceive the normal way. She'd run that night—from the men who had ruined her, from the killers who had taken her family—until she realized there was nothing more to run from. This man seemed safe, safer than most. She would take what she wanted from him and nothing more.

When she gets to the white truck, she walks past it without slowing, then along the muddy boardwalk until it ends and the parking lot's blacktop begins. She crosses the lot and when she gets to the front doors of the hospital they part before her with a whoosh. She stands a moment in the center of the lobby, the air-conditioning chilling her instantly. How long would she have to wait? However long, it's a waste of time.

But then Nermina reminds herself to perform the next step in her ritual. Straight across the lobby, the Java City Café is busy with morning customers. She reaches into her cloth tote and pulls out a small, red satin purse, the colored threads that form a pattern of birds and mountains fraying along the zipper. She waits behind a cluster of bleary-eyed nurses in green scrubs and then it's her turn at the counter.

"One black coffee," Nermina says. She drops her change into the jar. She bends slightly to drop the little purse into her bag and, as she turns, she feels the solid heft of a shoulder, a splash of hot coffee on her wrist.

"I'm so sorry...I didn't mean—" she begins. She looks up to see a man—him—standing in front of her. She hears a sharp intake of breath, her own. The expression on the man's suntanned face registers mild amusement rather than concern.

"No problem," he says. He raises his hands, palms out to her, as though in surrender. Then his eyes travel from Nermina's angular face, alighting briefly on her eyes, before moving on to the rest of her. She flushes under the man's casual inspection and she thinks how—in truth—her surveillance of him in the past weeks has been no different. She notices his eyes—dark brown but rimmed in amber—and how they seem to mock her now.

"It's all good," he says and winks.

Nermina tries to recall the words she's rehearsed with Raifa and remembers only how she'd smiled into the mirror, softening the set of her jaw, the intensity of her stare.

The man grabs a handful of napkins from the counter. "Here," he says. He reaches out and wipes the coffee first from Nermina's wrist and then the spot on his pale blue T-shirt where a brown stain has bloomed.

"I am clumsy," Nermina says.

"Nah. It could happen to anyone," the man says. He blots the spot on his shirt once more then tosses the balled-up napkins into the trash bin. "I'm Carl, by the way. Carl Ingram."

"I saw you..." Nermina stumbles, "the days before...the day before last."

"Yeah?" The man smiles when he says this, like he's making a joke. "I haven't seen *you*, though. You work here?"

"Yes, yes, in the radiology." Blood pounds behind Nermina's temples. She presses a wide smile across her face.

Carl Ingram folds his arms across his chest. Nermina notes the veins pressing just beneath the surface of his thick forearms.

"How long?" he asks. "How long have you worked at the hospital?"

"One year, I work one year now." Nermina beams.

"Cool," says Carl. His eyes flicker over Nermina's light

cotton skirt and top. "So, how long have you been *here*...I mean, here in the U.S.?"

Nermina flushes and with this, she also feels a flicker of anger. She hates explaining herself to people here. Hates carrying the traces of her former life so openly.

"I come here almost eighteen months ago," she says.

"Wow," says Carl, grinning. "Your English is awesome. You must be a fast learner."

"I study English in Bosnia," she says. "Everyone at my school. Also Latin and French."

The man's face grows thoughtful. He looks down at his work boots before raising his eyes to Nermina again. "Hmmm, I remember seeing something about that on TV. The war and all."

Nermina reminds herself why she's here with this man, *Carl Ingram*. She repeats the name silently, committing it to memory.

"Yes," she says. She flicks her hand the way Raifa might with Samir to tell him not to worry about the messy kitchen she hasn't had time to clean. "Very bad," she says, "but now I live much better."

Nermina smiles. She places her right hand on her hip and leans into what she imagines will resemble a more seductive pose. Her heart pounds.

The pensive look on Carl's face dissipates some. "So...you work every day? During the week, I mean?"

"Yes," Nermina says. "Like my workmates say, first J.O.B. then T.G.I.F." Now her face flushes with pride for remembering this Americanism.

Carl throws back his head and laughs. Nermina doesn't

need to pretend now. Her joy is genuine. She's one step closer to her baby.

"Hey, maybe we could get a drink sometime?" Carl says. He squints, his eyes hold Nermina's, and she feels a trickle of sweat at her temple.

"Yes, good," she says.

"I'll call you, then," he says, a matter-of-fact tone that makes Nermina uncertain. She looks down at her sandals, the rust-colored dust that has settled between her toes.

"Yes," she says. She ventures a direct look into the man's deep brown eyes.

A sly grin spreads across Carl's face. "You have a number?"

"Of course."

"Wait," he says. "You have a pen?"

Nermina searches through her bag—holding the coffee still. "Here," she says, triumphant again. The man—Carl—takes the ballpoint from Nermina. She recites the phone number and he scribbles it on his hand.

CHAPTER 17
WEEZ'S

Though he hates to admit it, Carl feels a little nervous about his date tonight. The girl—Nermina—seems different from the others. When he'd called her the week before, Carl suggested he could drop by Friday night around 7:30 or so. He figured he'd take her to one of those cheap, little restaurants near the university. He didn't imagine a girl like her would spend a lot of time out partying and thought it a safe bet she wouldn't have plans. She was a foreigner and he saw her more likely visiting once a week with some old couple from the homeland in their run-down apartment that stunk of onions and spices he wouldn't know the names of. He'd been right. Without hesitation, Nermina said Friday night would be fine. Most important, he'd chosen a Friday because this was the night Rebecca went out with her girlfriends.

Now he has some time to kill before he picks up Nermina. Joey and Neil should still be down at Weez's and when he drives around back he spots Joey's panel van right away. Carl chuckles. The thing's impossible to miss. A giant cartoon character of a dancing banana is plastered on its side. Despite this quirk, Joey is the most stable guy Carl knows and—because of that—the friend he depends on the most. He figures the van is the one last thing Joey has held onto from his bachelor days, just like Joey is the only friend Carl has held onto from his old life in New Jersey. And though he imagines Joey's wife, Elsa, hadn't been too keen on the idea, Carl had crashed with them—sleeping on a pullout couch—for his first six months in Portland. He'd even driven Elsa's Volvo wagon till he scraped together enough cash for his truck. And now it's been two years since he left Boulder for Portland.

Carl shakes his head as he walks through the door. Two years is a long time, the longest he's been in one place for a while. He feels a little twinge of nerves again and wonders if he'd made a mistake telling Joey about Nermina. Inside, he takes a second or two to get his bearings. His eyes sweep the booths and tables. To Carl *Weez's* feels just like the pubs he liked so much the summer he'd backpacked through Ireland: cozy, dark, and hardcore, all at the same time. "A *man's* bar," is how he'd described it to Joey when he first discovered it. Carl had convinced him to make the jump from a TGI Fridays where Joey and his office friends always went for happy hour.

"Hey," says Joey from his seat at the bar now.

Carl claps Joey on the shoulder with a beefy hand. "What's up?"

"Well, actually, Neil and I were just having a little debate before you walked in. Perhaps you can settle it."

"*Perhaps*?" says Carl, simultaneously catching the bar tender's eye. "A Black & Tan," he says over Neil's shoulder.

"Well, here's the deal: Elsa wants to take the game room and turn it into a laundry room to make it easier for when the baby comes—"

"Jesus Christ, this is the big, fucking dilemma you guys are talking about!"

"I know," says Neil. "It's just tragic, isn't it?"

"What I was about to say," says Joey, "is I agree on principle, but it's just that was *my* space before we got married and Elsa moved in."

"Your space. Now there's something," says Neil. "I think you're the only guy I know who buys a house and gets all nice and cozy before he gets married. You know, that whole nesting thing is a bit of a feminine trait."

"That's not even the point. It was an investment and a damn good one, I might add," Joey says.

"Jesus," says Carl. He lays down a ten on the bar and grabs his beer. "What the fuck're we talking about, here?"

"Joey's balls," says Neil. He breaks into a grin. "I think they're about to be crushed between a game room and a washer and dryer."

"Seriously," Joey begins, but they all burst out laughing and the topic is forgotten. Two rounds later, Joey is the first to say he has to get going.

"Oh, come on. It's still early," says Carl, "even for you."

Joey smirks. "Hey, forget about me. Don't you have your date or whatever with that Bosnian girl from the hospital?"

"Oh yeah," says Neil, "What's up with that? How's Rebecca

feel about your little night out?"

"It's none of her business," Carl snaps. He picks at the edge of the label on his beer. He could care less what Neil has to say, but he doesn't want to see the expectant look he knows he'll find on Joey's face.

"Really?" says Joey. "Last I heard you were sort of moved into Rebecca's place. Or did I imagine that?"

There it was, that goddamned preachy tone Carl had been dreading. But then, Joey and Elsa had been married for three years now, so Carl figures a lot of Joey's opinions these days are tied to Elsa's. That doesn't make it any easier to swallow, though.

"Who're you, my fucking mother?" Carl says, trying his best to sound amusing.

Joey, smiles. "Hey, calm down, asshole."

"I'm meeting her at her place in an hour," says Carl. "No big deal. We're gonna grab some dinner somewhere. That's it."

"Sure," says Neil. He places a sweaty hand on Carl's forearm. "It's no big deal—taking out some foreign chick you met one time, shacking up with another—"

"So what?" says Carl. "You jealous or something? Just cause you guys are old and married doesn't mean I can't check out some new scenery once in a while."

Joey's expression is serious now when he turns to Carl. "Sure, dude, that's fine and all. I'm just saying, then maybe you shouldn't have moved in with Rebecca so fast. How long were you two going out? Like a couple of months or something, right?"

Neil nods his head in agreement but, catching the glare

that settles into Carl's eyes, decides to keep his mouth shut. Carl takes a long swig of his beer and raises his hands in the air as a sign of surrender. He flashes a tight smile but sees that Neil and Joey aren't buying it.

"Hey, you know what? Gotta go," Carl says. His face portrays a child-like belligerence. He grabs his five off the sticky bar, leaves a couple singles for his end of the tip, and stalks out the door.

CHAPTER 18
BOSNIAN GIRL

Carl slams the truck into gear and heads out toward the university. The Rolling Stones' *I Can't Get No Satisfaction* blasts from the stereo. Carl sings along at the top of his lungs. He thrums the steering wheel with both hands, an accompaniment to his off-key singing. The night air rushes through the wide-open windows and tousles his hair. By the time he's crossing the Willamette, Carl feels a lot better, those little needles of guilt all but forgotten.

A few blocks from Nermina's he stops at a state store and buys a six-pack. And now, something nags at him again. He thinks about the way she'd looked him over at the hospital. Something he can't put his finger on, something a little off. This makes him remember a party during his first and only year of college. He'd been wasted and a pretty girl with long, brown hair was talking some stuff about the Russian novelists. He liked the way she had of weaving her tiny hands— fingernails bitten down raw—in patterns that went along with whatever she was saying about Tolstoy. Next thing he knew they were back in his dorm room. At first he thought he was just too wasted, but then he'd felt her lips and her tongue and her long hair, soft and sweet-smelling, against his thighs. Afterward, he'd found her huddled on the cold bathroom tile, rocking and crying, making no sound whatsoever. When he tried to comfort her, the girl's eyes seemed to look right through him. But this Bosnian girl, he tells himself now, this is a whole different story.

Once he spots the address, Carl circles the block three times looking for a parking space. He finally ends up in the church lot across the street from the ramshackle two-story house where the Bosnian girl lives. He hopes he won't get ticketed. Back home in Jersey he'd racked up so many parking tickets there'd been a warrant out for his arrest.

Carl walks up three crumbling cement steps to the door and rings the bell to the right of the hand-written insert that says "Beganović." This label is fitted underneath a plastic tab at the top of a narrow mailbox, next to two others that say "Jenson/Miller" and "Farquhar." When there's no immediate answer, he feels a stab of doubt that, for reasons he can't decipher, moves fast in the direction of indignation. But then a few seconds later he sees Nermina through the paned glass of the upper portion of the door. She's making her way down the stairs from the second floor. Her progress is deliberate and unhurried. She opens the scarred wooden door in the same measured fashion.

"Hi," Nermina says, seemingly not all that excited to see him.

Carl quickly assesses the woman who stands before him. Her hair, braided in the same style as when they'd first met, is wet, as though she's just showered. This fact is confirmed as a light, fruity scent from her shampoo engulfs him.

"Hi, I just happened to be in the neighborhood," he says with a smile.

Nermina's eyes stray to the six-pack that rests against Carl's hip. His jeans are torn at both knees and the T-shirt he wears—Bruce Springsteen 1987 European Tour—is pocked with tiny holes.

He follows her gaze. "Oh, I, uh, thought maybe we could have a beer or something before we head out to dinner." Then he smacks his forehead with the heel of his hand. "Oh, shit, I forgot. Muslims don't drink." When she doesn't respond, Carl rushes ahead. "I read up a little." He smiles again, desperate for her to appreciate his efforts. "The Bosnians, they're Muslim, right?"

"Yes." She seems to mull the question further. "Yes, but not all." She produces a nervous smile. "I drink. Sometimes. It's okay." She holds the door open for Carl and says formally, "Please, to come in."

She leads him through a foyer that's been painted bright purple, the color so vibrant it seems to be lit from within. The wood trim gleams with a tropical shade of green that reminds him of the little paper umbrellas that bartenders put into those fru-fru drinks Rebecca always orders. He notes with approval that the railing to the stairs, and the stairs themselves, are a rich mahogany, the wood meticulously restored. Aside from these features, the rest of the front room and an adjoining dining area are in complete disrepair. Here, paint that at one time may have been white is now a dingy gray and peeling in spots. The window frames and woodwork are in the same sorry state. Cardboard boxes filled with newspaper and magazines, piles of books, plumbing supplies, old lighting fixtures, and what look like someone's idea of abstract painting—more than a dozen canvases doused with crazy splashes and swirls of neon orange, pink, and florescent green—fill most of the floor and wall space.

Nermina leads him through these rooms and then outside through a set of sliding glass doors to a small deck that looks out onto a yard choked with a robust collection of weeds. "Please to sit," Nermina says. She motions to a small table with a mosaic top and two white, resin chairs.

Carl wipes his hands on his jeans and clears his throat. He places the six-pack on the table and pulls a beer from the carton. Nermina shakes her head when he offers her one.

"No, thank you. You drink, please," she says.

"So," he begins warily, "I was thinking, there's a little Mexican place down on Powell. Do you like Mexican food?"

"I don't know."

Carl notes Nermina's posture. She sits perfectly upright, her long legs crossed almost primly. But her toenails are painted a pretty shade of light pink and this softens her some.

"Ahhh, so, you've never tried it?" he says. His own legs are too long for him to sit comfortably at the tiny table. He scrapes the chair on the wood decking as he repositions himself, stretching his legs out and then crossing his sandaled feet at the ankles. He imagines this posture makes him look relaxed.

He feels, instead, an uncustomary apprehension.

"Not yet," she says.

"Then I guess we'll have to fix that." He tilts his head back and laughs. But when he looks across the table he sees a young woman, pretty, but not beautiful. Intelligent, maybe. But she carries her foreignness like those African women in *National Geographic* who balance huge and seemingly unwieldy bundles on their heads. He feels himself drawn to her and repelled at the same time. That day at the hospital, he'd sensed something brave and a little desperate in the way she'd looked at him. But he wouldn't say her interest in him seemed sexual. It seemed something else altogether, but he couldn't say what. And still—now—he knows he doesn't want to screw it up with her.

"Hey," says Carl, with a burst of enthusiasm; he remembers a joint tucked away inside his wallet. He takes it out gingerly, rounding out the flattened cylinder. "Do you...?"

"Oh, no," says Nermina, shaking her head again. "But, it's no problem. My landlord, he smokes here always. Go ahead. Please feel free."

"Okay, if you're sure it's cool..."

"No problem," says Nermina. Carl takes her smile as encouragement.

With a nice little buzz on, Carl puts his hand lightly on Nermina's back as they head across the street to his truck. His confidence has returned and he's tamped down any worries about slipping into the apartment, maybe long after Rebecca has gone to bed. Under the halogen lights that bathe the church lot in amber, Carl thinks Nermina's gauzy white top and her pale blond hair made her look very pretty. There's something about her, he thinks, something kind of mysterious, that might be worth the trouble here.

CHAPTER 19
ZÓCALO

Carl chooses a small restaurant called Zócalo. Nermina had passed it many times before but until now had never ventured inside. The brightly colored tiles remind her of the mosaics that covered so many of Sarajevo's old mosques. While school was still in session, she'd seen students and young couples from the neighborhood lined up around the corner, waiting to get in. But tonight, Carl walks directly to the hostess stand where a heavy-set Mexican woman with a thick dark braid and dangling turquoise earrings tells them they can sit anywhere they like.

"What about out there?" Carl asks. He points to a small courtyard they can see through the windows at the back of the room. Nermina nods in agreement and the Mexican woman, her earrings swaying against coffee-colored cheeks, motions for them to follow. Seating herself across from Carl, Nermina looks up at the strands of multi-colored lights woven through a lattice ceiling. Following her eyes, he says, "It's pretty here, right?"

"Yes, very pretty!" she says. She'd been quiet in the truck on the short ride here and meant to change that now. When the waitress arrives for their drink order, Nermina studies the menu intently.

"I'll take a Negra Modelo," Carl says. He smiles at the waitress, a woman equally as round as the hostess.

Nermina looks up from the large menu. "The same," she says. Like Carl, she gives the waitress a broad smile.

"Cool," says Carl.

When the woman returns with the beers, a basket of tortilla chips, and two small bowls of sauces—one green, one red—Nermina fears both will be too spicy. She'd had Mexican food only once before, a very long time ago when she and her family had vacationed in London. She and Mirsad had still been small children but that week their parents had treated them like grown-ups. The memory saddens her. Still, she forces a demure smile as she dips into the green sauce. She takes only the tiniest nibble, relieved to find it flavorful but mild. Carl loads a chip with the red sauce and brings it, dripping, to his mouth. A small bit of tomato slides off the chip and onto his chin without his notice. He chews thoughtfully for what seems a long time. Nermina watches his jaw muscles working, reminded of one of her co-workers, a doughy, older woman who sits behind her desk, munching away on a seemingly endless supply of pretzel nuggets.

"What is it?" says Carl. He looks at the food and then at

Nermina's face. "What's so funny?"

She understands that showing her amusement at Carl Ingram's less than perfect table manners is not polite. "Very good," she says and digs another chip into the bowl of green sauce. "Delicious!"

"Yeah, well, the food at this place is pretty decent. I've been here a few times with my buddies."

Nermina takes a sip of her beer. It's rich and just a little bitter, but it's good, she thinks, not like the watery stuff everyone ordered the first time the women from her office had talked her into joining them for happy hour. They'd gone to a sports bar named Rocky's, just a few blocks from the hospital. The place was packed, the music so loud she couldn't hear a word anyone said to her.

But now she tries on an expression—a sort of pout—she'd seen one of the younger women use whenever a male patron looked their way. Like her, Nermina leans forward, places her elbows on the table and makes a little support of her entwined hands, resting her chin in the center. She pouts. Carl smiles at her.

"What do you recommend?" she asks. She's grateful to see Carl wipe the bit of tomato from his chin with a paper napkin.

"Enchiladas are always a safe bet. Hey, you like Chile peppers?" Carl is suddenly animated, drumming his fingers on the edge of the table.

"I'm not sure," says Nermina, feeling foolish.

Carl throws back his head and laughs. He runs his large hands through his hair.

"You either *like* Chile peppers or you *don't*! They're spicy little suckers. Know what I mean?"

No, Nermina thinks, I don't. She feels herself blushing. An appropriate response refuses to materialize. She says nothing.

"Hold up," he says. He waves for the waitress. When she arrives he says, "Bring us a plate of your hottest peppers. *Caliente!*"

The Mexican woman raises her eyebrows in amusement. "Of course, *Señor.*"

Nermina is surprised at how well the rest of the evening had gone. She'd had another of the dark beers and Carl another two. He'd asked her many questions about her family, about her country. He was quite a bit smarter than she'd expected. He read the newspaper, knew many things about the world. But when she'd asked about his family, a stony anger passed quickly across his features.

"I don't have a whole lot to do with them anymore," he said, and she'd left it at that.

For her part, Nermina thought she'd done quite well. Without shedding a single tear, she'd told a perfect stranger that her entire family was gone, killed in the war. She'd seen his face go soft then, a look she recognized. She didn't want his pity, though; that she wouldn't tolerate from anyone. She hated it when her caseworker, or one of the counselors they'd made her visit, produced that look of blatant compassion. Their earnest gazes shamed her, made her feel naked. Exposed.

Now as Carl pulls the truck up to the curb in front of her apartment she decides there will be no more discussion of her past with Carl Ingram. From now on, she'll be as evasive about her family as he's been about his. Clearly, there is no good reason to delve any further into either of their pasts. She'll get what she wants without any of that nonsense to hinder her progress.

Carl turns off the engine then drums his fingers on the steering wheel for several beats. And when he turns toward Nermina, she sees that for the first time all evening he looks unsure of himself. He slides closer to her, across the seat, and she feels the warmth of his body as he pulls her into an awkward embrace. The smoky aromas of the restaurant cling to his hair and to his T-shirt. Nermina reminds herself again why she is here. She tries to squelch her rising panic. He kisses her, gently at first, but then forces his tongue inside her mouth, the thing probing and slick like a hungry animal. A wave of nausea rolls over her. Then he cups her breast in his hand, squeezing her nipple through the light fabric of her clothing, and she pulls back. He draws his square-jawed face back from hers and she sees surprise, perhaps a little anger, but this is the way Raifa said it should go. Make him want you, she'd said. Tease him a bit. Now Nermina forces herself to smile sweetly.

"Sorry," she says. "I should go now. It will be very late." She runs her hand along the frayed seam of the truck's front seat, imagining the rough nylon thread encasing a deep and ugly wound.

"Um, that's okay," Carl says. He sounds to Nermina almost bashful now. The driver's-side door groans as he opens it. She opens her side and feels around for the running board with her foot. As tall as she is, it's still a reach. Carl stands on the sidewalk waiting for her to slam the door shut.

"Listen, Nermina, I'd, um, like to see you again," he says

as they walk toward her door.

The drone of her heartbeat reverberates in her ears. "Sure, that will be nice."

"I've got your number," he says. "So, I'll call you." He balls up his fists and shoves them into the front pockets of his jeans.

Nermina thinks this makes him look like a frightened child. And just for a moment she sees little Esmer's face. "Okay," she says. "Thank you for the very good dinner. See you."

"G'night," he says.

Nermina waves from the top step as Carl starts up the truck. She remembers—especially those days in Ancona with Esmer—how tightly his little hand had clung to hers, how easy it had been to love him. How awful it had been to turn away from the little boy. She wonders then what boundless love she'll feel for a child of her own, the child she'll conceive with Carl. She stands outside a few moments longer, until the rattle of the truck's engine disappears into the hum of cicada song, until her own crazy heartbeat subsides.

CHAPTER 20
CONSUMMATED

Carl pulls a clean pair of jeans from the laundry basket on the bedroom floor and steps into them. He'd scooped the warm load of clothing from the dryer and tossed it here earlier with no intention of folding it. If Rebecca cared so much about whether stuff got wrinkled, she'd just have to deal with it when she got home from work. He rummages through the pile for a T-shirt and pulls out the first one he finds—pale blue with an old-school M & M's logo on it and two cartoon M & M's, one plain, one peanut. He sniffs the shirt, wondering if the flowery fabric softener smell will stay with it for long.

Then, as he pulls the soft shirt over his head, he recalls Rebecca's reaction a couple weeks before. First off, he hadn't expected her to still be awake when he got in. Second—and this was the part that really burned him up—she'd acted like he'd done something wrong. Shit, he'd kissed a girl goodnight. And for all Rebecca knew, he hadn't even done that much. He hated that he'd found himself explaining—making stuff up—to cover his tracks. He'd felt embarrassed, ridiculous. Besides, it was Rebecca who'd told Carl it was okay for him to move into her place. She'd *wanted* him to. He'd been pissed at Joey for not standing up to Elsa. So what if he crashed on their couch for another couple months—just till he got on his feet? But no way, she wasn't having any of it. Carl figured it was the pregnancy that'd really brought out Elsa's bitchiness. And now, here he was, living with a girl who expected him to punch a clock.

He sits on the edge of the bed to pull on his sandals. He remembers how Rebecca had turned her back to him that night, dragging the sheet and blanket with her, and leaving him bare-assed and horny. Literally out in the cold. If it hadn't been so damned aggravating, he thinks now, it would've been funny. But the whole thing had gotten ugly. Rebecca cried, they fought for a while longer, and then he'd slept on the couch. But the next morning he managed to smooth things over. That was two weeks ago already.

And that makes tonight feel kind of weird, Carl thinks. He hadn't given too much thought to Nermina since he'd called her the week before to set something up. And now he isn't exactly sure what he wants from her. Maybe nothing. She seems nice enough, a lot less opinionated than Rebecca so far. And pretty, too, but different from the girls he usually goes for. Nermina has those sharp angles to her—the cheekbones, that hollow at the base of her throat—but he remembers the soft yellow of her hair, the long braid.

Damn, he thinks, seeing Nermina again is starting to feel complicated. He hadn't lied to Rebecca outright. But then again, he hasn't been exactly truthful about where he's going tonight, just said he needed to help out a friend over by the university. A renovation project in the works. He might be late was all he said. He doesn't owe Rebecca anything, he tells himself now. Screw it, he concludes and grabs his keys from the top of the bureau. He doubles back to the nightstand, opens the drawer, and pulls out a couple condoms from the stash Rebecca keeps there. These he slips into his wallet before wedging it into the back pocket of his well-worn jeans. He smiles. You never know, he thinks. Better safe than sorry.

Nermina sprints down the stairs when she hears the bell. Her face is flushed as she opens the door, her hair a silky, blond curtain that flows softly over her shoulders. She sees the effect of this change on Carl's face. Raifa had been correct. She smiles.

"You come here, exactly on time."

"That's true," says Carl grinning. "Doesn't happen all that often, though, I have to tell you."

Nermina takes in Carl's appearance. Little has changed since their last date, with the exception of his hair—drawn back now into a thick ponytail. She can't help but compare this feature to her landlord's, which is scrawny, graying, and always greasy.

"Well, now you're here," she says cheerfully. She grabs the six-pack he's brought and leads him through the house. The kitchen's aroma of stewing tomatoes, lamb, and spices envelops them as she slides open the glass door to the rickety wooden deck.

"Wow, smells awesome," says Carl.

"Oh, you will like. Not so spicy as the Mexican food, but not too much bland. You'll see."

"That's cool," he says. "It's nice of you." He clears his throat, looks down at his sandaled feet. "It's nice of you to cook, I mean."

Nermina smiles, thinking again of Raifa. Without her, she'd never have gotten this far.

"It's easy," she says. "Besides, it's more..." She takes a few strands of her hair between her fingers, brushes the ends along her cheek, then looks up at Carl. "More personal, I think."

"Absolutely." He twists open one of the beers and hands it to Nermina.

"Oh, thanks," she says. Her tone is matter-of-fact, this affect also the result of Raifa's patient tutelage. He opens another for himself and takes a hefty swallow from the bottle. Nermina takes a small sip. Then she places the other bottles in a cooler she borrowed from her ponytailed landlord. "Good for you!" he said when she'd told him she was having company. He even suggested the beer assortment that now fills the cooler. Nermina wanted to be prepared.

"We will to relax now," she says. She pulls out a chair and sits down at the small mosaic-topped table. Dinner will be ready in a short while."

Carl stands with his back to the railing. Nermina sees how the light breeze ruffles a few loosened strands of his hair, just a shade or two darker than her own. And like the last time she'd been with him, she thinks she detects a hint of uncertainty in his demeanor. The air carries the delicious smell of a neighbor's barbeque, grilled steak and charcoal. And she remembers in a flash how all the smoky aromas from the *Baščaršija* wafted alluringly through the Sunday crowds. How she and Mirsad would dart from one stall to the next, yet never wander too far away from their parents' diligent surveillance. The happy memory unearths the familiar well of grief and her eyes fill. She turns back toward the house, away from Carl, and brushes away the tears with the back of her hand.

"Sure," he says, clearly relaxing as she'd suggested; she now recognizes another sweet fragrance in the air. She turns toward him. The smoke from Carl's joint curls around his face, and these combined scents—past and present—make Nermina feel as though she's lost all sense of time. She floats alone and aimless through inky darkness. Carl blows out a slow stream of smoke, stands up, and walks over to where she sits transfixed. Without saying a word, he holds the rolled paper to her lips. She hesitates a moment, afraid, and then inhales. Her throat burns. Her lungs feel like they'll burst. She coughs for what seems a long time and is grateful that now Carl won't know her eyes had already been wet with tears. She shakes her head no when he offers her another puff.

"No, no," she says, shaking her head even more emphatically when he persists. "As you see, I'm not so used to smoking."

"That's okay," says Carl. "Just take your time." He takes a couple short hits from the joint, holds it awhile, and leans down so that he's face to face with Nermina. Then he presses his lips against hers, releasing the smoke before she can turn her face away. This time the coughing is even worse.

"Sorry," she sputters, nearly upsetting the chair as she stumbles to her feet.

"No, I'm sorry," says Carl. He giggles then like a little boy. "Just thought you might like to try it that way."

"I stick to the beer," says Nermina, before lapsing into another coughing fit. "I need to check on dinner," she manages finally, then rushes headlong toward the sliding door. She stops just short of smacking into the glass. She turns back to see Carl grinning up at her sheepishly from his seat at the little table.

"I'll be right back," she calls, trying to reclaim her dignity as well as her confidence.

In the kitchen, she lifts the lid from the top of a steaming pot, stirs the fragrant contents, and takes a taste with the spoon. My God, she thinks, we haven't even eaten the meal yet. How am I going to make it through the evening? She'd planned everything so carefully, but now the thought of Carl touching her, Carl inside her, sends a shudder through her body. Can she do this after all? She sees the first soldier's eyes, bloodshot, feverish, the Chetnik skull and cross bones inked across his chest. She takes a deep breath through both nostrils and lets the air hiss out through her mouth, just as she'd practiced with the counselor when she first arrived in the United States. She does this several times more, each time feeling herself gain a bit more composure, a bit more control.

She reaches up to the top of the refrigerator to retrieve the loaf of sourdough bread she'd stored there earlier. She pulls out a wooden cutting board and sharp knife from the drawer, then slices the bread evenly, arranging it finally on a plain white plate. All of these kitchen implements she'd slowly, cautiously acquired since moving into her first real home here, grateful after each purchase that she'd begun to assemble the trappings of a stable life. And still the irony never escapes her; instead of bringing comfort, these household possessions—the pale lavender sheets, quilt, and pillowcases on her bed; the French press coffee maker; the ginger-jar lamp and milk-crate nightstand—serve only as reminders of everything she'd been forced to leave behind.

She knows she'll never have her family back; this loss is vast and irreparable. The material things, she tells herself, will be necessary if she hopes to provide an appropriate home for a child, though. Her *child*. And she assumes that the impression of normalcy will eventually lull her into a reasonable approximation of this concept. But here's the problem, she thinks now; the concept is *not* my reality. She laughs and hears the bitterness even through the fuzziness of smoke Carl had coaxed into her. She thinks about all the hours she's wasted—talking with her counselor in these silly, abstract terms. She's become as proficient in this language as she has in English. Talk, talk, talk, but how is all this talk supposed to fix her? To her mind, there's only one way to make up for all she's lost. She reminds herself again about the task at hand. Carl Ingram.

She searches inside a low cupboard and pulls out a bag of potato chips. These she dumps into a wicker basket nested among the clutter on the countertop. The kitchen's not nearly as clean and orderly as Nermina would like, but she's grateful to have the space to herself this evening, her roommates gone. She peers through the glass doors to the deck where Carl sits, tipping the metal chair back precariously, his feet crossed at the ankles, fingers laced behind his head. Nermina sees that his gaze is directed at the tiny sliver of moon, the handful of stars that have begun to emerge in the darkening sky. She takes another deep breath and slides open the door. He smiles at her as she sets the basket of chips on the little table.

"I thought you might be getting hungry."

"Good call," says Carl. He reaches into the basket and grabs a large handful of chips, then munches contentedly for a few moments before adding, "Nice out tonight, huh?"

"It is," says Nermina. She draws up the other chair and sits across from him. She can see that his giddiness has passed and she leans in closer until their faces are just a few inches apart. She sees the effect of her nearness reflected in his heavy-lidded eyes, the languid smile on his lips. Once again, Raifa had been right. She's aware of her heartbeat and the insistent rhythm of the crickets. Of a faint flowery scent that seems to underlie the heavier aroma of the spent joint that Carl had stubbed out on the mosaic table. Resting her hands on the edge of the table, she leans in further and kisses him lightly, tasting the saltiness of the chips, the slight sourness of the beer. Then, before he's had the chance to respond, she pulls away from him.

He stands slowly and goes to her, taking both of her hands so that she stands now too, her height, even in flat sandals, bringing them eye-to-eye. He puts his arms around her, pulls her close. She feels his heart pounding against her breasts. He brushes her hair away and buries his face in the crook of her neck. He begins to kiss her there softly, more tentatively than before. A metallic taste fills her mouth. He slides his hands down to her hips and pulls her closer still. She feels the hardness of his penis pressing against her thigh. This is what

I wanted, she thinks. This is how it will happen. At no time throughout her lessons with Raifa had they spoken of the soldiers. Instinctively, though, each woman had understood. She closes her eyes now, repulsed by the sweat-slicked faces above her, flinching at the quick blows to her cheeks, to her mouth. She tells herself to breathe, to swallow.

Then Carl kisses her on the lips and again he seems to her more cautious than he'd been that first night. She knows this is the time to play her part and so she threads her fingers through his hair—surprisingly soft—and holds his face to hers. She knows what she has to do. And then she is doing it. Now it's *her* tongue that's probing, insistent, seemingly hungry. She slides one hand down to the warm bulge in Carl's jeans and rubs him there with her palm. His breath quickens and he moans a little, then draws back from her.

"What're you doing? I thought—" Carl's voice is hoarse, as though he's just awakened, still groggy with sleep.

Nermina continues to rub him with her palm and flattens her other hand across his mouth. "Shhhh," she says softly. "Not everything is always as it seems." She leads him by the hand, sliding open the glass doors, and he follows.

In her room she pulls down the blinds. Carl stands there among her meager possessions, glancing at the bookshelf her landlord had helped her to hang on the wall, at the books there, and the single bed with its lavender quilt, at the framed posters of Paris and Florence that she'd bought at the flea market. Then she goes to him, holds his hand, walks him to the narrow bed.

"Please," she says, when he hesitates. "Sit here." He sits, looking so out of place to her, here in her little room. She feels powerful now, in control. Standing in front of him, she wraps her arms around his broad shoulders, pulls his face to her breasts. She feels his breath, his tongue, through the thin summer fabric of her blouse. She stands back from him then and begins to pull his T-shirt over his head. He raises his arms for her, wholly compliant like a child. She tosses the shirt on the floor. He kicks off his sandals and she kneels to pull off his jeans, his briefs. He reaches out to her and she sees his penis arching greedily at her touch. He stretches his hands around her narrow hips and pulls her body closer. She places small kisses along his neck, moving incrementally, taking her time. She strokes his penis with her right hand and pulls him closer with her left.

"In my wallet," he says, his voice hoarse like before. Nermina laughs then. "No need," she says. "I'll be right back." She smiles at him reassuringly. Then she slips out the door and into the hall bathroom she shares with her roommates. Here, she pees and then kicks off her jeans. She hangs them carefully over the towel bar. She washes her face and hands. Looking at herself in the mirror, she pushes her hair back from her forehead and, with her index finger, traces the scar, traversing this memento several times. She thinks about her mother, the way her cool fingers would smooth away the stray wisps of hair that had escaped Nermina's braids. She longs for her now and realizes it's become harder and harder to remember her mother's features. Still, she remembers her touch. She flushes. Her mother, she tells herself now, would understand.

When she returns, Carl is tucked beneath the covers, one

tanned arm exposed though, dark against the paleness of the quilt. His presence in the small bed—her bed—seems, again, improbable. The scene feels surreal. She thinks he may have dozed while she was gone but, if he has, he's roused himself now. Propped up on one elbow, he watches her switch off the lamp. "Thought you might've changed your mind," he says drowsily.

The velvety darkness that's dropped on the room emboldens her. "Not at all," says Nermina. She's surprised at the evenness of her voice. She undresses, letting her panties, her gauzy summer blouse, her bra, fall to the floor. She feels for the soft edge of the quilt and slips into her bed with Carl Ingram.

He pulls her to him and she feels his lips on her throat like before. He runs his hand along the flats and the curves of her body, cupping one breast and then the other. And then his mouth is there, his tongue flicking across her nipples until they grow hard. She feels the slickness of her own skin and of Carl's. She caresses his thighs, one and then the other, then strokes him again, feeling the stickiness on her hand. She lets him open her with his fingers, and she is ashamed when she feels how wet she is, how willing. She lets him kiss her as he enters her, and she even holds tight to his muscled ass, pulling him deeper inside her. She feels ashamed and then, briefly, unexpectedly, vindicated. She makes him pull out so she can climb on top of him. And then she's losing herself, thinking of nothing, her fingers woven through his hair, now loosened from its ponytail, the sensation of pleasure so wholly unexpected she dares not question it.

But when, a long while later, his body shudders beneath

her, she comes back to herself so suddenly it frightens and confuses her. She's almost surprised by Carl's presence. The bed is too small for them to sleep side by side all night, and Nermina knows now she wouldn't have wanted this anyway. Even so, she makes herself lie still, waiting for what she imagines to be the appropriate amount of time for the makings of her baby to mesh. She watches the numbers turn on the digital clock by her bedside for another fifteen minutes. Then she slides from his body and hears Carl's even breathing in the darkness as she shuts the door behind her.

She lets the shower run a long time, soaping her body tenderly. She realizes then that she's happy. She'll get what she wants, what she needs, after all. And in the end, this is all that matters. Her body wrapped in a clean towel, her hair piled atop her head and wrapped in another, Nermina pads into her bedroom. She places her hand on Carl's shoulder, shakes him gently.

"I think it's time for dinner," she whispers.

He rolls toward her, and she brushes the long strands of sandy blond hair away from his face. He smiles at her. "I *am* hungry," he says.

"That is good," she replies.

CHAPTER 21
SUCKERED

After dinner, Carl waits until Elsa goes back into the kitchen and he hears the water running in the sink, the dishes clattering against one another as she drops them into the tub. With his feet resting on the coffee table, he leans back against the couch and clasps his hands behind his head.

"She kicked me out," he says to Joey. Then watching Joey set his beer down on the coaster, Carl smirks.

"So the big love affair's over?"

Carl turns his head just enough to see the look he'd been expecting: smug but also slightly amused, a look that's changed very little since third grade. Only then, Carl and Joey had stood on the blacktop behind the school and it was Carl who'd sent the softball crashing through the cafeteria window even though it was Joey who'd missed the catch. It was Carl on the bench outside the principal's office till his mother retrieved him. Now, Carl hates the way Joey can still shame him so easily.

Carl takes a long swig of his beer. He winks at Joey then sets the bottle down gently on the cork coaster. "Who said it was love?"

"You, for one," says Joey, his face now drained of amusement.

"I was wrong," says Carl. "And I'm a big enough man to admit it."

"Jesus," says Joey. He glances toward the kitchen. "Do you ever think about who gets hurt? Last time it was Fern—"

"I don't need you to keep track for me, asshole." Carl forces a smile to lighten his delivery. When things had blown up with Fern in Boulder, Joey hadn't hesitated to help him out.

"The door's always open," Joey said then, but now Carl knows he's screwed. He knows this time is different. He knows, for sure, this time he's at fault.

"So, what happened? Did Rebecca find out about your Bosnian girl?" Carl sees the tightness in Joey's jaw, the color rising in his cheeks like when they were kids playing dodge ball in the street. Joey always the first one to call the game when a kid got really suckered.

"So what if she did?" Carl keeps his voice low and even. He digs his hands into the nubby fabric of the couch.

Joey shakes his head. "It's shitty, is all. It's a shitty thing to do to both of them."

Carl sees Nermina's expression that last time at her place. She'd rolled away from him, seemingly content, content to be in her own little world. Her affect, so unlike Rebecca's—clingy, sappy-sweet—should have assured him, but instead it had set him on edge. There were things about her he didn't understand, things about her he didn't *want* to understand. Nermina asked nothing of him and he'd liked that. But now he flashes on his mother, her expression empty, depleted. Carl knew he'd had a hand in that. His mother had given up asking. But had she given up wanting too? He swallows the hard stone of guilt that threatens to choke him.

"Fuck you," says Carl. "Fuck you and your perfect little marriage."

"Jesus, Carl—"

Carl is already on his feet when Elsa stomps into the room, dishtowel over her shoulder. Joey stands, looks from his wife's face to Carl's, and back to Elsa's. "What?" Joey says to her.

"Now," says Elsa.

CHAPTER 22
BLUE

‿⧓⧓‿

When her period was three days late Nermina called Raifa, but Raifa said not to get too excited yet. It was still very early. A week later the two women stood in the grocery store checkout with two E.P.T. boxes.

Even when both test strips turned blue, Raifa was still skeptical. "How many times did you and Carl...?" she'd asked Nermina.

Nermina remembered the bus ride home from Dr. Chong's office. The emptiness that supplanted all rational thought. She'd considered her choices that day. She could use the sharpened blade of her knife. Or she could follow her father's expedient example. She could draw the blinds finally on the images that haunted her. Her mother's shrouded body. The soldiers. The bits and bone of the dead in the streets. She'd made a plan and Carl had followed. She'd made a plan and her family would be whole again. Or at least she'd have some prayer of wholeness, someone to draw her away from the ragged grave of what was lost.

She'd had sex with him five times, the last just before he'd told her he was moving to Vancouver. "A whole different country," he'd said with child-like excitement, and her first reaction was panic; she wouldn't get her baby. But then—as though divinely planned—the nurse at the clinic confirmed what Nermina already knew. And when she said goodbye to Carl and said that she wished him well, she'd meant exactly that.

PART THREE

CHAPTER 23
ATIKA IS BORN

Nermina holds her baby daughter, Atika, to her breast. The sensation of a tiny mouth suckling there is both strange and welcome. Nermina is exhausted but has never felt so powerful. She's a mother. At times she can barely believe that this is true. She strokes her baby's warm scalp, smoothing the fine wisps of auburn hair that cover her daughter's head like a cap. She presses her lips to the unimaginable softness of her cheek, breathing in her milky scent.

But then, inevitably, she remembers her mother. How she'd always smoothed back Nermina's hair from her forehead with her hand, revealing the short, unruly strands of her cowlick. Her mother had called this Nermina's 'baby hair.' And when Nermina had grown into a young woman, this gesture, the silly, secret language between them, had transformed into a touchstone of their bond. The potency of this broken connection strikes Nermina now with renewed urgency. Her baby's arrival has brought the happiness she'd wished for but also rekindled her grief. She longs for her parents, especially her mother. She feels her absence all over again and with nearly the same intensity as when Nermina had first arrived in the United States.

She scolds herself gently for this digression; she now has all she needs. Since her daughter's birth—one week exactly—she's fought hard to keep the ghosts at bay. But today she allows herself to imagine her mother as her daughter's *nana*. She smiles sadly, thinking how beautiful her mother had been, how improbable that a woman so lovely and youthful could be called nana. The word seems suddenly coarse and old fashioned, nothing at all like her mother.

"We'll have to think of a more modern name, little one, won't we?" she whispers. She rocks her daughter rhythmically for a few moments and then, realizing that she's stopped suckling, lays the sleeping baby against her shoulder. She pats her back gently, waiting for the burp that Raifa insists is essential for an infant's proper digestion. This takes a bit of time and when she finally lays the baby in her crib, covering her with the soft pink blanket, Nermina realizes how truly tired she is. She remembers with relief that Raifa has already washed and folded all of Atika's things—the sleepers and blankets and onesies and bibs that seem forever in need of laundering. The bottles that she'll need later in the day for filling with the abundance of Nermina's surplus breast milk are washed and dried and neatly arranged on the drain board.

There is nothing left for her to do now except to nap beside her baby. She lies down on the bed in the room her friend has prepared for Nermina and Atika, and the waves of exhaustion wash over her. She feels the soreness in her limbs, the dull ache behind her eyes. She curls her legs to her chest, feeling as close to content as she dares. The pregnancy had been easy and she'd worked right up till the day her water broke. But Nermina understands that, without Raifa and Samir, she'd never be able to give her daughter the proper start she needs. Moving here has given Nermina the relative luxury of knowing that she and her child are not alone. That at least for as long as she needs them, she'll have a surrogate family of sorts until her own tiny family is sturdy enough to function on its own. And certainly, just as important, she knows that her friends have never once questioned her reasoning. Never once made her doubt her choice, nor judged her because of it.

Nermina had told only Raifa and Samir that Carl Ingram was the father of her child; that she'd kept this from him, and would likely do so for the foreseeable future, troubles her only in her weakest moments. Feeling the steady tug of sleep, she tells herself once again that she's done the right thing. She's done what was necessary. And Carl has made it easy.

CHAPTER 24
POSTPARTUM

Nermina sits on the sofa in her usual spot, her left hip wedged against the firmness of the rolled arm. She takes up only a small portion of space amidst a tasteful array of sky-blue, ochre, and sand-colored pillows, batik-printed to offset the crisp ivory fabric of the sofa. This two-person sofa—or *love seat* as the Americans say—has become Nermina's refuge and also her Nemesis. She's cultivated a love-hate relationship with this piece of furniture and a love-hate relationship with its owner, Shira Rosenberg, Ph.D., psychologist and mind reader.

It was Beverly, Nermina's caseworker, who'd made the recommendation and Beverly who painstakingly pestered Nermina to make the appointment. At first Nermina fought her, explaining in careful English, that she had no further need for therapy. In that first terrible year, she'd had no choice but to submit to the initial intake assessments, the constant referrals to specialists. But now she is perfectly capable of functioning without assistance. Aside from that, therapy subtracts fifty-five minutes from her life each week, fifty-five minutes she should be cuddling her baby daughter. Had Beverly not taken it upon herself to check in on Nermina after Atika's birth, Nermina would have swallowed the intermittent waves of sorrow that swept away that first perfect bubble of euphoria. After all, *now* her life is different. *Now* she has everything she needs.

Feeling Shira's gaze, like her baby's steady breath on her cheek, Nermina averts her eyes. As she's learned in the past four months, Shira Rosenberg sees all. Shira Rosenberg sees deep into Nermina's past and, if she (Nermina) had been the slightest bit religious, she might even suspect her *shrink,* as they say here, had established direct access to her soul.

"So, from what you're telling me, even the flashbacks are easing up some?" Shira asks.

"Yes. Only one last week." Nermina's finger glides back and forth on the sofa arm, noting the weft of the fabric, the intermittent golden, metallic threads—a bit thicker than the rest—that remind Nermina of the awful German fairytale about the little man who swindles a young mother of her newborn baby. She thinks of Atika, asleep in her crib, and her breasts tingle, then ache. Any moment now she'll be leaking through the only sweater she owns that isn't stained with spit-up and breast milk. An unexpected smile emerges on Nermina's lips. Shira nods, makes her gentle advance.

"You said you think you're ready to cut back our visits to

every other week. I'm not sure that's a good idea right now. Are you keeping the journal we discussed last time?"

It strikes Nermina that she owes her life here in America to a cadre of women: first Raifa, then Beverly, and now Shira. She quickly dismisses Dr. Chong, the shame and disappointment of that interlude. Aside from her, *these* women make it possible for Nermina to awaken each morning with something like hope. And they make it possible for her to breathe without feeling constantly the unfathomable weight of her demons. At work, her coworkers are always saying: "You saved my life!" A coffee delivered. A phone message transcribed. *No*, Raifa, Beverly, and now Shira, have saved Nermina's life in the most literal sense imaginable.

Nermina doesn't want to answer; she doesn't want to disappoint this woman who cares so deeply, who studies her each week like a rare and coveted book. Who looks at her the way her mother had. Instead, Nermina conducts her regular inventory. Each object in Shira's office Nermina has committed to memory. The willow basket filled with sand dollars, a cobalt vase of hand-blown glass, a small brass Buddha. As always, Nermina's gaze finds the ebony cat, meticulously carved out of stone, a talisman that has taken on such immense value, Nermina has to struggle with herself whenever Shira's attention—though rare—is averted. She struggles even now not to pocket this thing that doesn't belong to her and yet somehow does.

When Shira repeats the question, Nermina pulls herself back into the sun-filled room and away from her near-transgression, her brother's young face barely discernable now. The copper figurine she'd bought for Mirsad, though, this survives in memory. And in this room, the shattered porcelain cat—Her fault? Mirsad's?—this too, is whole again, returned intact to their mother's table.

"Not all the time..." she begins. Then after a moment, "But I do feel better. I do..."

Shira tilts her head and her eyes—dark, earnest—implore Nermina to continue. When she doesn't comply, Shira says: "Post-partum depression is common among women in the U.S. There's absolutely nothing to be ashamed of. And your history presents additional challenges." This coda she delivers in a tone at once kind and professional, a tone Nermina has come to appreciate, though at first considered condescending.

But now, Nermina's cheeks flush. Shame comes more easily and unexpectedly these days. She shuts her eyes against the onslaught. Again, the men's weight smashing against her body. Again, the crunch of gravel and glass as she struggles to her feet. Again, the look in little Esmer's eyes as she leaves him in the palazzo with his aunt and hurries away like a thief. Again, the heavy, pinching feeling in her breasts that prompts her each time to question her worthiness, her ability to be a mother to Atika. Again. Again. Again. But she coaxes her thoughts back from that darkness. She is here now, not in Bosnia. Here now, *in a whole new country*. She tumbles these words like pebbles in her fingers and realizes it was Carl who had spoken them.

"I know that," Nermina says. She forces a tight smile.

"We can revisit the possibility of medication once you're done breastfeeding."

"Maybe, but I'm sure I'll be much better by then. I'm sure..."

"Just promise me you'll consider it," Shira says. "It's just one option. You're working hard with therapy...sometimes people need some extra help."

Nermina cuts her eyes away from the ebony cat and hazards a brief connection with Shira's bottomless stare. "I promise," she says.

CHAPTER 25
FIRST LANGUAGE

Nermina lifts the felt pouches from the drawer one by one. Each is thick and heavy as she unrolls the soft, dusky fabric. Then she pulls out the silverware—forks, knives, spoons—that Raifa unearthed at a garage sale and gifted to Nermina once the bungalow was fit to live in.

"Service for eight!" Raifa announced then. Nermina slides her fingers along a swirling pattern of leaves and remembers how her friend's exuberance had canceled out her protests. "When would I ever use these fancy things?" Nermina was focused on moving, on Atika, on classes and work; she couldn't imagine entertaining dinner guests, let alone using formal accouterments like these.

But now she also considers those last family meals in Dobrinja, the rare times her parents' work schedules coincided. How her mother would lay the dinner table with an embroidered linen tablecloth and napkins, her wedding crystal and silverware and china. Nana's copper samovar and the petite matching cups would come out last. Nermina blinks back the dulled but persistent sadness attached to these memories. Sadness for times she hadn't given a moment's thought until they were gone forever. So, for the time being, she justifies her little indulgence.

Tonight, Nermina sets the kitchen table for three. This will do for now. A dining room set will have to wait. For practical reasons, she decides on the smaller salad fork at Atika's place setting. The high chair is long gone, the booster seat, too. Still, Nermina makes a mental note to forego her ban on apple juice, since a pale spill will render far less damage than pomegranate.

Amar will arrive at seven. Amar, a friend of a friend of a friend of Samir's that Raifa has recently thrust upon Nermina with no less vigor than the flatware. Of course, Nermina protested. Of course, Raifa wore her down. Two milquetoast dates—one to a coffee shop, one to a downtown craft fair—and now again, Nermina has succumbed to Raifa's good-natured command: "Invite him for dinner! Treat the poor guy to a home-cooked meal. You know what they say..." Nermina wonders if the vegan lasagna in the oven is what Raifa had in mind. This meal is one of three she can produce with confidence. Her face flushes as she remembers that very first dinner she'd made for Carl. It served her well and she'd gotten exactly what she wanted. And now? She has no goals. No agenda. And, despite Shira and Raifa's assurance her feelings could someday change, she has no desire to entangle her life with another's. With Shira's help, she's only beginning to learn how her losses have shaped her. It wouldn't be fair, she thinks, to drag someone else through this mess.

These thoughts are interrupted by a muted thud from her daughter's room and, in the space of a heartbeat, Nermina flies up the carpeted staircase. At the doorway, she takes in the scene: Atika on the floor, startled but not crying or maimed or bleeding. The toppled nightstand, Winnie the Pooh lamp, coloring books, and crayons scattered on the hot-pink area rug.

Nermina lowers herself to the floor and pulls the child into her lap so that their bodies meld and Nermina is certain Atika is unhurt. Then she eases back against the wall, holding the child at arm's length so she can see her face. Wisps of copper-colored hair lie damp on her little girl's forehead.

"What happened here, *dušo*?" Atika's green eyes stare back at her, wide, unblinking. Nermina scans the room once more and then she sees it: the bottle of nail polish lying on its side. Beside the toppled nightstand, a Rorschach of Hawaiian-Coral splattered over the blond hardwood floor. A long trail of coral droplets splashed along the baseboard. Her daughter's eyes follow her.

Nermina's voice emerges harsher than intended: "What have I told you?" She squeezes her daughter's shoulders, a bit harder than necessary. She feels the child's soft flesh—baby fat still—and the solid bones beneath that shift a little with her touch. Looking down at Atika's chubby fingers, she sees the haphazard application of coral polish on six of her ten fingernails. "No playing with Mama's makeup!" She sees, as though for the first time, that each of her daughter's nails is bitten raw. Then she forces her voice softer: "Do you understand, *dušo*?"

Tears brim and overflow her daughter's eyes. A shudder passes through the girl's body and reverberates through Nermina's.

"I'm sorry, Mama." Atika's voice sounds small inside the quiet room and Nermina feels the tug of guilt that replaces her anger with its swift and predictable current. She pulls the child into her arms again and holds her. This time, she breathes in her daughter's sticky-sweet smell of strawberry shampoo, of sweat, and the strong fumes of hardening nail polish. She wills her heartbeat to slow to a normal pace. For a split second, she feels her mother's cool hand on her cheek, the ghost of this gesture's assurance. Her voice softer still, Nermina says, "It's all right, little one, Mama's not angry anymore."

At 7:00 p.m. sharp Nermina opens her front door to Amar, a bearded young man even slighter than her old classmate at the medical faculty in Sarajevo. *Those* memories—of her and Hasan, of the city in flames and the barricade and what happened afterward—these she'd relegated to Shira's office only. But seeing Amar in her foyer now, Nermina's mouth goes dry. Amar hands her a bouquet of yellow lilies. She recognizes the crisp lime-green paper, the curled multi-colored ribbons that make the flowers seem more expensive than they are; she pictures Amar's progress as he would have paid the tattooed cashier at the market, then rounded the corner at the end of her block before making his way to her house. "Thank you," she says. "They're beautiful."

Amar produces a tentative smile; his eyes meet Nermina's

only briefly. He scans the room. "*Tvoja ćerka?*"

Rather than soothing her, this language—her first language—sounds harsh on Amar's tongue. "Oh, Atika will be down soon," Nermina says. "We had a little...well, a little accident." She flutters her hand toward the stairway. Amar glances toward the top of the stairs as if to conjure the child. The box fan that Raifa lent her blows a torrent of warm air toward them. It lifts several strands of the young man's hair from his forehead and then settles them back down. Nermina sees his uneasiness and silently scolds herself for keeping him standing in the foyer.

"Please, please, come sit down in here," she says finally. She leads him into a small parlor, empty except for two plastic sculpted armchairs that she and Raifa found at the curb.

Amar scans the high-ceilinged room. "This is...this home is very...good." His thin-lipped smile begs Nermina to appreciate his efforts.

"Oh, yes! We love it here!" She hears Raifa's words of encouragement and ratchets down her tone—false and nearly shrill. Certainly, she can do better than this. She sweeps her arm toward the archway Samir opened up just days after she'd made settlement. "All of this is Samir's handiwork." And when Amar's eyes convey incomprehension she adds: "*Ručni rad.* Handiwork."

"Samir?" Amar strokes his beard thoughtfully.

"*Njegov ručni rad. Da, da!*" Nermina gushes. "Yes, Samir!"

Throughout the meal Atika and Amar trade furtive stares but very few words. And when Nermina and Amar lapse into their first language—this she finally concedes the poor man—

her dinner guest has no idea the child understands every single word. Of course, Nermina knows. She knows, too, Atika's proficiency in the silent language she and her daughter are schooled in. Private. Exclusive. Nuanced. Nermina wonders if this secret language of love and pain will always remain so. She watches as her daughter raises the beautiful silver fork to her mouth. Even this smaller one looks oversized and unwieldy in the child's little fist.

Amar's words startle her. "*Hvala*, Nermina. Everything is good, is...delicious meal."

"*Nema na čemu*," Nermina says. She glances again at her daughter, the child's face impassive. "We hope you'll come again," Nermina says, but even as these words are spoken, she knows they mean the opposite.

CHAPTER 26
SCHOOL SHOES

Atika sits on the wooden bench in front of the office. Though tall for her age, her feet barely reach the floor. She pulls at a snag in her navy-blue tights and an inch-wide run zips from her ankle all the way up to her knee. Then she kicks her right foot—attached to the leg with the run—back and forth beneath the bench, scuffing the toe of her shoe. These are her school shoes. When she sees the minor damage accomplished—the floor is concrete, the shoe is leather—she increases the pace and intensity of the kicking. She begins to alternate, swinging one foot then the other. She falls into a comfortable rhythm she could have maintained for quite some time. But when Atika looks up her little-girl heart leaps into her throat.

Atika's first-grade teacher, Mrs. Vestri, stands just inches from her, gray-haired, flabby arms crossed over a large bosom that makes a convenient shelf just for this purpose. "What on earth do you think you're doing?"

Atika meets her teacher's angry stare. "I'm waiting for my mama," she says.

Mrs. Vestri seems to embody all the changes in the child's life. Nearly everything is different now. Her new teacher is nothing like Ms. Barnett from kindergarten, a first-year teacher who had showered her young students with an abundance of kindness and colorful stickers. This year too, Atika and her mother no longer live with Strina Raifa and Ujak Samir. Instead, they've moved into their own house, and Atika's cousins—Sabrina and Taki—won't be there except when they come for a visit.

"She's late," says Mrs. Vestri, "*extremely* late." And then under her breath she mutters, "Some people..." Atika picks up a couple of words from the ensuing tirade. *Inconsiderate* is the one that stands out the most. In Sabrina and Taki's room, adult voices never seemed to penetrate the cozy bottom bunk she'd shared with her cousin. But in her new bedroom, in her new house, Atika has developed a special ability to tease out the sounds of her mother's crying, even through thick walls and TV news and public radio broadcasts, all of the new sounds of their small household. As a result, her hearing has become exceptional.

Atika looks up at her teacher's face now—a blank expression on her own—and says, "My mama has to work." There is nothing overtly sarcastic or impudent in her delivery; the child seems to instinctively understand the nuance of such interchange with adults. Mrs. Vestri opens her mouth to reply but then changes her mind. The janitor—Mr. Johnson—pushes a huge, wheeled trash bin into the hallway from a classroom across from the office. Mrs. Vestri straightens her shoulders. She looks toward the dark-skinned man as he makes his way across the hall. Mr. Johnson nods to Mrs. Vestri just as she turns away from Atika and disappears through the office doors. Mr. Johnson smiles at Atika and she at him. She remembers his kindness, how he'd dialed the phone in the office and spoken softly to her mother, how he'd waited with Atika, waited until her mama arrived. That was a long time ago, one of the first times her mama had been late.

But now Atika jumps up from the bench. Still in green scrubs, hair in a ponytail, her mama is walking toward her. And then her mother is kneeling down to meet her eyes, smelling like rubbing alcohol, like pee, like sick people.

"I'm sorry, *malena*. Mama fell asleep. I'm so sorry." Atika feels her mother's hands pulling her close.

"It's okay." The girl chokes back the lump in her throat that is mostly sadness, but something else too. Perhaps Atika is angry with Mrs. Vestri for saying bad things about her mama. And perhaps she is angry with her mama for forgetting her at school. She wonders how it is that she can be angry with both of them at the same time. She presses her small hand to her mother's cheek. "It's okay, Mama," she says.

CHAPTER 27
THE STUDY

Atika creeps down the staircase in a wooly darkness that seems to swirl all around her in changing patterns. She knows not to switch on the light and avoids the floorboard two paces from the bottom of the stairs, the one that will produce a creak not loud but loud enough to awaken her mother. She touches her fingers to the wall and pads silently through the dining room, then freezes, imagining herself like the white-tailed deer she and her cousins had seen on their hike with Ujak Samir just the week before.

She stands outside a set of glass-paned French doors and, on tiptoe, presses her small face to one of the squares. Her breath clouds the glass as she strains to see into the room that Atika and her mother call 'the study.' This is where wooden bookshelves stretch all the way to the ceiling and so, a long time ago, her mother had put all of their favorite books—the ones she'd read to Atika when she was just a baby, plus all the books Atika can now read by herself—on the bottom shelves, well within her reach. The fancier books, the ones her mother collects at flea markets and auctions, sit on the top shelves, and these she's only allowed to look at with her mother's permission because reaching them requires a ladder. This is one of the things her mother is very strict about.

As her eyes adjust to the darkness, the blur of her mother's figure comes slowly into focus. She sees her there, curled tightly in the bentwood rocking chair, covered up to her chin with a soft blue afghan, one of the many Strina Raifa has made for them over the years.

Something tugs harder inside Atika then and makes her eyes sting. She hears her mother's words. *You're a big girl now. Eight years old.* And she knows this is true. But she longs now to climb into her mother's lap, to breathe in the lemony smell of her mother's skin, and just be held.

She fights this jumble of feelings as best she can, dabbing with her fingers at the tears that run hot now on her cheeks, along the line of her chin. *You're not a baby*, she tells herself sternly. In her head she mimics her mother's tone, not the usual one that is mostly patient, but the sound of her mother's voice during what she calls her 'sad times.' These always pass in a couple of days. And even during the worst of it, her mother never yells at her or spanks her. So, what is there to be afraid of? She can't say exactly, but she knows she hates the feeling more than any other. Hates feeling more like the crybaby her cousin Sabrina has begun to taunt her with.

And then, rather than climbing the stairs and returning to

her bed, she slowly turns the smooth glass doorknob—cold on her fingers—all the way to the right, the brass tumbler clicking, the panes of glass rattling only slightly. Still, this is enough. She hears the sharp intake of her mother's breath and knows at once that she's been crying, too.

"Mama," she says, her small hand still on the doorknob, her voice a whisper. She pushes, just a little, the door making a tiny creak. And when her mother returns no answer, the girl slips into the room through the narrow opening she's made. She nearly runs across the wooden floor, stopping only when her toes feel the thick carpet at the far end of the room where her mother is tucked into the rocker. The tall windows behind her mother reveal a nighttime darkness much deeper than inside the room; and this, too, frightens the girl.

"Mama," she thinks she's said. But she realizes that even this isn't right, that the tiny voice has only sounded inside her head. The girl freezes once more and again she thinks of the frightened deer, how it appeared on the ridge like a ghost and Ujak Samir had put a finger to his lips, instructing them wordlessly to stand silent on the trail.

Her mother shifts in the chair and Atika sees one slender arm slip from beneath the blanket, her fingers reaching for the lamp beside her. She hears the click as her mother pulls the brass chain, and the girl blinks in the soft light that seems to move out in rays, like in the pictures she'd drawn of the sun when she was little.

"I'm sorry, Mama," she says aloud now.

"What do you need, Atika? You should be asleep."

Atika hears it right away: the tone she'd been dreading. It's been hiding there all along, just as she'd imagined, coiled inside her mother's words like a snake in one of the picture books her mother read to her before she could read them on her own. Her heart thumps hard but Atika runs the few paces across the carpet to her mother anyway. In the lamplight her mother's face seems thinner than in the daytime, gray shadows smudged under her eyes and cheekbones like a scary mask. The girl's face flushes hotter and still, she shivers a little. Goose bumps rise on her arms against the thin cotton of her nightgown.

"You weren't in your room," Atika says. "You weren't in your bed."

"I'm here," her mother says. She draws the afghan around her body. "I'm right here."

Atika sees that her mother still has on the same clothes she'd worn the day before—a pair of jeans and a dark green sweater with three buttons along her collarbone. Loose strands of her mother's hair that have escaped a sloppy ponytail hang limp against her forehead and across her cheeks. She knows that her mother hasn't showered and the stale smell of her clothing and her body makes Atika a little queasy. She reaches out and places her hand on her mother's cheek, feels the streaks of wetness there. Her mother turns her face away then, a harsh movement that tightens the knot in Atika's stomach.

"You need to go back to bed." Her mother mouths the sentence as though reading it from the pages of a book but with none of the animation she'd add if this were actually the case. Her mother's voice is blank, a blank page.

"Can't I stay down here with you, Mama?"

"No, you may not. It's late. It's…" Her mother reaches for

a little brass clock that sits next to the base of the lamp and brings it close to her face. "It's 2:30," she says. She sounds a bit surprised but otherwise uninterested. "You need to go upstairs now." Her mother replaces the clock but adds nothing more. The room is silent except for the low thud of the heating system coming on and then a light rustle of papers on the antique desk in front of one of the windows.

Atika waits what seems a very long time for her mother to brush the messy strands of hair from her face, to smile at her, or even begin to wiggle her fingers and pretend she's going to chase her down and tickle her the way she used to when Atika was little. But as the seconds tick past on the little brass clock, Atika knows that her mother isn't going to do any of these things. Instead, the girl knows she's going to have to set the little alarm clock in her bedroom for 6:45 a.m. because it's unlikely her mother will be waking her with a kiss on the forehead in the morning. She knows she'll have to call Strina Raifa to tell her that her mother will be staying home from work. She'll pour her own cereal and try not to spill any of the milk on the counter. She'll pack her own bologna sandwich and an apple. And she'll walk three blocks to the bus stop to wait with the other children for the school bus.

Atika looks at her mother once more and again her face seems as cold and still as the statues in the park. She looks up at the tall bookshelves and at the fancy desk where her mother writes out the bills. She loves this room because this is where her mother has always read to her. And she hates this room because this is the place where her mother hides when she's sad.

Then the girl turns away from her mother and drifts like

a little ghost through the slim opening. She shuts the French doors behind her and, clutching the banister, starts up the carpeted stairs. The light from the study clicks off just as she reaches the top step, leaving the child alone in the darkness.

CHAPTER 28
STORM

The thunderheads build up quickly, and before the adults have the chance to debate, the rumbling is loud enough to make their decision unanimous: they're turning back on the loop trail and getting the kids back to the car as fast as possible. When the first flash of lightning crackles across the sky, Nermina grabs Atika's hand but her daughter pulls free from her grasp. At ten, her body has begun to lengthen considerably, the roundness of her little girl's belly now flattened and taut. The expression on her face—her jaw set tight and her green eyes wide with determination—reminds Nermina that her daughter is growing up quickly.

"I'm going with Sabrina and Taki," Atika says, a statement, Nermina understands, not a request for permission.

"But the storm—"

"It's okay, Mama." This last, the girl says with tempered patience. "Taki knows what to do. We all do."

Fear flutters deep inside Nermina's stomach as her daughter scrambles ahead to catch up with her older cousins.

Now fat raindrops begin to splatter the leaf-strewn trail and a few seconds later the deluge beats down on them. Nermina turns back. She sees Samir and then Raifa, a couple of paces behind her husband. Samir smiles and holds up his palms to the rain in a posture of submission. Raifa's expression—her lips pressed together in a straight line—reveals nothing beyond placid acceptance; neither seems worried, but Nermina struggles to quell her uneasiness.

She sets herself to the task of keeping her footing over clumps of rain-slicked tree roots. The terrain and the sudden turn in the weather remind her of a hike she'd taken with Carl. That day, the fast-moving clouds had snuffed out the sunshine from moment to moment as they picked their way along a trail much steeper than today's. Midway, they sat on a rock ledge to eat the lunch she'd packed. Goose bumps rose on Carl's arms. She'd asked if he were cold, if he wanted to go back to the truck. "I don't need a mother," he'd snapped. She remembers his silence on the drive back to the city, his face molded in the expression of a pouting child. Strange, she thinks, to be reminded of him now.

By the time they reach the trailhead, the storm has moved off. A dappled pattern of sunlit leaves falls across the hood of Samir's old Subaru station wagon. That morning he'd hauled out the ladders and rollers and paint cans so Nermina wouldn't have to drive out to the mountain with Atika in a separate car. Now Samir opens the back door and lifts it so the kids can climb in. Atika squeezes in with Sabrina and Taki, all three of them dripping and muddy.

"You must buckle in," Raifa calls. "Everyone."

Taki feigns fourteen-year-old disinterest, his thumbs already busy with his GameBoy. Sabrina whispers something to Atika that makes her laugh. Nermina's worries return. Only two years older than her daughter, Nermina thinks Sabrina is far more worldly than a twelve-year-old girl should be.

Raifa flattens one hand along the side of the car to steady herself while she scrapes mud from her boots with a stick. Samir kisses the top of Raifa's head, her hair slick across her forehead. Raifa rolls her eyes comically. Nermina observes this exchange, and then climbs into the backseat, alone. She squelches the urge to force her daughter to sit beside her.

When Sabrina and Taki fight over stations, Samir flicks off the radio. "That's it," he says. "No more." He eases the Subaru off the muddy shoulder and onto the road. His face, in profile, is placid now. A pushover, just like Raifa, Nermina thinks; Samir has already forgiven his children. Raifa slings her arm over the seat and turns back to face Nermina. "So now we have some peace," Raifa says.

Inside her own house, dry and warm, Nermina feels better. The bass from her daughter's iHome throbs above her, but she can't make out the lyrics. She hears a loud thud and then Sabrina and Atika's muffled laughter.

Twenty-five minutes later Nermina spoons organic marinara sauce onto three plates of steaming whole-wheat pasta. Atika carries two plates to the table and Sabrina the third. They eat in near silence—Sabrina asking Nermina to pass the salad and shaved Romano cheese, Atika going to the kitchen to refill her water glass.

"What's the matter?" Nermina asks when she can no longer stand the silence. She looks from her daughter's face to her niece's. With closer inspection, she sees that Sabrina has re-applied her eyeliner and mascara, her dark eyes sultry and teasing, the eyes of a woman, Nermina thinks, not a girl. Sabrina stares down at her plate, twirls a forkful of pasta.

Nermina looks across the table to her daughter. "Tell me what's going on here or you go straight up to your room and Sabrina goes home as soon as we're done with dinner."

"That's fine with me," Atika says.

"Atika, that's rude. Tell me now—"

"No, *she's* rude!" Atika stands and Nermina notes how expertly her daughter mimics Sabrina's posture, hands on her hips, the right hip jutting out seductively.

"She called me a little baby," Atika says, her eyes bright with unshed tears.

"Strina Nermina, I didn't mean it," Sabrina fixes a doe-eyed look on her aunt.

"No, of course not..." Nermina leaves off.

"It's *your* fault anyway," Atika says, the girl's glare cutting into Nermina like a straight-edged razor. "Sabrina said you treat me like a baby because I don't have a father."

Nermina's stomach clenches. Her daughter's face—leaner than just a few months before—seems vulnerable now, even as her eyes squint with anger. Nermina turns to her niece. "Did you say that, Sabrina?"

"Um, no, I just said you guys were, like, closer than

most..." Sabrina hedges. "Like, not in a *bad* way. Maybe it just came *out* wrong?"

Atika strides to the table and slumps back down into her chair. "That is *not* what she said." She turns to her cousin. "You should tell her the truth. You shouldn't lie," Atika says.

"I'm sure no one's lying here," Nermina says evenly. She turns from her daughter's angry glare to Sabrina's studied look of nonchalance. "Every family looks a little different," she continues. "Sabrina...your mother and father, you and Taki— you're Atika's family. *Our* family. You know that, *draga*."

Sabrina turns a sweet smile toward Nermina. "I know that," she says.

Atika slaps her hand down on the table. Her water glass jumps. "Stop it! Both of you. You're both liars."

"That's not called for," says Nermina. "Whatever Sabrina said, I'm sure she didn't mean to hurt you...Atika, you're old enough to understand now..."

"I understand I don't have a father because he didn't want us. Because he didn't want *you!*"

Blood throbs behind Nermina's temples. Again, she turns from her daughter to Sabrina and back again. The dread she'd felt on the mountain earlier wells up inside her just as before. "What's going on here? You know that's not true. Is this what Sabrina told you?"

Atika glares at her cousin, whose long dark hair obscures her face now. The older girl clears a hole in the center of her plate with her fork, shifting the pasta methodically to the edges. She works at this a couple of moments longer before speaking.

"She asked my opinion," Sabrina says. "I told her what I

thought."

"You had no right to say these things," Nermina says. "You're not her mother." Nermina remembers the day her father had announced his plan for her escape, her exile. He'd pushed her away. She'd left him behind. Both were true. "Atika, you know exactly how you were conceived. I used a donor. You know why I chose this option, *dragi.*" And there it was again, certainly a lie, but wholly justified, Nermina reminds herself. She thinks then, too, of the lies she'd told little Esmer when she left him. *White lies*, but lies nonetheless.

"I'm not a baby and I want you to stop treating me like one," Atika whines. She glares at Nermina. "It's *your* fault."

"My fault?" Nermina tries to smile but her daughter's angry face diffuses all hope of ending the discussion gracefully. Nermina presses the heels of her hands to her forehead.

"I think you'd better just go up to your room now," she says.

"You can't do that," Atika says. She smacks her slim hand down on the table again. "One minute you treat me—"

"Stop it," Nermina says. "That's enough." The panic she'd felt during the storm rumbles inside her again like the thunder that had chased them off the mountain.

"You're a very fortunate girl," Nermina says. "You have a mother...so many people who love you..."

Sabrina stands and collects the plates and silverware, her expression contrite now. A moment later Nermina hears the water running in the sink. She closes her eyes and then opens them.

"I just wish your *nana* and *deda* were here," Nermina says. "They would know what to do. They would know how to handle you..." Nermina hears these words as though someone else has spoken them.

Atika covers her ears with her hands. The tears finally slip down her cheeks. "Mama, I don't want to hear this part again."

Nermina feels the familiar weight drop around her shoulders. She can't say if this weight is a comfort, only that it's familiar. It's hers, alone.

"They took them from me," she says. "All of them...gone."

"Please," Atika cries. "Stop it."

The girl's voice is small again, not nearly as grown-up sounding as before. Nermina's heartbeat pounds in her ears. She sits at the table for what seems a long time while Atika cries silently.

"Fine," she says, finally. Rather than taking her daughter in her arms as she knows she should, she stalks into the kitchen and grabs her car keys from their hook on the wall.

"Let's go," she says to Sabrina. "I'll take you home now."

CHAPTER 29
STRAY
Athens, Georgia

Carl loads the rest of the tile into the bed of his pickup. He figures he should hurry if he's going to beat the storm. He wants to finish up the job and get paid. He'd sized it up three weeks ago, met the young couple at a brick ranch house they'd all but gutted. When he did the walk-through with them and settled on a price, he'd liked the husband—a soft-spoken, tall and wiry guy with a halo of curly, red hair—but hoped he wouldn't have to spend too much time around the wife. She was muscular with dirty-blond hair pulled back in a ponytail. She'd walked right past him and through the bare-studded house, yakking away on her cell phone like he wasn't even there. She reminded him of his brother's wife Lisa, a bad sign, Carl thinks now.

He pulls the weathered, blue tarp over the truck bed and starts to secure the clips into their rusted slots. Before he finishes, though, fat raindrops begin to splatter on the dirty windshield. The rain sends up a scent of parched earth that reminds him how much he hates this Godforsaken, shithole of a state.

Carl sprints back to the warehouse to settle up with the cashier. The rain's coming down steadily when he heads back to the truck. He's about to jump into the cab when he notices the flat tire. He looks closely between the treads: a nail with the head broken off. "Jesus-fucking-Christ," he mutters. "Just can't catch a break."

Carl slides back into the truck and slams the door shut. He doesn't have a spare. If he gets a tow to the station he's pretty sure they could just plug the thing and he'd be on his merry way. But the thieves at the station will charge him an arm and a leg just to tow him a few lousy miles. He can't call Tessa. She'll just get on him for not having a spare.

Carl thinks back to when he'd first rolled into Athens two years before. He'd just lost the business, nothing in the bank, but for some reason he'd still felt hopeful. Then—bam—he'd met this barmaid at one of the upscale places down on Washington. He'd noticed the slight gap between her two front teeth, the silver bracelets on her narrow wrists, and how they jangled against each another when she reached across the bar to grab a couple of empties. He'd liked that her name was Tessa and he thought the tiny lines at the corners of her deep-set, brown eyes made her seem like she was about to burst into laughter at any second. Later, when she'd asked him if he wanted to hang around till she got off work, he answered without hesitation.

He dials Roddy Flick's number now, not Tessa's. Roddy's one of the guys he hangs out with at O'Brien's, a dive that serves dollar beers and free food between five and seven on weeknights. Roddy's the kind of guy Carl's mother would call 'a pleasant young man,' but he'd pegged him as a chump, always trying to please. Trying *too* hard, he thinks, remembering the five grand he'd hit Roddy up for a couple weeks back. Roddy's maybe 30 and, in Carl's opinion, not too bright. Still, Roddy's father kept him on at the family's hardware store.

"I just got a flat over at Worth's," Carl says. "I'm sittin' here with a whole load of crap I gotta get over to the job. Any chance you can cut out early? I need a lift to the service station, is all."

"Well...sure, I guess I could do that."

"Awesome." Carl feels a prickle of guilt and then the familiar irritation that hits him whenever Roddy opens his mouth. Here it is again; the kid's ass-kissing tone reminds him of a puppy who'd follow him around from room to room, slathering him with unconditional affection and never knowing when to get out of the way. Same way his mother had always bucked up the old man, even while he treated her like dirt.

"Just give me a little while. I have to wrap things up here," says Roddy.

"Sure, sure, whatever. Just get here as soon as you can."

Carl sits in the truck and watches the rain streaming down the windshield. It's coming down in buckets. He thinks about getting the tile over to the job and getting set up. Then he thinks about Portland, how it would rain for days on end. He thinks about Rebecca, the yoga instructor he'd moved in with, the tiny tattoo of a rose on the inside of her thigh. He thinks, too, about Nermina—the Bosnian girl he'd slept with a couple times back then. He remembers her stillness, the way she watched him as he stepped into his jeans. How easy it had been to leave Portland when Rebecca kicked him out.

He cracks the driver-side window and pulls a cigarette from the pack he keeps wedged above the sun visor. Just this one, he tells himself. He's supposed to be quitting for Tessa but can't bring himself to get rid of his stash. Just in case he hits a rough spot.

By the time Roddy pulls into the lot in his Plymouth Neon, Carl has smoked three cigarettes. The inside of the cab holds the rank smell of dampness—his soaked-through jeans, flannel work shirt, and boots—and the un-emptied ashtray. Before Roddy can cut the ignition, Carl bolts out of the truck and pounds on Roddy's window.

"Where the hell you been?" he yells. The kid's baby-faced expression—blue eyes all wide and scared-looking—irritates him.

Roddy rolls down the window. "I had a customer. I got here as fast as I could," he says. He swings the car door open.

"All right, all right. Now that you're here, let's just get this thing done."

Carl leaves Roddy standing next to his car and trudges to the back of the pickup. He slides, head first, under the truck, the gravel in the flooded parking lot sharp against his back. He pulls the jack out from the empty space where the spare should be and gets to work. Once he has the lug nuts off,

Roddy squats down next to him to pull the tire. Both men are soaked to the skin. Roddy rolls the tire over to the Plymouth, opens the trunk, and heaves it onto a plastic tarp. He wipes his muddy hands on the towel he grabbed from the store.

"That wasn't so bad," says Roddy as he edges out onto the two-lane highway. The rain has slowed a bit and the wipers thrum rhythmically, soothing Carl's mood.

"Thanks for coming out in this." Carl feels unexpectedly grateful for Roddy's company and a little sorry, too, for giving the kid a hard time. "There it is, over on the right. The Texaco. Pull in there, buddy."

At least Carl has the satisfaction of being right about the flat. A simple puncture, probably the nail he'd suspected in the first place. No tear and no shredding, but the afternoon's shot now. He might as well drop off the load of tile at the job, then meet up with Roddy and the others at O'Brien's.

Now, half an hour after saying goodbye to Roddy, Carl backs the truck into the muddy side yard. It takes several trips with the handcart to get the tile inside the breezeway in the encroaching darkness. He'll start fresh in the morning with the front foyer, get there before any of the other workers, and make a good dent in the job. Roger, the husband, had given him a key so Carl wouldn't have to be tied to anyone else's schedule. Now that the drywall guys are done taping and sanding, he's good to go. He thinks about unloading his tile cutter and leaving it along with the rest of the supplies in the breezeway but the wind and rain have started up again with a vengeance. The now-steady downpour is pounding the puny saplings the landscapers just put in, bending them nearly to the ground. A yellowish light—one Roger told Carl he'd set on a timer—switches on outside the breezeway door. He hears the sharp crack of a branch from behind the dumpster, just beyond where he'd parked.

"What the hell?" he mutters. Carl darts out the breezeway door and jogs over to the slate-blue dumpster. Peering in, he sees that it's nearly filled with debris from the demolition and remodeling. Nothing else. Nothing moving, anyway. He checks around the Johnny-on-the-Spot, opens the door to the sickly, chemical-sweet aroma and finds nothing amiss. But, shutting the door, Carl hears what sounds like a soda can rolling around in the flatbed. His breath catches in his chest and a wave of adrenaline washes through him. He picks up a length of two-by-four from a pile of scrap lumber near his feet. Walking slowly and as quietly as possible, he approaches the back of the pickup. He holds the two-by-four like a bat, ready to use it if he has to. Then with sudden clarity, he recalls a summer thunderstorm when he and Jeff were kids. He'd felt paralyzed by the low rumbling thunder that reverberated in the pit of his stomach.

Like then, he tries to push the fear down into his gut, but Carl's heartbeat is drowning out even the loud rush of wind and rain. Still approaching, he thinks he sees a hunched shadow moving inside the truck-bed. He'd left the blue tarp tossed over the tile cutter and, at first, he thinks that maybe it's only the wind blowing the rain-slicked thing around. But as he comes closer he sees the bulky form of what looks like a man huddled against the cab of the truck. A trickle of sweat snakes down between his shoulder blades, now tense with the effort of holding the board in his ready stance.

"Come on out, motherfucker!" he yells, still inching forward. The soda can skitters across the corrugated metal in reply. He transfers the board to his right hand and, grasping the cold rim of the opened flatbed, lunges onto the platform. From beyond the tarp-covered equipment, two piercingly blue eyes meet his.

"A fuckin' dog!" he says, his heart flopping in his chest. Still gripping the board and holding it out defensively in front of him like a sword, he leans in to see more closely the animal's unyielding but not unfriendly gaze. The dog sits patiently on its haunches as though it has been expecting him. Carl puts out his other hand—palm up, the way his father had taught him so long ago—and waits. The dog assesses him with restrained attention, a look of intelligence, he thinks. Rain beads on its thick, powder-white fur and sparkles like tiny ice pellets in the near-darkness. Stark, black markings, like a photo negative, define the dog's wolf-like face, outline the icy, blue eyes. He decides it must be a Siberian husky. Or some breed damned close to it.

"Hey, boy," he says, setting the board down carefully. "You scared the living shit out of me." Encouraged by the dog's good behavior—it hasn't even barked—he brings his hand closer still. Palm up. The dog turns its large head abruptly and Carl takes a quick step back. He keeps his hand still, though, and the dog sniffs, then laps at his upturned palm. He runs his hand over the wet fur, first the solid, muscular back and haunches and finally—more certain of the dog's disposition— he strokes the bristled fur just above its ears. He feels around on the blue canvas collar for a tag but doesn't find one. The dog looks well cared for. Not underfed or injured. If it had been, Carl imagines, the animal would have taken his hand off.

The dog is a female and he figures that whomever she belongs to is pretty upset. He thinks of the young couple but, remembering their little, two-door BMW, rules them out as likely dog owners. His mood has changed since discovering the husky; he's put the flat tire episode behind him. He puts out of his mind, as well, his current financial state—not encouraging, but he's been through much worse. Things will turn around. He thinks that maybe, in some weird way, the dog is a good sign. He's changed his mind about meeting up with the guys at O'Brien's. Instead, he thinks about Tessa and how he'll pick up a bottle of wine on his way back to her place. They can sit out on the deck when she gets home after her shift and just talk like they used to when he'd first moved in with her. A fine rain still peppers his face but, from the look of the fast-moving clouds, the storm will be long gone by then.

"Whad'ya do, girl, run out on your folks?" Carl asks. He grabs a piece of plastic strapping that's slipped off one of the boxes of tile and loops it through the dog's collar. He wraps the other end a couple of times around his fist. He laughs out loud when he thinks about how scared he'd been just a few moments before. The neighborhood, a thirty-year-old, middle-class development, isn't exactly what anyone would call menacing.

He figures the dog probably hasn't wandered too far from home. He might as well check around the neighborhood to see if anyone recognizes her. He's a little uneasy about going door to door like one of those Greenpeace crazies, but maybe he'll get lucky after a house or two, he thinks. If not, he can drop her off at an animal shelter. That thought, however, troubles him. He bends down and strokes the surprisingly soft fur of her neck. "You're somethin' special, girl, are'ntcha," he says. He doesn't want to dump her off at a place where she'd be penned up with a bunch of mangy strays. Or worse. He knows he can't do that.

The rain has all but stopped and the pavement—sidewalks drawing the half-circle perimeter of the quiet street—smells like what Carl remembers of those coming summer storms when he was a kid. What had he been so afraid of then? The thunder? Being home alone with no one but his big brother Jeff to watch over him? Remembering his mother's nervous instructions before she went out, he thinks how scared *she'd* always seemed back then. He recalls the look of panic in her eyes every time the tires of his father's Chevy chewed into the gravel driveway. I guess she'd rather have left us alone than with the old man, Carl concludes.

He stuffs that thought, too, and walks up the driveway to a tidy rancher. The garage door is open and a white Volvo station wagon sits clicking in the center of a bunch of kids' sporting gear—roller blades, bicycles, fishing rods — all hanging from hooks or stowed on red plastic shelves. Carl smiles and shakes his head seeing this picture of American family life. "Not for me, girl," he says to the dog.

He rings the front door bell and notices the husky straining at the makeshift leash. "It's okay, girl," he says. "Is this where you live? Is that it?" Carl hears the yip-yipping of a much smaller dog inside the house. He hears a kid running on hardwood flooring, then, "Momm-myyyy, someone's at the doo-ooor." He hears heavier footsteps and the increasingly frenzied yip-yipping of the small dog inside. The husky tugs hard on the strap, the thin plastic biting into his hand.

"Stay," he says sternly. "Sit!" The dog obeys. "Good girl," Carl says, running his hand—again and again—along the strong ridge of backbone he feels even through the thick fur. It's beginning to dry now that the rain has slowed. He feels foolish crouching there with the dog, listening to what sounds like chaos inside the house; he feels like a peeping Tom. What the hell, he thinks then. I'm just trying to do the right thing.

The door opens and, straightening to his full height, Carl faces through the outer storm door, a plain-looking woman in her early thirties. Her chin-length brown hair is pulled back from a broad forehead and held in place with a white headband. A little girl—maybe three years old—clings to the woman's thigh, peering up at Carl.

"Can I help you?" the woman asks. The little dog is kicking up a racket in another room and he hears, even over that, a TV tuned to cartoons. The woman, tall, but with an athletic stockiness, assesses him suspiciously.

"I, uh, found this dog across the way," he says, pointing across the street as though this will explain his inquiry. The commotion inside the house seems to be getting louder. The little girl begins to whine. The woman hoists her up on her hip. The child wraps her spindly legs around the mother's waist, her arms around her neck. Watching him cautiously, the girl—wisps of drab, brown hair clinging to pale cheeks, turns her head and presses her face into the woman's sturdy-looking shoulder.

"I don't understand," the mother says. "You found the dog where?"

Carl notices the purplish shadows beneath the woman's brown, wide-set eyes, the cluster of tiny pimples at her hairline, just below the headband. He feels foolishly tongue-tied. "I thought maybe...this was your dog?"

"Oh, no, no," the woman says, shaking her head so that her short brown hair swings from side to side. "I wasn't sure what you were asking. Excuse me a sec." She turns away from Carl and hollers in the direction of the TV, "Ryyy-annn, turn that *off* please!" She turns back to him. "Sorry, you know how kids are," she says with an apologetic shrug. "So, you found...the...I'm sorry," she says. She opens the storm door a crack, "I can't hear myself think."

Beyond the woman, Carl sees a boy run across the living room and, just after, a streak of white fluff racing behind the kid. The little dog's yapping is a monotone of constant, ear-splitting noise. The husky yanks against Carl's grip and lets out a long, searing howl. The little dog darts through the slightly opened doorway and, in one seamless motion, the husky lunges at the white ball of fluff. She has the little dog between deadlocked jaws, shaking it back and forth like a plush toy.

"No, girl, no!" he hears himself yell. He yanks on the strap. He hears the thud against the door and sees the little dog flail for a split second before it rolls onto its stomach and lies trembling. The woman pushes through the door and shoves Carl aside. He sees the boy then, and the little girl, their faces pressed—wide-eyed—against the glass.

"What? What?" the woman shrieks.

The husky retreats with a look of resignation. Carl feels the weight of her against his thigh. He sees a few droplets of blood—barely visible, like the prick from a needle—on her thick, white fur. He feels a rush of fear for the second time that night, as if he'd just been startled awake at the wheel to find himself driving into oncoming traffic. But most of all, he feels the familiar punch-to-the-gut of guilt. Like he's seeing, simultaneously, into his past and his future, forever screwed.

"Miiiistyyyy," the woman wails. She stoops to pick up the little dog, its white fur coated with blood, but it turns suddenly at her touch and snaps at the air, dangerously close to her face. Carl reaches out toward the woman.

"Here, please let me—"

"Don't touch her!" she yells. "Don't touch her!"

"I'm sorry, my God, I'm sorry, Miss, let me...please—"

The little dog's mouth is open a little and a string of saliva leaks onto its fur. Carl is aware, then, of the instant the dog's body goes slack. The woman's face is washed in grief, tears streaming down her cheeks. Her mouth works furiously, moving like she's mouthing a silent prayer, until the words pour out again.

"You killed her! That monster killed her!"

"Miss, let me help you," he pleads. "I didn't mean to—"

"Get away, pleeeeez, just get away," she wails.

"Miss, calm down, if you'll let me..."

The woman sweeps up the little dog in her arms and crushes it to her chest, the blood mottling her T-shirt. Carl feels a wash of sadness, the same as when his father died. It isn't the death itself, but the hell he'd put Jeff and his mother through that comes back to him. The way they'd looked at him when he finally arrived—unannounced and with no explanation—two weeks after the funeral. He hadn't understood how his mother could grieve the man who'd all but destroyed their family.

The woman is sobbing, the kids still terrified to come out the door. Carl places his hand gently on the woman's shoulder; she is remarkably warm. She pulls away from his touch. The husky sits between them, panting mildly, obedient; she watches Carl with a look of patient expectation.

"I don't know what to say." He imagines that he sounds juvenile, insincere. "I can help you now, um, with the—"

"No, my husband will be home soon," the woman interrupts. It seems to Carl that she's passed from that earlier, out-of-control anger into something much deeper. "You just go. There's nothing more to do."

"Well, I feel responsible. I'll pay..."

"Oh, no," she says, shaking her head slowly. That won't be necessary."

"Let me give you my number," Carl says.

"No," says the woman. Her blocky, square-jawed face is set resolutely. He feels something then that might have been anger. Why the hell couldn't she just blame him outright and get it over with? Wasn't that the drill? He thinks again of that last year at home before he'd cut out for good. He pulls a pen from his shirt pocket, then rummages around in his wallet for a scrap of paper. He scribbles down his name and cell phone number and hands it to the woman.

"Thank you," she says coldly, "but I told you, there's nothing more you need to do here."

Her face looks numbed and empty, the way Tessa's looks in the aftermath of one of their blowouts. The tears always seemed to wash away her anger, but they washed away something else, too. The calm that came over her carried a price and he figured that with each surrender she'd lost just a little bit more faith in him to make things right between them.

The woman turns her back to Carl, pulls open the storm door, and steps inside holding the little dog in a one-armed embrace like a sleeping baby. She slams the inside door on him and the husky. He bends down and strokes the dog's lean flanks. She sits patiently on her haunches as though understanding the man's indecision. When he stands and says, "Come, girl," there's no need to tug on the leash. When he opens the door to the pickup she leaps inside.

Carl drives forty-five minutes west of the city to a rural stretch of land. The dog sits panting beside him. In the moonless night his headlights pick out a lone stand of loblolly pines and an abandoned shack in the distance. He pulls the truck off the road, the tires spinning a little in the sandy soil, and jumps down from the cab. "Come," he says, his voice rough and tired. The dog observes Carl quietly. She spreads herself across the seat, taking over the place that he's vacated, her front paws splayed in front of her. "Come," he says, more harshly now. The dog bounds from the truck, then sits attentively at the man's side. He bends and unties the strap.

"I guess we fucked things up again," he says quietly. He crouches next to the dog and scoops up a handful of sand. It smells like the pines and the rain. He lets it sift through his fingers. Then he stands up quickly and slaps the dog hard on her flank. "Get outta here!" he yells. "Just *go!*"

The dog runs a few paces toward the trees, then halts and sniffs at the cool night air. She lowers her head and strides back to Carl. He crouches next to her again and runs his hand over her thick fur. He feels the sturdy texture of each bristle beneath his fingers, but then the slick, glossy coating, too. Finally, he wonders what in God's name he's going to tell Tessa.

CHAPTER 30
SCHOOL CLOTHES

Atika struggles under the load of clothing—corduroy jeans in several colors, sweaters, and a couple of long-sleeved T-shirts. An older woman with a powder puff of gray curls nested on her head takes the stack from the girl, a little rudely, Atika thinks, and slowly (too slowly!) hangs the items on a tall rack. The woman counts them, screeches the hangers together on the rack, and hands the cluster of clothing back to Atika along with a white plastic number 9. The girl pushes open the door to one of the fitting rooms and drops everything on a low, hot-pink padded bench that takes up a third of the room. She yanks the door shut and makes sure to lock it. Undressing, she flings her own clothes to the floor where they scatter a large clump of dust bunnies into the four corners of the room.

Then she stands in front of the mirror—actually three

mirrors that show a person from every conceivable angle—and assesses her figure; she sees the same narrow hips and long, willowy arms as her mother's but, also, what she perceives to be the flattest chest of all of her thirteen-year-old classmates. For purposes of comparison, Atika also considers her older cousin Sabrina who, by age twelve had already 'fully developed,' as Strina Raifa put it, the most telling example of Atika's sluggish crawl toward maturity. Sabrina's deep cleavage, those plump breasts looming from what seem to be an endless array of low-cut tops, make Atika equally uncomfortable and envious.

But today she's excited because her mother has agreed to let her pick out some of her own school clothes. In fact, her mother has even begrudgingly agreed to leave Atika alone in the juniors department for forty-five minutes. The girl glances at her phone—*Just for emergencies, Atika*—and feels a little prickle of annoyance. It would be nice to do all of this on her own, she thinks, or maybe even with Sabrina. Then she pulls a stretchy teal-green sweater over her head and, standing in front of the three-way mirror in just the soft sweater, her socks, and panties, she's almost shocked to see how the garment, with its scooped neckline and clingy fit, hugs her body so perfectly. It makes the small swell of her A-cup breasts appear almost voluptuous. She giggles and turns away from the mirror, grabs a pair of cords from the pile and unclips them from the hanger.

But before she has the chance to step into them, she hears her mother's voice: "Atika, are you back here?"

The girl's heart sinks. She'd wanted to have everything picked out already, to simply hand the pile to the saleslady and say: We'll take these!

"Atika, which one? The lady says you're back here in one of these." Her mother's voice is getting closer, more insistent.

"This one, Mama," Atika says. She wiggles her foot beneath the gap at the bottom of the fitting room door, bracing herself against it protectively. "Here," she says. She feels her mother's presence on the other side, hears her try the knob.

"Can I come in?"

"Not yet," says Atika. "Wait just a second."

"Atika, open the door please." The girl calculates her mother's mood on a scale of one to ten, one being 'fine' and ten being 'really mad.' She figures she still has some wiggle room.

"Mama, I said just wait!"

"I gave you time—" She hears the struggle in her mother's voice to stay pleasant. To stay—What? Normal?

Atika unlocks the door and opens it a crack. Her mother stands there for an instant, a small shopping bag dangling from her wrist, the strap of her brown leather purse slung diagonally across her body. Then she pushes the door fully open and fills the remaining space of the little room. "Really, Atika—"

"Mama, I didn't mean..."

Her mother slides the pile of clothing to the edge of the bench and sits down. She places her shopping bag on the floor. Atika feels the air in the little room changing. It's charged, she thinks. Like in those experiments in Mrs. Lehman's science room. Static electricity. Strands of Lydia Rosselli's thin blond hair straining up toward the balloon Mrs. Lehman held above Lydia's head in second grade.

"Wait," Atika says again, but this time the word carries some of the earlier excitement she'd been feeling before her mother had intruded. She steps into the pair of pants still in her hands and pulls the soft corduroy up and over knobby knees, nonexistent hips, and zips them triumphantly. The hems come to the girl's ankles without an eighth of an inch to spare.

Her mother's eyes meet Atika's in the center mirror.

"The sweater's very pretty, Atika, but the pants—look, they'll shrink after one washing."

Atika looks down at her feet then back to her mother's earnest face. "They're perfect," she says.

"Atika—"

"You always do this."

"Do what?" Atika hears the bite creeping into her mother's tone and she knows she should stop.

"You told me I could pick out everything on my own."

"Yes, I did, but you can see they're too short."

"But they're not. They're just right."

"Don't they come in another length?"

Atika has no idea if this brand comes in different lengths; she'd grabbed the first pair that said 24 on the waistband. She wipes her damp palms down the outside of her thighs, feels the ribbing of the fabric.

"I don't know," she says.

"Let me go check."

"No!" This is just what she *doesn't* want. Her mother will bring back a bunch of stupid clothes. Probably the most babyish things she can find. Atika pouts into the mirror. She digs her hands deep into the front pockets of the pants and twists a quarter turn so she can see the little bubble of her rear in the mirror. "Mama, *please*?" Atika tries.

"Absolutely not. It's a total waste." Her mother sweeps the clothing from the bench into her arms and hangs each item, one by one, onto the two hooks on the wall. Then she plucks a pair of gray cords from their hanger and inspects the label.

"R," she says. "The length on these is 'regular.' You need 'long' or 'tall.'"

Atika feels her skin prickling beneath the wool of the sweater. Her chest just above the edge of the neckline is hot and itchy.

"Mama—"

"This is ridiculous. They're all too short. You have better sense."

Her mother sits back down on the pink bench. She still holds the pants. She aligns the edges of the hems, smoothes the ribbed fabric with one hand, folds the pants in half and then precisely—lengthwise—into thirds. The way she'd taught Atika to do when she was still a little girl. Her mother concentrates on the task, smoothes and smoothes the fabric beneath her long fingers, her eyes fixed on the folded gray object on her lap. The girl feels the tug. She resists.

"I want these," she says, trying as best she can to mimic her cousin's blasé tone.

The crease between her mother's pale eyebrows slices deep into a face Atika knows better than her own. She's studied it for years, and now she sorts through the range of familiar expressions, flips them up, one by one, like the stack of tarot cards Sabrina had tried to explain to her. But the cards, like the changing topography of her mother's features, can always hold more than one meaning. Sometimes she watches her mother surreptitiously—leans silent against the French doors outside the study—trying to read from the curve of her mother's body in the rocker, the set of her lips, whether she should open the doors and go to her. Whether, instead, she should leave her there, alone. Her mother might go months and months without a single 'sad time'—her mother's words—and Atika's adolescent life lurches ahead as usual. In those times chaos erupts only of her own making, when Sabrina or a school friend gets under her skin and her careful armor crumbles. Now her mother sits silent.

"Mama, did you hear me?" she ventures.

Her mother leans forward. She holds her head between her hands, elbows on her knees, and her green eyes meet Atika's pleading gaze in the center mirror again.

"I wish your *nana* were here," her mother says flatly. "She'd know what to say to you. She'd know how to deal with such nonsense."

Atika feels the muscles in her throat squeeze tight. They twitch a little, the way the muscles in her thighs do after she's stopped running laps after school.

"Mama—"

"I just wish ..." her mother's voice continues, then flattens into nothing. The girl knows what's coming next but can't stop herself now.

"What? What is it?" Atika turns from the mirror to face her mother.

"I wish you understood how fortunate you are."

Atika crosses her arms across her chest. Her fingers press hard through the itchy wool and into the muscle of her upper arms. This hurts and she decides she doesn't want the hurt to stop right away. It helps somehow.

"I *know* how lucky I am." The words, the way she says them, feel nasty on her tongue, like biting into a plump grape tomato turned sour.

"No, I don't think you do." Her mother sets the folded gray pants on the bench next to her. She reaches for the shopping bag on the floor, stands up, not looking at Atika's face. Not looking at anything at all. She stands there, Atika thinks, like a blind person afraid to step off the curb. But then finally her mother completes the required steps toward the door and puts her hand on the knob.

"Don't," Atika says. "Don't you dare! You always have to do this."

The girl is horrified and also a little thrilled. But when her mother turns to face her again she sees the raw pink edging her eyelids, how her face is nearly translucent in the over-bright lighting of the fitting room. And she sees the blue vein at her mother's right temple, just below its film of pale, pale skin. It pulses there, like a heart beneath thin flesh.

"You may not speak to me that way," her mother says.

"I'm sorry." The girl says this, but she isn't. Not completely.

"I'll meet you at the checkout," her mother says.

"No."

"What do you want from me, Atika?" Her mother's fingers still clutch the doorknob.

"I want you—I want us—to be like everyone else. To be like *normal* people."

Her mother emits a quick, strangled sound, too harsh

Atika thinks, to have been intended as a laugh. Neither of them moves.

"I don't understand—" the girl begins.

"No, that's clear. You don't. You don't know what it's like to be alone."

Atika glares at her mother. "Look at me, Mama!" the girl demands. "You're not alone." She knows for certain now it's a landmine she's unearthed. Her mother's pain. Her mother's past. Frantic phone calls for emergency sessions with the psychologist her mother still sees whenever she needs to.

Her mother takes a deep breath, even this sound, amplified it seems to the girl, so that this—breathing— becomes yet another offense. This one heaped atop all the others. "This isn't about you," Atika continues. "You always make it into that. You—"

"No," her mother says. "Right. I forgot. I should know this. The world revolves around Atika. That's the point. Correct?"

Her mother's voice is deeper now, raw and tired. Atika hears the slight guttural diction that punctuates each word, the foreignness that still clings to her mother's perfect English. She thinks of how Sabrina imitates her parents, their Bosnian friends who come over for huge, endless meals. "People from the old country," Sabrina would say with equal parts ridicule and pity.

"Mama, I just want to pick out my own things. I don't want to fight with you. I don't want to have to feel guilty about *everything*!" She draws out the last word in an elongated whine.

"Stop it." Her mother says this quietly, her voice a sharp, icy, weapon.

"I'm supposed to be grateful that you give me all these things. That's just what normal people do, Mama."

Her mother turns toward her then, and her slim body slinks to the floor in a graceless movement depicting nothing beyond exhaustion. She draws her knees up to her chest. Her back pressed against the door.

"I can't, Atika," she says. "I just can't do this anymore. *My* mother...I can't—"

"Mama—"

"Her face was purple with bruises," her mother says. "There were welts. Open welts the size of your fingers."

"Stop it," Atika says. The girl kneels down in front of her mother. No air remains in the little room. The anger drains from the girl's voice.

"They wrapped her in a plastic tarp. Bright blue. The kind they use for painting indoors, so you don't ruin the floors."

Atika reaches out and places her hand on her mother's shoulder. Her mother swats the hand away. "Don't," she says.

And when the girl withdraws, her mother continues: "You should know this. They beat her. Several men, they raped her. The doctors, they can tell such things." Her mother rifles her fingers blindly through her short, cropped hair. "She was torn," she says, her voice catching on the word. "She was ruined."

Atika feels the familiar lump rising in her throat. "Mama," she says, tears burning her cheeks now.

"My father—your *djed*—he wiped away the blood from her face. The filthy slime from between her legs. And he knew. He knew she was already gone from us."

The girl sobs now. There's no air and she imagines herself

drowning, slipping beneath a dark skin of thick tepid water, and floating there, motionless. She hates her mother. Hates her for revealing these awful things. These awful truths. For forcing her to hear it over and over again. And *was* it true? All of it? How would she ever know differently? She hated her mother for sitting there now on the floor, her eyes looking straight ahead. Dead. Her eyes looking at nothing. Seeing nothing. She hates her mother for not crying when she, herself, can't stop.

"Mama, look at me!" she demands again. "Look at me," she says more softly then.

"He risked everything to bury her. The snipers. He dug the earth himself."

"Please, stop it," Atika whines. She hates hearing her mother's words and she hates hearing her own voice, too, drained of the assurance she'd started with. And finally, she hates that she's been born. Born to her mother. This mother.

"They took him, too," her mother whispers. "They took my father..."

Now Atika imagines her escape. She sees herself pushing past her mother. Leaving her there on the floor. "Strina Raifa," she'd say into the little phone. "It's an emergency. Come get me at the mall." She'd leave her mother right there and she'd ride home in the rusting, creaking Subaru, next to *Strina* Raifa, who never seemed to be anything but happy and, when they arrived, she'd take the stairs two at a time up to the second floor and jump into Taki's bed, the bed that used to be hers, and pull the covers up to her chin, just like she'd done when she was a little girl.

Instead, she goes to her mother, and this time her mother

doesn't push her away. The girl places her hands on her mother's shoulders, nuzzles her face into the smooth curve of her neck. She feels the deep hole of her mother's grief, her own grief, she understands. The two so entwined as to be nearly indistinguishable from one another.

CHAPTER 31
JEFF'S BREACH
Afghanistan — 2009

The Skype image of Lisa and the boys keeps freezing, muting Lisa's chatter mid-syllable. Her face, her hair a little greasy, pulled back in a ponytail—all pixelated. She angles the laptop so Jeff can see a six-inch crack in the drywall above their dresser.

"Jesus, Lisa," Jeff says. "That? It's no big deal."

"It makes me nervous."

"Forget about it."

A few seconds later Jeff sees his baby boys scuttle across the pale blue carpet like two diapered crabs. He remembers the rush of happiness when he and Lisa got the news. Double trouble, they'd joked when the doc said twins. Then he got called up.

"Okay, it's nothing," Lisa says.

Her tone is flat, dead calm, but somehow it crackles with dangerous current, the way the treeless highway feels at the start of every convoy.

"And the icemaker's not working again," she says.

Jeff sucks in his breath. "Lisa..."

A couple seconds of silence, then a long thin wail shrieks across the time zones, exacting and swift like tracer fire in the night. Jeff feels the familiar ache of guilt-and-anger-anger-and-guilt. The screen shows nothing but pale blue carpet.

"Oh, sweetie," Lisa coos then. "It's okay, baby. It's okay."

Jeff's heart is pumping like right after the blast. He hears Lisa shushing one of their sons. Cooing and shushing.

"What the fuck's going on, Lisa? Who's hurt? What the fuck?"

No crying then. Nothing. Radio silence.

Lisa comes back on. She cradles the laptop and both boys. Ethan's round cheeks are splotchy from crying, Tyler reaches with one pudgy hand for Lisa's earring. Jeff's breath returns. His lungs ache with relief.

"I gotta go," she says. "They're hungry."

"Yeah," he says, and then a hair's width of a second after Lisa logs off, "I love you."

Jeff lays on his cot in the early morning darkness, Rodriguez and Peters still asleep. He pictures Lisa, back in their bungalow in Portland, sleeping, too. Not the Lisa he'd left alone with their sons, or the Lisa on the Skype calls, but the Lisa from before. He tells himself this shit is normal. Him and Lisa, they know the drill. They've done it before, but this time he feels more alone. Exposed. He's the old man on this tour.

Thank God for Rodriguez, the only other NCO in his unit over forty.

Bullshit, he thinks. He grabs his shaving stuff from his footlocker. He's just doing his job. And he's lucky this time: hot showers, a weight room, and a rec center whenever they get back on base inside the Green Zone in Jalalabad. During his last deployment, two years before, he'd been stuck for all twelve months at an FOB, one of the outposts that overlooked what command liked to call a population center. It hadn't looked like much to Jeff, just a bunch of crumbling stucco and mud houses and some dreary-ass patches of farmland. His squad's quarters were even worse. Not even a lousy Port-a-John. Had to wrap up their shit in foil bags and burn it.

You never knew when the enemy would fire off an RPG from higher ground or strafe the outpost with sniper fire. Now though, the province is mostly cleared of insurgents and when their Humvees roll out, Jeff figures they've gained something in exchange for those long dusty months.

He grabs the soft, blue towel that Lisa sent in her first care package. She'd included pictures of Tyler and Ethan. Their pudgy-cheeked little faces look down at him now from where he taped the photos inside his locker. In the five months he's been gone, the twins have morphed from babies into full-fledged little humans. He sees his own gray eyes in both of his boys, the pale red hair that's still peach fuzz, but will likely darken up to the same rusty shade of red his is now. His eyes sting when he thinks of Lisa's pixelated face, of his boys. He shuts the locker on the pictures of his sons, more real—and therefore more heartbreaking—than his real children, his real wife, and wonders why this should be so.

In the shower, Jeff turns the water as hot as it will go. The spray peppers his shoulder blades like gravel. He tries to shake off the bad thoughts, the fear. Crazy thing is, he doesn't feel any safer inside the gates now than he had in '06 at the FOB. The enemy's actions were unpredictable then, and no less so now. If anything, they seemed more brazen. Desperate.

On his squad's first night back from their mission into Gardez, the Taliban fired rockets—just outside the base—but they hadn't breached the concrete barriers. Roused from a dead man's sleep, Jeff heard the warning sirens and the car alarms, so loud they nearly canceled one another out. The blast ignited everything within a two-block radius. Charred bodies lay in the dust and rubble like smoldering logs. Jeff's company commander ordered his squad to tally and gather the dead. He'd never escape that smell of burning flesh. Most vivid, though, Jeff remembers pulling a young Afghan boy and his mother from their burning car, their flesh like melted candle wax. Dead before the medics could get to them.

After that, morale went south. Five months in country and his guys were bitching. Jeff tried to cajole them, but he was no better off. They'd all seen what they'd seen at the blast. Some of them had seen worse. Still, the innocents—the kids, the women—it wasn't so easy to suck it up after that. Those burned-up bodies stuck in his head. He can flip through the gruesome images like pages of the photo albums Lisa makes up of their boys.

At the mess hall Jeff sits across from Rodriguez. He's not

hungry but he forks eggs and bacon and syrupy pancakes into his mouth anyway and chews and swallows, but without tasting any of it. He forces each mouthful and when he can't stand Rodriguez's eyes on him a second longer he looks up just long enough to warn the other man off.

"You gotta call her, man," Rodriguez presses. "I'm telling you."

"Not now," says Jeff. "Not yet."

Rodriguez and his wife have six kids. They pray together over Skype calls. They fucking pray. Maybe that's how they do it. Three deployments in six years—just like him and Lisa. He should be pissed by her bitchiness, but then he remembers her face at the parade grounds the day, his boys bundled into their strollers. Tears smeared her makeup. Two lines of black mascara bled down either side of her face.

"You gotta put things right," says Rodriguez. He slides the Styrofoam food tray a couple of inches closer to Jeff's so the two rectangles nearly touch, the pads of Rodriguez's fingers pink, shades lighter than the fingers themselves. Lighter than the hands that could crush a human skull if necessary. Jeff swings his legs over the bench and grabs the empty tray. He can't look Rodriguez in the eyes, doesn't want to. He strides to the row of trash bins and shoves the tray deep into its open gullet.

Jeff is happy when the orders come down. Relieved. As squad leader, he commands two five-man teams of infantry soldiers. His sergeants, Rodriguez and Peters, will take three of the privates in their vehicle and the other three will ride with Jeff. The two Humvees will provide an escort—diplomatic security detail—for some NATO brass into Kabul.

At 0600 the sun is just peeking above the horizon. Jeff orders PVT Rissling to man the turret gun on the vehicle he'll be driving. Rodriguez takes his post on the other. Like old times, Jeff thinks. Rodriguez had been with him when their unit got yanked two weeks into Task Force Rita in '06 and all of them packed off to Afghanistan. Jeff remembers the big man's lips moving in silent prayer, those wooden rosary beads clicking against one another as the others slept. He believes Rodriguez saved them all.

Looking out over the hills, Jeff wishes he could pray. He tries to shut it down, but he thinks about his boys. How they'd felt slippery in his hands the first time Lisa made him bathe them on his own. He'd been scared to death of doing something wrong but Lisa said not to worry. He could do it. And he had. He remembered the way their skin felt when they were warm and dry from the soft towel after the bath, then slippery again and smelling sweet from the baby lotion Lisa said to use. He'd touched his lips to each of their foreheads when he was through. He'd felt unimaginable relief. He'd bathed his baby boys and hadn't harmed them. All of them— he, Lisa, the babies—they were safe.

At ten kilometers out on Jalalabad Road, Jeff reaches his platoon commander, Second LT Richmond: no negative intelligence to report from Kabul. Truong, a nineteen-year-old from Denver, rides shotgun with Richmond, his M-16 at the ready. Jeff glances off into the dusty hills. The sky is robin's-egg blue. It makes no sense, he thinks: something that perfect spread out over a shithole like this. A second later he hears the blast. He feels the Humvee flip, feels himself powerless as he slams against the roof or the floorboards—he can't tell which. He sees the flames, and hollers for Truong to get the others out.

He tries to move but something heavy is crushing his leg. Hot steel singes his flesh. Flames thrash, reaching for him, the heat a monstrous beast. His eyes burn—blinded now—as black smoke billows. He breathes the acrid smell of explosives. He calls out for Rodriguez and Peters.

"Get them out!" he yells. "Get every last motherfucker out!"

CHAPTER 32
WARRIORS

Jeff lies perfectly still. With his eyes shut, he feels the pain gnawing greedily at the edges of his sleep. He feels the thin sheet and blanket like an extra layer of agony tucked in around him. It keeps coming. He sees it in the blackness behind his eyelids: jagged peaks in neon green and orange that dance in crazy patterns, some kind of chaotic rhythm that eventually syncs up with the throbbing in what remains of his leg—this stump. He feels it there, but he feels it in the part that isn't there, too. That's the worst of it. The searing pain that pulses through the calf and the foot that's no longer there. The pain always starts out wild like that. Then it settles down, taking on a certain regularity inside the chaos that Jeff has begun to perversely appreciate. At least it's a *predictable* bastard, he figures. The slightest movement of his torso, thighs, or even his head, can set it off, sending the hot, glowing monster into a frenzy again. He's learned to lie perfectly still and to regulate his breathing. He's learned to put off opening his eyes for as long as possible.

He tries for a while and fails to let the sensation pull him under, to drag him back into the dense, black cave of sleep. When he can't stand the pain a second longer he pushes the button on the morphine pump that the night nurse had wedged next to his right hand. Without opening his eyes he waits for the numbing bliss that will buy him a half an hour or so of sanity. He buzzes for the nurse and tests, with a flutter of his eyelids, the effect of the morphine. Almost there, he thinks. He opens his eyes fully. The room hums with hospital light, an impersonal glare that never changes from day into night, a fact he's discovered over the last few days. He takes a deep breath and presses the button to raise the head of his bed. The mechanism's whir blends with the undercarriage of pain that still grips him, but the edge has blurred some, just enough to make sitting up bearable. "You're a sorry motherfucker," Jeff mutters. "Guess you're gonna have to give it a rest for a while."

"Can I help you?" asks the cheerful voice bursting through the speaker behind the bed.

"Yeah, I need the shitter."

"Be right there." Jeff recognizes the voice. Meghan. Sweet, little Meghan. He hates like hell to have that girl carry his shit away. He thinks about what it might be like to fuck her, how soft her skin would feel. He wonders if it would be different now, if he even could. But then, there she is in the room a minute later, all creamy skin, big blue eyes, and blond ponytail.

"*Good* morning, Sergeant Ingram. Let's just get you situated." Using the bottom sheet for leverage, she deftly rolls her patient and slides the pan beneath him. Jeff winces and looks toward the window, the heavy, blue curtains not yet drawn. "You just buzz me when you're through," Meghan says. "I'll bring in your meds then. How's that?"

"Sure," says Jeff. He avoids the earnest look he knows he'll find on her clean-scrubbed, young face. He's grateful that the girl then briskly exits the room, doesn't stop to fuss with the water pitcher or the curtains like that other one, Stella, he thinks her name is. He closes his eyes again, concentrates on the mission at hand. *One fuckin' thing at a time.*

By 0930 the tech, a serene-faced black man in maroon scrubs, has helped to sponge him down and pull on a T-shirt and sweatpants. Jeff sits on the edge of the bed, the foot of his good leg sheathed in a white athletic sock. He watches as the tech gently folds the thick fabric of the sweats and then safety pins it around the bandages of the stump. The cocktail of pain meds he'd swallowed earlier is holding the beast at bay.

"Ready?" Jeff notices the man's voice, like his touch, is also gentle. He takes in, too, the thick bundle of ropey braids, pulled back from a face that isn't young or old. The bundle is cinched loosely with an elastic hair tie, the kind Lisa used to leave all over till the babies were born. Then he glances at the man's ID badge for the first time.

"Let's roll, Charles," Jeff says.

The tech carefully gathers the catheter tube, hooks the quarter-filled bag of urine to the chair, and wheels over the IV pole so that it stands within reach.

"At the count of three, Okay?... One, two, *three.*"

Jeff pushes off the way the PT had shown him and feels Charles's strong hands under his armpits, steadying him, as he lowers his body into the wheelchair. Okay, that wasn't so bad. He'd get through his PT by 1030. *What the fuck am I gonna do for the* rest *of the day?* But then a scorching jolt shoots straight through his leg. It hits him, so hard and so fast, he can't think. He forgets how to breathe. A clammy sweat breaks on his forearms and his face. He hears Charles say something, but can't understand him. A high-pitched screeching pulses in his ears. Next, he feels the crush of heavy steel, smells the sickening stench of burning rubber. He sees the pool of surprisingly bright red blood on colorless sand, the sun beating down with no mercy. He can't move. His leg is pinned somehow and he can't free it.

"You okay, buddy? Hey, just take a breath, man. That happens sometimes."

Jeff bends forward until his head is between his knees. His heart feels like it might beat its way right out of his chest. He tastes the gritty bile that comes up in his throat and thinks he's going to puke.

"Hey buddy, you need me to call someone?"

A moment later Jeff's face is flushed and glistening with sweat when he lifts it to the soldier in front of him. He struggles to get out from under the overturned Humvee but can't move. The soldier's hands feel like vice grips on Jeff's shoulders as the stronger man holds him down.

"Let's take it easy, Okay?"

"Just shut the fuck up! Where the fuck's Peters? Where's Rodriguez? Gotta get 'em out!

"Listen, man—"

"I'm giving you an *order*, Private. You hear me? Get those men out now!"

Charles holds Jeff in the chair with one arm pressed across his chest and reaches for the call button with the other.

Within seconds a woman in a cotton skirt and T-shirt sweeps into the room. "It's okay," she says to Charles, registering his doubtful look. "I'll take it from here."

Charles backs off from Jeff and the woman positions herself directly in front of the patient. Jeff sobs. She glances at the chart the tech thrusts at her, then searches out the patient's red-rimmed eyes instead. "Sergeant Ingram," she says softly. "Do you know where you are?"

Jeff holds his head between his hands, his broad shoulders hunched forward in the chair. After several seconds, he looks up at her with a blank stare, his hazel eyes gazing into a landscape she views with sad resignation. She watches his face—notices how the reddish stubble follows the line of his square jaw—waiting for the moment of recognition. She waits, listens to the choking sobs until he seems to tire. Several minutes pass.

"Go ahead," the woman says to Charles, still standing next to her. The two exchange a look of understanding before he walks quietly from the room. The woman pulls over the room's only chair and sits so that she faces her patient. Her narrow hands rest in her lap. She waits another few moments before she speaks again.

"Sergeant Ingram, do you know where you are?"

Jeff rubs the tears from his face with the back of his hand. He meets the woman's eyes—green and wide with a sadness that tries hard to be something else, he thinks—and feels like weeping all over again. *What the fuck's the matter with me?*

"Portland VA Medical Center," he says.

"That's right. And where were you a few moments ago, before I got here?"

Jeff shakes his head and looks down at his hands, grasped in front of him. "I can't really say, ma'am."

"Please, Sergeant Ingram, call me Nermina if you like."

Jeff looks at the woman who sits across from him. She's pretty—maybe forty or so — her short blond hair softening an angular face. Her eyes look huge in that pretty face, but there's a hard edge, too, a stubbornness in her jaw that makes him a little uneasy. He sees that she's dressed in street clothes, isn't wearing a white coat over them like the rest of the docs, and tries to figure out her rank in this place. At Landstuhl there'd been no civilians and it was easy to figure out who was who. He reads her badge: Nermina Beganović, DrNP, APPN.

"You're a doctor, Ma'am?" Jeff asks tentatively.

"Oh no, I'm sorry, I should have introduced myself properly. I'm a nurse practitioner—psych—with the post-trauma clinic."

Jeff shakes his head again and feels his anger rising. "No disrespect, ma'am, but I don't need any shrink."

Nermina's face remains placid. "No disrespect taken, Sergeant, but I think you'll find it helpful to speak with me. We don't have to do it right now, not if you're not up to it."

Jeff struggles to make sense of what this woman is saying. He'd filled out the A-4s at Landstuhl and then again at Walter Reed. He'd answered no to all of their idiotic questions and thought that was the end of it. But here he is again. Another shrink, another set of questions. Why did they all want to get inside his head so badly? Jeff thinks about the irony of that; all he wants to do is get the fuck *out* of his head. He looks up to see the woman's face, set patiently, green eyes sizing him up but, unexpectedly, with a seeming lack of outright judgment.

"Maybe some other time," he says, surprised by the gentle tone that creeps into his voice.

"I'll stop by tomorrow, Sergeant, and we'll visit for a while then." Her eyes soften the statement, making it sound somewhat more like an open-ended question than an order.

"Okay, then."

"Would you like me to call someone from PT, or will you be all right on your own?"

"I'm good, ma'am, thank you." He waits until she returns the chair to its place near the window, then rolls the wheelchair closer to the bed and grabs the call button. Once she's left the room, though, he drops it back on the bed.

When Meghan comes in with the little paper cup of meds half an hour later and touches him gently on the wrist to wake him, he swings so hard that her cream-colored cheek purples within moments.

CHAPTER 33
FIRST LOVE

Atika lies sprawled on her unmade bed. Her head rests against a stack of pillows stuffed against the headboard, the comforter and sheets—a matching print of bright, oversized, purple flowers—rumpled beneath her. The girl clicks away on the keyboard, her knees bent at just the right angle to cradle the laptop. She shakes her head in time with music that throbs through her earbuds. Her limbs, long and lithe like a dancer's, are relaxed, as is her face. She stares straight ahead at the screen, smiling whenever Keith's dialogue box pops up among the others. The fingers of her right hand search out the tiny silver ring that pierces her lower lip, worrying it gently as she thinks about the way Keith's tongue flicked over it like tiny sparks of electricity—teasing her—then pressed against her lips until they'd parted. Her face flushes when she remembers the way he'd unzipped her jeans with one hand while the other caressed her breasts.

Now she feels rather than hears her mother's presence on the other side of the locked door. Her mother pounds several times before Atika sets aside the computer, yanks the earbuds from her ears, and extricates herself from the tangle of bedding. The girl stands with her hand gripping the doorknob and opens the door only slightly.

"What?" she says, making little effort to disguise her annoyance.

"I wanted to talk with you a minute," says Nermina. She peers through the narrow sliver her daughter has ceded. "I thought you were supposed to be doing homework."

"I am," says Atika.

"It doesn't look that way."

"Well, I am."

Atika pushes against the full force of her mother's body on the other side of the door but finally yields. She flops dramatically back onto the bed with a loud sigh.

Her mother paces the room twice, then moves the stack of papers and books from the chair that's shoved under an antique roll-top desk, and sits down. She turns the chair toward her daughter's sullen figure and clears her throat. "I need to talk to you," she says.

Atika turns away from her mother's stare. "Well, okay, let's talk," she says.

Nermina reaches into the back pocket of her jeans and pulls out a handful of brightly colored packets of condoms. She tosses them on the bed. Atika props herself up on one elbow and eyes first the condoms and then the serious expression on her mother's face. She silently curses herself for being so careless, for not choosing a better hiding place. She also feels a wave of guilt wash over her—not because she's slept with Keith exactly, but because she's kept this development to herself. Away from her mother. Separate from her mother.

"Would you like to tell me why you have these in your room?" her mother asks.

"Would you like to tell me why you're always snooping through my things?"

"First, I'm your mother. I still have the right to know what you're doing. To know if you're...well, if you're doing something that might be harmful or self-destructive."

"Oh, *really*? Aren't you being a little dramatic?"

"No, I don't think so."

The girl's eyes light up with amusement. She leans back against the pillows. Traces of a smirk appear and then vanish.

Nermina stands and hooks her thumbs in the front pockets of her jeans. "I'm sorry, I really don't see what's so funny."

Atika follows her mother's gaze as she takes in the mugs and plates and glasses that sit in various states of use or abandonment on the nightstand, the bureau, the desk, the windowsill. A snort of laughter escapes the girl's mouth as her mother makes these rounds.

"*You're* funny," says Atika.

"Very nice," Nermina says. The girl recognizes both hurt and anger in her mother's measured syllables. This infuriates her.

"So, what is it you think I'm doing that's so terrible?" she says finally, presenting Nermina with a look of disregard, an expression she's worked hard at perfecting these past months.

"*Draga*," Nermina begins again, "you know what I'm talking about."

"Do I?"

"What I mean is, I would have hoped you'd come to me first to talk this through. I really think—"

"I don't *want* to hear what you think right now." She can't stand the look on her mother's face, the overwrought concern pulling down the corners of her mouth.

"Are you having sexual intercourse?" Her mother's voice is calmer still.

The girl turns away. "What?" she asks. She feels her mother's eyes boring into the tense muscles of her back.

"It's a simple question. Yes or no."

Now Atika hears the sharp edge of anger displacing her mother's concern. A metallic taste singes the back of her throat.

"Jesus! Why are you asking me this?" She pulls one of the pillows from behind her and hugs it to her chest.

"Because I deserve an answer."

"Yeah? And why's that?"

"Because I'm your mother," Nermina snaps.

Atika considers the repercussions of telling the truth. What if her mother refuses to let her see Keith anymore? What if Keith doesn't even *want* to see her once she's told him her mother knows about them? Sitting cross-legged now on the bed, she tucks one hand under each thigh to still them. She listens to the whir of her laptop as it powers down into sleep mode. Her mother stands there in silence—hovering—for what seems to Atika like hours. The ticking of an old-fashioned alarm clock on her nightstand marks each second of the standoff. All the while, Atika's mind churns out a stream of thoughts. Thoughts of what will happen if Keith meets some college girl. Thoughts of spending almost another whole year in Portland with her mother watching her every move. Thoughts of whether she'll actually have the guts to move away for college and leave her mother behind.

"I want an answer," Nermina says. "Are you having sex?"

"Of course not," Atika blurts. "I don't know why you'd think that."

Nermina snatches the foil packets from the bed and holds them in her open palm.

"Okay, fine. Then, why do you need these?"

"They gave them to us at school," Atika hears herself say. "We had this safe sex assembly. They gave them to everyone. You know, the public health program about STDs, HIV, all that." The lie came easily. "It was very informative."

"Oh," says Nermina, "I thought that was just for freshmen."

"Nope, they're doing it all four years now."

"Hmmm," says Nermina. "That's interesting."

"Isn't that exactly what you've been telling me all these years? Practice safe sex. Use condoms."

She tosses away the pillow, gathers her legs to her chest, imagining she looks more complacent in this posture. Her copper-colored hair is plaited into a long, thick braid, and she unconsciously plays with the soft brush of hair the ponytail holder makes at the end, moving it like a powder puff along her jawline.

Nermina lowers herself into the chair and Atika watches her.

"Sure. We've talked about all that. About the risks and the..." Nermina trails off.

"I know that. You've done a great job, Mom. Really. You have."

Atika feels her mother's steady gaze and she wills herself not to look away.

"There's just a lot involved," Nermina says. "I want to make sure you understand, well, it's complicated. A mature sexual relationship is...complex."

Atika's eyes lock onto her mother's and she concentrates on keeping the saccharine tone of her voice as steady as her gaze. "Mature? Now that's an interesting word for you to use. How do you mean mature, Mama?"

"Well, I guess I mean mature enough so you really *know* yourself. That you know you're ready to be in a loving relationship with someone...with another person. It's a big responsibility..."

Atika swings her legs off the bed, kicking one of the pillows to the floor. She walks to the window and yanks the cord for the blinds so that they clatter down to the sill. A yellow mug thuds onto the carpet. She kicks this, as well, sending it under the bed.

"*What*?" she whines, glaring at her mother as though she might kick her too.

"Are you done with your little outburst?"

"No, actually I'm not." Atika smiles grimly and continues. "You're just exasperating. Do you know that?"

Nermina removes her hands from her knees, crosses her jean-clad legs, then clasps her hands together in her lap. "What is it that's set you off? What horrible thing have I said or done to you now?"

A quizzical look on her face, Atika holds her mother's gaze. "It doesn't strike you that talking to me about maturity is a little hypocritical."

"I'm not sure what you're getting at."

Her mother's voice is calm again. The girl flings herself back on the bed. "We're talking about *maturity*, right? Responsibility? Who is it that takes care of stuff around here when you can't?" She knows she's headed in the wrong direction now but doesn't know how to turn back around.

"That's not fair," says Nermina. A slight hoarseness saturates her voice. She crosses her arms in front of her. "Everything you do is appreciated. You know that. We're talking about a completely different thing here."

Atika can hear that her mother is trying. That she's hurt. Still, something urges her on.

"Right," comes her curt reply. "The yard, the shopping, the laundry. I guess I just don't know many kids who have the *maturity* to do all that stuff whenever their mom can't get out of bed..." She lets her voice trail off, sounding bored and (she knows) obnoxious. Even cruel. She tells herself she doesn't care.

"That's not what I mean by maturity," Nermina snaps. "We were talking about having sex. About you—not me—growing into a mature woman. Maybe getting married. Maybe having children someday. We were talking about something else entirely. You do see that? We're *not* talking about me."

A swath of pink covers her mother's neck and cheeks. Atika feels the lump rising in her throat. She fights back tears. "Oh sure. I get it. Do as I say, not as I do."

The words are out and with them the hot flicker of vindication, the sinking feeling right after. Atika's heart races and a sour taste fills her mouth. She clenches her fists, balls them underneath her thighs. She lets her knuckles dig into the muscle until it hurts.

"I see where we've ended up. Same as always these days," Nermina says.

Her mother's voice is flat, the same monotone, emotionless flat that has served as a warning flag to Atika since she was little. She knows all her mother's moods. It's impossible not to, always just the two of them since they'd moved from Strina Raifa and Ujak Samir's. Just the two of them, minus the buffer of family—at least the closest she can claim.

"What is it you want from me, Atika? What do you want me to say?"

"I don't know. Maybe I just wish you'd stop pretending."

Her mother's face is a mask now, red and splotchy, her green eyes fixed on something beyond Atika. Beyond the window, beyond the tree branches that sometimes scrape the window in the night, the lonely noise that had frightened the girl, causing her to run to her mother when she was younger, even sometimes when she was much older, to be held and comforted.

"How am I pretending?" her mother asks.

Tears threaten to spill; Atika refuses to succumb, and this effort feeds her anger. "You're pretending that's what *you* did. That you had a mature, loving relationship. That's ridiculous. You got inseminated. You got pregnant. You had me. End of discussion. Right? Isn't that how the story goes?"

Nermina flutters her hand in the air as though to brush away the gnats that hover above the compost bin in the yard.

"We've been through this before. The circumstances were different. Much different. You know all about that. I did what I needed to do. I don't need to apologize to you or anyone else."

Atika hears her mother's pronouncement—a well-worn script—the whole of it delivered evenly and without a trace of anger or conciliation. Maybe her mother is happy with her decision, happy with her life—just the two of them—but that doesn't make it fair. She remembers how Ujak Samir would scoop her up in one arm, Sabrina in the other, and carry them to their bunk beds to tuck them in. Jealous is the word that describes what she'd felt once she was old enough to understand that she'd never have what Sabrina and Taki had. She'd never have a father. And this was her mother's doing.

Nermina rises and walks over to one of Atika's bookshelves, trails her fingers along the spines, nudges back a little brass figurine of a cat—just a bit—from the edge where it perches among a jumble of other trinkets. She brushes the dust from a stack of *National Geographics* on the top shelf with the side of her hand. Atika glares at her mother's back, willing her to turn around *now* so she can demand an answer, demand an end to this stupid game.

But when, finally, her mother turns, she stands mute, leaning against the bookshelf, her hands tucked into the back pockets of her jeans. Her face is almost placid now, pretty. This makes Atika remember there were good parts, too. A fifth-grade outing, her mother a chaperone at the roller rink. Her mother, skating easily, gracefully, one leg crossing in front of the other, the almost ridiculous contrast to their teacher, gray-haired Mrs. Rush, her short, blocky figure stumbling around the edge of the rink, her round face red and winded. She was proud of her mother that day.

"I'm not asking for an apology," Atika says now. "But maybe I deserve to know who my father is. Do you get that?" Much of the nastiness has drained from her tone and a heavy sadness settles over her. She realizes that of all the things that hurt her, not knowing her father is the worst. She's not a little girl anymore—especially now, with Keith—but somehow the hurt still follows. Exacting, it knows just where to find her.

"Of course, I do," her mother says. "But we've been over this a million times, draga. It was anonymous. The clinic keeps donor records anonymous on purpose."

Her mother's tone has warmed a little now, too. And Atika sees that she's being silly. She's asking for something her mother simply can't provide. But still Atika wonders, not for the first time, if there's a way to hack into the fertility clinic's database. Would they even save records for sixteen years? She puzzles it out again, but the concept strikes her, inevitably, as futile. If a guy—a man, maybe even a *boy* Keith's age—would do something as disgusting as selling his sperm for money, he probably wouldn't be the kind of person who'd want a daughter calling him up out of the blue. She can picture it now: Hey, you don't know me, but you provided half my DNA. Guess what? You have a daughter!

"I know that," she says.

Her own voice sounds to Atika so tiny now, so childish. Deflated. And when her mother goes to her, she stands and lets herself be hugged. She breathes in the fresh-laundry smell of her mother's thin sweater. Allows her tears to dampen the soft cotton. She presses her face to her mother's shoulder and feels the sinewy strength of her mother's arms lock around her. A least for now, she lets herself be mothered.

CHAPTER 34
CATERPILLAR

Atika wipes the tears from her face with the back of her hand. There is nothing gentle or maudlin about the gesture. Just talking about the stupid argument, she's indignant all over again.

"Classic," says Keith. "Your mom's overcompensating, playing up her parental role now. She's just not ready to let you go."

Atika feels the guilt encroaching again like a bratty kid in the supermarket, whining and whining until someone takes notice. Until one of the exhausted parents finally gives in and hands the kid the candy or the little plastic toy. She hates this rush of doubt that floods her as soon as her defenses are down. And she hates, especially, for Keith to see it.

She knows this and, as always, it makes her both angry

and sad. She knows her mother is suffering, *has* suffered. And Atika knows if she gets into Brown, her mother will likely suffer a whole bunch more with her only daughter thousands of miles away at college. But how is this her fault?

"Whatever you call it, she's driving me nuts." Atika lies with her head on Keith's naked chest. She feels the even rhythm of his heartbeat against her cheek. His skin is still slick and she calms a little now, taking in the smell of him—the musk-scented deodorant that doesn't quite cover the salty-pungent aroma of sweat and sex.

"I'm telling you, it's classic separation anxiety."

Atika only half listens. Since taking his first psych class this semester, Keith is always going off on this stuff. She figures he makes at least a little sense, but she knows it isn't that simple either. Her mother knows a lot about human behavior, too. She'd put herself through school—a psychiatric nursing program—while Atika was still in middle school, and now she counsels soldiers who've been blown up or shot up in Afghanistan and Iraq.

"Maybe, but with us—my mother and me—it's always worse."

Keith's only reply now is the rising and falling of his chest. Atika's own heartbeat quickens.

"She found some condoms in my room," she says. "That's actually what started the whole thing."

"You didn't tell me that part," says Keith. The two of them—both tall and lanky—fit only precariously in the single bed. The bed itself is wedged into one corner of the tiny dorm room. The other bed is empty, the result of careful pre-arrangement on Keith's part. He'd given his roommate a joint and instructed him not to come back before nine.

"Does your mother know about us, then? Does she know we're sleeping together?" Keith's clinical tone has segued into what Atika construes as alarm.

She props herself up, placing one hand against the wall and the other pressing into Keith's taut stomach. She feels him pull the muscles tighter.

"Well, no...I don't think so." She eases herself back down so that her head lies against his chest again. "I told her we had an assembly at school and they gave out condoms to the whole senior class," she says. "You know: Get your free condoms! Practice safe sex!"

As soon as the words are out of her mouth she wishes she could take them back. The excuse sounds silly, unbelievably immature. She raises her head, searches his features for any clue of disapproval.

"And you think she went for that?" Keith raises an eyebrow. "She's not stupid."

Atika gauges the gathering clouds of misgiving she reads in his blue eyes. This is what she'd been worried about. "Well, it's plausible enough..."

"Where does she think you are right now?" Keith wraps his arms around her and together they tug themselves—like a giant caterpillar, Atika thinks—until they're both sitting upright against the headboard.

"I told her I'd be at Margo's but she probably knows I'm with you." She thinks glumly about the other thread of the argument she'd had with her mother. She isn't sure she should talk about this with Keith. She isn't sure what he'd think. When she and Keith first started to hang out together, he'd seemed really impressed with her mom, with the idea that she'd been so bold—"such a brazen feminist" was how he'd put it then—to do the whole *in-vitro* thing and then raise a kid on her own. To do this "so purposefully." When Atika was much younger, she accepted her mother's explanation and rationale with little dispute. Lately, though, Atika has decided her mother has just been remarkably selfish. Her mother made a unilateral decision to raise a kid with no father. How is that fair? But, at the time, she'd found herself nodding in agreement with Keith, feeling all superior and somehow enlightened. *Like she'd had anything to do with any of it!*

And now Atika thinks how absurd her situation really is. She feels sorry for herself and, even though this is also embarrassing, she feels completely justified. She watches as Keith draws slow circles on her thigh with his index finger. It's warm and stuffy in the room—neither had thought to open a window—and the light pressure of his finger feels hot on her skin. He stops and regards her with a look of sincerity, a look Atika takes as a challenge.

"What are you going to say if she calls you on it?" he says. "She could give this whole condom thing more thought. A lot more thought. I mean, she's your *mom*. She's probably really freaked out we're—

"I don't know," Atika cuts in. "Maybe I'll just tell her the truth. I mean, why shouldn't I be able to have a mature relationship with my boyfriend?"

Keith reaches down to the heap of clothing they'd shed on the floor earlier and pulls on his boxers. Then he swings his legs over the edge of the bed and sits with his back to Atika. His vertebrae stand out in relief as he leans over, resting his elbows on his knees, his fingers enmeshed in the mass of his dirty-blond curls. Atika reaches out and runs her fingers slowly down his spine, touching the spaces between each bone like a blind person, feeling with her fingertips the precision and perfection of the human body. This body. Keith's body. She thinks about the way his body shuddered against her, *through* her, when he came. She moves to hug him from behind and her nipples stand erect against his still-damp back.

"Jesus, Atika. You're *sixteen*," Keith says, as though he's only just discovered this. A prickle of anger shoots through Atika's nervous system. There'd never been any discussion about her age before. At first they were friends and then something else. It happened naturally. No guilt or drama.

"So?" The word and the way she delivers it sounds juvenile to her. Atika swallows hard.

"I'm serious," he says. "She's worried about you. She's concerned—"

"*So*?" There it was again. When had she started to sound like such a whiny baby?

Atika pulls away from Keith when he doesn't respond and yanks at the tangled sheet so that she's covered herself to the chin.

"Just before...you weren't so worried, but now, all of a sudden you are? You're worried because my *mother's* worried?"

"Well, I guess when I think about it now...when I think about it from, you know, from her perspective—"

"Why are you taking her side?" Atika demands.

"I'm not, I'm just saying, like, as a parent...I can see the moral—"

"Oh *Je*sus, what are you, some kind of preacher now?"

Keith turns away, his body rigid on the bed beside her, and she feels the shift—subtle but certain. He's pulling away from her. She remembers last semester, when they'd studied tidal flats in her AP Science class. The slides of mud couplets, alternating layers of sediment and fossils, all of this revealed or hidden as if by magic, controlled by the constant pull of the moon. She reaches out and places her hand on Keith's wrist. "Are you mad at me?" Again, she hears the babyish voice Sabrina had always taunted.

Keith shakes his head from side to side. His face, with the high color that flushes his cheeks whenever he's warm, looks wholesome, even angelic, Atika notes.

"I'm not mad. I just..."

Outside it's chillier than she would have imagined. Atika clutches her sweater at the collar to hold it closed. She fumbles to push the thick buttons through the holes. The campus streetlights flicker on and when she turns to Keith again his hair seems to glow, haloed like in those Renaissance paintings of the faithful in art history class. When they hug this time Atika feels the tide slipping back, away from her and Keith. For now, her tears are buried in a deep layer of grief, an ancient one. Maybe she'll get into Brown. Maybe she won't. Either way, she's losing him. She pictures her mother, the yawning summer ahead. As always, just the two of them.

CHAPTER 35
SURVIVORS' GUILT

Nermina waits, impatient, as the young clerk stands at the hulking copier. When the machine finally spits out the last copy, the clerk hands a disheveled bundle of papers to Nermina without a word. "Thank you," Nermina says. She turns curtly from the girl and pushes open the glass door to the corridor.

In the nurses' lounge she sits on one of the long benches. She skims the chart first, then goes back to read more carefully. SSGT Jeffrey P. Ingram, 49 years old, Oregon Army National Guard, 41st Infantry Brigade Combat Team. Married with two children, ages: 20 months. "Twins," Nermina murmurs, "but no mention of family of origin." She continues, noting that Ingram had been on his third deployment, the first a twelve-month tour in Iraq in 2004, another in 2006. This time, he'd been in Afghanistan for five months when an RPG struck the Humvee he was driving in Jalalabad. The file says Ingram's unit was on "diplomatic security detail" when the incident occurred. Two American soldiers killed. They'd Med-Evac-ed Ingram to Bagram for the first surgery—his right femur crushed under the vehicle—and then to Landstuhl for the amputation. Some of the skin grafts were performed at Walter Reed. All of that and he'd survived.

She remembers the shame she'd seen in Sgt. Ingram's eyes. The soldiers who'd died were under his command. She knows that shame, too, and feels the weight of those ghosts he carried home from the desert on his back. With this reminder, her index finger seeks the V-shaped scar at the edge of her hairline. She feels the bristle of cowlick there, more prominent with the short hairstyle she wears now. How silly, she thinks— growing her hair back after escaping Bosnia was the only thing she'd been able to accomplish without the well-intentioned but humiliating help she needed then.

She closes her eyes and takes a couple of deep breaths. Even so, the memories flood back with their usual intensity. The cloying sweetness of the woman's perfume, and still the rancid smell of her beneath it. She'd dragged Nermina by the hair from behind the metal drums the U.N. set up throughout the city, protection from the snipers. But the Serbian soldier appeared out of nowhere. No older than Nermina, a black leather jacket, a pair of tight jeans, no proper uniform. The soldier threatened to kill her but then settled— unaccountably—on shearing the hair from her head. The razor gouged deep into Nermina's scalp. Why had she stopped there?

The soldier forced her to watch as one of her comrades shot a young mother in the head. Even after Nermina had shuttered her eyes, the image remained: the flesh opening like a crimson rose where the bullet had penetrated her forehead. The woman crumpled to the ground. And the child crying, a little boy, clinging to the dead woman's body until two more bullets silenced him, as well. Why *that* woman and not her? Why had she been spared? Why had she survived? After all these years, even Shira has no answers.

And now she sees again the haunted look in Sgt. Ingram's eyes. She understands he'll be asking himself a similar set of questions, perhaps for the rest of his life. Gathering herself, she returns to the chart. After what she's just seen in his room, Nermina knows without question she'll recommend transferring Ingram from the main hospital to the post-trauma unit as soon as he's medically stable. She'll speak to Dr. Harris immediately.

Again, she envisions Ingram's eyes. Beyond his pain, she remembers something else there, too. Something equally familiar. The strong cut of his jaw made her feel the weight of Carl Ingram's face as it pressed against her neck, the prickling stubble against her skin. How he'd cried out that first time, as though in agony. She knows, of course now, that the two men are brothers.

CHAPTER 36
COLLATERAL DAMAGE

Nermina had requested one of the small family conference rooms and she waits here, checking her watch, although her appointment with Lisa Ingram isn't for another ten minutes. She looks around at the room's décor: a small sofa and matching chair, the nubby, beige fabric worn and soiled, the round table where she sits, composed of cheap particle board. The room's only effort toward aesthetics, Nermina decides, is a poorly executed seascape, a print at that, and inexpertly framed. She's left the door open, and the hospital's noises and smells drift in on waves of overly air-conditioned air: the rumbling of a passing gurney, the limp aroma of institutional meatloaf blending with antiseptic. She looks up to see a tall, solidly built woman peering tentatively into the room.

"Oh, excuse me, do I have the right place?" the woman

asks.

"You're Mrs. Ingram," Nermina says. "Lisa, right?" She rises from the table to greet her. The woman nods, still eyeing the room uncertainly.

"Please come in. I'll shut this door so we have a little privacy."

Lisa Ingram chooses a seat on the dilapidated couch and Nermina sits across from her in the armchair. "I really appreciate your coming in to speak with me. I know this has been a difficult time."

"It has," says Lisa, fingering the quilted fabric of her purse. "For all of us," she adds after a moment's hesitation.

"I was hoping I might meet your children today," Nermina says, smiling.

"Oh, no, I decided it would just be easier to get a sitter."

Lisa Ingram's face features a broad forehead, hazel eyes, narrow and somehow feline. Her heart-shaped lips give her a pouty appearance. Her limbs are long and muscular, her overall appearance that of a former athlete. Lisa's clothing—a khaki skirt and baby blue, sleeveless polo shirt—is conservative, or preppy, as Nermina knows Atika would say.

"Well, I won't take any more of your time than is necessary. As I said on the phone, I wanted to meet you in person and see if you had any concerns—"

"Well, *shouldn't* I?" Lisa cuts in.

Startled, Nermina tries again. "Sure, well, of course you'd have concerns..."

Lisa looks around the room. "My husband doesn't seem in a big rush to get out of this place, for one. *That's* a concern."

"I sincerely doubt that," Nermina says. "I know your

husband is working very hard at his physical therapy. He's making tremendous progress."

"That's great," Lisa says, "and what about his emotional progress? His psychological progress?"

Nermina sits rigid in the chair. "I'm not...well, I'm not at liberty to discuss specifics—"

"No, of course not." A tight smile flickers across Lisa's pouty lips and then vanishes. "Here's the thing, though. Since being back, he's checked out. Completely."

"Meaning?"

"Meaning, he's built himself a sort of...cave, I guess you'd say. And *we're* not allowed in."

"You and the children?" Nermina says as gently as she can. "I can imagine that must be very frustrating."

Lisa turns her eyes away from Nermina's and steeples her hands, holding them tensely against a taut stomach.

"Well, *yes*," says Lisa. "It's one thing to have your husband gone in Afghanistan, but now that he's home, well...I just don't get it. He should *want* to be with his family, right?"

"I think what you're describing is really not all that unusual for people who've experienced the kind of trauma your husband has. It can be difficult for the survivor to open up."

"To his own wife?"

"Well, sometimes, especially...The people we love the most are the hardest to...to let in, as you say."

Lisa takes a section of her hair—it's shoulder-length and sandy-blond, pushed back from her wide forehead with a fabric headband that matches her polo shirt—and listlessly smoothes it between her fingers. A couple of moments pass.

Nermina feels the weight of the silence but decides to give Lisa a little more time.

"You know what?" Lisa says finally. "I think I'm just a little tired of all this. I *know* that sounds awful. I *know* Jeff's been through a lot. I get that, but I'm at home with two kids in diapers. My friends? My sister? There's only so much you can ask people, you know?"

Despite her best efforts, Nermina feels a rising irritation with this woman, a red flag, she knows. She'd imagined—perhaps idealized—Lisa as Jeff's devoted wife, a woman eager to help her husband recover. But this woman is suffering, too. Parenting two young children alone. Nermina remembers those first exhausting months with Atika, the depression that nearly swallowed her. But she also remembers the heavenly feel of soft down when she pressed her lips to her daughter's scalp, the milky scent of her. She'd been so in love with her baby girl, so grateful that, with Raifa and Shira's help, she and Atika had survived.

"I can only imagine how difficult things have been," she says, "but I *do* know your husband is going to need a strong support system when he leaves here. Frankly, in my experience, the most difficult time is still ahead of him."

"I know that," Lisa snaps.

"Look," Nermina says. She leans forward in what she hopes will be taken as a gesture of compassion. "There are services available for both of you."

"Right. Counseling. All that Family Readiness bullshit. Blah blah blaaah."

"I know it may feel like I'm asking a lot of you right now...I am, there's no question, but for Jeff to move forward, to do the hard work he's got to do, he's going to need you."

Tears glinting in her eyes, Lisa levels an angry glare at Nermina. "What is it you want from me?" she says, fisting her hands in her lap.

"I just want you to try," says Nermina calmly. "Try to let go—"

"Oh, *God*," Lisa whines. "You're all the same. You shrinks are all the same." She stands abruptly, grabs her purse from the couch, and slings it over her shoulder. "I have to go," she says.

"Wait a minute, Lisa. Just give me another moment, okay? What about the rest of the family? Are there parents...or maybe siblings, that Jeff might feel comfortable speaking with?"

Lisa looks at Nermina and shakes her head, her irritation apparent. "Jeff's mother lives in New Jersey in an assisted living facility. She's frail and can't travel. His father died a few years ago. Want to know how many times they came out to see us while he was still alive? That would be zero. Oh, wait, then there's the deadbeat brother," she says. "Maybe we can get *him* to come out and spend some quality time with Jeff. That is, if we had any idea where the hell he was."

"I'm sorry," says Nermina. She senses that Lisa's diatribe is far from over. "I was just thinking out loud. I was thinking that maybe with another family member here, it might take some pressure off *you*. I know what I said before, but it might help Jeff...to open up a bit."

Lisa shakes her head in disgust. "You'll have to excuse me now," she says. "I have to go visit my husband."

Nermina listens to the slap of Lisa's sandals as she walks

out the door and down the hallway. Her thoughts return to what she'd said about her in-laws. Two precious little boys who wouldn't get to know their grandparents. Then she smiles—a small, inward expression of grief—when she tries to recapture her own parents' faces. She imagines them fussing over *their* granddaughter, the absurd overindulgence with which they would have showered Atika.

But then another thought begins to fight its way to the surface, at first opaque and unformed, taking shape of its own accord. Despite her efforts to push it back under, the thought bubbles up and grows clearer. She wonders, finally, whether Carl would even *want* to know his daughter.

CHAPTER 37
JEFF'S PT

Jeff grips the bars on either side of the walkway in the PT room. His shoulders and forearms ache badly and a dull pain throbs in his good leg. He takes another halting step. The temporary prosthesis extends from his right thigh and sports a brand-new Nike running shoe. Lisa had dropped off the shoes the week before, along with an assortment of other items, packed neatly inside one of the rolling suitcases they'd bought themselves for their seventh wedding anniversary last year. The visit went badly and he'd told her he wasn't ready to see the twins yet. He felt like shit saying this out loud, but he couldn't imagine touching them. Couldn't imagine putting the same hands on his little boys that had zipped up that ooze and flesh and bone into body bags for counting. *Remains.* Even the word nauseates him. Touching his boys so soon after; this doesn't seem possible.

With sweat rolling down his cheeks now, Jeff sees the look on Lisa's face when he'd said this: equal parts hurt, exhaustion and—if he was really being honest with himself—rage. She might never say it, but he knows it's there. Four years of trying to have a baby on their own and then the grueling rounds of fertility treatments had edged Lisa to the brink. When they'd found out it was twins, Jeff felt a huge weight had been lifted. Nothing could have made him happier. But when he got called up again, Lisa morphed into a different person. Even in the choppy satellite image on the base computer, he saw the strain, dark circles under her eyes, the ticking bomb of anger hastily stowed. He shakes his head to clear the image and takes another step on the walkway.

"*That's* it," says Craig, the PT who's been working with him all week. "You're doing great, Sarg." Jeff leans into the railing, holds himself steady with his left arm, and wipes the sweat from his face with the front of his T-shirt. Once his right hand is free he snaps Craig a salute. Last week, he'd been all set to hate the kid: bulked-up chest and arms, brush-cut blond hair, and clean-shaven baby face. The kid's twenty-*six* for Chrissake and still lives at home with his parents. What the hell could *he* know? But when Jeff couldn't figure out how to attach the prosthesis and was already twenty minutes late for his first PT session with the new leg, Craig came into Jeff's room and, with an astounding amount of patience, showed him what to do.

"See, you turn the silicone liner inside out before you roll it onto the stump, but the key is to center it. You want to get the pin exactly centered—that can be tricky—so it fits right into the socket of the prosthesis," Craig explained. Then after he showed Jeff the whole procedure, Craig depressed the lock button and talked him through it all over again until he'd gotten it right on his own.

Now Jeff walks the next few steps toward the kid and feels, for the first time in weeks, fairly pleased with himself. "What's next?" he calls out.

Craig consults his clipboard and then his watch. "We still have time for some range of motion exercises if you're up for it."

"Damn straight, I'm up for it. Bring it on, son."

Jeff throws his arm around Craig's shoulder, and the two men make slow progress to one of the floor mats in the far corner of the room.

"You should be using the walker, Sarg—"

"Yeah, yeah," says Jeff, as Craig helps him to ease down onto the mat.

"Hold up a minute," Craig says. He grabs a green nylon strap from a peg on the wall. "Fifteen out to the side, okay? Both legs. Remember how?"

Jeff looks at Craig, a flicker of uncertainty.

"Okay, we'll do your good leg first. Out to the side."

Jeff pushes through the set with no problem, but when he switches to the other leg, he barely ekes out three reps before the pain kicks in.

"Take a break, sir," Craig says, squatting next to him. "It's okay."

Jeff lets out a long, slow breath and feels the familiar lump forming in his throat. He looks down at the edge of the bandaged stump that emerges from a pair of mesh running shorts, the alloy rod, and the ridiculous-looking sneaker. He remembers those trips to the K-Mart for school clothes with his mother, the humiliation of showing up on the first day of school with no-name sneakers, and his little brother, Carl, still too young to care and oblivious to the whole dilemma. He lets out a throaty chuckle at that but thumbs a tear from the corner of his eye.

"That's plenty for today, Sarg. You did great."

Jeff shakes his head no. He swings the leg out slow, slower than before, the pain liquid now. It travels in throbbing cycles—his hip, his thigh, his knee—but always winds up right back in the crushed femur, in the leg they'd taken at Landstuhl, and here it burns like the limbs they'd shoveled into stacks. Sweat drips from Jeff's face onto his T-shirt, the gray stains dark around the neckline, down the center of his chest.

"Sarg," Craig says.

Jeff pushes another rep. The hand holding the strap shakes hard. He smells the burning bodies, remembers how they'd retched, all of them, even the LT. He thinks about Lisa, imagines how the soft flesh of her breasts would feel under his calloused fingers. The bile rises in his throat.

"Sir," says Craig. The boy lays a meticulously clean hand on Jeff's shoulder. The boy's eyes are blue and clear. An innocent. Jeff lets the green strap fall to the mat. He feels his shoulders cave a little. Jeff's hand still shakes and he steadies it on the mat. He'll wait it out. He'll wait out the bastard if it takes all fucking day.

CHAPTER 38
STANDARD MAINTENANCE

Raifa twists halfway around toward Nermina, slings her arm over the seat, and slowly, very slowly, backs out of the driveway.

"Thanks for doing this," Nermina says. She drops her purse on the floor by her feet and then immediately retrieves it. She clutches the bag in her lap and brushes away the bits of crumbs and tissue that instantly cling to the brown suede as if attracted by a magnet.

"Stop thanking me," says Raifa. Nermina gazes out the window as Raifa commandeers her creaking Celica through a neighborhood of houses and yards as lovingly tended as Nermina's.

"It's just a standard maintenance. They said it'd be ready by—"

"It's fine," Raifa says. On the service road, she flicks on her right turn signal and inches toward the line of traffic streaming along the interstate. After an interminable length of time, Raifa finds a gap and then increases her speed just enough to merge into the slow lane without getting rear-ended. Nermina takes in her friend's placid profile and bites down gently on her lower lip.

"Well, I know how busy you and Samir—"

"I told you, it's no trouble."

The two women are silent then. Nermina knows Raifa will wait for her opening, just as she'd done with the traffic.

Her heart pounding, Nermina had awakened at dawn to one thought, one truth: Carl Ingram's flight had landed in Portland this morning. Of all people, it was Lisa who informed her of this development. She'd been contrite, said Jeff's mom was the one who arranged it. Lisa thought Nermina would want to know. And since Lisa's call two days before, she'd wanted to talk with Raifa. Raifa would know what to do. But now Nermina's not even sure she's ready to hear her friend's advice.

"How's Taki making out?" Nermina asks finally. She sits back against the cloth-covered seat for the first time since they left her driveway and takes a deep breath now that Raifa has finally reached the minimum speed limit.

Raifa laughs, throaty and full, a laugh that had always made Nermina envious for its ease. "They're buying a dishwasher and garbage disposal at Sears today. Samir's going to help Taki and Meredith install them."

"That's nice," says Nermina. Seeing Raifa so happy allows her to put her own worries aside, at least for the moment. "Is the place ready for them to move in yet?" Nermina knows she's stalling now, but gives herself a pass.

"They've got all the other plumbing in."

"Is the drywall up?"

"I think so."

Now Nermina smiles despite her worries. She knows Raifa could care less about such details—whether a house is habitable or not. What she cares about is that her son has finally found 'a nice girl.' They'll have a house of their own and then lots of babies for her to fuss over.

"Well, that's important," Nermina says thoughtfully. "You don't want them to be living with all that dust. Believe me, I've been there—"

"Yeah, I remember. I was there, too." Raifa keeps her hands tight on the wheel. Even in profile Nermina can make out the look of pride on Raifa's face.

"I know that," Nermina says. She remembers how she and Raifa would sit on the front steps while Samir and the others hammered and sawed and drilled. Atika running around in the muddy front yard with Raifa's children. She'd watched the little bungalow transform from a moldy, broken-down shack into the immaculate home her daughter grew up in. "It seems like such a long time ago," she says. "Another lifetime." She thinks how much easier it had been to mother Atika back then, how much easier to lie to her.

"It really was." Raifa laughs again, softly this time. She flicks on her signal and, after a slow, wide-angled turn into the Toyota dealership, circumnavigates the entire lot. Nermina sees Atika and Taki and Sabrina, all of them scrubbed clean and sound asleep on Raifa and Samir's bed. The ceiling fan paddling above them while the adults drank wine and told stories late into the night. It had taken Samir almost two years to finish the renovations but it had been worth every moment of waiting. Nermina tries to imagine Carl sitting with her and Atika on the back deck of their house now or at the kitchen table. Carl in the home she'd created for Atika. For their daughter.

"And now Samir gets to do it all over again for Taki and Meredith," Nermina says.

Raifa begins a second loop around the lot, passing the service bay without notice. "He loves doing this kind of work. Don't let him tell you—"

"Wait! Park there." Nermina gestures to an open space in front of the showroom. She sucks in her breath as Raifa inches into the space with barely a couple of inches between the driver's side of her dented Celica and the brand-new Prius on her left.

Nermina opens her own door slowly, careful not to bang the BMW to her right, and steps out of the car. "You don't mind waiting a minute? I'll just go check—"

Raifa flicks her hand, a gesture of disregard. "I'll wait—"

"You sure?"

Raifa pulls the keys from the ignition and tosses them in the seat Nermina has just vacated. "Go see what they say. I'm *waiting*." Raifa sets her face into a stern look she might give one of her adult children.

Her hand flat on the roof of the car, Nermina ducks her head inside. "Okay," she says. "Be right back."

Nermina's Prius is still two from the top of the list. Raifa and Nermina, each with a cup of strong coffee, sit across from one another in the dealership's café. A soundtrack of ambient music wafts in and out of the noise—a screeching blender, the occasional voice on the loudspeaker calling a customer to the service desk or a salesperson to the showroom.

Raifa leans back in her chair. Nermina sees how the fabric has frayed along the neckline of Raifa's T-shirt. From the cut, a deep V, and the color, bright pink, Nermina determines the shirt once belonged to Sabrina. Her eyes alight on the Victoria's Secret logo over Raifa's left breast, and the incongruity makes Nermina smile. Most days Raifa wears the same bland palette of beiges and browns, the same shapeless items from one season to the next.

"What?" Raifa says.

"I'm sorry." Nermina shakes her head. "I was just thinking..."

Raifa raises an eyebrow—this gesture as far along the scale of sarcasm as she's apt to travel. "So, are you going to tell me what's going on?" Raifa smiles, passes her hand over the wisps of hair that have come loose from her ponytail. Nermina notes the patch of gray that's claimed territory at her friend's right temple.

"I wanted to...but I just..." Nermina begins. "That's really why I called..."

With the side of her pinky, Raifa sweeps a few grains of sugar into a little pile on the paper napkin in front of her. She touches her pinky to her tongue, presses it to the granules, then touches the pinky to her tongue again. Nermina watches her. "So, talk to me," Raifa says when she finally looks up.

"This is bad..." Nermina wraps the fingers of both hands

around her Styrofoam cup of coffee. She thinks about their 'lessons'—almost comical as she remembers them now—Raifa playing the male role. Nermina batting her eyes and pouting. A plan of seduction Nermina never would have been able to execute on her own. "It's about Carl," she says. But then speaking his name out loud makes her situation real again and not funny at all. She sees her daughter's angry face, feels the tug of guilt as it forms a sickening knot in the pit of her stomach.

Raifa's expression returns to its natural state of candor. "What *about* Carl?" she asks, her tone serious now. There had been perhaps a handful of occasions when the women discussed Carl over the years, and these only when Atika had truly worn Nermina down. But even then, she could never have imagined contacting Carl, inviting him into her life with Atika.

"He's here in Portland for his brother."

Raifa's face registers confusion. "His brother?"

"Jeff. *Ingram.* He's one of my patients." Nermina tamps down a surge of annoyance as Raifa considers this information in silence.

"Carl is Jeff Ingram's brother," Nermina continues slowly as if she were speaking to a five-year-old. "He's in Portland...who knows for how long...to help out with Jeff's care." Nermina feels the ache behind her eyelids. She'd slept only fitfully the night before. "Are you listening to me?" She nearly shouts this into the din of the café.

Raifa reaches across the table. She places one cool hand over Nermina's. "Did you really think you'd never see him again?"

Nermina swallows hard. "I hadn't thought about it. I honestly hadn't. I didn't think I'd have to—"

"But that's a little...unrealistic, don't you think?" Nermina's jaw tightens as she watches Raifa's face—cool, placid, unchanged.

"Well...no, not really." Nermina understands there isn't another soul on earth who would ask her this question. With Shira, she'd buried the most important details of Carl Ingram's role in her life. In Atika's. When Shira first inquired about "the father" Nermina told her a half-truth: "I slept with the man a couple of times. I didn't know I was pregnant till after he'd gone." And when Shira pressed further, Nermina replied, "No, I don't *want* to find him." That part had always been true. A flush creeps across Nermina's throat.

"But now he's here in Portland," says Raifa calmly. "So, are you asking me what to do about this?"

Raifa's tone is so rational Nermina wants to scream. "No," Nermina says. She pulls her hands out of Raifa's grasp. "I don't know. At first I wanted to..." She looks past Raifa to the little clusters of families milling around out in the showroom beyond the café. These people seem universally happy. Normal. Everyone happy and normal and going about their lives without a care. "I don't know what to do," she says, unable to meet her friend's eyes.

"So, you haven't talked to him yet?"

"No!" An elderly couple at the next table cranes their heads toward Nermina. "That's what I'm saying. I don't even know if I should."

Raifa turns toward the couple and gives them each a polite nod. "Okay," she begins calmly. "If he's already here in

Portland...*and* he might be here for a while—maybe a long while—then what would be the harm? People change. You're a different person now. Maybe he is too."

Nermina forces her voice to an acceptable volume. "The harm is...it could ruin everything." She tells herself that, as a mother, Raifa will understand this. But Raifa has been married to the same man since she was twenty. She has two children with this man. She has a husband. Nermina has one daughter and that is all. That is all that has ever mattered. "Maybe he won't even want to know about Atika," she says. "Maybe he won't believe that she's his."

"Why don't you give him the chance to decide?"

Nermina thinks she detects a hint of righteousness in Raifa's suggestion. Still, in the deluge of thoughts that have overwhelmed her these last few days, this one had never occurred to her. "I don't know," she says. "I'm not sure if I really want to."

When she'd first decided to get pregnant—Raifa had raised no objections. She'd said it was a worthy decision—not one she'd make for herself—but one she understood. She told her to choose wisely, to be careful. So why is Raifa betraying her now?

"He came here to be with his brother...but maybe there's another reason—" Raifa begins.

Nermina swats her hand in the space between them. "I don't believe—"

"What don't you believe?" Raifa takes the lid off her coffee cup and dumps in another packet of sugar, stirs the thick mixture with her finger.

Nermina envies Raifa's faith. She remembers the cool aqua

tiles of the mosque her family had visited only on holy days, but she'd found no reason to put her trust—blind trust—in any sort of God once they were all gone. Once they'd all been taken from her.

"For one, I don't believe in chance or fate or—" she begins.

"Believe what you want," Raifa says evenly. She looks past Nermina, makes a sweep of the café customers before returning her attention. "What about Atika? Are you going to give *her* a choice in this?"

Nermina's stomach clenches tighter. She can see Atika stomping around her bedroom, furious, slamming the door and locking it. She knows Raifa's intentions are good—Atika is old enough to decide, has every right to know her father if that's what she wants—but the question feels like a rebuke. A montage of quarrels flickers like a slideshow. Nermina sees the smirk on her daughter's face, the hurt underneath. Atika had begged her. She wanted to know her father.

"I don't want to set her up for a big disappointment."

"She's a big girl," Raifa says. "She's probably a lot stronger than you think. A lot more level-headed." Nermina considers their latest argument, Atika hammering away at a similar point, and she knows Raifa is right but she doesn't want to admit this now.

"And what if he wants nothing to do with either one of us?" Nermina bends over the table miserably, her chin resting in one cupped hand.

"Then you're no worse off than you were before." Nermina sees nothing in Raifa's face beyond a candid logic, nothing to make her think she's over-simplifying what had seemed an impossibly complex puzzle at four o'clock that morning.

"He might be angry," Nermina says. The flush on her throat has traveled to her face, her chest. She wishes she could crawl out of her skin.

"Yes, he might be."

"And Atika—"

"She'll probably be angry," Raifa says. "At least at first."

Nermina bites her lower lip. "I just don't know..."

Raifa leans forward and Nermina sees in her friend's expression the same look she'd turn toward her children, her husband, toward Atika. It's a look of unconditional love that Nermina has no reason to mistrust.

"The choice is in Allah's hands now," Raifa says.

Nermina concedes a sad smile. "No," she says, "that's not exactly true."

CHAPTER 39
BROTHERS' REUNION

The brothers lean against a chest-high concrete wall in the hospital courtyard. The area reeks of spent cigarettes. A row of dead arborvitaes line one of the concrete walls. Patients and visitors have turned the long stone planter into an ashtray, butts sprouting among pansies and salvia. Nearly the same height and build, the brothers conform to an identical stance, arms crossed in front of their chests, legs wide apart.

But Carl's eyes are drawn again to Jeff's prosthetic leg. The thing emerges from a pair of mesh workout shorts, titanium rod stuck inside a Nike running shoe. A white athletic sock pools around the top of the sneaker. On the good leg the sock comes midway up his calf, still thinner than it should be, but at least this one is normal, Carl thinks.

He pulls his attention away from the damned leg, swallows

hard, a tinny taste at the back of his throat. It had taken *this* to bring him back. Carl hears his mother's voice again on the phone, pleading, biting back whatever anger or disappointment she may have felt toward her baby boy. Carl listening, resentful, fearful, the old shame revived in an instant.

Jeff brings a cigarette to his lips, sucks in a long hit as though it's his last. He squints through the stream of smoke and surveys the parking lot again. As Carl waves the smoke away, he sees in his brother's profile a near replica of his own. Same square jawline—and if you get close enough—the same dimple to the right of their full lips.

"She's here," Jeff says. He jerks his head to the right, cigarette tight between his lips.

Carl turns and watches his sister-in-law push a double stroller across the asphalt wasteland. Jeff waves the hand with the cigarette, a brief motion resembling a salute. Getting closer, Lisa flashes them a fake, beauty queen smile Carl remembers.

"Hey," Jeff says. He drops the cigarette to the pavement and grounds it out with his good foot. Lisa receives her husband's peck on the cheek. She bends down in front of the double stroller and peers into carbon-copy faces. One child is sound asleep with his thumb in his mouth. The other reaches out a dimpled hand to her. Carl watches Lisa's face light up, a real smile now.

"Okay, Pooh Bears, ready to go see Daddy!" Lisa says.

The awake baby waves both of his chubby hands. "See Daddy," he parrots.

Lisa turns her gaze to Carl, a smirk ghosting her upper lip.

"Hey Lisa, how's it going?"

"Never better." Carl feels his sister-in-law's eyes travel the full length of his body and when they linger beyond the point of politeness, he matches her stubborn stare. For a split second he gets that weird *deja vu* feeling, and then he's grateful when a gaunt, older man—his wrinkled arms covered in tattoos— wheels his IV pole up to Jeff.

"Got a light, man?" Jeff hands the man a pack of matches, waits while the guy blows a stream of smoke into the air.

"Thanks, buddy," the guy says to Jeff. He nods to Lisa, drags the pole a few steps away from them, then slumps down against the wall to smoke.

Lisa beams another showy smile at Jeff. "We're not staying long, honey. How about we get the kids inside." Her voice matches the same register she uses with the twins. Carl shoves his hands into the front pockets of his jeans, squats down in front of his nephews. He squints up at Lisa. "Tell me again which is which. Damn, they look alike!"

"They're *identical*," says Lisa.

"Duh!" says Carl. He looks from one boy's face to the other.

"Look," Lisa says, as though she were talking to one of her children. She unfastens the straps on Tyler's side of the stroller. The boy's eyelids flutter and then, wide-eyed, he looks from his mother's face to his uncle's. A half-beat later, the child sends up a long, ear-splitting wail.

"It's okay, it's okay sweetie, time to wake up anyway," she says. She lifts the crying child from the stroller and cuddles him to her shoulder. Carl stands up beside her. "Look," she says and gently smoothes back the damp curls from the boy's forehead. "See that, Uncle Carl?" She runs her finger back and forth over a constellation of three dark freckles on her son's porcelain skin. "If you ever get stuck, that's how you can tell the difference. This is Tyler."

"Cool," says Carl. He reaches out and ruffles the boy's hair.

"Honey?" says Lisa, her eyes steady on Jeff's. "We have a lot to do today. Can we head upstairs now?"

Carl watches his brother's impassive face, then turns and snaps Lisa a quick salute.

"Yes ma'am," he says, smiling. He holds out his arms to the sleepy-eyed child. Tyler clings to Lisa's neck. "Hey, buddy, how 'bout a ride with Uncle Carl?" he ventures.

Tyler squirms in Lisa's arms and he reaches out his dimpled hands, palms up, toward Carl. A look of resignation washes out a poorly concealed smirk. Carl lifts the child to his shoulders, his hands then on Tyler's knees, steadying him, as a half-beat of alarm flashes in the boy's eyes then disappears. A guileless smile spreads across the boy's face.

"I got'cha," says Carl. "You okay, buddy? Ready to roll?"

The boy sinks his hands into Carl's hair and gurgles his approval.

The elevator doors open and the odors of disinfectant and warmed-over meatloaf hit Carl full on. He swallows hard and wonders how Jeff—or anyone—could ever get used to that smell. Lisa leads the march down a poorly lit hallway, past the nurses' station, and through a door that says "Family Conference Room." The room is small, its pea-soup-green walls reminding Carl of the series of dank youth hostel dormitories he'd bunked in throughout those first years of his travels. Now the smells of coffee grounds, popcorn, and Lean

Cuisine lasagna take over, an improvement, Carl thinks, but the combination of all this in such close quarters gives him a closed-in feeling that turns his stomach.

Jeff ambles in after Carl and slumps into one of the three, plaid-covered, heavy wood-framed sofas. The furniture resembles the kind of stuff that had been in their family's rec room, the basement their father haphazardly remodeled when they were kids, but never finished.

Crouching down on the mottled carpet, Carl grasps the fleshy sides of Tyler's waist, lifts the toddler over his head, and sets him down gently in a smooth arc. He feels Lisa's eyes on him, feels the current of—What? Disapproval? Outright hostility? Whatever it is, it's coming through loud and clear. They'd never liked one another. This he knew. But now he also knows, with these boys, the idea that his brother's kids were connected to him, too, that there's something else he needs to account for. He can't name it exactly, but when he feels the pressure of Tyler's little hands clinging to his pant leg, it seems he has no choice except to...well, to accommodate her. That's the word Tessa would use here.

"Up, up, up," Tyler chants but, before Carl can respond, Lisa takes the child's hand. She coaxes him toward the ramshackle pile of toys that Ethan has upended from a red plastic milk crate in the middle of the room.

"Here we go, sweetie," Lisa says. "Look, they have lots of nice books here." She pulls out a square picture book with thick cardboard pages and holds it gingerly by the spine. Before handing it to Tyler, though, she swabs the pages with an antiseptic wipe she's pulled from a package in her bag. Kneeling down so that she's eye-level with her children, she gives the rest of the toys a quick once over with the wipe. When Carl puts out his hand to help her up, she waves him off. A brisk smile that could have been that smirk again appears, then vanishes. Carl's jaw tightens. He shoves his hands into the front pockets of his jeans, looks down at the toes of his work boots, and when he looks up, Lisa has crossed to the other side of the room. A set of white laminate cabinets, countertop, microwave oven, and mini fridge hunker along the wall and a white laminate table and four chairs are shoved into the only remaining space. Carl watches her unpack, swiftly, efficiently, like fucking Mary Poppins, enough neatly cut squares of peanut butter and jelly sandwiches to feed them all.

Jeff, his good leg resting on the scarred coffee table, leaves through a *Sports Illustrated* he picked up from the pile of magazines and newspapers.

"Lunch time," Lisa says. She scoops Ethan onto her lap and hands him a square of sandwich.

"Honey?" she adds in a syrupy tone, when Jeff doesn't snap to. His eyes remain fixed on the pages for another long moment before he tosses the magazine onto the pile and turns blankly toward his wife. He stands, a little unsteadily Carl sees, walks the few steps to where Tyler sits with the book, and bends down to pick him up. The move is awkward and Jeff winces, shifting his weight to the good leg. When he lifts Tyler to his chest the boy opens his mouth, hesitates a moment, and then lets out a long, piercing wail.

"For goodness sakes, Jeff!" Lisa says. She's instantly there, her lean, tanned arms pulling her son from his father's embrace, her legs solid and muscular as she sways back and forth, cradling the child against her body.

"It's okay, sweetie. Daddy didn't mean to scare you." As if on cue, the child instantly quiets.

"Jesus, Lisa. What do you want from me?" Jeff stands, a full head taller than his wife.

She smoothes back the strawberry-blond curls from Tyler's forehead, turns an angelic face to her husband.

"Sorry, honey. We all have a lot to get used to, I guess." She pauses a moment, then adds: "Now that you're home."

Jeff glares at her, his eyes unblinking, his hands fisted against his thighs.

Carl watches all of this, takes it in. He thinks about the way he'd wake up in felted darkness and hear his parents sniping at one another, his mother's voice bitter and brutal, a full register lower than the one she'd use with him and Jeff in the morning. She'd hand them their lunch money, send them out the door as though the previous night's fighting had never taken place. In the night, their father's baritone also carried a special quality. An angry desperation that now, Carl realizes, would have been too heartbreaking to witness in the daylight hours. As nasty as his father had been with him and Jeff, the old man had always saved the worst of it for their mother. But it was also with her that their father had seemed most vulnerable, the belligerence a shitty cover-up for whatever disappointment, whatever doubt, he'd carried onto that battlefield of marriage with their mother.

Carl had only just begun to understand this. Or if not to understand it, then to perceive it on some gut level, he had to admit, he'd likely never have recognized without Tessa's persistence. Carl's guilt swells now, a hard lump in his throat.

He should have done more for his mother. Especially after the old man died. He'd felt for her then. He feels for her now. But there was always something lingering there between them that kept him from fully trusting her. Maybe even from fully loving her as he thought he should. That she'd stayed with the old man all those years. That she'd *taken* it from him.

He tries to remember exactly how Tessa put it. The fighting, the sniping, that was the only way his parents knew how to be with one another. It was embedded. That was how Tessa explained it. And now Carl sees that same thing happening here with Jeff and Lisa. He feels bad for his brother. He sees things going south between these two. But what can he do? What right does he have to butt in now? He'd promised his mother he'd be there for Jeff. Well, he's here now. Damned if he knows what comes next.

Then Lisa claps her hands. "Okay, everyone. We've got lots of goodies here." She beams at Jeff and turns the same beauty queen smile on Carl. "Let's eat," she says.

CHAPTER 40
TILLIE'S DINER

Nermina parks her car in one of the head-in angled spaces in front of Tillie's Diner. The old-fashioned silver-clad building, shaded by tall spruce and oaks, is one of Nermina's favorite places in the city. She has sweet memories of spooning oatmeal into Atika's mouth while Raifa scolded Taki and Sabrina for tearing open sugar packets and dumping them into their water glasses. And in recent years she and Atika have indulged in huge Sunday breakfasts—stacks of blueberry pancakes, sausage and eggs—a ritual as important to Nermina as church for the most devout. They'd sit at a favorite table, surrounded by boisterous families and wan college students still hung over from the night before.

Today Nermina murmurs hellos to the regulars at the counter as the hostess leads her to a booth next to a big window overlooking the street. Though Carl isn't due for another ten minutes, she peers out, her stomach fluttering like it had the day he'd first spoken to her at the Java City Café in the hospital. But today her anxiety is tied to an entirely different fear. She startles when Lily, a twenty-something waitress with a platinum-blond beehive hairdo, leans over the table with a pot of coffee.

"Sorry 'bout that," Lily says. "Didn't mean to sneak up on you." She holds the coffee pot aloft and raises her penciled eyebrows.

"Sure," says Nermina. She forces a smile while Lily expertly fills her mug. "Thanks. I'm waiting," she says, trying her best to sound casual. "I'm waiting for someone."

"Take your time," Lily says before hustling off to the next booth.

Nermina stirs in a packet of sugar and some cream and when she looks up again she sees Carl coming through the door. Her hand shoots out in a wave. Feeling immediately silly, she looks back down at her coffee and stirs it intently. And then Carl is there at the table, some gray among his sand-colored hair and much shorter than when they'd first met. Even so, she sees the image of his younger self—a black, leather lace around his neck, what looks like a lacquered shark's tooth hanging at the base of his throat. With his face a weathered bronze and wrinkles fanning out around his eyes, she thinks he looks now like an affable, middle-aged surfer.

"Hi," Carl says. "Am I late?"

"Oh, no. I was...well, *hi*," she says, her voice sounding to her like a nervous middle-schooler's.

Nermina stands and they come together in an awkward

half embrace. Carl smells of Dial soap and his flannel shirt and jeans, though wrinkled, seem recently washed. She'd told him who she was on the phone, reminded him about their time together all those years ago. And she explained her connection with Jeff and how she'd discovered they were brothers.

Now she sits down gratefully in the diner booth with the wide expanse of flecked Formica between them.

The bee-hived waitress arrives as Carl folds himself into the booth. "Coffee?" she asks. She gives Carl a pretty, red-lipsticked smile.

"Yeah," says Carl. He picks up the plastic-coated menu and lays it back down on the table. Lily looks from Carl to Nermina. "Need some time?" Nermina's eyes meet Carl's. She can't imagine consuming food now, though her stomach is empty. It's lunchtime. She'd eaten half a peach for breakfast before tossing the rest into the trash bin.

"Yeah, give us a few minutes," Carl says. And once the waitress retreats, "So this is weird, huh?" Carl shows Nermina a crooked smile, his full bottom lip protruding slightly, just as she remembered. We dated a couple of times, she'd said on the phone. *Dated.* Carl hadn't missed a beat. "Yeah, Bosnia, right? I remember you."

"I know," Nermina says now. She imagines Carl will expect she wants to talk about Jeff. She hadn't said otherwise on the phone. All she'd said was she wanted to meet. "I appreciate your coming here..." She hears the absurd formality in her tone. She smiles then—deploying a look of calibrated compassion—just as she would with a family member of any of her patients. "Well, it's good to see you, Carl."

"Yeah, you too." Carl takes a sip of his black coffee. He clears his throat. "So, you're a nurse now? That's great."

"A DNP," Nermina says, and when she sees the blank look on Carl's face, "I have a doctorate as a nurse practitioner in psychiatric medicine." She flushes then, hoping she hasn't embarrassed him. "It sounds like a much bigger deal than it really is. I counsel patients like Jeff."

"No, that's really impressive. That's awesome...I remember you were going to apply for some kind of nursing school..."

"Are you hungry?" Nermina asks. "I already ate, but feel free..." She waves toward the menu, again feeling silly.

"I'm always hungry," Carl says. He picks up the menu. "What's good here?"

"My daughter and I always get the blueberry pancakes." Nermina's mouth goes dry. *My daughter*. She has no idea how these words have escaped her lips.

Carl looks up from the menu. "You have a kid? That's cool. How old?"

"She's sixteen."

"Wow," Carl says. His eyes dart to Nermina's hands. They're wrapped tightly around her coffee mug. "Married?" he asks.

Okay, Nermina thinks, this is happening. She'd meant to give herself some time. She'd ease herself—and Carl—into the conversation slowly, carefully. She shakes her head, produces a thin smile. "Nope, not married."

Carl takes what seems a long time to consider this. "Divorced?"

"No, never married."

"Hmm," Carl says. "That's cool, I guess."

Nermina feels a jolt of indignation. Was he *judging* her?

"I'll try your blueberry pancakes," he says a moment later when Lily returns. "Side of bacon." He smiles as he hands her the menu.

"You got it," she says.

Nermina's stomach turns a little flip. "Nothing for me," she says.

"I like kids," Carl says thoughtfully. "Just met my nephews for the first time." He shakes his head and his smile now—wide and genuine—lights up his suntanned face. "They're awesome little dudes."

Nermina takes a deep breath. "That's so nice. It's good you've made that connection." She remembers how she'd felt that first night with Carl in her bed, so certain she'd get what she wanted. If she'd loved him then, even a little, she'd surely been too broken to know it. She glances out the window, at the row of bicycles, each tipped into their slots along the rack, and then turns her eyes back to Carl. "It's really good you're here for Jeff," she says.

Carl's smile clouds over. He picks up the saltshaker from the chrome container against the window and rolls it back and forth between his hands. When Nermina says nothing further he sets it down on the table carefully.

"Just being a good brother," Carl says finally.

"You are," Nermina says. She clears her throat. "You're a good brother to come here now."

"Jeff, man...I know that's what—"

"Carl, listen. That's not why I asked you to meet me here." Nermina feels the damp fabric of her T-shirt clinging to her back. She leans forward in the vinyl booth. Carl's face—same square jaw as Jeff's, same hazel eyes—looks almost frightened now. "It's kind of crazy, the way things work out sometimes..." She swallows. "But here's the thing..."

She remembers Carl's hair had smelled like coconut and that his body next to hers in that tiny bed had provided an odd and completely unexpected sense of comfort. She'd trusted him for no good reason. He looks at her now, his full lips nearly pouting, child-like.

"*What*?" he says.

"When you left Portland..." Nermina leans her elbows on the table and rests her chin in her hands. The waitress arrives and sets down the pancakes, a smaller plate of bacon, a pitcher of syrup, in front of Carl. "Can I get you two anything else?" Nermina looks up and murmurs no though she's not quite certain she's said this aloud.

"'K," says Lily. She gives Carl a wide smile. "Enjoy."

Carl appraises the food and then Nermina's face. "What the hell's the matter?" He pushes the plates toward the middle of the big table. "Look, about Jeff, I told that social worker lady I'd do my best. I've got a life, too, you know. I have commitments—"

"This isn't about Jeff," Nermina says. "It's about you."

A look of belligerence washes over Carl's features, a look Nermina recalls without hesitation. "What *about* me?" he says.

"My daughter," Nermina says quietly. "Her name is Atika and she's sixteen years old."

Carl tilts his head. Again, Nermina feels the belligerent glare trained directly at her.

"What're you talking about?"

Nermina looks down at her hands. She spreads her fingers wide on the table in front of her. She finds a few grains of sugar and worries these with her fingertip for a second or two. "She's yours, too," Nermina says.

Carl grips the edge of the table, straightens his arms so that he's sitting bolt upright against the back of the booth. He shakes his head. "I'm not sure I heard you right."

"I know this isn't..." Nermina tents her hands in front of her on the table, presses her fingertips together until they turn white. "I didn't tell you then. I didn't..."

"What the *fuck*?" Carl mutters. "What do you want?"

"I don't want anything. I needed to tell you. I just needed you to know..."

Carl picks up the saltshaker again and Nermina fears for a moment he might throw it. "You wait sixteen years. Why bother to tell me now? Why the fuck should I believe you?"

Nermina forces herself to swallow, to breathe. "I'm telling you the truth," she says. "I have no reason not to. Atika—"

Carl flings his right arm along the top of the booth and stares hard at Nermina. He grips the vinyl with one large hand. "Jesus," he says.

"I'm sorry Carl. I see I should have—"

"Forget it," he says, and Nermina remembers how quickly he'd turned on her that day on the mountain, his stony silence as the truck rounded the switchbacks on their way back to the city.

Carl slides out of the booth, digs some cash out of his front pocket, and throws a crumpled twenty on the table. Nermina watches him stalk by the counter—filled now with lunch customers—and the row of booths. She hears the bells jingle above the door as he stalks out onto the shade-covered street. When Lily comes back to fill her coffee, Nermina places one trembling hand over the top of the mug. She shakes her head no, the tourniquet of her throat rendering her mute this time without question.

CHAPTER 41
COMPOSTING

It's Saturday morning and Nermina is not on call. The whole day lies ahead of her but she has no idea how to occupy her time. She stands in the hallway outside Atika's door. She'd hoped the two of them might wander through the farmer's market this morning, the way they'd always done. Nermina corrects herself: the way they'd done before Keith. But it's already ten o'clock. Her daughter's door is closed and, uninterrupted, Atika will likely sleep till noon. Nermina doesn't want to wake her.

She begins down the staircase, stepping silently the way she'd done when Atika was a baby, asleep in the tiny room they shared at Raifa and Samir's house. Back then she'd hoped to steal a little time of her own for studying while her baby slept. And now? She decides that the more her daughter sleeps, the more time she'll have to figure out what to say about Carl and how to say it.

In the kitchen she pours herself another cup of coffee and sits down at the scarred oak table that was her first possession in her very own house. She remembers how she and Raifa had shouldered it onto the porch and how Samir had to come over and remove the front door from its hinges to get the thing inside. There are muted streaks of colored marker on its surface and glitter in the center crack where the table comes apart to add an extra leaf. The finish is worn away in places where she and Atika had rolled out mounds of Play-Doh, and real dough for baking cookies. She spreads her fingers wide, flat against the clean, grained surface. How many hours have the two of them spent at this table?

But Nermina's heart sinks when she muses on their last argument. This wasn't one of the silly spats that spring up daily now like milkweed among her flowers. She'd wanted to talk about the condoms lying at the bottom of Atika's laundry hamper. Her daughter, her beautiful baby girl, is having sex with a boy. With Keith, Atika's boyfriend. She'd wanted to have a rational conversation with her daughter, but it had all gone wrong. Atika twisted the conversation. Atika lashed out. And then *she'd* lashed out. The worst part—Nermina sees now—is that she'd had the perfect opportunity to tell her daughter the truth. Instead, she wasted it. Carl's angry face at the diner, her daughter's angry tirade the week before, this convergence swirls and swirls through her thoughts. She feels the inevitable weight of her long-ago lie pushing her forward. But where?

Nermina scrapes her chair back from the table. She stands

and walks to the sink. She runs the water long enough to rinse out the remains of her coffee, then dries her hands on a spotless white dishtowel that hangs on the stove. She looks out the French doors to the deck and scans the yard. The wheelbarrow, filled with grass clippings and leaves, stands next to the compost pile, exactly where her daughter had left it two days before.

She slips on the pair of old Keds that she keeps by the door and lets herself out. The wet grass soaks through the thin canvas of her sneakers as she crosses the yard. When she tries to lift the handles of the wheelbarrow to flip its contents into the pile, the rain-drenched load won't budge. She stomps over to the squat garden shed just a few feet away, unlatches the hasp, and pulls open the wooden door. The musty odor of soil and fertilizer hangs heavy as she ducks inside. She lifts a long-handled shovel from its hook. Then searching for the pitchfork, she remembers Atika left this out in the rain as well—left it there to rust—leaning against the chicken-wire cage that holds the compost.

And then instead of ducking through the shed's low doorway, as she should have done, as she's *always* done, Nermina feels the hard thwack of a two-by-four against her forehead. The blow brings tears to her eyes. She curses her own stupidity and then Atika's carelessness as she ducks and makes her way out of the shed. She stomps across the yard, then bends down, one hand against the screen-door frame, and peels off her muddy sneakers. These, she tosses next to the doormat.

In the bathroom mirror she sees the purple bruise and egg-shaped bump already rising. She winces as she holds the ice pack to her forehead. Her head throbs. Then, with no further thought, she crosses the hall to her daughter's room and pounds on her door. Nermina hears Atika's feet stamp down, first on the rug next to her bed, and then onto the hardwood floor as she crosses the room. The girl opens the door, blinks at her mother, and then crawls back into the tangle of bedding. The room smells to Nermina like candle wax, spent matches, dirty laundry, soured milk.

"Get up," she says. Nermina sits down on the edge of the bed, feeling the weight and the warmth of her daughter, curled up beneath the covers like a snail, her back to Nermina. Inscrutable. "It's time to get up," Nermina says. She glances at the clock on Atika's nightstand. "It's late."

"What is it?" Atika presses her face into the pillow. "What happened to your head?"

"What happened is you left all the garden stuff out to get rained on."

Atika throws off the rumpled covers and sits up to face her mother. Sleep crusts the corners of her eyes, the mass of coppery curls coiled into a messy bundle on top of her head. She looks remarkably young to Nermina, a baby still.

"What's that got to do with anything?"

Nermina's eyes travel to the tiny hummingbird tattoo on her daughter's left shoulder. The blue-green creature hovers near the thin strap of her camisole. Nermina had been furious when she first spotted it. But it was too late. She'd had to let it go. She couldn't go back and remake each of her daughter's decisions. Just as she couldn't remake her own.

"I had to go in the shed—"

"And that was my fault?"

"Yes," Nermina says, "I shouldn't have been out there in the first place."

"That's crap." Atika grabs for the alarm clock and holds it in front of her face for a split second before setting it back down on the nightstand. "It's not late. It's early," she says. "You *like* being out there at the crack of dawn."

"It's not early and you have chores," Nermina says. "You're helping me with the mess you left." She holds her daughter's incredulous gaze. "Now," she says. Nermina gets up from the bed and stands, hands on her hips, until Atika kicks the blankets to the floor and scrambles out of bed.

"Fine," Atika says. She grabs the hoodie from the back of her chair and wiggles both arms into the sleeves, then shoves her feet into a pair of Adidas sandals on the floor. "Let's go." Arms crossed in front of her, Atika stands at the foot of her bed. Nermina notices the pair of boxers her daughter wears, green-and-blue plaid, the elastic rolled so that the waistband stretches across Atika's narrow hips. She wonders if these are her daughter's or if they belong to the boy. "You'll be cold," Nermina says.

"I won't."

Wordlessly, mother and daughter shovel the rain-soaked leaves and clippings from the wheelbarrow onto the heap. Nermina's forearms and shoulders ache. The exertion warms her. The bump on her forehead stretches tight. The pain eases some. Then Nermina hands Atika the pitchfork. She watches as her daughter turns up the thick, dark sludge and with it the rotting smell that is not unlike human waste.

Her daughter hoists the muck again, folding in the bright-green grass clippings at the top. Nermina breathes in the thick, earthy smell of it. She tries to imagine how her life with Atika will change. She tries to imagine how the two of them would make room for Carl. The equation sprawls out to infinity. There is no clean answer, nothing exact, always a remainder. Carl—Atika's father—is the remainder in the problem. No, Nermina thinks, Carl is the X in the equation, the unknown. When Atika was little, that part had been simple. Children adapt. Children believe what they're told. Nermina sees the packets of condoms at the bottom of the hamper, the foil packets in bright primary colors like Mylar balloons from those long-ago birthday parties when her daughter would still allow such a silly indulgence. Atika is no longer a child.

Nermina walks the few steps to where her daughter still plunges the pitchfork into the muck. She places her hand on Atika's shoulder and the girl shakes her off.

"What's the matter?" Atika says. She shows Nermina a belligerent glare, but her cheeks are flushed, auburn corkscrews of hair cling to her forehead. Her daughter smells of sweat and mud and outdoors, just as she had when she was little. But Atika is no longer a child. She's nearly—but not quite—a grown woman.

"Now what?" Atika demands.

"That's good enough," Nermina says. "You should eat some breakfast. I'll make you something."

"I don't need you to make me something to eat. I'm not six." Atika stabs the pitchfork into the pile and strides toward the house. Nermina stalks after her, but stops short as Atika lets the screen door slam rather than holding it open for her mother. Again, Nermina kicks off the soaking Keds.

Inside, Atika stands in front of the open fridge. Nermina stands behind her. "What?" Atika asks without turning.

"Sit down," Nermina says. "You're being silly." Nermina reaches up, rests her hand along the top of the fridge door beside her daughter's. Atika ducks under Nermina's arm and leaves Nermina standing alone. Nermina pulls out eggs and milk, a package of English muffins, a jar of jelly, methodically setting each of these items on the counter.

Atika slides out a chair from the table, screeching its wooden legs on the floor. "Are you satisfied?"

Nermina turns from the counter to face her daughter. The knot in her stomach makes her want to climb the stairs and curl up under the covers the way Atika had done earlier. "Yes," she says. She sits down at the table across from her daughter, sits at the same spot she's occupied nearly every day for the past 12 years. But now she finds no comfort here. The awful ache in her gut tells her that everything is about to change, that there's nothing she can do now to stop it.

"Good," says Atika. "Now that you've ruined my morning—"

"Can you stop a minute? Can you just listen?"

Atika fixes her mother with a glare. "I don't know what you want."

"I want you to listen. We need to talk—"

"No, I already told you! Keith and I—"

"Atika!" Nermina hadn't meant to raise her voice and she catches herself now. "It's not about you and Keith."

Nermina holds her daughter's gaze a moment, then turns away. She bends her head and gingerly touches the bump on her forehead. The flesh is tender, sore. And then her index finger finds the scar at her hairline, traces it gently. She turns back to her daughter and takes a deep breath. She doesn't know where to begin and so she decides to leap, just as she and Mirsad had done, running and diving into the surf headlong, rather than prolonging the agony of wading through the still-cold Baltic each spring.

"You have a father," Nermina says. She's surprised that the words come so easily. Her daughter regards her in silence, thick like the mucky compost in the heap, impermeable. When Nermina speaks again her voice seems to come from far away: "Do you know what I'm saying?"

"I don't know. I'm not..." Atika's voice carries no trace of its earlier venom.

Until now, Nermina had only thought about Carl when Atika forced her there. In her mind's eye he'd remained just as he was the first time she'd noticed him—tall, muscular, handsome—and she'd chosen him for that alone. Sex with him had surprised her. That she'd enjoyed it then, even a little, this was a surprise.

"*Draga*—"

"Mama, I'm sorry. You really don't need to—"

"Listen to me." Nermina had given no thought to the kind of man Carl might turn out to be. She hadn't needed him to stay. She hadn't wanted him in her life then. Once she was pregnant, it didn't matter if he was there or not. It hadn't been so difficult to shut him out. It hadn't been so difficult at all.

Nermina takes both of her daughter's hands in her own. They're warm and damp, just like when she was a baby. Nermina remembers how she'd lift her from the crib, how it felt to have those tiny hands reaching up to her, to touch her face like a gift. "What I'm saying is... there was...someone. There was a man—"

"I know that. An anonymous man. Sperm. A man's sperm. Really—"

"No, I mean there was a man I *knew*," she says then. "A man I *know*." Nermina's forehead begins to throb again. Carl had been leaving Portland anyway. A new job some friend had gotten him. And then she was busy and overwhelmed with caring for her child and going back to school. Making a life for herself and her daughter. That was the only thing that mattered then. She'd never thought of Carl as Atika's father and this shames her now. She cringes as she remembers the constellation of emotion his face had revealed at the diner. There'd been more than anger, she realizes now. There'd been hurt. There'd been pain.

"Oh," says Atika. Beginning to register the meaning of her mother's words, her eyes are wide now, riveted on Nermina. "*Really?*"

"Atika—"

"All that crap you told me. How you'd chosen the donor sperm. For all the right genes. For all the right reasons. You *said* that."

"It didn't happen the way I said it did."

"Oh really? No sperm bank? No artificial insemination?" Atika's grimace dares Nermina to continue. "There was a man, but he didn't matter to me. I just—"

Atika jumps up from the table nearly upending the chair. She stands against the kitchen counter, her fingers gripping the edge of the marble slab behind her. Her cheeks flush pink, just as they'd been outside.

"Wait! So, you just got pregnant with some *guy*. Is that what you're saying? That I was a mistake?"

"Absolutely not!" Nermina shouts. "You were planned, Atika. I planned for you. I *chose* him," she pleads now, hearing the absurdity in her argument. She wishes she could go back to before she'd started to unravel her life this way. It would have been difficult though not impossible to perpetuate the lie. She could have left things just as they were.

But Carl had come to Portland for Jeff. Despite their differences, despite their estrangement, they'd needed one another. She sees this clearly now. Jeff and Carl, they are *still* family.

"Seriously, what are you saying? If it's what I think, then that's totally disgusting. You just picked out some random guy—"

"No, we were friends," Nermina hears herself say. "And I told him I wanted a baby. I asked him if he would do this for me and he said yes." This newest lie slips out of her mouth so easily, but even as it does she knows she has to retrieve it.

"Well, then what the hell was wrong with *him*? What kind of a guy does something like that and then just walks away?"

Atika's cheeks are mottled red now, slick with the heat of her anger. Nermina remembers kneeling on the cold tile floor in Raifa's bathroom, kneeling there as Raifa thrust two-year-old Atika into a bathtub filled with ice. Her daughter's screams reverberating throughout the tiny room and Nermina thinking it would never stop. But then the fever broke. And her daughter hadn't died. And she'd never felt more grateful.

"What about all that preachy crap about love and responsibility?"

Nermina says nothing. She has no answer. She'd never allowed herself to wander this far in her thinking. Her plans had never accounted for Carl's place in their life, in their family.

"Well?" Atika demands.

"It still applies," Nermina says softly. "Of course it does. But my situation was different then. I had no other choice."

"Oh my God. We *all* have choices. Isn't that what you're always telling me?" Atika's voice is shrill in Nermina's ears. It frightens her.

"*Draga,* this is so...hard. Can you give me a chance to say what I need to say?"

Nermina feels the trap tightening around her ankle. She knows she needs to tell her daughter the truth. All of it.

"Come sit here. Please." Her voice holds steady now, and Atika joins Nermina at the table, slouching into the chair opposite her, as before. Nermina grasps the girl's hands again. They're long and thin, so much like her own. She feels Atika straining to pull away, and she holds on even tighter.

"Look at me," she demands. Atika stares at her defiantly. "Here's the truth," Nermina continues. "Here's what you need to know. There's a man. His name is Carl Ingram. I knew him a long time ago. I needed him. I needed him so I could have you. And...truthfully...I didn't care much about him. I know that must seem awful."

Nermina feels a trickle of sweat at her temple. It traces the painful bump on her forehead. She watches her daughter's face. The girl eyes her in flinty silence.

"I never told him I was pregnant. I didn't want him in my life. All I wanted was my baby. I didn't have money for artificial insemination. I was a clerk at the hospital, for God's sake! I didn't have money for anything besides food and rent."

All of this rushes out of her, and now Nermina feels surprisingly relieved. Grateful. Remarkably and stupidly grateful—she recognizes in a flash of clarity—because she really has no idea what will happen next.

"Wait," says Atika, "so you tricked this guy—my *father*—into getting you pregnant."

"I didn't trick anyone. We were two consenting adults. We slept together a couple of times. That's all."

"You *fucked* him. You fucked this guy." Nermina feels the thwack of her daughter's words like the blow to her head earlier. A flush creeps across her neck and cheeks as though the girl has actually struck her. Atika yanks her hands from her mother's grasp.

"Well, yes, if you want to put it that way. I guess I did."

Atika crosses her arms in front of her chest and glares at her mother. "Jesus! Why the hell are you telling me all of this *now*?"

Nermina feels foolish. She'd never pictured having to defend herself and this alone is absurd. But which is worse, she wonders: believing she'd be able to keep this secret from her daughter forever, or thinking that revealing it now would earn her daughter's forgiveness?

"I'm telling you now because I need to," she says. Tears slide down her cheeks. And to her surprise, this, too, is a great relief. "Because he's here now, in Portland, and I needed to tell him about you." Her voice breaks and she thinks, for the first time, that this might actually be the truth.

"Why? Why would you do that?" Atika's voice is thick with

unshed tears. She sits, straight-backed against the chair, utterly still.

Nermina rakes her fingers through her hair. "Honey, I can't tell you how sorry I am, how much I regret—"

"What? What do you regret? Actually, that interests me."

"That I never told you. I know it wasn't fair."

"You're damned right, it wasn't fair."

"But I can't go back and change it now. Do you see that?"

"I don't know." Atika pushes the chair back from the table. She draws her knees up to her chest, wraps her arms around herself like a tidy, impenetrable package. "I don't know what to think. You lied to me. All this time, you fucking lied."

Again, Nermina flinches at the words. "But I didn't mean—"

"I don't care what you *meant*. It never crossed your mind I might want to know?"

And then like a flicker on a screen, Nermina sees her father's ashen face the day they'd uncovered her mother's body. Her own loss so large then—her mother gone—she'd never consoled him. She sees this now. She hadn't been able to in those first days. And then it was too late. She'd carried that loss like a stone in her pocket. And then certain in her logic, she'd perpetrated a fraud. Against Carl Ingram, against her daughter. With impunity, she'd buried that lie in the same earthen graves of those she'd lost.

"No...I suppose I wasn't thinking about that," she says. She rocks the kitchen chair slightly, incrementally, back and forth, back and forth. Eventually, she rights herself. She remembers sitting in Raifa's darkened living room, rocking her baby daughter back to sleep, the solid, warm weight of her head against her shoulder. And she remembers Carl, tipping back in the chair on her little deck, the first night they'd had sex. "I wasn't thinking then because I couldn't. I was...*Draga,* I can't explain it—"

"So, what now? What happens next?"

"I don't know," Nermina admits.

Nermina had decided to tell Carl. *She* decided. She imagined—and now she wonders how she'd come to this conclusion—that Atika would be angry, but then ultimately, also anxious to know her father. "I'm not sure," she says. "What do you want to happen?"

Atika presses her fingers to her scalp amidst the coppery curls. "I don't know," she says. Her eyes are puffy and red, and Nermina sees the pain she has caused, the damage.

"Do you want to see him?"

Atika shakes her head. "I don't know. Did it ever occur to you that maybe...this guy, my *father*, maybe he wouldn't even want to know about me?"

Nermina remembers one of the few real dates she had with Carl. They'd walked out of a downtown restaurant and Carl spotted the parking ticket pinned under the wiper blade. He'd grabbed it and stood on the sidewalk cursing, indignant and angry. At the diner the week before, she'd seen this again, but then something more.

"Yes," she says now. "Of course, I considered that."

"What's the point then?" Nermina hears the weariness in her daughter's voice. War weary, she thinks, and this brings her back to Jeff Ingram and then to Carl and she remembers how frightened Carl seemed in Jeff's hospital room, as though it had taken every ounce of his courage to remain there fidgeting in the chair at his brother's bedside.

"I don't know," she says. He's here...maybe there's a reason this is happening now—"

"*Jesus*, Mom." Atika presses the heels of her hands to her cheeks. When she pulls them away a pair of creamy imprints remain for a moment before turning pink again. "You sound like Strina Raifa," she says. "That's a bunch of crap."

"It is," Nermina says. She ventures a quick glance into her daughter's eyes, presents her with a weak smile. "I know it. At least we can agree on that."

CHAPTER 42
A DAUGHTER

Carl parks his rental car—a lime-green Ford Fiesta—at the curb. Nermina's directions were good and the ride over from the Motel 6 took a lot less time than he'd expected. He thrums his fingers on the steering wheel. He doesn't want to get out of the car and walk up to her house, but he doesn't want to sit cramped inside the economy-sized rental car either. He rolls down the driver's side window and squints into the sun-glare. It's one of those few and far between April days in Portland, not even a hint of rain in the chilly air. The trees have all begun to leaf out, green like some Crayola color that doesn't exist in real life. He'd forgotten how pretty this place could be in the spring.

He studies the house, a two-story craftsman with gables over the front windows that remind Carl of eyelids, and a nice, wide front porch. The place looks a lot like Joey and Elsa's had. Like theirs, Nermina's place is pristine. Grass and hedges perfectly trimmed. Big, overflowing planters on either side of the door. The guy across the street starts up a leaf blower and Carl feels a jolt of irritation. It's Sunday, for Chrissake.

He looks at his watch, a black, rugged-looking thing with all kinds of timers and stopwatch features that he never bothers with. Tessa had given it to him for his birthday, so he wears it. The digital numbers say 10:45. As he rolls up the window, the short exchange he'd had with Jeff starts on replay again. Somehow it had gotten all turned around and he'd felt like Jeff was scolding him. That old streak of righteousness coming through loud and clear. Just like the good old days. "Guess it's time to man up," is all Jeff said when Carl told him what Nermina claimed. About the kid and all. But now Carl thinks about his little nephews there in that lousy hospital dayroom—shy at first, but when they finally warmed up to him—how they'd climbed into his lap for a hug. They giggled and belly-laughed when he roughed them up a little. He'd liked the sweaty-outdoors smell of them, the simple look of trust on their identical faces. Twins for Chrissake! His brother has twins.

When he tries to put a finger on the way he feels now—about his *own* situation—he'd have to say it's like having a 255-pound bar over your chest, then hitting the wall with no spotter in sight. Nothing left inside to push the monstrous thing off.

He'd barely known Nermina then. What was it, maybe three or four times they'd actually slept together? A couple of dates. No, he wasn't in stellar form back then. He'd be the first to admit it. After Joey and Elsa's, he'd moved in with Rebecca. Maybe it was love. But looking back, Carl figures he'd split from Portland because he was too afraid to find out. He'd messed around with Nermina, the Bosnian girl, just because he could. Neither had been *real* love, Carl decides now. Tessa had taught him that.

Still unsure as to what tack he's going to take with Nermina, he pulls the keys from the ignition, opens the door, and unfolds himself from behind the steering wheel. The breeze feels nice on his face, his skin tingling a little. He'd shaved, not so much for Nermina, but for Atika. He didn't want to look like some deadbeat, even if that's what the kid likely thinks. He walks up a short, flagstone path to the house. The welcome mat—*Welcome Friends*—taunts him while he works up the nerve to ring the bell.

"Hey," he says when Nermina opens the door, pretty sure but not certain he's gotten control of his voice. She looks the same to him, maybe not as tired as the last time. Her eyes— the thing he'd remembered most from all those years ago—are outlined in brown, a thin line that makes the green look brighter. Maybe that's it. Maybe that's what's different now. They hug awkwardly, just like in the diner the week before. She's nearly as tall as Carl and her cheek brushes his as she pulls away. Her scent, like clean laundry from the dryer, registers for a split second longer.

"Thanks for coming. I hope this is okay. Coming here, I mean."

She leads him through a little foyer where a mirror in a whitewashed frame hangs on the wall. He catches a glimpse of his face there, surprised that he still has his work tan, but more so by the little pouches of flesh on either side of his mouth, an unwelcome change he's recently begun to notice. He sees his father's face for half a second and shoves his fists deep into the front pockets of his jeans.

"Sure, sure, this is fine," he says.

"Can I get you anything? Something to drink?"

Carl sees that she's trying hard. Trying to be polite and civil. And that's good because this whole thing is nuts and he doesn't know any more now than the week before. He doesn't know what to think or how to get his head around this thing she claims as fact.

"No, nothing. I'm good," he says.

He takes in the light-filled room, everything soft. Soft colors: cream, aqua. Blond floors. Nice hardwoods every-where. He lowers himself into a plush, cream-colored sofa, taking his cues from Nermina, who curls herself into a big armchair—the same soft fabric—across from him. She tucks her socked feet up underneath her. He imagines she's trying to look relaxed—home-court advantage and all—but he knows she isn't. Then he hears the heat kick on. His eyes follow the slight stir of sheer white curtains at the two front windows; they sway a little at the bottom. It reminds him of a pretty flower-printed dress that Tessa wears a lot and he sees her legs, tanned and sexy, as she'd stood waving from the curb at the airport.

"So, um, where is she anyway? Where's Atika now?" he asks.

Nermina holds Carl's eyes but busies her fingers, runs them through the silky fringe edging a pale blue pillow she's pulled onto her lap.

"With some friends. I...um...rethought the game plan a little. I wanted us to have a chance to talk first. I hope that's okay with you."

He swallows. What he wants to say is: Why bother asking? For the past 16 years you've done perfectly fine on your own. For the past sixteen years you've made any damned decision you wanted.

What he says is: "Sure, fine by me," his tone flatter, meaner, than he'd intended.

"Carl," she says. "I know this is awkward."

He feels her gaze but doesn't look up. Instead, he examines the jagged cuticle around his fingernails. *The elephant in the room* is what he thinks. It's what that shrink said a million years ago. He'd been maybe ten, Jeff twelve. His dad sitting there, his face nearly blank, just the hint of a smirk. His mom with a wadded-up tissue, dabbing at her eyes. She'd talked a long time and then the shrink leaned forward and said that thing about the elephant in the room. Back then, Carl had pictured a cartoon Dumbo, but now he knows that the elephant the shrink meant was a whole lot scarier. It was the thing you couldn't face. The thing you didn't *want* to face. And since his mom had never tried to get them back there again, Carl figured his elephant theory was probably right. Now he has his own to deal with.

When he finally meets Nermina's eyes, she rushes ahead. "This situation is entirely my doing. I know that, so maybe...well, could we just start from there?" She uncurls herself in the chair, crosses her legs, then places her hands on the armrests.

"Sure, why not? You've got the whole thing figured out."

He stops himself from saying more. The house is completely silent inside now, just the muted drone of the leaf blower again.

"No, it's actually the opposite," Nermina says. "I've no idea what happens next. I've no idea why I didn't leave things as they were. I just felt..." She trails off and goes quiet again. He thinks she might break down a little, maybe offer up some explanation, an apology.

"You felt guilty?" he says.

"No, not exactly."

"Well, maybe you should." He places a question mark at the end of the statement, which he imagines takes a little bit of the sting out of what he means. But, really, he *wants* her to feel bad. He wants her to feel like shit. Whichever way you cut it, she's done a shitty thing. And now, for some reason, he's the one who feels like he needs to prove something. He's pissed at her, and maybe even more pissed at himself, and he wants her to fix it.

"Really?" says Nermina. "Would that be better? Would that change anything now?"

Yeah, he thinks, actually it might.

"The only thing I care about right now is my daughter," she says evenly.

Carl holds her gaze, refuses to look away. Now he remembers the first time he'd touched her. They'd been sitting in his pickup, outside the run-down place she lived then. All he'd wanted was to get in her pants. But then he'd kissed her and her body went as rigid as a cinder block. He thought that'd be the end of it. Figured the girl had some deep kind of problems he didn't want any part of. He knew where she'd come from, the whole bit about the war. When he thinks about it now, he knows he should've walked away.

"You mean *our* daughter?" he says.

The words surprise him and he feels a subtle tightening deep inside his throat, a rush of heat to his face. He thinks he sees tears welling in her eyes before she turns away from him. They sit there then, for what seems to Carl a long time, neither saying anything. Then Nermina clears her throat, runs her fingers through her hair. She looks, straight into Carl's eyes, holds them.

"Okay, that's a fair shot," she says. "That's right. This is the thing, though. I think what I was thinking about when I called you, when I knew you'd be back in Portland for Jeff, well it was about doing the right thing. I wanted to be fair."

She leans forward, tents her hands together in her lap. Prissy now, Carl thinks. He lets out a short, bitter laugh. Joey had asked him how he knew the kid was his. His first night back in town, they'd sat at the bar at Weez's, shooting the shit like old times. And when he told him about Nermina, about the kid, Joey flipped out. "She's looking for a sugar daddy," is what he'd said. Not what he would have expected Joey to say. Joey, the devoted family man. Still, with a few beers in him, Carl found himself agreeing. The woman was shaking him down. But now, after going over it a thousand times in his head, Carl knows Joey's reasoning makes no sense. Nermina would've known he didn't have a pot to piss in. He pegged her as a woman who'd have done her homework. Now he tamps down the urge to get up and walk out the door.

"Fair thing?" he says. "How is this fair, Nermina? You get a sixteen-year head start on things, then bring me in just for the hell of it?"

His own voice sounds tired, he thinks. Hollow. He isn't yelling. He's learned his lesson living with Tessa. Yelling would get him nowhere. Just Tessa crying, the bathroom door locked tight.

Nermina stands up and walks to the spotless bay window. Her hands resting on boyish hips, she stares out. The white curtains are pushed to either side. Pristine. Her jeans and long-sleeved, collared shirt seem expertly pressed.

"I didn't think I had a choice." She sounds tired too, Carl thinks.

"Yeah, you did. You could have told me what you wanted *then*. You could have maybe asked me? Maybe told the truth?"

Now Nermina laughs. The sound is thin, as bitter as he knows he sounded a few minutes before. The two of them, he decides, are in a bad, bad place. He gets up from the sofa and goes to her, stands beside her at the window. He wants to shake her. She turns toward him and they're nearly eye-to-eye, her clean-laundry smell unsettling Carl with its nearness.

"Really?" she says. "You have no idea what brought me to that decision back then. What I was going through. I mean, what I'd just come through."

The dead calm of her voice frightens him. Though he can't say why, this calm is much worse than if she'd been yelling. A wave of regret begins to work its way through his body, a bitter taste in the back of his throat, like the first day of the flu, before you admit you're sick. Before you know you have no choice but to give in to it.

"So, tell me about it then. I'm thinking I deserve that much," he says.

"I'm not about to share that with you now. My *history*."

She spits the last word out at him.

"I didn't mean—"

"Forget it," she says.

He remembers a little of what she'd told him and it had been all over the news back then. The girl escaped a war zone, for Chrissake. He knew she didn't have any family—all of them killed—just another Bosnian couple she hung out with in Portland back then. That much, he knew, but that was all. He'd never bothered to ask.

"Hey, I'm sorry—" he says.

"I said forget it."

"Fine," he says, and when it's clear they've hit another brick wall: "Really, Nermina. How'd you expect me to react? You've had all kinds of time to plan, to figure things out. What *I'm* trying to figure out is why bring me into this now?"

Nermina strides back to the chair she'd been sitting in and drops into it. She leans forward and places her hands on her knees. Carl stands there for a moment. Between a rock and hard place, he thinks. Then, not knowing what else to do with himself, he returns to the sofa and sits down again.

"I know I must seem like a horrible person to you. So much has changed from when ...from when we knew each other."

She's calmed herself some, or is trying to, he sees. Most of the anger has drained out of him. He's a little surprised by this but mostly he's exhausted.

"I was desperate to have a baby," she says, "and I've never regretted it for a second. But I do see I was unfair to you. I do see that. I should've given you the option to say no. I was just so afraid it would never happen. I needed for it to happen. I needed Atika."

"You needed to have a kid? Right then?"

"Yes, I did."

Carl gets up from the sofa and paces a few steps. He'd imagined this conversation with Nermina would be rough, but he hadn't factored in how completely ill-prepared he'd feel 'in the moment,' as Tessa would say. He pictures her face—that pretty mass of curly brown hair piled on top of her head—and he misses her even more now. They've talked on the phone and still he can't find a way to bring it up, *this* part. She'd offered to take off work, to fly out with him to be with Jeff. Jesus, what a mess that would've been. An even more screwed-up mess than he's in right now.

"I'm gonna be honest here, okay? I'm not sure I have that much to offer. As a father, I mean. I don't have much saved..." Carl sees the sheen of sweat along Nermina's cheekbones, across her forehead.

"It doesn't matter," she says. "I'm not asking you for money, for financial support of any kind. Do you understand that? That's *not* why I told you."

"That's what you're saying now, but—"

"And that's exactly what I mean."

Carl thinks of his father. Dead for how many years now? Six. Or maybe it's seven. He feels the old lump of guilt-and-anger-anger-and-guilt that makes it tough for him to swallow. Why had things with his old man always been so goddamned hard? Each time Carl thought things would change between them, they'd always wound up right back in the same place: the old man taunting him and Carl taking the bait. Carl hated losing his temper with him. Yelling, slamming out of the house. All of this comes rushing back and it shames him all over again.

"Then what do you want? I mean, why am I here?"

"I don't want anything from you. I just wanted to do the right thing. I thought this was the right thing. To give you the opportunity..."

Carl sits down again. He leans forward, rests his elbows on his knees as Nermina had done just before. He places his hands on either side of his head, laces his fingers behind. He pulls forward a little, feels the muscles of his neck: tight, painfully tight. He feels the weight of the whole damned mess. He sits a while like this—both of them silent—then he unlaces his fingers. He lets go and the tension eases up just a little. He imagines what it would feel like to let go of everything. Then he ruffles both hands through his hair, still long for a guy his age, but not nearly as long as it had been when he'd first met Nermina. He rights himself and a smile ghosts his lips.

"What?" she says. "What is it?"

"Nothing," he says. "I'm sorry. I know you're being serious. You always struck me as a serious girl."

Nermina smiles then, too, and Carl knows this is only for his benefit. She leans forward, the muscles in her forearms where her rolled-up cuffs end, her hands grasping her thighs, tight, everything tight.

"You came along at a very strange time in my life," she says. "Back then, I mean. Everything felt so urgent. Well, it still does. But *then,* I really had nothing. I was alone. Do you understand?"

He thinks how weird it is that life could be so random. How crazy that Nermina—of all people—would wind up taking care of his brother. He believes *that* part of what she'd said; if it hadn't been for Jeff, she'd probably have gone right ahead with her life, she and her kid, without giving him a second thought. He sees that now. She didn't need him. From the looks of everything here, she's done just fine. She doesn't need his help or anyone else's.

"I guess so," he says. But he doesn't understand. He really doesn't understand because it hadn't just been about her. It'd been about him too. He wonders now what he would've done if she *had* told him she was pregnant. After the fact, of course, but before he'd left for Vancouver. Would it have changed anything? He knows the answer. No way would he have hooked up with Nermina then to raise a kid.

"Look," he says finally. "I need a little time to think this through. Okay?" Now he's glad the girl isn't here. He wouldn't have been ready to face her. He can see that now.

"Of course. It's completely up to you. I told you that last week."

Her voice has softened some and so has her expression. She looks relieved, Carl thinks. And in one way he's relieved, too, but then he isn't. If what she says is true, he has a kid, a sixteen-year-old daughter. And no one is telling him he has to do *anything*. But she's told the kid about him already. She's told the girl she has a father.

Carl sees himself then at sixteen, at the girl's age. Those were his worst years at home with the old man, alone, once Jeff was out. And then there's something else he remembers. Like a punch to the gut, he remembers Laurel. He lowers his head, afraid he'll tear up, or worse, that Nermina will see. He picks up the glass paperweight from the low table in front of him, pretends to admire the swirling colors inside: dark blue, purple, yellow, a bright pink that Tessa would have an exact name for. The thing is heavy, feels solid in his hand, the glass smooth—soothing even—against his calloused thumb.

They'd been so young, he thinks. Only kids. Why hadn't anyone stopped them? It'd been too damned easy. He even remembers Laurel's pink bedspread, the stuffed animals and the dolls kicked to the floor. And Laurel's mom still on her shift at the A & P across town. Laurel had been the same age as his supposed—he tries out the word—*daughter*, and his stomach clenches.

He keeps his head down, turns the glass sphere in both hands. It's warm from his handling it. When he hears his name he nearly drops it.

"Are you okay?" Nermina is asking him.

"Yeah, yeah, wow," he says. He looks up then, forces a smile. "Just a lot to think about. That's all." Carl is so exhausted he can't imagine ever moving his legs again. Getting up and walking out into what used to be his life.

"I know," she says. He searches her face, calmer now, and tries to gauge if the kindness he imagines now is for real.

"What do *you* want me to do?"

She laughs, not the bitter laugh like before, but plenty wary still. This he can tell. A thought occurs to him now. Maybe Nermina had really hoped he'd simply walk away. She would tell him, settle the score, but then he'd walk, just as he'd always done.

"To be honest," she says, "I'm not really sure yet."

She leans forward and he sees now in her angled cheekbones a reminder of the brittle beauty that first attracted him. And most of this is still intact, he thinks. What a rush it'd been when she pulled him into her bed all those years ago. The foreign girl. The mystery girl. And Rebecca back at her apartment waiting up for him when he walked through the door. A prickle of embarrassment inches up his spine. Again, he thinks how crazy, the randomness of things. And he doesn't want to see it, but then he does. The old man cussing him out. His mother crying, but taking charge of the mess he and Laurel had made. They were stupid, stupid kids. They'd waited. Maybe they'd thought the whole thing would just go away?

"I guess we take it one step at a time," Nermina is saying. "This is new territory for me too."

He shakes his head in agreement, places the paperweight back down on the table.

But the thing—Laurel's pregnancy—hadn't gone away. And it'd been worse, they said at the clinic, because it was so late. It was ugly and Laurel's father said he'd kill him if he ever caught Carl near his daughter again, just like in some B movie. And then Laurel's family had packed up everything from that crappy house of theirs and moved away.

"Hey, let me show you something," Nermina says. Her voice is brighter, but Carl fights to hold back a wave of sadness so big he thinks it might drown him.

"Sure," he says, "I gotta..." he trails off. He glances down at his watch.

"This won't take long," she says. "I promise."

She gets up from her chair and walks over to one of the front windows and, beneath it, she opens a long bench—hand-built and solid. Carl focuses on this—the careful mitering, the thickness of the wood panels—still fighting for control. She takes out a photo album, walks back to where he sits on the couch, bolt upright now, and eases down next to him. He looks down at the album she's placed on the table in front of them. She opens it to the first page where she'd slipped under the plastic what looks to Carl like the official document of Atika's birth: two little footprints pressed onto the yellowed paper and her weight (six pounds, eight ounces). But before he's had the chance to read the rest of the details—like parents' names, he thinks wearily—she's already flipped to the next page.

This one shows a tiny pink baby wrapped up in an aqua-and-pink-striped blanket. The woman holding the bundle to her cheek looks flushed, her long hair pulled back from her face in a ponytail. Carl can see that the flimsy hospital gown Nermina wore then was drenched in sweat. He sees where it stuck to her bloated belly and breasts. He feels a rush of embarrassment; the intimacy of the photo, of the event that it captures, makes him feel like he should turn his head away and he almost does, but he feels her hand on his arm.

"I'm so sorry," Nermina says softly. "We'll do this another time. I can see I've upset you."

He clears his throat. The sun slants across the hardwood floor, matching the pattern from the blinds, and Carl thinks how, being a Sunday, Tessa will probably be out in the garden, weeding between the rows of tomato plants or deadheading the zinnias and dahlias, the ones she picks all summer long to put in a vase on the kitchen table. Her T-shirt will be soaked through with sweat, her hair tied up like another bunch of flowers, dirt streaked across her cheeks and under her fingernails.

Carl thinks he feels a little spark of understanding now. Not all of it, but a little. He knows that no matter how he's ended up here, the outcome is the same. He has a kid. He's fairly certain of that. It isn't about money or anything like that. And he isn't going to be able to walk away from her now. He's in it. He realizes now that he was in it from the moment he'd given in to his mom and bought his plane ticket West. There isn't any going back now and he knows it. The girl, his daughter, Atika, he'll have to see her. He'll have to do whatever it is a father does. And much more than his father ever did.

"Sure," he says. "Another time."

Nermina flips the album closed, then rises quickly and stows it back in the bench. When she comes back she hands him a framed portrait: a pretty girl with long, coppery hair. A mane of it! The long dress—some kind of peach color—sets it off to look even brighter, almost like it's glowing. She stands, tall and confident, next to a sandy-haired boy in a tux, his bowtie the same color as the girl's dress.

"That's Atika's junior prom," she says, a smile softening her face.

His brother Jeff has red hair and so do his nephews. Carl feels his heart skitter.

"She's beautiful," he says.

Nermina holds out her hand for the photo and when he releases it she smiles again. "Yes," she says. "She is."

CHAPTER 43
ATIKA'S MESSAGE

The message is already a few hours old when Carl notices the red light blinking on the motel phone, the thing itself a hulking relic he'd never thought to use. He tosses the empty beer bottle from the nightstand into the plastic trash bin. It clinks against the others there. Then he sits on the edge of the bed, the flowered spread waxy beneath his hand, and holds the heavy receiver to his ear. He listens to the message and his mouth goes dry. He listens to the message three more times, memorizing the words, memorizing the inflections.

He tries to match the voice to the pictures Nermina had shown him. Tries to figure if the girl's voice sounds more scared than pissed. It isn't friendly. Neither is it shy or sweet. And since he has no frame of reference, nothing to compare it to, all he has are these few words. And this isn't much. This isn't shit, he decides.

He paces the room a half dozen times, then squats down in front of the cooler he'd picked up at the Wal-Mart on his way into town that first night. He opens the lid and grabs the neck of one of the bottles floating there, the ice long melted. The bottle drips lukewarm water on the worn carpet and he pays it no mind, just twists the cap and tips the bottle to his lips. He paces some more, sits down on the bed again.

Is this his kid? Is this his *daughter*? He tries out the word, speaking it aloud into the dank air of the motel room, into the long, long night ahead.

CHAPTER 44
BONE TIRED

Atika stands at the corner along with the other commuters. The mist creeps under her too-light hoodie, beneath the thin T-shirt that clings to her body. She'd showered quickly and dressed in the dark, not taking the time to dry her waist-length hair, and now she shivers, even though the digital sign at the bank says 50 degrees. It's probably wrong, like everything else, Atika thinks. Barely awake, her stomach growling with hunger, she glares at the tight cluster of people sitting on the metal bench under the enclosure, and at the others—like her—shuffling along on the gritty sidewalk.

It's easy for her to pick out the working people, the woman in green hospital scrubs, the gray-haired man in a tan overcoat, a blue canvas briefcase slung over his shoulder. A young mother in a prissy business suit jostles a baby on her hip while she talks into her cell phone about price points and revenue streams. The rest of them, Atika figures, are probably students or people who have nowhere else to be at this ungodly hour. She wonders if her so-called father ever stands at a bus stop like this. She pulls out her cell phone: 5:28 a.m. It doesn't matter, she tells herself. Her aunt will be awake.

But imagining Strina Raifa's face at the front door, Atika feels the familiar ache, the feeling she gets whenever she's scared or uneasy. It grabs her deep inside her gut, the same feeling that's dogged her since she was a little kid. And then she remembers her aunt holding her and rocking her. Her mother at work? Or maybe the time she'd gone to Seattle to sit for her first set of nursing boards? And Strina Raifa sending her oldest cousin, Taki, into the kitchen for a Popsicle. Her aunt's hand so cool on her face, then peeling the wrapper from the treat for her—an orange one—and putting it to Atika's lips. Cool again.

"You just had a bad dream, *draga*," she'd said. Then the sweet, orange taste on her tongue and, with her aunt holding the Popsicle steady, a fat, syrupy splotch landing on Atika's thigh. She sees her little-girl finger dabbing at the sticky orange spot, touching it to her tongue, the taste sweet and salty. How old was she then? Atika tries to puzzle it out, though it really makes no difference now. Still, there were so few times without her mother's hovering presence, she wonders if the memory holds some special meaning.

She twists the damp bulk of her hair twice around her fist, makes a thick bundle at the nape of her neck, and pulls up the hood of her sweatshirt to cover her head. Gazing into the mist along with the others, she wills the Number Six bus to arrive.

Atika tells herself she hasn't acted irrationally, slipping out of the house before her mother awakened. Not even a reason to be quiet or to rush—her mother sleeping heavily, the Ambien making sure of that—but Atika had been careful, nonetheless, her heart throbbing as she'd locked the door behind her. The last thing she wanted was to have to rehash the whole thing with her mother *again*.

All she wants is the truth. Her mother's a liar, and in light of this *fact*—she underscores this word purposefully—how can she possibly know that what her mother tells her now is, *in fact*, the truth? As opposed to the lie she's maintained for the past sixteen years? Every understanding they've had between them—as mother and daughter—is based on a lie that she, Atika, had believed. *Like an idiot*, she thinks now. Well, she'd wanted to believe it. Of course, she did. Who wouldn't? Your mother's egg and some anonymous man's sperm had made you. Your mother, a refugee from a terrible war. Alone. And she wants only you. Not some random man. Just you.

She assures herself again that her aunt will tell her what she needs to know. Her aunt will tell her the truth or, at least a more accurate version than her mother is capable of delivering.

Then through the gray mist, the Number Six bus approaches the stop. The diesel hangs heavy and damp in the air as the bus idles. Atika crowds into line behind the others. Her lungs sting from the fumes; she tastes the grit in her throat. When a few seconds pass and the door has not yet opened, she feels the collective impatience of the people around her like a buzzing hive.

Finally, a side door on the bus slides open, and a

mechanical lift slowly lowers a man in a wheelchair to the street. The device makes a loud, grinding screech at the end of its descent, and Atika sees the young mother wince and turn away, the cell phone still at her ear. The man in the wheelchair seems young to Atika, despite a face covered with a thick, dark beard. A morass of tattoos blooms up and down his bare arms, and one of his pant legs is tucked up around the stump that had been his left leg. Atika smiles politely, but the man's face remains expressionless, his brown eyes hooded and empty as he wheels past her. The main door louvers open and she boards along with the other passengers.

Once in her seat on the bus, she watches through the dingy window as the man waits at the traffic light, then disappears into the mist with the thickening crowd of pedestrians and cyclists. The image of the man stays in her mind for a long time and she feels some of her anger at her mother mixed up with the sadness she feels for the man, though she isn't sure why.

She'd dozed a little, but awakens with a start when the old woman in the seat next to hers pulls the bell for her stop. Atika rouses herself and feels around in her bag, through spent tissues and pens and loose change, for her cell phone. Her heart races now and her face flashes hot. She wants the truth. And then maybe she doesn't.

Atika walks three blocks to the tiny, two-story house she knows as well as her own. She pulls the metal latch on the gate at just the right angle to open the fussy thing her uncle insisted he'd fixed, but whose subtle trick strangers can rarely figure out. She sees how the ivy has encroached along the iron fence and the gate so that it nearly obscures the white paint she and her cousins had applied in one of her aunt's great sprees of home improvement. And then with her stomach turning flips, she knocks on the delft-blue door, though she could have just as easily used her key. Too early in the morning, she reasons. She imagines her uncle, hunched intently over the morning paper, his coffee mug perpetually full. Give him a chance to throw on a T-shirt, she thinks.

Her cousin Sabrina opens the door, twin mascara smudges under her eyes, long, jet-black hair pulled into a sleep-mussed ponytail. She gazes at Atika blankly for a long moment before unlocking the screen door.

"Who died?" Sabrina asks.

"Jesus," says Atika. She yanks the screen door open and pushes past her cousin. "Thanks a lot. It's nice to see you, too."

"You know what time it is?"

"Early," says Atika. The two girls stand nearly eye-to-eye, and Atika feels silly and prudish, wishing she didn't have to encounter her cousin's voluptuous body, barely clothed, at 6:15 in the morning; Sabrina's nipples stand erect through her tank top, her flat belly displayed above a tiny pair of shorts, the waistband folded down for maximum effect, Atika thinks. But then Sabrina pulls her into a quick hug. Atika inhales the mish-mash aroma of her cousin's leave-in conditioner—coconut—and body wash—cucumber—and, underneath it all, the unmistakable smell of cigarettes.

"Sorry," Atika says as Sabrina releases her. "I know it's early." Her voice catches a little. "She's up, though, right?"

"Uh-oh," says Sabrina, "you guys fighting again?" She grabs Atika's hand, crushes it inside her own, still warm from sleep. The girls had grown up like sisters, almost as though they each had two mothers. Recently, though, Atika prefers her aunt to her mother, especially now. She'd come to her aunt the night that she and Keith broke up for good. She'd sobbed her heart out and now here she was again.

"No, not really. Well, sort of." Atika unzips her hoodie and yanks it off. Now she's hot, sweating.

"C'mon," says Sabrina. Atika follows her into the kitchen. The room feels remarkably tiny and safe, everything familiar, a miniature version of her childhood. Atika plops down at the table, right at the spot that has always been hers.

Sabrina's eyes sweep the room. "She must be in the shower," she says. "I'll tell her you're down here, okay?"

Her cousin's voice has slipped into a disconcertingly gentle tone, and this irks Atika.

She's the little girl with the Popsicle again, the little cousin, so needy, so *sheltered*. She remembers the first time she'd tried cigarettes. Following Sabrina's lead, she spewed a billow of smoke out the upstairs bedroom window. Atika remembers coughing and gagging, Sabrina only laughing. And then her uncle pounding on the door, scolding them equally. The two of them grounded. The two of them guilty, but Atika crying, while Sabrina let fly a stream of curses Atika could never have conjured then, let alone uttered to an adult.

"Sure," says Atika now. "I'm not going anywhere." She watches her cousin's retreat, watches the block letters that spell out PINK on the back of her shorts swaying from side to side as she scuffs into the hallway.

Atika gets up and walks to the kitchen counter. She grabs a Lands End catalogue and flips through the pages. It's one among many that lie inside a big wooden bowl. The thing has been here, in her aunt and uncle's kitchen, for as long as she can remember. She smiles a little to herself, imagining that if she dug to the bottom of the bowl she'd likely find a catalogue or magazine from the year she was born.

When she looks up from the pages, her aunt is plodding into the kitchen, her hair still bundled inside a towel on top of her head, and the same coconut scent as Sabrina's surrounds her. Atika goes to her, tears welling in her eyes. She fights them back. "I'm sorry, Strina Raifa," she says into her aunt's shoulder.

"It's fine, *draga*. What is it?" Raifa holds Atika out at arm's length then, her strong hands grasping the bony knobs of the girl's shoulders.

Now that they're face to face, Atika can't think how to begin. She wonders if her mother has already called. It wouldn't surprise her; her mother seems to possess amazing powers for tracking Atika's every move. Maybe she'd sensed her absence and struggled out of a dead man's sleep to alert her closest friend. So what? Atika decides; she's here for a reason.

Raifa guides Atika to the table—like a small child, Atika thinks again—but she slumps right back down into her usual chair, the rungs solid against her back, cradling her.

"Okay, now tell me what's going on." Raifa stands with one hand holding her toweled hair in place and the other on her hip.

"Where's everyone else?" Atika's eyes dart to the archway that leads to the hallway and the staircase, as though the rest of the family might be lurking there.

"Your Ujak Samir drove up north last night. He's helping Taki and Meredith install new kitchen cabinets."

"That's good," Atika says. She knows she's stalling, but that's okay. She needs to. She needs to show her aunt that she—unlike her mother—can behave like a rational adult. She can ask rational questions and—with her aunt—maybe even get some rational answers.

"He should have put his foot down and told Taki to hire someone. This is too much work for your uncle." Raifa's face forms a stern expression that Atika knows is mainly bluster. Her aunt and uncle have always 'gone easy' on their kids—her mother's words—and Strina Raifa is particularly soft on her oldest. Maybe, Atika thinks, it's just a matter of proportions. Her own mother has no one else to manage. No one but Atika.

Raifa unwraps the towel and tosses it behind her onto the back of the chair. She runs her fingers through her still-wet hair. Atika thinks how such an infraction in her mother's kitchen would never be tolerated. She searches her aunt's face and it's clear: Strina Raifa knows why she's here. Still, Atika worries how to begin. Her aunt's lashes flutter, obscuring for only a split second her gray eyes, a color duplicated in both of Atika's cousins, but in no other person Atika has yet to encounter. The girl takes a deep breath and the knot in her stomach eases just a little.

"Has my mother talked to you about Carl Ingram?" She knows the answer, knows there's likely nothing the two women keep from one another, least of all something as important as this. Atika feels her aunt's eyes on her, intent and patient.

"Yes," says Raifa, "She has." And while Atika considers

again how to proceed, Raifa adds. "She knows, *dušo*." Raifa leans forward. Her damp hair paints dark splotches on the faded brown fabric of her T-shirt. "She knows this is a hard thing to accept. She knows you're angry,"

Liar, Atika thinks. Her mother has lied, unaccountably. And, *yes*, she is angry. She's furious. Her hand goes instinctively to the two little silver beads that pierce the skin above her left eyebrow. She turns the top bead between her thumb and index finger, feels the solid cast of metal. She remembers the expression on her mother's face when she'd first seen it—the piercing—disappointment, disgust. And anger, anger that her little girl had dared to go against her, dared to choose for herself what she wanted.

"I'm not angry," says Atika, surprised by how steady her voice sounds now. "I'm confused. I'm...shocked, I guess."

Raifa spreads her hands, palms down, on the bright, flowered tablecloth in front of her. Her hands are as small as a child's, the nails short, the thin, gold wedding band—the only jewelry Atika has ever seen her wear—dull on her finger. A pink ponytail holder is cinched around her left wrist.

When it's clear that Raifa is waiting for her to continue, Atika says, "I don't understand why she couldn't have just told me the truth from the beginning. Wouldn't that have been better?"

"Better? I don't know. Your mother...your mother was very determined..." Raifa runs her fingers through her hair again. Drying a little now, it forms its usual waves. A bright shock of gray at her right temple stands out against the muted brown of the rest.

"Is Carl Ingram my father?" The question seems to Atika

to have materialized without her knowledge or consent.

"Yes," says Raifa. Her eyes hold steady on Atika's and, under this gaze, the girl places her elbows on the table. She lets her head drop into her hands and feels the full weight of it there.

"Did he *know* he was my father? I mean, before now?"

"I don't believe he did," says Raifa. She hesitates a moment and then, "I think he had no idea."

Atika wonders then if her mother had ever loved Carl Ingram. Her mother said no. She'd been emphatic. But if she'd said, yes, Atika thinks, she'd be even more disgusted than she is right now.

"Isn't that unfair?" she asks. "I mean ..." and now Atika feels a righteous anger building. "Isn't that, like, *deceitful*?"

Atika thinks about when she and Keith had first made love in her own bed, her mother working her long shift at the hospital. She remembers how she and Keith had fumbled at first with the condoms, but then become expert. The terror of getting pregnant so easily extinguished, replaced by unimaginable pleasure. Her face flushes now and her mind sets off on an unexpected tack. What if something *had* gone wrong? What if she'd gotten pregnant? She imagines keeping this secret from Keith, from the person she loves—she corrects herself: *loved*—more than anything. Impossible, she decides. Even with her wounds still fresh, she's certain she could never do that. Or could she?

Raifa tents her small hands in front of her on the table. "Yes," she says. "But, I think at the time, your mother felt completely..."

"What?"

"I think she felt, well, justified. I think I understood it that way, too. There were things that happened before...things she couldn't tell you—"

"What difference does it make?" Atika says. "What difference does it make what happened before? She lied to this guy, this guy who got her pregnant. She just used him. And then she lied to me."

Raifa gathers her damp hair behind her head and slides the pink elastic from her wrist. She pulls the shoulder-length mass into an untidy ponytail that Atika knows will be the full extent of her aunt's hairstyling for the day. Even so, the girl feels her impatience growing again when Raifa's hands linger a few seconds more at the task.

"Atika," Raifa says, "sometimes a lie can be much kinder than the truth." Her tone is even and unhurried and this infuriates Atika. Now her aunt is treating her like a little girl too. A child who can't be trusted with the truth.

"That's wrong," Atika says. "I don't think it's kinder to deceive someone. It's cruel—"

"Draga, listen to me. The choices your mother made then, the decisions she made, may not have been...so, so correct, but she had the right...I think the right intention."

Atika's not so sure her aunt believes this. What *had* her mother intended? Maybe she'd hoped to keep her little girl tucked away in a private world only she—her mother—controlled. Forever and ever, the grown girl thinks, like she's some sort of prized hothouse flower. A picture pops into Atika's mind of the terrarium Keith's parents kept on a low table in their den, a thick, domed jar and, inside the glass, tiny ferns and succulents, each pressed into the dark, moist soil. A perfect, miniature ecosystem, droplets of moisture clinging to the inside of the glass. The first time Keith's mother had pointed it out to her, Atika lifted the lid and thought the little garden was beautiful but also a little sad. And now Atika can see exactly why. It isn't natural. She thinks of the garden that surrounds her own house, how it overflows in abundance. She thinks how happy it makes her mother to separate with a knife, thick clumps of lilies and hostas and coneflowers each spring to share with their neighbors.

She puzzles through all of this now, stealing glances at her aunt's patient face. She sees a subtle pleading there. Still, indignation prods Atika further.

"But she never gave me the chance to decide if I wanted a father in my life," she blurts out. She hates how she sounds—the whiny kid again—but can't stop herself. "She never gave him the chance either."

Raifa spreads her small hands in front of her on the table again. She turns the thin gold band a couple of times on her finger. "She's giving you the chance now," she says. "Both of you."

Atika knows this is true. Her mother had told her Carl was coming to the house to talk; if she wanted to meet him then she could. And, of course, she'd refused. She would decide when she was ready—if she'd *ever* be ready—to meet him. Her mother is getting off too easily. Carl Ingram, *my father*, Atika thinks, practically dropped onto their doorstep; it didn't seem a big stretch for her mother to come clean now. It didn't seem she'd had to do much of anything to reach her decision. The choice had been made for her, Atika thinks. The choice had been dictated by circumstance, by chance, and now she's the one who feels stupid. Tricked somehow. She's the one who feels like she's being pushed into a corner. It's just not fair.

Raifa's eyes dart to the clock on the microwave and then back to Atika, and the girl knows her aunt's morning—and her own time here—is fast slipping away. Her aunt needs to do laundry and shop for groceries. She needs to drive Sabrina to her job at the salon and talk to Ujak Samir when he calls from Taki and Meredith's.

Atika's mind races. She tries to remember what she'd been so desperate to say to her aunt, what she'd hoped to hear in return. Had she thought her aunt would reveal a secret that would make it all better, like some ridiculous fairy godmother? Besides, what does it matter now? What would change?

"Why don't you give her a chance to make things right?" Raifa's question hangs in the air between them. The girl turns it over a couple of times before answering.

"What choice do I have?"

Raifa eyes her evenly. "You know, you're not helpless in all of this. You can do as you please. If you want, you don't have to do anything."

"But I already have," Atika says, almost to herself. The words have slipped out and, in response, the knot in her stomach clenches again like an angry fist.

"What do you mean?"

"I called him."

"I didn't know that." Atika hears the shift in her aunt's voice from patience to something else. "I know your mother contacted him and that they talked. They met a couple times. She said you weren't ready to meet him yet. I thought that was all. There was more?"

Heat spreads across Atika's face, her chest. She'd called him herself, left that stupid message at his motel. She'd called out of anger, really, nothing more. Like an idiot. Like a child. And he'd stepped up. A man she'd never even heard of before last week agreed to come and meet her. Which of the two of them was more pathetic, she wonders now. Each of them caught up in her mother's lies.

"What? Just tell me," Raifa says softly.

Atika feels wrung out. 'Bone tired'—her mother's words come to her now. She tries to think what more there is to say. Her mother had made it possible, but she—Atika—had pushed him. She'd forced this man, a stranger, into her life. And now she doesn't know how to stop it from happening.

Atika scrapes her chair back from the table and stands, along with Raifa. She goes to her aunt, and the two women—Atika taller by a good three inches—embrace. Atika snuffs back her tears. She clings to her aunt a while longer until Raifa moves away. She holds Atika at arm's length, just as she'd done earlier.

"He'll love you," Raifa says.

Atika searches her aunt's gray eyes for clues. How can she know this? How can anyone? And, still, she knows how very much she wants to believe her.

CHAPTER 45
MAKE LOVE, NOT WAR

Carl stuffs himself into the rental car and heads for Nermina's. *This* time he's going to meet his daughter. "Why didn't you call the cell?" he'd asked the girl the night before. He asked the question only to fill the awkward silence on the line. And it hadn't even struck him till this morning that she'd never answered him. But the thing is, Carl thinks now, this is what he'd really wanted. He just wanted to know the girl wanted him as a father. And if she hadn't—no matter how pissy or cold she sounded on the phone—why would she even bother? She'd been the one to call him. Right?

He parks at the curb again and wastes no time walking up to the house: same pristine garden, even the cement steps and landing spotless, like they'd just been power washed. Nermina opens the door only seconds after he rings the bell. She looks pretty, he thinks, clean-scrubbed. She has on jeans and a soft, white gauzy blouse that reminds him of one she'd worn all those years ago, the night they'd gone to that Mexican place. The night he'd first kissed her in his truck. And as he pictures this he feels a sinking in his gut.

"Come on in," Nermina says. "Atika just called. She'll be here any minute." Carl feels Nermina's smile now like some kind of offering. He figures this meeting can't be easy for her either. He wonders why Atika isn't home now waiting for him, and then he squelches the thought. He doesn't want to start off on the wrong foot. He has no right, really, to wonder where she is, why she'd set up a time and then not be here.

Inside, Carl and Nermina stand in the living room like strangers. "Did you have any trouble—" Nermina begins, and he answers, "No, once I've been to a place..." and leaves it at that. And he tries to think what to say next, but then—just like Nermina said—the door opens and here she is. His daughter.

Atika stands in front of him, her earbuds draped over one shoulder like a stethoscope.

"Hi," she says, a general greeting, addressing both him and Nermina.

"Hi," he echoes.

He'd thought he would feel more nervous—he'd built up the thing so damned much—but Carl is surprised now to find himself more fascinated than frightened. The girl—Atika—is as pretty as she'd been in the pictures. Her hair is thick and long, and it carries the scent of summer sweat. A 'pony smell' is what his mother had always called it. Funny, the things you remember. An image of him and Jeff when they were little kids: flushed, sweaty, rolling around on the blue shag carpet in their room before bedtime. His mother demanding they get into the tub and the two of them ignoring her.

Atika shrugs off, first the backpack that looks to Carl like it weighs more than she does, and then a denim jacket loaded with all sorts of buttons; the first one to catch his eye—Make Love, Not War—makes him smile. That's pretty old school, he thinks he might say, but then he doesn't. He says nothing. He looks from Atika's face to her mother's. The two exchange an unhurried look that Carl can't decipher. He doesn't care now, he tells himself. He doesn't care what might or might not have gone down between them in the past few days. And he doesn't even care if Nermina has maybe talked shit about him, though he figures that's likely not the case. What would that gain her now?

But he doesn't know what to do next, so he thrusts out his hand toward the girl, and she receives it. She shakes hard, like a guy. They shake hands like two old buddies meeting up after a long time apart.

"You're Carl," says the girl. He sees the little muscle twitch above her eyebrow—same as her mother's—the blue vein just under that pale, pale skin at her temple. He sees the piercing she's got there too and it makes him want to wince and he hopes he hasn't. She doesn't look away, and Carl holds her gaze a little longer, then pulls his hand from hers. He looks down at his boots, shoves both hands into the front pockets of his jeans.

"Yeah," he says. "And you're Atika." He feels a flutter in his gut then but stays his ground. He clears his throat. He stands there for what seems a long time. And then he's grateful, so crazy grateful when Nermina reaches out and places her hand on his shoulder. A surge of tension releases from his muscles into her fingers, a tension he hadn't even known was there. It scares him, how easily his body has yielded, how wrung out and desperate he feels at her touch. It scares him to realize that he's in so far over his head.

"Look," Nermina says, "this is strange, right? I know it. I put you both in this...in this ..."

Carl waits and when she doesn't finish the sentence he steps back beyond her reach. Nermina crosses her arms in front of her and he feels the absence right away, the tension seeping back into his shoulders.

"Oh, for God's sake," she says then. "This is insane." She rakes her fingers through her hair and then walks to the front door, the door Atika had come through only moments before.

"Maybe I should just go out for a little while. Give the two of you a little time? Carl, would that be better? Atika?" She looks from one to the other. Carl's heart is pounding inside his chest. *God, no*, he wants to say. Now that he's here, now that push has come to shove, he's scared. He's scared shitless. The girl's face, purposely blank he thinks, reveals nothing.

"No, stay," he hears himself say. "Maybe you could fix us some coffee?"

"Sure," says Nermina. He hears the relief in her voice and her features settle into the same determined expression he remembers from their first meeting all those years ago at the hospital café.

He looks to the girl. "You drink coffee?" He knows he's smiling, a nervous smile, probably looking like some kind of raving lunatic. *To hell with it*, he thinks.

"Yeah, I do," Atika says, and then to Nermina, "I'll make it,

Mom."

She moves past him, briskly, with confidence, her pony smell hitting him again full on. The tight feeling in his gut eases up a little, and when he settles himself at Nermina's kitchen table he feels a little better. His mind scrolls through all the things he'd thought about the night before, all the things he'd planned on saying to her, his daughter. He thinks again about Tessa and what she would say. Watching Atika now, he has no doubt that she's his. He sees, in the set of her shoulders, her jaw, the outline of his—and damn—of his *and* Jeff's features melded there. How does that work? It's an insane and awesome thing to behold.

He thinks about Ethan and Tyler, how solid their little bodies had seemed to him, how he'd seen both Jeff and Lisa in their faces, too. As screwed up as things have gotten between those two, he thinks, they did that. They made those kids. And he thinks about his father then, tries to picture him as a young man. Before him and Jeff. Was there a time, Carl wonders, when the old man had even wanted kids? Dreamed of making another little human being from his own DNA?

And then it hits him—no matter how watchful, he can never head it off in time—the old guilt grabs hold again and gnaws. He does his best to shove it back down inside.

He watches as Atika fills the carafe with filtered water from the faucet. Her movements are quick, precise, just like her mother's. He admires this, and when he looks around Nermina's kitchen—at the wide crown moldings that meet the ceiling, the white subway tile behind the sink, the small squares of glass tile in between with their bright pops of color, the way the bull-nose has been set so evenly, expertly, against the countertop—he admires all of this, too. He watches Atika scoop coffee from a stainless-steel canister into the basket of the coffee maker, then flip it into place. She reaches up to the highest shelf of the glass-fronted cabinets and pulls down a small, white pitcher.

Sitting across from him at the table, he sees Nermina smile at her daughter.

"That's nice," Nermina says.

"Well, it's a special occasion, isn't it?"

He can't tell whether Atika is being smart-assed or not, but he thinks not. He doesn't know her yet and has no point of reference, but he figures he's been around enough teenagers—Tessa's nieces to start with—to trust his gut now.

"I'm glad you think so," he says.

Atika fills the little pitcher with half-and-half and sets it on the table in front of her mother, next to the matching sugar bowl already there. Carl sees something more in the girl's movements, a kind of grace, as Tessa would say. He compares her again to Tessa's nieces—two leggy blondes, a year apart, whose names he can never seem to keep straight. Both have the nasty habit of cracking their gum the whole time they talk, and Carl cringes now recalling this.

"Come sit with us," Nermina says. Her voice is calm and she smiles again. She's gotten herself under control, Carl observes, and this helps him, assures him, that they're going to get through this thing. This first step.

Atika pulls out one of the straight-backed chairs and sits down. She folds her hands in front of her on the table, a mirror image of her mother's gesture. Carl sees now the tiny silver hoops that fill the piercings all along Atika's right ear, even the cartilage. He can't say how many. He notes again the little studs that pierce her right eyebrow. He's repulsed by this but cannot look away.

"What?" She smiles at him, a little snidely, he thinks, her full lips an exact replica of his own.

"Nothing," he says. "Sorry."

"You really—"

"Really, *what,* Mom? He's staring at me."

"Atika, my God, that's rude!"

Nermina slides back her chair and gets up from the table. Carl watches her take out three mugs and pour the coffee. She takes three spoons from the drawer, clusters the mugs into formation. She carries this all easily to the table like the waitresses at the restaurant where Tessa tends bar.

"It's okay," he says as she puts one of the mugs in front of him.

"I don't know what I was expecting," Nermina says. She sits again, takes a sip of her black coffee.

Carl isn't sure whether the comment is meant for him or Atika. He rocks back in the chair now, a habit that Tessa hates, laces his fingers behind his head. He figures he might as well take a shot.

"I'll tell you what," he says. "I'll start. How's that?"

He turns to Atika and, again, she wears that same poker face, a look of studied boredom, her green eyes hooded, yielding absolutely nothing.

"I'll take that as a yes." He makes himself smile. "Why don't you tell me about school?" And then as soon as the words are out of his mouth he realizes his mistake. What a stupid thing to ask a kid. He sounds like one of his old aunts.

"Oh, school's just dandy," Atika says.

She seems eager now to rub it in, Carl thinks. Kids are brutal that way.

"You know, I skipped two grades? Did my mom tell you that? I figure that's the sort of thing you'd want to know."

"No," says Carl. "She didn't."

He pours some of the half-and-half into his coffee and stirs it with the spoon. And then he tries matching her poker face with one of his own.

"Well, then I should definitely fill you in. I'm sort of a genius."

"Atika—"

"*What*?"

Carl rights the chair, drums his fingers on the edge of the table. He looks again from mother to daughter. He sees the beginning of a belligerent curl on the girl's lips and he recognizes it instantly as his own. She's scared too. He's sure of it now.

"Hmmm, a genius," he says. "That's pretty intimidating."

"Not really," she shoots back. "I hang out with some pretty intelligent people. It's not intimidating to them at all."

There's an edge to her voice now, sharper than before. Is she implying that he's an idiot? He sees she's playing with him and he *does* feel like an idiot now. What does she want from him? He can't answer that, might never be able to. The girl probably doesn't have a clue herself.

"Well, then I guess I'll just have to step up my game. Hit the books again, huh?" He smiles at her, a genuine smile, a pleading smile, Carl is ashamed to admit. He wants the girl to like him.

"Maybe you could tell Carl about where you've applied," says Nermina. "I'm sure he'd like to hear."

He knows Nermina is trying, but—damn—he feels hung out to dry here. He feels like an outsider. He *is* an outsider.

The girl shoots her mother a smug look. She scrapes her chair against the tile floor as she shoves herself away from the table again. Carl watches her saunter from the room. A few moments later she lays a pile of glossy pamphlets on the table in front of him. He picks up the one on top and riffles through the pages—a hodgepodge of photos: smiling co-eds of varying skin color, ivy-covered buildings, bright green athletics fields. Stanford. When he looks up, the girl has slid her lean body back into her chair, her face deadpan again. Nermina stretches the fingers of both hands around her mug, cradles the thing, twists it a quarter-turn in either direction before setting it back down on the table. She opens her mouth to speak and then doesn't. Carl feels the heavy silence between the three of them like the sweat-drenched work clothes he peels off at the end of the day.

"Wow," he says. "You're shooting high. That's good, right?" His old man had given him two choices: until he got his grades up, community college or a state college twenty minutes down the road. He'd chosen neither but applied instead to a third-rate college in Scranton, Pennsylvania. It was in the Pocono Mountains and he'd wanted to learn how to ski. He remembers the Pontiac station wagon ticking on the asphalt, the old man scowling behind the wheel, his mother standing with him in the parking lot, sniffling a little into a Kleenex, and finally pressing some extra cash into his hand. He hadn't lasted a year.

"My guidance counselor recommended it," Atika says. "She said I have as good a shot as anyone, but, like, then you have your safe schools to fall back on, too."

Carl isn't sure he's understood her. He waits half a beat, hoping she'll explain, but then plunges forward anyway; at least he's got her talking.

"They get a lot of *incidents* at Stanford?" he asks. "I wouldn't think that at such a nice place you'd have that sort of thing."

Atika stares at him blankly. Carl's face flushes hot.

"No, no," Nermina says. She flutters her hand in front of her. "The kids now, they apply to lots and lots of schools. The safe schools are the easiest to get into. That's all she meant."

Jesus, Carl thinks. He wishes someone had warned him. Nermina smiles then, so he does, too. Again, he feels like an idiot, but he reminds himself why he's here. He dares himself to look at her, to look at his daughter. He dares himself to see her.

And then a sensation takes hold of him, a sort of drifting, and he remembers it. How it would feel after he and Jeff had been in the ocean for hours on end. His mother and his aunt, standing at the shoreline, the outline of their tanned bodies, waving them in. And he and Jeff would come stumbling out of the surf, waterlogged, skin stinging. Then the hot sand, soggy white bread, licking grape jelly from their salty fingers. And that rocking, drifting, like he was still riding the waves.

Now he spreads his hands wide, one on each thigh, feels the soft weft of his jeans under his calloused fingertips. The drifting eases a little.

"Riiiight," he says to Nermina, and then turns his face to

Atika. "It's a lot different now, I guess. I mean, it's different from when I was a kid." He figures he'll go for broke. "Look," he says. "So, we're all sitting here. Trying. Well, I guess we're trying to be polite. I know that..." He studies both of their faces now, mother and daughter, each silent, motionless like the studio models Tessa hires sometimes for her paintings. He sees the slight wearing of age at the corners of Nermina's lips, again the plumpness, the fullness of their daughter's. He remembers that first time with Nermina, how hungry he'd been for her. How easy to lie to Rebecca, to lie to himself. And then, he supposes now, how easy he'd made it for Nermina to carry out her own lie. He sees the part he's played, sees it clearly now.

"I don't know what..." he tries again. He stands up and goes to Atika. Before that very instant, he'd no intention of doing so. He places his hands gently on her shoulders, the way Nermina had done earlier with him, and the girl stands, too. She crosses her arms in front of her and he sees tears pooling in her eyes. Lashes pale as corn silk, lashes like his little nephews'.

"What do you *want*?" she asks. The hard edge is gone now from her voice. A thickness clogs Carl's throat. He doesn't trust himself to speak.

"Tell me," she demands. He thinks he hears her pleading, too, just as he'd been pleading before. He looks to Nermina and her face holds nearly the same expression as her daughter's. They each want the same thing, he thinks. All three of them. They each want to know they aren't being lied to. They want something solid. Something that's not a moving target.

"I want to try," he says, the words shaping themselves. "I want to try to be in your life. To be your father."

Atika's tears finally fall. She cries deeply and silently, her mother silent, waiting, as well. He shakes his head from side to side then, passes a rough palm across his forehead.

"Jesus," he says.

He wants to hug her. He thinks this would make it okay. Again, his eyes are drawn to the little studs piercing the girl's eyebrow, the tiny silver hoops all the way up her ear. He thinks how this must have hurt her at the time. He thinks of all the hurts she's likely suffered and all the hurts that lie ahead.

But then she slaps at her tears with the back of her hand, looks first to Nermina and then to him, her pretty face morphed into an impassive glare. "I hate you both," she says. Her voice is small. Whatever conviction she'd hoped to convey is swallowed up in the sorrow Carl imagines she's feeling. He stands there, wanting to open his arms to her, wanting to hold her, but then she brushes past him and slips through the archway to the stairs as though she'd never been there in the first place.

CHAPTER 46
A DIFFERENT KIND OF LOVE

Carl checks his watch again. She isn't late. Not yet. But he begins to worry that maybe he's gotten the address wrong. There are three Powell's downtown now. Each with a coffee shop. Each probably identical to the others, Carl imagines. The downtown has changed a lot since he'd been here last. He thinks of the places where he hung out, little hole-in-the-wall establishments with mismatched furniture, stained cushions, crumbs all over the tables. The restaurants and coffee shops here now seem painfully generic by comparison.

He looks around at the clientele: hipster twenty-something guys with tight jeans and threadbare sweaters. A girl hunches at the table next to him in a tank top and a scarf, her arms an angry swirl of colors, nipples standing hard against her too-thin top. A wave of embarrassment sloshes over him and he shifts his eyes away from her. The girl never looks up, just taps away at her keyboard. He's invisible, and just as well.

He worries again that maybe he's in the wrong place. Maybe she won't show up at all. He realizes he needs to take a piss but doesn't want to go around back to use the unisex restroom he knows he'll find there. He's afraid he might miss her, doesn't want her to come in looking for him and think that he's stood her up. *I wouldn't do that*, he hears himself saying to her mother. He'd never do that to her. He shoots a furtive glance at the tattooed girl again. How old can she be? Eighteen? Twenty? He can't seem to tell these things anymore. He feels old. But he isn't *that* old, he tells himself. Not really, but he's sure as hell old enough to be this tattooed girl's father.

The guy behind the counter—his earlobes stretched around huge rubber discs—powers up an industrial blender and the loud, high-pitched churning grates on Carl's nerves. He blames the coffee, a large cup on the way over and a grandé here, for his present state. He pulls the cell from the back pocket of his jeans—no messages—and debates whether to take his jacket to the restroom or leave it on the chair. He needs to pee badly now and thinks in a near panic how he wouldn't want to have to excuse himself to do so once she's arrived.

He leaves the denim jacket hanging on the back of the chair, his grandé on the table. The place has grown uncomfortably loud and when Carl finds the restroom the door is locked. He can hear the hand dryer going but can barely make out the muted female voice from inside saying "hold on" or "just a second;" he can't tell which. And when the door opens with the overpowering scent of strawberry deodorizer, the girl who begins to push past him looks up. The girl is Atika.

"Oh, hi," she says, like she meets up with him all the time. Her absent father. Like maybe she isn't as scared shitless as he is. Like she hadn't said she hated him.

"Hey," he says. His arms begin to stretch out toward her, as though he might give her a hug, but then he doesn't. She doesn't move closer to him. She doesn't say anything. His heart thumps inside his chest—audibly, like some crazy cartoon heart. It doesn't matter now how they'd left off last time. She's here now.

"I gotta..." he gestures toward the restroom door. "I got us a table," he says. "The denim jacket. Look for the jacket. I'll be right back," he says, smiling madly, insanely, like before. Atika blinks at him, unfazed. He lets himself into the restroom, half afraid she'll disappear before he gets back to the table. But then he flips up the seat and feels his relief blasting the inside of the bowl.

When he gets back to the table he finds Atika, his daughter, texting on a phone ten times nicer than his own. She glances up at him, then back down to the phone, her thumbs moving impossibly fast on the screen. He hears the message fly into the ether. He registers her eyes on him then.

"Thanks for meeting me," he says. "Something to drink? You hungry? They've got..." He eyes the glass case a few feet from them. "They've got yogurt," he says. "They've got hot chocolate."

She looks at him, a smile or a smirk starting at the right corner of her lips. "I'll just have some coffee," she says.

And then he remembers how she'd been the one to make the coffee at the house, her house and Nermina's. "Just a grandé. Black," she says.

"Nothing else?" he says. "Maybe...like a muffin or something?" He doesn't want her to think he's some kind of cheapskate. The tattooed girl at the next table looks over at them—dull stare—then back to her computer. Her fingers fly across the keys. Carl notices how tiny the girl's hands are, her fingernails gnawed down to pink nubs. His eyes go reflexively to Atika's hands then; they're long, thin like her mother's, and he's lost there for a second or two, contemplating this.

"Just the coffee," she says and then "Thank you," when he sets it on the table in front of her a few minutes later.

"Sure," he says. He arranges his features into what he imagines to be an expression of parental assurance. He's here. He's listening. He thinks about how Tessa would slip out of the living room, ten minutes gone by and his eyes still glued to the game, before he'd notice she was gone. This is different, but it's also the same. Tessa has taught him that. He feels a flutter of panic, thinking how he'll tell her. How he'll tell Tessa he has a daughter. But that'll come later he assures himself.

He tents his hands on the table in front of him. "I thought this would be a good start," he says. He clears his throat. "I know this is...it's a little strange, I know. You and me. We don't know a lot about each other..."

Atika unzips her hoodie—navy blue, bulky—and shrugs out of it, drapes it over the back of the chair. Underneath she has on one of those white gauzy tops with embroidery that all the girls had worn in the '70s. A peasant top, he remembers they'd called them then. She has on a thin silver necklace that brushes her collarbones, a tiny silver hummingbird dangling at the hollow of her throat. This view of the girl is so—he searches for the right word—so vulnerable, he concludes.

"You're right," she says softly. "You don't know a fucking thing about me."

Carl recoils. He's grateful that his hands are already engaged. He clasps them tighter now.

"Right. That's the point. That's why we're doing this."

He watches her face, studies it as she studies his.

"Did you love my mother?" she asks after an uncomfortable silence. "Did you *ever* love her?" The girl keeps her voice steady. No wavering. No tears now.

He's a trapped animal. He swallows, the hard knot in his throat making even this a challenge.

"What did she tell you?" he asks next. "What did your mother tell you about me?"

"What does *that* matter? I asked you a question and you didn't answer. I want you to answer."

"Sometimes it's not that simple," he says.

"That's bullshit. It *is* that simple. A simple question: Did you love my mother?"

He sees the tremor in his hands and removes them from the table, grips the underside of the chair with his fingers, a wad of gum there, a rough spot in the wood.

"Okay," he says. "Fair enough. Maybe it's the way you say it is. Simple. Nope...no, then. I don't think I loved her. You seem like a smart girl, though. You've got to know it's not always like that. That's not always the way these things work."

"These *things*?" she says.

Red splotches cover her throat, her face, but her voice

holds steady. Whatever she's feeling now she isn't about to share with him.

"That's not what I meant. You know that, right?" He watches her face, the little cluster of freckles sprinkled across her nose and cheeks that he hadn't noticed that day at the house. The girl is in the middle of this mess. But she's not the cause of it. He knows that. He can't blame the kid. He tries to put himself in her place. Tries to imagine how he would feel, what he would have done. But it's impossible for him to imagine his own mother doing what Nermina has done.

"I don't know. I don't know you well enough," she says. The girl is not going to show her hand; that he can see for certain.

"Here's the thing," he says. "Your mom and me, maybe it wasn't all storybook romance or anything...I think you already know that part—" He stops himself. He doesn't want to hurt her. He doesn't know, not really, what Nermina has told the girl. Maybe she'd built him up after all.

His daughter peers up at him, the belligerent curl of her lips so similar to his own. She shakes her head back and forth, a slight movement that lasts only a split second, but in that moment he sees the same defiant movement Tessa might make. The girl is strong, he sees. The girl won't take any shit from anyone.

"What I'm saying," he continues, "is that we—your mom and me—we were only together for a little while. Your mom told you about this; your mom wanted to get pregnant and she did."

"Right," Atika shoots back. "And then you left. Just like that."

"Nooooo." He draws the word out long. He shakes his head back and forth as she'd just done. "That's not how it happened. I think you really need to know this—"

"I think I *know* what happened," she says.

"But you don't," he says. "You really don't know because you weren't there and you're going to have to trust us now because..." He doesn't know how to finish.

"Because what?" she says. "Why on earth would I trust either one of you?" Her eyes are liquid, the same green as Nermina's. She's fighting hard now, fighting the tears that will surely come. He wants badly to reach across the table and thumb the first one away, to somehow keep the rest from coming.

"Because we're all here now. I guess that's it. It doesn't matter how we ended up here. You see that, right?"

She glares at him and he knows how hard she must be working to sit there in that chair, to keep up the front. He'll wait her out. What other choice does he have?

"Did you love her?" she demands.

He drops his head into his hands, feels the tension at his temples when his fingers find their way there. He waits for whatever comes next.

"No," he says. "And your mother...she didn't love me either." The words are out and he only half wishes he could take them back. He didn't want to hurt her and now he has. He didn't want to hurt her and yet he knows there was no other way to answer. More lies would never fix the first one. How could you hope to build something solid on top of something as shaky as a lie?

"Fine," says his daughter. "That's all I wanted to know."

CHAPTER 47
OLD DEBTS

Outside of Powell's Carl sits behind the wheel of the rental car. His phone hums in his shirt pocket and when he pulls it out Tessa's name and number flashes on the screen. He lets the call go to voicemail and slips the phone back into his pocket. Not yet. He needs to be on top of his game when he tells her and right now he's feeling an unsettling combination of terrified and hopeful, rattled in a way he can't describe. The girl—his daughter—had conceded a miserly smile as she heaved that heavy backpack from the floor and slung it over her shoulder. Then she'd left him standing there, left him not knowing whether he should hug her or shake her hand or just walk out the door. Finally, though, she'd reached out and touched her fingers to his forearm; the whole experience lasted half a second, but he'd felt something there, something sweet and uncertain and—so far as he could tell—something genuine. She'd even agreed to meet up with him again before he headed back to Athens. Back to Tessa.

But now he's driving blind again. No maps or GPS. He's got a daughter, and now what? His mind makes another quarter turn and his thoughts are back to Tessa. What will she think? He grips the steering wheel. The thing feels flimsy under his fingers. He rests his forehead there, the fake-leather grain damp and sticky against his skin. He wants Tessa to tell him he can do this. He can be a father. As he leans back from the wheel his phone buzzes against his chest again. He pulls out the phone and answers.

Tessa's first words are measured: "Hey, honey. How come you didn't call me back before?"

Carl fumbles, "Hey, Tess. Sorry. I was tied up. Everything okay there?"

"Yeah, everything's great, but Roddy stopped by. He was asking..." Carl's face burns where the phone is pressed to his cheek. In that split second of hesitation on Tessa's end he knows exactly what's transpired. He imagines Roddy in his perfectly pressed red flannel shirt and khaki pants. Sees him toeing the gravel in spotless work boots, too shy to meet Tessa's eyes.

"Tess, listen—"

"Carl, you promised all this stuff was behind you." Her voice is still measured, careful. Even so, Carl senses tamped down fury beneath the Southern lilt.

The feeling settles on him like the dense fog that socked in the city the morning he arrived in Portland, a sad inertia that seemed to follow Carl wherever he'd landed. With Tessa, he thought he'd finally outsmarted it but he sees now that he was wrong.

"I know it," he says. "I'll make it right." But even as he mouths the words the old heaviness presses in around him. "I'll pay him back. I mean it." He feels Atika's fleeting touch, that little jolt of promise. Hope. "I'll make it right, Tess, I—"

"Sure, sweetie," Tessa cuts in. "I just wanted to let you know the situation."

And now it's like he's back in that cul-de-sac, the little dog limp in the woman's arms. Of course, this is his fault, too. All of it, and still no flat-out blame. And because of that, no clear-cut path to forgiveness. Nothing but overgrown roots and thicket.

"Tessa—"

"Give Jeff a big hug for me," Tessa says. Then silence. Certain and sickening, the familiar sound of failure.

CHAPTER 48
DISCHARGE ROUNDS

The first to arrive, Nermina takes a seat at the conference room table. As always, she makes a point of avoiding the chairs at either end; although there isn't supposed to be a hierarchy among staff at discharge rounds, these seats are always filled by doctors. She flips through the stack of patient files she reviewed the night before, and now finds herself rereading all the notes she's made in Jeff's chart since the day security sent her to his room to intercede. That day, had she taken a just few moments longer to arrive, Jeff may have strangled an orderly. It's going to be difficult to remain objective or—at the very least—to appear so now.

In these past three weeks she's watched Jeff struggle with the same determination she imagines he'd shown in combat. He's made good progress, but he hasn't hit emotional rock bottom yet, and this worries her. Until he's experienced the worst, there's likely no place for him to go but down. That's when the real work would begin.

But before Nermina can delve any further into these concerns, Rachel Mullen, chaplain for the post-trauma clinic, pokes her head through the doorway, and Nermina flips the folder shut on Jeff's recent history. Rachel, a short, compact woman with seemingly boundless reserves of energy and compassion, raises her hand in greeting when she spots Nermina in the far corner of the room. She walks around the long oval table and slides into the high-backed chair on Nermina's right. Immediately, she swivels toward Nermina. Rachel's round face fixes her with the beatific expression that Nermina thinks of as their chaplain's hallmark.

"Hi, Nermina. How are you?"

Rachel's voice brims with good humor and Nermina wonders how anyone can be so chipper at 6:25 in the morning.

"I'm fine, Rachel. And you?"

"Oh, I'm doing well." Rachel smiles again. Then she scoops Nermina's hands into her own and draws them to her, an action that Nermina would have once found disconcerting. But throughout a decade of working together, she's grown to appreciate, and perhaps even welcome, Rachel's demonstrative warmth; this, a quality Nermina feels she's never fully mastered, even in her private life. And instead of pulling her hands free and turning away, as she surely would have done with the majority of her colleagues, she sits as she is, soaking up Rachel's good energy like a sponge.

Within the next few minutes, the room fills quickly with staff—Saul Robson, director of physical therapy; Bonnie Clark, another advanced practice nurse practitioner; the MDs—two from an outlying VA facility and three from their own center. Jack Larson, the burn specialist, and Harold Schwartzman, chief of psychiatry, sit, respectively, at the head and foot of the table. At 6:32, Barbara Edmunds, a new staff social worker, rushes through the door with a travel mug clutched in one hand and a crumpled manila folder in the other. The young woman slips into the free seat on Nermina's left and mouths a breathless sorry as Dr. Schwartzman starts off the panel with not so much as a good morning as preamble. Nermina feels the energy in the room shift into the frenetic pace typical of these proceedings; each person here, each stakeholder, has his or her own agenda to advance. Even the overhead lights seem to buzz louder, to grow brighter and more intense.

The list had proceeded alphabetically and Dr. Schwartz-man rushed them all through four cases before they reached Staff Sergeant Jeffrey P. Ingram's. Nermina had reported on two of these earlier cases—the other two were Bonnie's—and not hitting any snags, now Nermina feels a bit more confident about what she'll say on Jeff's behalf.

"So, we've still got Sergeant Ingram on the Heparin," says Schwartzman. "He'll need to be monitored after discharge. My recommendation is to discontinue the Risperdal for now. The rest we'll assess at his thirty-day check-in. I don't want to cut the pain meds entirely. Not yet." He peers over the rims of his glasses at the faces around the table. "Anyone else?"

"He'll need to be fitted for the final prosthesis," Saul Robson says. "I believe Jackie's got him on the list already. Let's see, that puts us into next week."

"That's fine," says Schwartzman. He prods the nosepiece of his glasses with his index finger. "We can handle that as out-patient. Right, Saul?"

"Will do. And we've set him up for PT. Three times a week," Robson says.

"Excuse me. Dr. Schwartzman?" says Barbara Edmunds timidly. "I, um, I've met with the wife and I..." she trails off. Nermina feels the neurons and protons swirling faster and faster now throughout the room. "Well, I've met with Sergeant Ingram's wife," Barbara continues, "and there seems to be a problem."

"Ms. Edmunds, what sort of problem are you referring to?" Schwartzman asks. He delivers the inquiry without looking up from the papers in his hands, and then sends a withering look toward Nermina's end of the table.

Barbara looks first to Nermina, then down at her paperwork, finally raising her eyes toward Schwartzman. "Doctor, it's my understanding that the wife, Mrs. Ingram, is moving—she and the children—well, apparently Mrs. Ingram plans to move out of the marital home and in with her sister in Erie, Pennsylvania."

"Excuse me?" Schwartzman says.

Nermina remembers her only face-to-face with Lisa Ingram, how Lisa had shut her down before she'd even begun to discuss a plan for Jeff's after-care. Lisa had a different agenda. She'd looked exhausted, stressed out. Two toddlers, alone, but Nermina can't imagine a wife—*any* wife— abandoning her severely injured husband just as he's finally coming home.

"Mrs. Ingram slammed out of our conference last week,"

says Barbara. "I tried calling her for three days—both numbers—and nothing. Then last night I get an email; she's not comfortable having him—her husband—around their children."

"Harold," Nermina says to Schwartzman. "May I?" Then she turns to the young social worker. "Excuse me, Barbara. I didn't mean to cut you off. Were you through?"

The woman throws up her hands in a gesture of frustration, then turns to Nermina, visibly relieved to let someone else take up the issue.

"Okay," says Nermina. "I've also met with Mrs. Ingram." She turns briefly to Barbara again. "This was right after Sergeant Ingram was admitted. Perhaps I should have seen the red flag. She was actually, well, I guess you'd say rather hostile."

"Toward you?" asks Schwartzman.

"No, well, maybe a little," Nermina begins. She remembers the contrition in Lisa's voice when she'd called about Carl's arrival. "She's extremely angry with her husband. This is really where all of the anger stems—"

"Nermina," Schwartzman interjects. "I'm sorry." He looks down at his watch and then back toward Barbara and Nermina. "This is a problem of logistics. Am I correct?"

Nermina feels the chaplain's hand touch hers lightly. Rachel rises from her seat at the table, something Nermina has witnessed on many occasions over the years, though none of the rest of the staff follows this convention. Part of her thinks that Rachel stands for dramatic effect but another part of her admires her colleague for quietly asserting herself.

"Harold, I'll be working with the family on this. Obviously,

Sergeant Ingram will need to make some other arrangements for his after-care. For transportation and whatnot. Barbara and I will work this out." Rachel holds Schwartzman's eyes a moment and then turns the same beatific look toward Barbara. "We'll work on logistics," Rachel continues, "but I imagine we're going to need a couple more days to make some calls. To set up Sergeant Ingram's support network." She looks down at the social worker again. "If you work on the Tri-Care piece, Barbara, I'll go ahead and reach out to the others on Sergeant Ingram's contact sheet."

"Fine," says Schwartzman. "Nermina, we need to set him up for his weekly group therapy, out-patient."

"Of course," Nermina says. She'd been prepared to argue for more time and she's fairly sure that Schwartzman would have agreed without much of a fight. But now she's gained a couple of days for Jeff. All thanks to Rachel. It isn't much, but it's something. And she hasn't had to expend any of her political capital to achieve this. Most importantly, she hasn't had to risk sounding as though she's personally involved with Jeff Ingram's case. Her professional duties fulfilled, Nermina's pinky finger finds the scar at her hairline, traces it gently, mindlessly. She thinks of all the broken men she's tended, and yet with Jeff, she knows that something's different. And this difference is both so distinct and so nebulous, Nermina forbids herself to delve any deeper now.

"That's it, then," says Schwartzman. "Private Belinda Jennings." This is one of Bonnie's patients. Bonnie flips a page in her copy of the chart. Someone's cell phone vibrates at the other end of the table. Nermina takes a deep breath, grateful to snap back into a realm she understands.

"TBI and PTSD," says Schwartzman. "Martin," he says, turning to one of the MDs from the Hillsboro satellite office. "Is this one of yours? Are we terminating speech therapy this week?"

Despite her best efforts, the current tugs and Nermina's mind drifts. She thinks about the last interaction she'd had with Jeff. Carl had just left for the café and Jeff seemed at his most anxious. All he'd talked about was getting strong enough, getting in shape for another deployment. The new resiliency protocols were designed for just such an outcome, but the possibility of Jeff returning to war terrified her. And still, when Nermina conjures the waning images of the family she's lost, she understands the impulse. She and Jeff are both survivors and no amount of therapy will ever completely extinguish that glint of doubt they could have done more. They could have saved the ones who perished.

She thinks again about Lisa's demeanor on the phone, so much nicer than she'd been in person that first time. Maybe this was because she'd already made up her mind. She thinks about Jeff's contacts—Carl, now at the very top of the list. She sees her daughter's tear-streaked face, hears Atika's angry words and, this impulse too, she understands. What she doesn't understand is how she's arrived here—at the center of a mess *she's* single-handedly created. She sets her hands together on the table in front of her. Schwartzman's voice drones on a few minutes longer and then stops abruptly. Nermina bows her head for an instant, a mirror image of Rachel's gesture now. But as Nermina sends up her prayer to the heavens, she attaches a mental footnote, reminding herself that—unlike Rachel—she is no longer a believer.

CHAPTER 49
MAGIC MUSHROOM

Carl parks the rental car in the lot at the arboretum. Only a handful of cars and trucks fill random spaces, their windshields and windows filmed with mist. The visitor's center—vaguely familiar to him—is still shuttered. Carl locks the car and heads for the trailhead. He stops at the little wooden pavilion where the trail maps are posted and leans in close to read them. He and Nermina had taken the four-mile Wildwood Loop Trail. That part he remembers distinctly. It went two miles in, straight up, almost from the very start, before switch-backing into a relatively easy downhill return. He chuckles, thinking how cocky he'd been that day, how he'd frozen his butt off trying to be the tough guy. He refused to take the windbreaker she offered him, the extra layer he'd never thought to pack. She was a smart girl, even then. And he'd been a prideful asshole.

Carl takes one of the envelopes from the plastic bin and slips a five-dollar bill inside. He grabs the ballpoint pen, tethered there by its ratty string, and jots down the license plate number of the rental car. *The honor system*, Carl thinks as he pushes the envelope through a thin slot in the padlocked wooden box. He understands that there was a good chunk of his life when—even in a situation as simple as this—he wouldn't have bothered to do the right thing. Hell, he would have gone out of his way to *not* do the right thing. Why, he wonders now, had it seemed like the rules had never applied to him?

He thinks about Roddy, about the money he owes him, and how he'd promised Tessa that he would straighten out his debts. A few weeks before his mom called with the news about Jeff, Tessa had started dropping hints about getting married. He figured, yeah, maybe it *was* time to ask her. Now his face flushes with embarrassment. The goddamned debt. One mistake after another. He'd panicked when he saw the stack of bills. He'd gone behind her back, hit Roddy up for cash—a drop in the bucket—but now Tessa knows. Tessa knows he lied. Then his thoughts gather speed: Tessa, Nermina, Atika, and Jeff. Nermina, Atika, Jeff, and Tessa. He wonders, in turn, what each of them *really* thinks of him. He wants to say it doesn't matter, but of course he knows it does. This all comes at him faster now, every choice a big one. A big deal, every single one.

He bends down to tie the lace of his work boot and startles a little when a young couple—neither older than twenty—walks up to inspect the trail maps. They hold hands, each offering Carl a contained nod, but nothing more.

"Morning," Carl says.

"Morning," the young guy mumbles. He slips his arm around the woman's waist. She's slim, blond, ponytailed, a female version of her chiseled boyfriend. She leans into him, gazes past Carl like he's invisible.

Carl walks back to the car and grabs a half-filled water bottle from the console, lukewarm from sitting there overnight. He hadn't intended to hike very far—just wanted to clear his head some—but seeing the young couple has changed his mind. He doesn't know why and he tells himself it doesn't matter; he doesn't need to figure it out right now. Maybe he'll even do the loop trail. The whole thing.

The first ten minutes on the trail have him sweating through his T-shirt. He unbuttons his flannel shirt, shrugs out of it, and ties it around his waist. By the time he crests the first ridge, he's drenched. The fog has burnt off completely. Beyond the dense cover of Douglas firs, the sun feels strong on his face. The warmth feels good. He runs his thumb and forefinger against the stubble on his cheeks, along his jaw. He looks out over Portland, over Mt. Rainier, and the other four peaks— whose names now escape him—etched against a sky so perfect it could be fake. The thought makes Carl chuckle, but the view *is* beautiful. In all those years pin-balling across the States, those couple of trips he'd wrangled to the UK, he'd always been a sucker for this kind of natural beauty.

He thinks about Tessa again. About those first dense, sticky nights in her place, the air so still you felt its subtle pressure on your skin. He'd stayed in Athens because of Tessa. But he also remembers the mind-numbing inertia that had settled over him. Yes, he'd fallen in love with Tessa. But he'd also been lonely. And maybe the truth is he'd just been tired of running from the old ghosts, from ducking his own shadow. Till now, Tessa had kept him safe from both.

Now he decides he'll push on a little further, at least to the next marker, before heading back to the car. On the next switchback the trail narrows. It winds downward, around a little island of tall hemlock. A canopy of mountain laurel shades the undergrowth—ferns, trillium, ropey tree roots, dark and lush—but Carl spots a bright orange mushroom at his feet, the thing so bright it seems to be glowing, doesn't even look real. He bends down to inspect it. He wants to pluck it from the soil to see it better but decides he'd better not. It *belongs* there. Instead, he squats lower and brings his face close to the solid-looking flesh of it. It smells like the earth, like rain, like moldering leaves. He knows it's corny—superstitious even—but he gets the idea that maybe this thing is a sign; it's there to tell him where he belongs, what he should do about Tessa. He loves her but does he love her enough to change? *Can* he change? And then he calls back that light touch to his arm that his daughter had bestowed. His *daughter*. In his mind the word sounds exotic, even sacred, like it belongs to some ancient language he's only discovered by chance.

He stands—maybe too fast because he feels the dizzy rush to his head—and then both boot soles slide over a clump of slick tree roots. His feet fly out from under him. He lands hard, flat on his ass, his tailbone, and he sits there more startled than hurt. What an idiot, he thinks. Then he hears the crackle of boots on underbrush. He looks up. The couple from earlier— neither sweating, still pristine for Chrissake—take three or four perfectly placed steps down to where Carl lies sprawled on the ground.

"You okay, sir? We heard you hit the ground," says the guy. "Can you move?"

Carl feels a bruise rising around his tailbone, a throbbing pain just coming into its own. Still, he thinks he'll laugh then. *Sir?*

"I'm fine." He wants to add *Son*, but the girl's blue eyes, wide with alarm and Carl thinks, also potential pity, lock onto his. "Yeah, I can stand," he says, turning away from the girl. He starts to push up with the heels of his hands, but feels the pain there, too. He holds his hands out in front of him and sees how both palms have already purpled, pinpricks of blood rising on the right, his dominant hand. "Let me help you," the young guy says. He's lean and, now Carl learns, also strong; Carl feels the guy's fingers lock solidly, high up on his ribs, under his armpits. He feels himself being lifted and he wants to resist. And then it's too late. He's on his feet. He stands just a few inches from the couple, their youth, their vitality, a seeming reproach.

"Can you make it back down?" the guy asks.

"Sure, I can," says Carl. "I'm good, really. Thanks."

"We can wait with you if you want," the girl says. "I mean, we'll hike down with you." She shoots her boyfriend a look that Carl reads as a tepid apology. "Yeah—" the guy starts.

"No need," Carl says. He wants them gone. "I'm fine. Really. Got the wind knocked out of me is all." He forces a chuckle.

The couple exchanges another look. "Okay, cool," the guy says. "Take care." He slips his arm around the girl's waist and then the two scurry down the trail like cartoon jackrabbits. Carl shakes his head. He would laugh, but his back is seizing now, the spasms shooting down his right thigh. The same thing had happened when he miscalculated a ladder rung on a painting job a couple of years ago. He thinks about Jeff, wonders what it would feel like to have your leg blown off, what god-awful pain his brother must have endured.

Carl blots his palms—streaked now with blood, with dirt—on one of the loose sleeves of his flannel shirt—and begins what should have been an easy trek back down.

Behind the wheel of the rental car, the spasms ease up a little. He knows he'll be stiff later, but hopefully not out of commission. He tells himself it's no big deal. He thinks about the couple on the trail again, how the two of them seemed to meld together into one creamy substance, the way Tessa's cornbread batter folded in on itself as she worked the mixer blades around the bowl. He thinks about the stupid mushroom and then Tessa. And then he pictures his daughter. He pictures Atika. His heartbeat shifts to a faster pace. Two completely different kinds of love, these. He knows he'll never have to coax the second. Already, his love for her scares him.

Carl grabs his phone from the glove box, taps out Tessa's number, and waits for the dial tone.

CHAPTER 50
BUTTERFLY GARDEN

Nermina waits behind a threesome of medical techs with identical maroon scrubs and matching Crocs. When it's her turn, she orders a grandé with a little frothy cap of soy. The barista, a robust black woman with a magnificent bundle of tiny braids, twisted and folded atop her head, hands the to-go cup to Nermina.

"Thank you, LaWanda," Nermina says. She stuffs a dollar bill into the jar in front of the register.

"Have a blessed day," the barista says.

"And you as well," Nermina replies, completing their daily ritual.

Then readjusting the strap of her bag so the ache in her shoulders eases, she takes a swallow from the cup. The coffee is hot and decent. She thinks of the strong Turkish coffee she'd shared with her family all those years ago. Thick and bittersweet, and poured from her nana's samovar in little copper cups. She shakes off the memory—aware she's procrastinating—and heads toward the elevators.

When the doors ping open Nermina's pulse speeds up. She steps onto the elevator and walks straight to the back. She avoids eye contact with any of her fellow passengers, an American social norm she's grown to appreciate, especially at the moment. Despite staying calm during discharge rounds, now Nermina's stomach churns. She wants to get everything right with Jeff, and the first step is getting him on board with the idea of continuing his therapy, the one-on-one counseling she's recommended. She knows Jeff will be onboard with out-patient PT, but the counseling he'll likely blow off if no one pesters him about it. Now that Lisa is temporarily out of the picture, she hopes Carl will be the one to do the pestering. Nermina smiles then. She remembers how careful and sweet Carl had been with Atika, how hard he seemed to be trying. Not once since he's met their daughter has that trademark belligerent smirk crossed his face. Maybe people *can* change, Nermina thinks.

The doors slide open on the fourth floor. Nermina edges her way to the front of the elevator and steps out into the hallway just across from the nursing station. She nods to Reese, charge nurse for the floor. The purple halos ringing the older woman's eyes tell Nermina that she's just coming off her twelve-hour shift. She remembers the wrung-out exhaustion of her own early morning bus rides home from the hospital, entire years of exhaustion, and she's grateful—again—that those days are behind her.

She knocks on Jeff's open door, though she sees the sheets pulled tight over the freshly made bed, Jeff sitting in the only chair.

"May I come in?" she calls from the threshold. Jeff looks up from the book he holds in his hands.

"Yes, ma'am," Jeff says. He stands, closes the book, and places it on the crisp white sheets. He stands in front of the bed, straight and tall, while she walks toward him. She imagines him with his unit and believes with immediate certainty that this man would rather have died than failed any one of them.

"Sergeant Ingram...Jeff, please sit," she says. She smiles, as much to calm herself as to put Jeff at ease.

"No, ma'am, I'm fine," he says. "You sit." His eyes, clear of pain meds, piercing and blue, hold hers briefly before he looks away.

"Okay," she says. Nermina shifts the strap of her bag on her shoulder. "How about we take a walk?"

"Sure," he says. He walks past Nermina and then stops at the door to wait for her.

She sees how his gait has improved, even in the past few days. They walk side-by-side down the corridor in silence. When they get to the nursing station Nermina places her hand on Jeff's forearm. With the other—clutching her coffee cup—she motions to an alcove to their left. "I'm just going to get rid of this thing." She pats the canvas messenger bag at her hip and then pulls a set of keys from a zippered pocket on the outside.

"Sure," Jeff says. He smiles. "I've got nothing but time." His voice and delivery convey a subdued humor, a side to Jeff she's yet to witness.

Nermina feels something loosen up inside her. "Here, this one," she says. She points to one of three doors in the poorly lit alcove as she fidgets with her keys. She unlocks the heavy wooden door and steps into the small office she shares with Robert, another advance practice psych nurse. The room smells of orange peels and burnt coffee. Nermina glances at the coffee maker to make sure Robert hasn't left an empty pot on the burner, something they've each done on more than one occasion. She slings the strap of her bag over a hook on the back of the door. All the while, Jeff stands rigidly just inside the doorway. Nermina turns to face him. "Oh, I'm sorry," she says. "Just give me a minute." She unzips a compartment on the bag and pulls out her cell phone. This she slips into the pocket of her white coat. She leans over the desk and slides the computer mouse around on its pad. She clicks a couple of times and scans the screen. "These'll wait," she says, almost to herself. Then turning back to Jeff, "So, where to?"

Jeff shrugs. "Up to you, ma'am."

"Okay, I have an idea," she says. She feels herself smiling. "One thing, though, you have to stop calling me 'ma'am.' After all, we're...well, we're sort of..." She looks down at her right hand where she's clutching the ratty back cushion of the desk chair. Her cuticles are jagged, her fingernails, just nubs really, unpainted. "Well, we're connected," she says finally.

"Yes ma'am," Jeff says, the moment she looks up again to meet his eyes. Nermina sees—and hears—that buried humor trying so hard to work its way to the surface again.

"Very clever, Sergeant Ingram." She swings the door fully open and motions for him to exit. "Have you ever been to the butterfly garden?" she asks.

"Didn't know there was one."

"Ah, then, you're in for a treat." She thinks about the first time she'd stumbled upon this place. The little garden has become her favorite spot when she needs to escape, even if for only a few short minutes, the unnatural glare of fluorescent light and re-circulated air in the hospital. She looks up into Jeff's eyes.

"You okay to walk a bit?"

He answers with a quick salute. "All right, then," she says. "Let's go."

They take the elevator down to the lobby level. Nermina leads Jeff past the cafeteria where the pervasive aroma of fried chicken mingles with the greasy smells of the morning's breakfast staples: fried eggs, bacon, scrapple, sausage, and hash browns. They walk slowly now, through a corridor whose exterior side consists of floor-to-ceiling windows. Nermina notes exhaustion in the hollows beneath Jeff's eyes.

"Just a little further," she says.

"I'm good," Jeff says, though Nermina hears the strain in his voice now, too.

When she pushes against the metal bar on a set of double doors, Jeff takes a couple of long breaths before testing the prosthetic leg on the first of two shallow aluminum steps. Nermina's heart plunges. She reaches out instinctively, the fingers of both her hands now circling the unyielding, broad muscle of his arm. He doesn't shake her off. They take the second step in unison. She feels a subtle opening inside her. Beyond them, a small square of grass, almost unnaturally green, and a sculpted border of purple coneflowers, yarrow, and buddleia—butterfly bush—soothe Nermina almost instantly. She lets go of Jeff's arm and gestures to a bench only a few steps away. The weak sunlight has begun to make its way beyond the medical office towers looming behind the main hospital building.

"How're you doing?" Nermina asks.

"AOK," Jeff says. He stretches out his good leg in front of him and pats his shirt pocket where a pack of cigarettes protrudes.

"Oh...geez, sorry Jeff. I'm sorry. There's no smoking out here." Nermina's arm sweeps out in a wide arc, seemingly of its own accord, and she points to a sign affixed to the blocky structure that houses the Garden Club's equipment. "I should have said something before."

"It's no big deal," Jeff says. He leans over, rests his elbows on his knees. Then he presses his hands together as though in prayer and Nermina follows the jittery path of movement, from the good leg—tapping in double-time into the grass—up through his hands and jostling his chin as he rests it there on his hands.

"Nice out here, though, isn't it?" Nermina asks.

Jeff scans the flower border, the low brick ledge surrounding a mosaic-tiled fountain, and finally a thin path of pale green grass fighting to take root in a spot that had, until quite recently, still been paved over. Two birch trees spread their limbs over the little garden shed, shading its shingled roof.

"It is," says Jeff. He shakes his head approvingly. "Reminds me of a little park me and Lisa used to go..." He clears his throat. "Before we were married, before all..."

Nermina searches Jeff's eyes to see if there's more that he'll share, but when he tilts his face up to a slightly brightening sky, she follows suit. She thinks about the day she'd first noticed Carl at the construction site for the new building, the building she now works in. She almost laughs thinking how determined she'd been then, how positive that she'd get exactly what she wanted: her baby. She looks down at her hands, clasped in her lap, and then to Jeff's face, his profile, as he stares straight ahead now. She sees again the undeniable similarity in their faces, Carl's and Jeff's. She thinks of her daughter, the lovely curve of her cheek, and then that same sleek plane of muscle and bone beneath. The same as in these men, these brothers.

"I know this is going to be a tough time for you," Nermina says. She works to keep her voice steady. "I know about Lisa taking the boys to her sister's. Celeste, right?"

Jeff lets out a long breath that hisses a little through his teeth. He rubs his right hand over the red-blond stubble of his brush cut. He says nothing for several moments. Nermina waits.

Then finally, he says, "Yeah, the lady chaplain...Miss Rachel?...she came to talk to me about all that. She said you guys had some kind of big powwow." He emits what sounds like a choked-off chuckle.

Nermina turns on the bench, turns her entire body toward Jeff's voice, which sounds at once defensive and frightened.

"Yes, we do that...for everyone, for all our discharged patients, I mean."

"I know," says Jeff.

"So, what I wanted to talk about—well, the hospital, we're

373

going to keep you another couple of days until you've had the chance to put some...to put a support—"

"Yeah, I know all that," Jeff says.

Nermina hears him biting something back. Anger? Relief? She hasn't spent enough time with Lisa to truly gauge her *or* the relationship that she and Jeff have. Lisa had been exhausted. Furious. In retrospect, Nermina thinks, Lisa is probably deeply hurt. She imagines that—rational or not—Lisa blames her husband for being deployed, holds him accountable for leaving her alone with their babies. Maybe she even blames him for his injuries. This wouldn't be the first time she's encountered this reaction, and part of her gets it. Part of her sympathizes with Lisa, though most of her doesn't.

"Do you think you can get some help...at home, I mean?" Nermina begins.

Jeff leans forward again and, with his knees on his elbows, he cradles his head in his hands. Nermina sees how the vertebrae of his bent neck stand out in relief, vulnerable in the gathering sunlight. And then something Nermina hadn't noticed before: a notch in Jeff's left ear at the top. She sees how the remaining bone and cartilage has been fused to compensate for what was gone. For what had been taken from him. She imagines placing her lips to that space. She imagines tracing each knobby bone of his spine with her fingertips. But then her fingers move instead to her own wound, to the scar on her scalp. She loses herself for a moment or two. She aches for this man. She aches for the both of them, yet the sensation is not wholly unpleasant.

"I'll be okay," Jeff says without raising his head. His voice is muffled.

Nermina places her hand lightly on his wrist. "Jeff," she says. "You're going to need some help." She clears her throat and withdraws her hand.

"My brother's here," Jeff says. Nermina hears a raspiness in his voice now that goes beyond exhaustion.

"You'll need a driver. For a while, at least," she says.

"I know that."

"And you'll need to keep up with the counseling."

Jeff slides his hands down to the bench and grips the edge. He straightens his torso and Nermina sees the muscles in his arms tighten as if he were about to raise himself—the complete weight of his body with the power of his arms—just as she's seen him do in physical therapy.

"I get that," he says. "I get it."

She holds his eyes and he doesn't look away. She feels his body, close, solid beside her on the bench and they sit then in silence. They sit in what she imagines to be peace. She watches a monarch drift down through the birch leaves—the first to arrive. It lands on a fluffy purple plume of buddleia, its wings fluttering softly, in cadence with her heart.

CHAPTER 51
FLESH AND BLOOD

The first thing Jeff thinks to do is call Lisa's sister, Celeste. He'll plead with her if he has to, get her to talk some sense into Lisa. But before he's worked up the nerve, Celeste calls him. Same chipper go-getter as when he'd first met Lisa's family the year he and Lisa got engaged.

"It'll be good for everyone," Celeste says on the phone. "You'll see. It'll give you and Lisa a little break. Our girls can fuss all over Tyler and Ethan. We've got tons of room, Jeff. *Tons* of room for the kids. Besides, Lisa's a wreck. I'm sure you can see that."

He wants to say: *What the fuck?* But she doesn't give him an opening—or he doesn't make one—and then it's too late. She's telling him she's hopping on a plane and Greg will "hold down the fort" till she and Lisa drive back together from

Portland to Erie with the boys. *His* boys.

And now he thinks that maybe he's brought this whole thing on himself. Lisa taking the kids. He thinks about Rodriguez. *Six* kids. That crumpled-up picture of his wife, his kids. The way Rodriguez would peel it from under his Dragon Skin after a mission, Saran-wrapped over his heart. Rodriguez, dead now. Crisped. Those kids with no father and him—Jeff—just letting his kids go. He slams his fist down onto the pile of magazines, then shoves the whole pile of them off the table and onto the floor. He can't read this shit anyway. Can't read anything. Can't concentrate. The docs say it will take a while yet. He levers himself out of the sofa and gets down as far as he can. He kicks the outliers with his good foot and scrapes together the pile, scoops them all up in one hand. Then he fans out the magazines on the table the way Lisa would on the coffee table at home. The way she always did before the kids were born.

The three women come in together: Lisa, Celeste, and Nermina. A trifecta, he thinks. Celeste—tall, muscular, almost Lisa's double, but darker—rushes over to where he sits on the crummy sofa and leans down to hug him. She smells like coconut, like goddamned Coppertone. "Hey, Jeff, how're you feeling?" She touches his arm. "You doing okay, buddy?"

He pulls his arm away. "Never better," he says.

Lisa hangs back a little. She has on one of those preppy dresses she likes to wear. Just like a polo shirt, baby blue and short, her long legs suntanned. She looks pretty now that she's lost the baby weight, even prettier than Celeste, Jeff thinks. But there's a hard edge to Lisa now, too, and that makes him sad because he'd always thought that once she got pregnant, once they'd had the boys, Lisa would be happy. Everything would be good. He pushes himself up from the couch and he thinks maybe he'll give his wife a peck on the cheek, *make an effort*, but she won't look his way.

"Let's all sit down," Nermina says. "Okay? Is the table all right, Jeff?" She smiles at him, a sweet smile, not nervous, not fake, and Jeff takes a deep breath. Nermina has on her doctor's coat, some kind of silky pants and top underneath. He wonders if she wears the white coat now on purpose, figures it's one way to take the upper hand. That day in the garden she'd left it behind and she seemed a lot softer then. He'd liked sitting there with her. He'd felt—for the first time in a very long time—just the tiniest hint of peace.

Jeff shrugs. "Fine by me." They all pull out chairs and sit at the white laminate table where Lisa had served him and Carl lunch. He hates this room almost as much he hates the rest of the place. Then he thinks about the garden again. He catches Nermina's look and he knows she has his back today.

"So, this is...a little unorthodox," Nermina starts. She unzips the canvas briefcase he remembers from the week before and pulls out a fat manila folder. This she lays on the table in front of her. "Typically, this would be Rachel's, um, Chaplain Mullen's, purview..." She looks to her right—Lisa, grim, a smirk dying to make its way to her lips—and then across the table to Celeste, her face poised angelically. Expecting *what*? Jeff wonders. Nermina turns back to Jeff. "So, first Jeff...I do understand...I know this is kind of, well, awkward, but Celeste was kind enough to facilitate this, um, meeting—" Nermina breaks off her little speech and opens the folder. He watches her fingers riffle through the pages. The fucked-up story of Staff Sergeant. Ingram's fucked up life, he figures. She has it all there in front of her and yet he doesn't get the feeling she thinks of him this way. She'd sat with him that day, like an equal, not judging, not pitying.

He can see Celeste is chomping at the bit to jump in and he has to hand it to her because she's keeping her mouth shut, same as Lisa. "So, as I was saying," Nermina continues now, "Jeff, you're going home, but the circumstances..." Jeff thinks he sees Nermina shoot a laser-quick look at Lisa. "Well, the circumstances have changed," she says. Now she locks eyes with Celeste. "So, Celeste and Lisa are going to get you all squared away...make sure you have everything you need—"

"I've got it under control," Jeff says. He glares at Lisa. "My brother and I—"

"Well, either way, Jeff, we're going to need to monitor the Heparin for another month. And you'll need to come in for PT. There's a lot..." Jeff watches Nermina's face, the bluish vein at her temple. He thinks he sees it pulsing. "There's an awful lot to keep track of," she says.

"I'm aware, ma'am." It isn't Nermina's fault. It isn't Celeste's fault either. "They gave me the list already." He won't mention that he had to read it three times before any of it sunk in.

"We had a good talk with Carl," Celeste says, breaking her silence. She turns with all her super-mom intensity to Jeff. "He's on board completely. His girlfriend Tessa is going to send up some of his things. It was really sweet of him to watch the boys today—" She stops short, her face going wide-eyed. Jeff chokes back the urge to topple the lame-ass table, smash the cheap thing to pieces.

"Jeff," Nermina says. "This is just temporary." He can feel Lisa across from him, feel the anger coming off her in waves. Lisa keeps her face down, picks at the cuticle on her left thumb. He tries to remember when things were still good between them and comes up blank. He imagines the smirk that would be there if she *did* look up. He'd slap it off her arrogant face.

"Lisa and Celeste will drive you home now," Nermina says. "You can spend some time with your sons before they get on the road...It'll be okay." He sees the muscle twitch above Nermina's lip and he knows, in that moment, that this arrangement isn't temporary. Lisa is going and his boys are going. But he doesn't know how to stop them. His family—*his flesh and blood*—is heading to Erie, Pennsylvania, but to Jeff, it may as well be Fallujah.

"Jeff?" Nermina says. She places her hand lightly on his wrist and he closes his eyes. He feels the room dissolve, lets himself float in space, but mostly he waits for the wave of sadness to recede. He doesn't want her to see his tears.

CHAPTER 52
TESSA

Carl waits in the cell phone lot for Tessa's text message. According to the Delta site, her plane is on time. It should land in fifteen minutes. And then after that he'll tell her he's not coming back to Athens. For how long he can't say. All he knows for sure is he needs to be here—with Jeff, with Atika— for now anyway. He checks the time on his watch again, Tessa's gift. Fourteen minutes till landing. He turns off the engine and rolls down the front windows of Jeff's Jeep Grand Cherokee. Then he opens the door and gets out. Mist still hovers over the great expanse of blacktop and concrete, jet fuel and diesel fumes greasy and sharp. Carl can taste it in the back of his throat. He leans against the roof of the Jeep, his elbows resting along the edge, and watches an E-Z Park van lumber out onto the service road. He imagines himself inside the van, maybe heading to Cancun. Hell, maybe even Europe. He'd treat Atika to a high school graduation trip. It'd be like some sappy movie.

And then he shakes his head and checks his watch again. Eleven minutes. Carl pulls his phone out of the front pocket of his jeans and lays it on the roof. He thinks about how different his life would have been if Nermina had told him when she got pregnant. Would he have stayed? Would he have done *the right thing*? His whole life has blown up in the last few weeks. Still, in some ways he knows he's better off. *Way* better offer, when it comes to Atika, even when it comes to Jeff. Goose bumps climb Carl's arms. He rubs his hands briskly up and down, feeling the taut muscle under the skin, but feeling older than he's accustomed to, feeling ancient.

He'll be starting all over again. *Again.* He lets himself wonder if Tessa's coming to Portland will change anything? A stupid way to think, a dangerous way to think now. When the phone vibrates against the roof he grabs it like the thing is a live grenade. He texts her back—his thumbs clumsy—Will B @ ground transport in a fww.

He pulls up as close as he can to Delta arrivals—taxis, cars, limos, weaving in and out of traffic, airport security waving cars on. He sees her standing at the curb, long teal-and-white-striped skirt, soft over her hips, denim jacket, her hair twisted into a knot. She looks pretty. She waves, her wrist full of bracelets, as he gets closer. When he hugs her she smells like lavender. She smells the same as before.

"Hey," she says, holding him at arms' length. "Let me look at you."

He smiles. "I should be saying the same." He grabs the

upright handle of Tessa's suitcase, holds his hand out for the tote bag on her shoulder. He wants to say something more but isn't sure what. He waves toward the Grand Cherokee, hazard lights flashing in sync with his heartbeat. "I'm over there," he says.

He pays at the booth with his credit card and as he merges into the airport exit lanes, he catches Tessa's profile, her expression calm, angelic, the way she looks at the end of a yoga session. He tries to imagine what she's thinking now. He doesn't want to hurt her. Before she'd said she wanted to come out, he thought he knew what was right. *The fair thing to do.* He remembered how Nermina had used these words when she'd told him about Atika. Nermina had come to the conclusion that telling him he had a daughter—sixteen years late—was the fair thing to do. She'd turned out to be right.

"I missed you," he says once he's pulled onto the interstate. He hears the wavering in his voice and wonders if Tessa hears it, too.

She turns her face toward Carl. "I missed you, too." She unwinds the elastic from her hair and the whole wild mess of auburn curls falls over her shoulders. He forces himself to keep his eyes straight ahead on the road.

"You sure it's okay for me to stay at Jeff's?" she says after a few moments. "Will I be in the—"

"More than okay. He insists on it. My brother..."

"It's good to hear you say that."

Carl clears his throat. If it hadn't been for Tessa he wouldn't have come out here in the first place. She—more than anyone, really, more than his mother, even—had convinced him: this was where he needed to be. Then his face flushes hot. He thinks about the money he still owes Roddy. It'll take a while now to pay him back. He has nothing to offer Tessa. He's starting from scratch. Again. And, still, she's here.

"It's not perfect between us," he says. "Between me and Jeff. We still have our shit." His head makes a quarter turn toward Tessa and he sees her smile.

"We *all* have our shit, Carl."

Carl pulls the Jeep into the driveway at Jeff and Lisa's place. He's already started to do some work. Four replacement windows lean against the outside of the breezeway where he'd left them the day before. He and Jeff are regulars now at the Home Depot. This thought makes Carl smile. He rolls Tessa's suitcase up to the breezeway and she follows him in through the side door. He leads her through the living room—nice little fireplace against one wall, framed pictures of the boys, of Jeff and Lisa, over the mantel. They walk through the archway to the kitchen and Jeff is at the table, every inch of it covered with papers. He pushes himself up and out of his chair. He's wearing a white polo shirt, a pair of khakis, loose over the prosthetic.

"Jeff, this is Tessa," Carl says. He feels shy all of a sudden. He thinks how their father would scowl over the top of his newspaper when either of them brought a friend home. Jeff puts out his hand and Tessa shakes with him, then she places her hands on his shoulders, hugs him lightly and steps back. Jeff's face goes red but he fixes Tessa with a level gaze. Polite, respectful. "Every bit as pretty as my brother said." He rubs his hand across the top of his buzz-cut head.

Tessa laughs. "We'll see what else he's said about me." And then Carl watches Tessa's expression turn serious, the slight dimple at the right side of her lips disappearing. "Jeff, I'm really...I'm just so glad to finally meet you."

"Same here." Jeff shifts some of the papers around on the table. "Sorry about this mess. We've got..." He glances at Tessa. "*I've* got a mess of bills here."

"Hey, Jeff?" Tessa looks toward Carl, then back to Jeff. She taps the handle of the suitcase. "I'm just going to stash these things, splash some water on my face, and then you and me, we're going to get started on whatever projects need doing here. Okay?"

Jeff shakes his head. "Hell, no. Your first time in Portland. My brother's got big plans for you. Places to go. People to see."

Tessa rests her hands on her hips—Carl knows the look— and raises her eyebrows. "We'll see," she says, her eyes still on Jeff.

Carl watches her appraising the kitchen, the dirty dishes in the sink, crumbs on the counter, the overflowing ashtray in the middle of the pile of papers on the table. His fingers reach for Tessa's wrist, worry the cluster of bracelets there with his fingers. Tessa and his brother in the same place. Crazy. He feels light-headed, giddy almost. "Come on," he says. "You have to be exhausted. Let me show you..." He clears his throat. "Let me show you our room."

"Give her the grand tour," Jeff says from where he sits at the table again.

"Yes, sir," Carl says.

The place is small, but Carl has to admit Lisa has done a nice job. He opens the door to the twins' room—the walls painted periwinkle blue, white curtains, bright white wood trim, a border below the crown molding, yellow moon and stars against a purple sky. Two white-slatted cribs, white bureau, white wicker rocker, and changing table fill the cozy space.

"Oh, it's precious," Tessa says. She grabs Carl's hand. Her eyes sweep the room again. "It's got to be breaking his heart."

"He's holding up." Carl's jaw muscles go rigid. "She's been calling every night, putting the twins on the phone."

"That's something..." Tessa walks over to the bureau and picks up a small plastic snow globe. She shakes it and a thousand confetti bits snow down on a miniature Seattle skyline. "Still got to be brutal, though. His babies..."

Carl feels a lump filling his throat. If he hadn't told Tessa that Lisa had left, taken the kids, maybe she wouldn't have been so anxious to come out here. Had he lured her? The idea that he'd capitalized on his brother's fucked-up situation strikes him hard now. Sure, he and Tessa had talked about the money. And he'd promised her he'd fix it, but even in her text messages, he still heard the silent question: Could she trust him? *Could* she? And now he's twelve again, awakened in the night to his parents' shouting. His mother's venom hisses up the stairwell: *How can you expect me to trust you?* It was always about money.

"Jeff has his moments," Carl says now. He places his hand on the small of Tessa's back and motions to the door. "I'll show you the rest."

Jeff and Lisa's guest room holds a double bed, the bedspread and pillows—lots of them—a teal, brown, and ochre swirling print against a white background. Tessa runs her hand along the edge of the bed, surveys the 1960s-style lamps with their patterned bases, the low brown credenza. "Wow, the girl's got style," she says. "Got to give her that." She pulls the blinds and she and Carl look out to a fenced yard, Little Tykes play set for climbing, a few shade trees, tidy brick patio. Carl thinks he'll rebuild the shed; the thing is listing badly, one of the wooden doors rotting at the bottom. He sits down on the edge of the bed. He imagines fixing up a place of his own someday. Maybe a place nearby.

"Tess," he says, his voice hoarse, unsteady again.

Tessa sits down on the bed next to him. They sit a few moments in silence, sit there, hip to hip. "Tess," he says again. He slides his arm around her waist, pulls her even closer. He holds her. He thinks about the night he'd brought home the stray, Tessa asleep on the futon in the living room, and the slow smile that lit her face when the dog lapped at her with gratitude.

Tessa cocks her head. "What?" she says.

Carl's lips brush her neck. He buries his face in the soft fountain of curls there, breathes in her lavender scent. "Nothing," he says. "Nothing."

CHAPTER 53
PROPAGATING

Her arms stretched around a new bag of potting soil, Nermina nudges the door handle down with her elbow, pushes against the screen with her hip and, once through the narrow opening, lets the door slam behind her. She settles the bag on the deck and drifts toward the railing. The wood is still slick from an earlier downpour and the air scented with roses and lavender, the honeysuckle remarkably sweet. A new-birthed sheen blankets each leaf and flower and stem.

Nermina places her hands on the railing. Her eyes come to rest on a wide swath of purple flowers that Raifa calls turtle head. The plant has grown tall and vigorous, seeming to have leaped from the ground and tripled in size since Raifa handed her the clump of roots a couple of years before. Nermina has never bothered to learn the proper names—the Latin names—

of all the plants in her garden as her mother and grandmother had. But she enjoys digging in the earth and watching the bright green sprigs push through the soil each spring with a constancy that still amazes her. She loves her garden nearly as much as she loves her house, the cedar-shingled bungalow with its large windows, the frames of thick mahogany, and the wide front porch. The deck she stands on now had taken Samir the better part of a summer to complete, and this she loves, well. For all of this she is grateful.

She hoists the bag of soil in front of her again and carries it to a far corner of the deck where a large blue-glazed pot sits empty. She pulls a set of pruning shears from the back pocket of her jeans, but then instead of cutting open the bag as she'd intended, she wanders down three wooden steps onto the spongy-wet grass. Walking the perimeter of her small yard, she stops, first to yank out a clump of weeds around the nasturtium, and then to admire one of the plants she does know the proper name for—a vine called sweet autumn clematis, *clematis paniculata*—that winds its way up and over a wooden arbor (another of Samir's projects), and sweeps a profusion of little white flowers in a fluffy arc that makes Nermina smile when she spots it from the kitchen window. Now on closer inspection, the wispy yellow threads at the center of each flower, the thick perfume rising from rain-wet petals, surprise her all over again.

But then she shivers, her feet cold inside her soaked canvas sneakers. She remembers the large terra cotta urns that stood on either side of the wide entryway to her childhood home in Dobrinja. She can no longer remember even the common names of the flowers her mother planted in these each spring, nor can she conjure her mother's face as she'd been before the war. Not a single photo of any of them remains. The last image of her mother—her face bruised and caked with blood—haunts her still. It is her mother's ghost that wanders here, especially.

Nermina squints up at the halo of white flowers, the leafy vine weaving through the lattice. Her experience has taught her that this is a *thin place*—a time and a place, really—this moment when sorrows coalesce, when the dead and the living clasp hands with one another. She thinks of everyone she's lost. Her parents and Mirsad and all of the others in Bosnia. She thinks of Jeff Ingram and the men—he'd called them brothers—he'd lost in battle. She thinks of Jeff's little boys, his own flesh and blood, but children he doesn't yet know. And she thinks of Lisa, too. Maybe Lisa and Jeff will learn to love one another again and maybe they won't. She thinks about Carl, of his own constellation of loss. She thinks of her daughter, *their* daughter. And Nermina thinks how she'd needed Atika—needed a child—so desperately she'd been willing to lie to her, to lie to Carl, for far too many years. Sorrows, all of these. But, also, an opportunity to make amends, she sees now. The chance, if not to erase, then perhaps to lessen these sorrows.

Nermina turns away from the arbor and climbs the three steps to the deck. Here she slits open the bag of soil with the clippers and dumps two-thirds of its contents into the blue-glazed pot. She digs with her gloved hand in the soil and drops three robust lavender plants—each in their soggy peat containers—into the place she's made for them. These plants, cuttings Nermina had taken from a huge woody clump in Raifa and Samir's front garden, were the first she'd ever propagated herself and she is proud of them. She is proud of what she's grown.

Then, remembering the other tasks on her list, Nermina walks back down the steps to the yard. She squishes again through the wet grass and stoops to pluck a few big leaves of basil. She'll buy tomatoes at the farmers market later and everything else she needs at the grocery store. She'll cook a meal for the whole big bunch of them. She'll cook it for her family.

CHAPTER 54
THE BIG ENVELOPE

Mother and daughter sit at the kitchen table, both unaware how they mimic one another's posture so perfectly: spines erect, long, thin hands steepled in front of them. Moments into their silence, Atika fans out the smaller envelopes—bills, solicitations for charities—and the bigger pieces of junk mail, catalogs, and sale flyers. All of this, including one large white envelope, she spreads across the scarred wooden table where dozens of family dramas have unfolded. Atika riffles through an Urban Outfitters catalogue and then places it on top of a sale flyer for Home Depot. She gently bites her lower lip, plucks Nermina's car insurance bill from one stack and places it on top of another. Nermina snatches the bill from the pile and fans her face with it. "Well?" she says, unable to follow her own best advice and keep her mouth shut.

Her daughter tilts her head to the side and squints. Gingerly, as though handling a rare book, she lifts the white envelope. "What if it's not what you think? Mama, I..." In that moment, Atika is six years old again, pleading with Nermina to lie in bed with her a little longer. To assure her the tapping sound outside her window is neither a monster nor a ghost.

Just as Rachel Mullen had done at the hospital, Nermina reaches out across the table and pulls her daughter's hands into her own warm grasp. Atika's hands are cold, freezing, and Nermina rubs them briskly. "Draga, what else could it be?" As much as Nermina dreads the answer, she wills false cheer into her voice. Raifa had prepared her for 'the big envelope' and now it's *her* job to be—or at least appear to be—every bit as happy as her daughter. When Atika applied for early decision at Brown the prospect of her acceptance seemed to Nermina as far away as that distant New England state. That her daughter would move across the country to Rhode Island, that her daughter would leave her, seemed nearly impossible.

Now Atika slides her finger under the flap and tears open the envelope. The sheet of paper she reads from is stark white. Even from Nermina's vantage, she gauges its thickness, the paper, the message, substantial. Her daughter's green eyes flicker across the page. An instant. A heartbeat. Atika shrieks, "I got in! Oh my god, I got into Brown!"

And now they're standing in the middle of the kitchen and hugging and shrieking, their arms intertwined, and their tears—of joy, anguish, relief, pride, regret—churning into one great wave of emotion. Then, like a single oyster shell dislodged from its jagged bed, the long-ago lie scrapes at

Nermina's conscience until she can no longer ignore it. She'd worried that Carl's reappearance would drive Atika away from her, the lie finally unearthed. But she sees now her daughter was bound to leave her anyway. If this is her penance for perpetuating that lie, then perhaps she's getting off easy.

She pulls away from her daughter's embrace and—her own fingers chilled now, too—clasps Atika's slender shoulders. She holds her daughter at arm's length in front of her. "Draga, I'm so very proud of you." The old term of endearment slides across her tongue and, with it, bittersweet echoes of her own mother's voice and these very same words. She rights herself quickly. "You need to call Strina Raifa and Ujak Samir right away!"

"And Sabrina," Atika says. She swipes the errant tears from her face with the back of her hand. "And Keith?" Her hand flutters to the silver stud above her right eyebrow. She worries it gently with her index finger. "We broke up, you know..."

"I didn't," Nermina begins. She scrubs any hints of relief from her voice. "I'm sorry, sweetheart."

Atika slumps against the kitchen counter. She drums the granite with her fingertips, tapping out an adolescent tale as old as the Greek and Roman myths Atika devoured in elementary school while her teachers were assigning chapter books.

"I guess it's just as well? I mean, I'm leaving anyway. But maybe I should tell him I got in? He was sort of the one who pushed me to shoot for Brown in the first place."

"Well, how did the two of you leave it?" Nermina asks. She is careful now, ever so grateful Atika has confided in her. Ever so grateful—at least for the moment—she needn't worry about unearthing another secret stash of condoms.

"We're..." Atika toes the spongy rug in front of the sink. "We decided we'll stay friends for now."

Unbidden, Hasan's earnest face appears above Nermina's. The sun shines through low clouds. The bench beneath her is solid against her back. Her whole life is before her. Her friend, Hasan, smiles.

Nermina smiles now, too. "Then I think if you and Keith are friends you should tell him your good news."

CHAPTER 55
FAMILY DINNER

Nermina cracks four eggs into the mixing bowl and whisks them until they are frothy. She measures out the flour, sugar, vanilla, and cream. The walnuts, raisins, and coconut she throws in less judiciously, following instinct rather than recipe. Then she spoons the thick batter into a greased pan and sets the oven timer for twenty minutes. Give or take a few minutes, this is about the correct baking time for the *sočni kolač*, the cake her mother and nana had always presented at the end of family dinners.

Then she reaches up to the highest cabinet and pulls out the *džezva*; they'd serve *bosanska kava* with dessert, even though it might be late by then for such a strong jolt of caffeine. She doesn't care. This is a special occasion. When she'd first suggested her dinner idea to Atika, Nermina was surprised she didn't immediately shoot it down. Far from it. She'd seemed excited, and she, Atika, was the one to suggest they serve the sweet cake and Turkish coffee that was always a staple at Raifa and Samir's. And then setting the copper pot on the stove for later, she thinks of that first and only meal she'd cooked for Carl, the small kitchen she shared with her housemates. She'd produced a beautiful meal. And, among the deluge of thoughts and emotions that had propelled her actions that day, she remembers feeling the nearness of her mother as the aromas wafted from the single pot on the stove.

Nermina peers through the glass of the oven door and sees her own face reflected there, a woman, she now decides, she understands much better today than she had a few weeks ago and leagues beyond that first time with Carl. Then turning her face to the side to catch the angle of light, she flicks away a smudge of flour from her cheek with the back of her hand.

Nermina fills the plastic washbasin in the sink and sponges clean the mixing bowl and the whisk and cup measures and spoons. Her cuticles sting from the soapy hot water and her mind re-traces her rationale for raising Atika on her own—her *choice*, she maintains—to stay single all these years. Just as it had been her choice to leave Carl out of the equation from the start. And now his choice, it seems, to be a father to Atika. Even now. And this is a good thing, a sweet thing like this cake baking in the oven.

Still, a slender needle of doubt slides beneath her skin. With or without Carl, her life is about to change. Atika will be leaving for college. Her daughter will be living an entire continent away from her. She'll be alone. She blinks back sudden tears. *Silly, ridiculous.* But then she defends herself.

These feelings are valid. Normal. She's a normal mother whose only daughter is about to move three thousand miles away. Nermina takes a long, slow breath, marveling at the strange equilibrium that settles on her now: equal measures of sadness and happiness, sadness that Atika will be going so far away, and happiness that she's raised a daughter who isn't afraid to do so.

She rinses each item and sets them on the wooden drying rack next to the sink, then dries her hands on a clean white dish towel. This, she returns to its place on the oven door. She slides an oven mitt onto her hand and again peers through the glass. Tiny brown bubbles rise and fall at the center of the pan, the creamy batter jiggling when Nermina pulls open the door and shakes the pan—just a little—the way her mother and nana had.

She sits down at the kitchen table. In another five minutes she'll turn off the oven and leave the pan inside for another half hour or so. The cake will be perfect and she'll have time to cool it in the fridge for a couple of hours before Atika ices it; her daughter had made her promise. Everything is moving so quickly now, Nermina thinks. Or perhaps the events of her life have always been moving at this pace but she'd never noticed before. But how is that possible? How have such precious days and minutes and hours escaped her notice? Silly again, she decides, a silly way to think.

When the oven timer buzzes Nermina jumps. She laughs at herself. Laughs softly at the idea that she could slow time, that anyone could. But even as she accepts this fact, she realizes how time *has* curled back on itself, for her and Atika. And when she worries this concept a little further, she sees how it is Jeff who has brought Carl back to her and to Atika—full circle. Her life has come full circle and for this she is grateful. And she knows there is more that Jeff has brought her. She'd felt it. The *possibility* of love. Precious, uncertain, but worthy of pursuit.

CHAPTER 56
A TOAST

The doorbell chimes only twice before Atika is there beside her so that when Nermina opens the door to her guests mother and daughter stand side by side, the same expectant look—half excitement, half trepidation—on their faces. They both speak at once. "Come in!" And then nervous laughter titters from each when they realize they've spoken in unison. Carl, Jeff, and Tessa—Carl's Tessa—step through the doorway of Nermina's home. They all hover in the foyer, a space that has never before seemed so crowded.

"It's so good to meet you," Tessa says, the first to break the ice. She clasps Nermina's hand in her own. Nermina feels herself drawn into the younger woman's embrace, her scent of lavender soothing and sweet. When Tessa releases her, Nermina says, "It's good to meet you, too." She feels off balance and giddy when she hugs first Carl and then Jeff.

Tessa turns to Atika. "Oh my gosh, Carl wasn't kidding. You are...a beauty. So lovely!" Tessa takes both of Atika's hands and holds them aloft. Nermina watches the tension drain from her daughter's face. She feels tenderness wash through her—a resurgence of love and appreciation for Atika that had been waylaid these past months—seeing her daughter through this other woman's eyes and knowing how blessed she is to have her.

"Thank you," Atika says. She puts out her hand politely to Jeff and shakes. "I'm Atika," she says, and then laughs. "I guess you figured that out."

"I guess I did," Jeff says. His voice reveals the same hint of humor that emerged that day in the butterfly garden. Nermina places her hand on his shoulder. She feels the muscle beneath his polo shirt, solid like his presence here, so different from their time at the hospital together.

"It's good to see you, Jeff," Nermina says.

"Good to be here."

They exchange a quiet look, each, Nermina believes, acknowledging the subtle shift. They'll have to wait and see. Perhaps it's as simple as that.

Atika's eyes seem to grow larger as she looks toward her father. Carl stands, smiling but uneasy, Nermina thinks, until Atika approaches him. His chambray shirt—mustard-colored—and jeans are crisply pressed. His scent is crisp as well—Dial soap and Old Spice. Her daughter raises herself on tiptoes and places a tentative kiss on Carl's cheek and Nermina witnesses what she hadn't even known she'd hoped for. For the second time in moments, she witnesses a subtle opening, the permeable passage between a time and place she'd vowed to wall off permanently. She thinks of those early days with Carl, her single-minded purpose. She thinks of the grief and longing that had driven her so relentlessly. For sixteen years, she'd guarded herself as best she could from the wandering ghosts of her past. But now she lets herself imagine there will be no further need for such constant vigilance. A sudden pang of panic yanks her back and then just as quickly releases her.

"Let's all come in, "she says. "This is..." Nermina flutters her hand toward the living room. "Crowded!" she finishes. "Come in, please." She leads Jeff to the sofa and relaxes a bit as he stretches out his legs—the new prosthetic on the left—beneath the coffee table. They all sit and it seems everyone is speaking at once. The volume of their voices, the combined energy of these souls, bounces from the high ceilings, from the clean, blond wood floors. It sinks into the plush sofa cushions and soft curtains. It catches in the updraft and swirls with the ceiling fan's gentle rotations.

When the doorbell chimes again, Atika flies out of the room and returns seconds later with Keith. Her daughter's 'first love' Nermina thinks, amused that this term would enter her vocabulary. But as she looks at him now—the soft sand-colored curls, his thin waist and hips, the way his wrists seem vulnerable as they peek out of the buttoned cuffs of his shirt—she sees how very young he is. Older than her daughter but still so very young. And then, moments later, Raifa sweeps into the foyer, her arms cradling a huge covered dish, and Samir a couple of steps behind her. A set of pearls encircles Raifa's neck, the strand bright and festive against her black dress and her heels adding uncustomary height. Nermina and her closest friend exchange a wordless hug. Sabrina is last through the door, her glossy black hair drawn up in an elegant chignon, the style so reminiscent of Zulfeta's that Nermina is momentarily speechless. She holds her arms out to the beautiful young woman, but their brief hug is interrupted as Atika and Sabrina throw their arms around one another. They Pogo and screech, just as they'd done when they were little girls.

When the introductions have gone round again, Nermina stands. She clears her throat. "Okay, now that we're all here," she begins. She looks at each of the people in her living room, still amazed by the joy that has supplanted the recent weeks of agony. Gone is the stranglehold of fear, the certainty she'd destroyed her daughter's trust in her forever. Her eyes settle on Atika and she realizes the two of them are walking a *new* path now. New, and perhaps even better than the one she'd imagined. "Honey," she says, "I'll need your help in the kitchen." A wide smile spreads across her face. "Excuse us," she calls over her shoulder as they walk from the room. She feels like a schoolgirl and hopes she doesn't sound to her guests as giddy as she now feels.

In the kitchen, Nermina takes out the chilled bottle of Veuve Clicquot and wraps it in one of her white dishtowels. She peels off the foil and untwists the wire around the cork. Then she wraps the towel over the top part of the bottle as she's seen waiters do. Atika goes to the counter where nine champagne flutes stand in a perfect line. The leg of lamb—still sputtering on its roasting pan inside the oven—emits a rich, intoxicating aroma of rosemary, cracked pepper, and mustard.

Mother and daughter shriek when they hear the pop and Atika holds each glass as Nermina pours. Nermina carries the silver tray with the glasses and Atika follows. Nermina holds the tray while Carl takes two glasses and hands one to Tessa. She sees the way his hand lingers a moment on Tessa's.

The potency of this gesture fills her. She sees her father's light touch on her mother's wrist—reads their silent language—and she feels Mirsad's hand entwined in hers as they charge into the sea. Then little Esmer's that last time, holding on so tightly she thought her heart would crack open. But it hadn't, and each of them had done their part. Each of them had brought her here, into the center of this messy family. Messy, yes, and undeniably hers.

Keith stands now and takes a glass, as does Jeff. Jeff smiles up at her—shy, sweet—and she imagines him as a little boy, but still the big brother, watching over Carl. And now the brothers have traded places, she thinks. Raifa, Samir, and Sabrina each take a glass. Nermina sets the tray on the coffee table and hands a glass to her daughter, then takes one for herself. She holds tight to Atika's hand and raises her champagne flute in the other.

"This is a special occasion," she says. She looks at each expectant face. "We have a lot to celebrate, so I'd like to make a toast." She leans in and kisses her daughter lightly on the cheek. "I'm so proud of you, Atika," she says, and her voice catches, just as she'd known it would. She begins again. "And I'm grateful to each of you for being in our lives..." She'd wanted to say much more. She'd planned to, but now the words won't come. And when she realizes that it's Jeff who hands her a clean, white handkerchief from his pocket like some old-world gentleman, she takes a sip from her glass. The bubbles tickle her nose, tears trickle down her cheeks, and she laughs.

CHAPTER 57
DRIVING LESSONS

Carl grabs the gas station coffee from the cupholder and swings the car door shut with his foot. Shoving the keys into the pocket of his jean jacket, he goes straight up the pristine little path to the front door. All of this familiar now. Then he rings the bell once and hears steps coming right away. The girl opens the door. A smile breaks across her face, wide and true.

"Hey," Carl says.

"Hi," Atika says. Carl hears a moment of hesitation and then: "Come on in." Then before he's all the way through the door she turns and calls over her shoulder, "Mom, he's here!"

Carl feels a weird flutter inside his gut, a little like how he'd felt that first night with Tessa at the restaurant. But this is a whole different thing. He knows the stakes are just as high, even higher now. He knows this with a sureness he hasn't felt in a very long time. He stands there in the bright foyer while the girl bounds up the stairs. He runs his fingers along the whitewashed bench, catches a glimpse of his face in the mirror above it, and then she's jogging back down the stairs, Nermina behind her.

"Hi," Nermina says. She smiles then, too. "It's really sweet of you to do this. You really don't—"

"Oh, no. I want to. This is great. It'll be fun." He looks at Atika, flashes a sly grin. "You ready to tear up some highway?" She has on the same navy-blue hoodie and jeans she'd worn the day he'd met her at Powell's. She bounces a little on the balls of her feet. "Yes!" the single word so full of teenaged zeal Carl almost laughs but immediately checks himself.

"Oh, I don't think she's ready for any highways—"

"I'm only kidding," Carl says. He almost laughs again but sees the two lines that stand out in high relief between Nermina's eyebrows. "We'll stick to the neighborhood for now," Carl says. He looks from mother to daughter. He sees a flash of himself with Jeff, Jeff at the wheel of their father's Pontiac. Feels the rush in his chest as they spin out, doing donuts on the icy A&P parking lot. "I promise," he says.

"Can we swing by Strina Raifa's?" Atika asks. "*Please*? I want Sabrina to see me driving." The girl holds Carl's eyes a long moment then turns the same intense gaze on her mother.

Nermina bites her lower lip. Carl sees the struggle there on her face. He thinks about the way Lisa had clutched Ethan to her chest that day at the hospital, the fierceness on her face when she grabbed the boy away from Jeff.

"Where do they live?" Carl asks.

"University Park," Atika supplies before her mother can

intercede. Carl searches his memory for the web of secondary roads that crisscross the city. He settles on a roundabout route, one that will avoid any major left-hand turns.

"Piece of cake," he says. He places his hand on Nermina's shoulder. Nothing soft there, just hard bone, taut muscle. To say he feels love for her is certainly true. But *this* love is tricky, not like any he's ever known. "It'll be fine," he says to Nermina. She shows him a brave little smile in return.

"Yay!" Atika says. She grabs Carl's hand and he feels it all over again. But now he really gets it. He loves this girl, his daughter and—unlike his feelings for Nermina—there is nothing complicated about it. He lets this sink in a little. He feels a smile spread across his face. Everything but this moment falls away. He turns to Nermina. "We'll be back in an hour or so," he says.

Nermina pulls her daughter into a brief, hard hug. "You be careful," she says. "Listen to what...listen to what Carl tells you," she says. "Okay?"

By the time Carl slides into the passenger seat, Atika is already behind the wheel of Nermina's Prius, the seatbelt clamped across her body. Carl clicks his own seatbelt into place. She grips the wheel and looks straight ahead. He sees the muscles working in her jaw, remembers how eager he'd been to get hold of their dad's Pontiac.

"Okay," he says. "What's the next thing you need to do?"

Atika turns her head to face him. She looks for a moment like she's been caught off-guard in class by one of her teachers. And then he almost hears the click in her brain.

"Foot on the break." She says this with assurance. There's

no moment of hesitation when she presses Start and the engine emits its quiet hum.

"What next?" he asks.

"Check the rearview mirror," she says, smiling now.

Carl swings his left arm over the back of the seat and peers into the mirror along with Atika. "Okay," he says. "You're good to go."

She shifts—an automatic on the console—into reverse. At the end of the block Atika flicks on the right-hand turn signal and he listens to its steady rhythm a long time as a procession of cars streak by. Finally, Carl's daughter eases the car onto the road. She hugs the right lane for a mile or two. "Okay," Carl says smoothly then, "let's give it a little gas."

ACKNOWLEDGMENTS

Nermina's Chance was born amidst a group of generous writers at the Rittenhouse Writers' Group, led by the inimitable James Rahn. Growing beyond the confines of a short story, the book took shape over many years, nurtured—as I have been—by love and support, first and always from my husband, and the numerous friends and fellow writers who have encouraged me along the way. Our daughter Alyssa, of brilliant intellect and insight, has been my ever-faithful reader of myriad drafts. Many thanks to the intrepid RWG contingent: Caren Litvin, Stefanie Cohen, Deb Edmondson, Tom Teti, Andie Tursi, Beth Overly-Adamson, Anmiryam Budner, Alina Macneal, and Saral Waldorf.

Had it not been for two remarkable women, Nancy Gold and Liz Kronisch, I may never have given *Nermina's Chance* the opportunity to mature into a full-fledged novel at UNCW. Many thanks to my MFA thesis advisors and professors: Clyde Edgerton, Dana Sachs, Robert Anthony Seigel, and Wendy Brenner. Jill and Philip Gerard: the heart and soul of Chautauqua (the place) and *Chautauqua* (the journal) contributed knowledge and friendship of infinite value. Jamie Lynn Miller, MFA classmate and dear friend, provided targeted doses of humor and unpacked her fair share of literary baggage on my behalf.

Mindy Agnoff, Susan Polizzotto, Mary Sanza, and Dave Theissen helped me to become a better teacher, friend and writer. Natalie Italiano, Jennifer Knodle, Yael Gold, Juul Bruin, and Barbara McDonald: your friendship and wisdom is a gift.

David Bright, Ursula DeYoung, and Joe Ponepinto found merit in my writing and a place for my stories and chapters among the pages of their beautiful journals. Diane Sorensen and Doug Hansen, truly a dynamic duo: I don't know where to begin—perhaps Wilmington, NC., perhaps Chautauqua—but always close to my heart. Zrinka Bralo gave Nermina voice, authenticity and, ultimately, the will to survive.

About Atmosphere Press

Atmosphere Press is an independent, full-service publisher for excellent books in all genres and for all audiences. Learn more about what we do at atmospherepress.com.

We encourage you to check out some of Atmosphere's latest releases, which are available at Amazon.com and via order from your local bookstore:

Saints and Martyrs: A Novel, by Aaron Roe

When I Am Ashes, a novel by Amber Rose

The Recoleta Stories, by Bryon Esmond Butler

Voodoo Hideaway, a novel by Vance Cariaga

Hart Street and Main, a novel by Tabitha Sprunger

The Weed Lady, a novel by Shea R. Embry

A Book of Life, a novel by David Ellis

It Was Called a Home, a novel by Brian Nisun

Grace, a novel by Nancy Allen

Shifted, a novel by KristaLyn A. Vetovich

Because the Sky is a Thousand Soft Hurts, stories by
    Elizabeth Kirschner

ABOUT THE AUTHOR

Nominated for The Pushcart Prize, Best Small Fictions, and *The Millions*, Dina Greenberg's poetry, fiction, and creative nonfiction have appeared widely in such journals as *Bellevue Literary Review, Pembroke Magazine, Split Rock Review, Tahoma Literary Review, Barely South*, and *Wilderness House Literary Review*. Dina earned an MFA in fiction from the University of North Carolina Wilmington, where she served as managing editor for the literary journal *Chautauqua*. She teaches creative writing at the Cameron Art Museum and provides one-on-one writing coaching for victims of trauma. Her work leading creative writing workshops for combat veterans resulted in writing *Nermina's Chance*, her debut novel.

CPSIA information can be obtained
at www.ICGtesting.com
Printed in the USA
FSHW011225061021
85257FS